Women of Summer

I. B. Wells

First published by Dog Ear Publishing
4010 W. 86th Street, Ste H
Indianapolis, IN 46268
www.dogearpublishing.net

ISBN: 978-160844-823-4

This book is printed on acid-free paper.

This book is a work of fiction. Places, events, and situations in this book are purely fictional and any resemblance to actual persons, living or dead, is coincidental.

Printed in the United States of America

*"I know I am but summer to your heart
and not the full four seasons of the year."*

Edna St. Vincent Millay

Acknowledgments

My sincere appreciation to Anthony Radd who encouraged me to pick the book up off of the (electronic) shelf where it had sat dormant for ten years; dust it off; and re-write it.

The publisher's editor was excellent, but I had two others, Faye Hollowell and Richard Smith, whose eagle eyes and wise advice and counsel are as much appreciated as their friendship.

Special thanks go to my wife, Sue, who supported me in both efforts and both versions and who read every line with an English teacher's practiced eye.

For Sue, a woman of the full four seasons of my year.

Prologue

It returns to the Virginia Highlands every year after the dismal winter cloak falls away. Then spring creeps forward subtly, always tentative at first, to decorate the mountains in delicate suggestions of green that give faint definition to the graceful ridges and steep, plunging valleys. Finally, year after year, always a surprise because of its sheer magnificence, the glorious garb of spring bursts forth. After spring comes, it reveals itself, first becoming visible in the afternoons. It stays until fall, when the smoky golden hue of Indian summer starts to fade and the nights grow chilly again. Then it goes away. It is the pale pastel color, the hue that in elegant simplicity gives description and name to the Blue Ridge Mountains.

Those mountains do not rise dramatically and majestically toward glistening, ice-capped crowns, but as the deer and wild turkey know, snow blankets the barren forests and meadows in higher elevations until spring. The mountains do not beckon from a great distance to draw one to famous summits. They do not become their own monument to themselves. They simply grace one end of the horizon to the other, choosing flowing ranges as a means of expression. From a distance, they look blue in summer, their elegance understated.

The blue is cool and evasive. It can be seen only from a distance. Travel too close, and, like the shadow of a dream that is apparent for a moment then gone, the blue fades from perception. One must take great care with the blue, or it ceases to be. The lives of the inhabitants of the Blue Ridge can be as fragile as the hue. Careless or evil intrusions into those lives by accident or design can make reality imperceptible and the lives vulnerable. They too can fade like the blue hue.

Some say that God flung the stars about the universe and sculpted the magnificent mountain summits with His hands. Possibly, when He gently laid down these ridges, for an extra touch of grace, He breathed the hue into the Blue Ridge Mountains. He set running the sparkling cold mountain streams of White Top and Mount Rogers, gushing constantly as they plummet with abandon, misting banks of mountain laurel in their spray and cradling rainbow trout in their pools. The crackling, turgid rush of gurgling mountain waters can be heard in the forests before the streams are seen. That sound, an additional gift of nature, sings timelessly to those who listen. The freshness of the early morning air in the Blue Ridge, another passing gift, makes the act of breathing an exquisite exercise in being.

Some believers hold that God made perfect His natural creation, but most would admit He does not sculpt and form the lives of the inhabitants of the Blue Ridge or any other place. He does not interfere, it seems, with those who live in the savannas of the low country or on the tundra of the high plains or along the shores of the oceans where life first oozed forth. For whatever reason, the lives of this island planet home were spared the incredible boredom of being predictable, of being made good; yet, with that measure of freedom comes inevitable pain and sometimes flights into insanity. Because of the scheme of things, we can become isolated and desperate, vile or deadly, but most of us also have the nature and the capacity to be loving and good and at times joyous. Occasionally, we rise above our natural inclinations and, for a few flickering moments, moments of grace, we become better, better than we actually are.

Those who make the journey, the struggle, together share an undeniable commonality. Regardless of how little one's existence may overlap another's in time and space on the planet, we are all in this life together. For that reason, the story of each of us, at least in some measure, is the story of us all.

Chapter 1

"The wind blows where it chooses, and you hear the sound of it,
but you do not know where it comes from or where it goes."

John 3:8

The graceful bare limbs of the trees in the Blue Ridge Mountains stood in stark, wintry elegance the day the secret was revealed. Like the lovely, naked forest stripped of its leafy mantle, the truth, if only in part, was exposed, adorned solely by its own harsh reality. Most who heard the news would not, could not, believe it as fact. It was, after all, an unbelievable story. Many Scotch-Irish fundamentalists, Southwest Virginia mountain people, shook their heads somberly, unmoved in detached resignation. Most were certain that their God, full of wrath and fury, had intervened, sending swift and terrible retribution for unpardonable sin. But a few introspective souls realized that truth, like an actress in the footlights, sometimes masquerades as illusion. They knew too that truth's sweet cousin, illusion, moves forever in murky twilight, always parading as truth.

It was one month to the day past Christmas, bleak and bitterly cold, in the late afternoon darkness of January 1910. The swirling Southwest Virginia winds of Mount Rogers and White Top whipped about unpredictably, angrily. Then, raging downward in frigid vengeance, they raced unrestrained through the gaps and across the knobby lowlands, but when they reached the town, they mellowed like weary travelers mesmerized by a long journey. Now, dissipated by their own fury, more glacial breeze than fierce highland wind, they brushed against icy windowpanes, moaning in the darkness. They called softly to those people who chose to hear, but call was all they did. The winds move where they please and whisper to whom they choose, but it is left to the souls of those who hear to give language to the wind.

The secret was revealed in winter before the earth's renewal, but, as always, it followed its own course, eventually turning winter to spring.

"How long, O simple ones, will you love being simple."

Proverbs 1:22

On a Saturday afternoon in late May of 1908, eight King College boys stood huddled together on the platform, looking westward waiting for the marvel of the age, a magnificent black Norfolk and Western steam engine. Finally, they saw it, barely visible as a speck of light in the distance. As if mesmerized, all stood immobile, gazing down the tracks like cadets on a parade ground. Their destination, Martha Washington College, "a finishing school in Abingdon for fine young ladies," was fifteen miles away. As always with the arrogance and madness of masculine youth, they fed on themselves, convinced that their station in life existed only for their own glorification. For all the young men but one, the abandonment and madness were heightened because their school year was drawing to a close.

The conforming rebels were drawn to the quest simply by the adventure itself, by the sheer excitement of rail travel and by the compelling force of their lives, churning testosterone. Because that condition eradicated rational intellect, none could see that their goal was as obvious and transparent as the retractable isinglass curtains on the carriages of the day.

As the train came to an elongated stop, twenty-two-year-old Bentley Thompson pulled himself up the steps into a coach. He was a few years older than the others, but because of his boyish good looks and small stature, no one noticed. At five feet eight inches, the shortest of the group, he also stood apart in another way. He was clearly the best turned out, the best dressed. His pale blue eyes, incapable, it seemed, of true intensity and his light brown hair cast him more like a prep school boy. Bentley, ironically, had recently dropped out of college to work full-time at J. S. Simpson's, the best clothing store in Bristol. He took courses from time to time working toward an accounting degree. A natural salesman perfectly suited for the clothing business, Bentley kept a significant following from the college crowd. Although he did not have a close friend, he was popular and well liked. His engaging personality and quick sense of humor allowed the others to forgive him for a subtle but pervasive arrogance.

As the train jerked forward, Bentley sat beside Big Jim Hoggard, a young man of six feet four and two hundred forty pounds. Hoggard's thick black mane of wild, uncombed hair flew as he threw his head back, roaring with laughter at "The Bent." Hoggard's outrageously full mustache twitched as he grinned at his traveling partner. His deep-set eyes, dark as small pieces of coal, twinkled under thick, unruly eyebrows, while his clothes failed to conform to his gargantuan hulk. His rumpled appearance seemed worse in contrast to the immaculate Bentley. The antithesis of Bentley in another way, Big Jim possessed a sweet disposition and an unaffected and simplistic approach to life. He remained an academic freshman after two years at college, two years during which he had struggled and applied his meager mental resources to their fullest. A happy person, Hoggard took playful delight in feigning a sinister disposition to intimidate friends and strangers alike with his dark, imposing looks; but those who knew him well realized that occasionally his frightening threats were legitimate. At first the giant had a limitless reservoir for alcohol, drinking for hours; yet, sometimes he reached a dark threshold in which he would sit, eyes glazed, until his anger burst forth, unleashed by the slightest provocation, real or imagined. In a flash the dark shadow of his soul could erupt, turning the simple boy into a menacing man, a danger to anybody. His friends were thankful that the metamorphosis occurred rarely. All who witnessed the profound change feared the big man, knowing that the possibility of his madness always loomed darkly in the background.

Bentley, an intuitive person, understood better than most that the balance of Big Jim's dual personality weighed heavily on his sweet, innocent side, so Bentley knew that cultivating the friendship and loyalty of Hoggard enhanced his own power. It worked easily, as Jim Hoggard, the laughable left-footer, liked Bentley Thompson best of all.

The banter and laughter continued until the train slowed as the engineer eased back on the throttle, preparing to stop. Soon they heard the steam whistle's mournful wail, but to them it was like the sweet siren's song calling, "Martha . . . Martha . . . Martha."

The eight young men infiltrated the festive crowd gathered to meet the train, then walked toward Miller's Boarding House. Upon arrival, Hugh Carrington, a serious young man and a natural organizer, asked, "Who's gonna go in?"

"How about The Bent? The Bent hasn't been up here in a while!" came the response from the group.

Hugh stepped forward, announcing, "It's resolved, then. Bentley will go in, and for good measure, you go in with him, Big Jim."

"Me?" asked the perplexed giant.

"Yes, you," confirmed Carrington.

"Yeah, the Hog Man might have to kick some ass!" offered a recruit.

"If Mrs. Miller doesn't kick Bentley's ass first!"

Margaret Miller, an anathema to some, was, if the truth were admitted, sexually appealing to the rabble. At forty-four, she was a thin, angular woman with moderate bosoms and no reluctance to reveal them as teasing dimpled cleavage, usually displayed in low-cut dresses. Coal-black hair matched eyes that could quickly flash in anger. A widow, she ran Miller's Boarding House like a field general, leaving no question about who was in charge. A typical mountain woman, she possessed a suspicious and confrontational nature. Although her mature yet sexy looks attracted the King boys, most were a bit afraid of her. Secretly, Margaret Miller became the hook on which many of the boys hung their sexual fantasies.

Five minutes after the discussion began, Bentley Thompson and Jim Hoggard climbed the steep steps of Miller's Boarding House, stopping near the top of the stairs. Bentley moved upward two more steps, turned, and adjusted Big Jim's wrinkled string tie. "For God's sake, Hog Man, why don't you let me sell you some stylish clothes?"

"My clothes are in style, Bent. It's my body that's out of style. I can never look neat like you little needle-dick runts!" chuckled Hoggard.

"Okay, okay, I understand, but I could help you immensely. Listen, here's the plan. You begin, and if you don't have a problem, I won't say a word. If she gives you any grief, I'll come to your rescue. Remember, tell her we want two rooms, and promise that only two of us will be in each room."

Entering the door, they faced a long wooden table that served as the guest registration desk. On the left, they saw a dismal, smoke-filled sitting room where a number of dingy men sat in their undershirts, drinking beer. All the men eyed the college boys with suspicion and visible disdain.

Mrs. Miller, sitting at the desk, did not disappoint. She was adorned in a short blue dress, the low-cut front drifting open to display uplifted bosoms. As she glanced up, her expression formed a practiced, commercial smile, but that look vanished quickly into disdain and suspicion as she stood, facing the two before her.

"We'd like two rooms, please, ma'am," said Hoggard softly, hunching forward with shoulders stooped.

"Got no rooms for the likes of you two," she responded, as a murmur of subdued approval came from the men in the room to her right.

Bentley glanced nervously to his left toward the men, but Big Jim, paying no attention to the audience, questioned, "You got no rooms?"

"I got no rooms for you and your bunch!" she snapped. "The last time you was here, five or six of ya stayed in one room and made noise late in the night. And one of 'em, he relieved hisself out in the yard. I got my regular boarders to think about. Don't need your kind here!" she responded defiantly.

Bentley, afraid of the crude and rough men, stepped forward, nevertheless, and spoke in a low voice. "Excuse me, miss. I mean ma'am. What if we pay extra?" he asked.

"Pay extra?" she questioned slowly, suspiciously.

"Yes, ma'am. We are willing to pay seventy-five cents extra for each room. And on my personal word of honor, I will assure you that no more than two of us will be in each room," offered the designated negotiator.

"Well, I do got two rooms . . ." she mused.

"We thank you so much, Mrs. Miller. I assure you that you will never regret your decision," interjected the salesman quickly, closing the deal.

Turning abruptly, Bentley walked out the door, but Big Jim lingered momentarily, befuddled and frustrated by the encounter. Ambling to the room on his left, he paused at the door, staring menacingly. His intense black eyes flashed, and his jowls were set firm, the look his friends called "the gaze." Recognizing the challenge and the size of the threat, red, watery eyes turned away from Big Jim as the room grew silent. Then he walked out, allowing the screen door to bang closed.

Mrs. Miller stood at the door watching. "Hell," she said to the boarders, "I ought to have the big kid here all the time if he can make you guys behave!"

"Come over here, darlin', and I'll show you how good I can behave!" came a response.

"You wish! You damn wish," she answered, smiling wryly.

The two envoys returned to the group to explain the arrangement. A short time later, Ron Sutton, Hugh Carrington, Big Jim Hoggard, and Bentley Thompson climbed the steps of Miller's Boarding House. After dark the other four would infiltrate inside.

At twilight, the youthful band marched to Martha Washington College, prepared to marshal an assault on the Spring Fling dance. All looked very presentable, like young gentlemen. The big man still looked slightly disheveled, but his concentration on proper bearing compensated enough to present a facade of youthful dignity. The army, upon entering the double doors of the Martha Washington College ballroom, immediately broke a cardinal rule of military engagement: It not only divided forces but disintegrated into eight components, each intent on its own skirmish of natural selection.

The night was sheer Southern romance, with the ballroom bathed in the soft glow of candles flickering in the drafts from the open windows. Traces of light and shadows danced on the walls as the pale glow illuminated the swirling forms in the subdued candlelight. As the string ensemble played, properly restrained conversation was occasionally broken by eruptions of sweet laughter from the Martha girls. Even the homely coeds, those seldom attracting attention, looked lovely in the soft light of the spring night as the young men responded in courtly superficiality. This splendid night Big Jim Hoggard morphed into a refined young man of great stature, drawing attention from several Martha girls. Looking up, one plain young woman saw a giant approaching; moments later, walking onto the dance floor, he told her she was very pretty. At the moment, she was.

Jean Deaton, a handsome twenty-four-year-old Martha graduate standing at the punch bowl where she acted as a hostess, vaguely remembered seeing Bentley when she was a student.

Later, standing alone, Bentley realized all his comrades were engaged with Martha coeds. All the King boys sought a date for the Martha picnic the next afternoon. Because the dance was carefully chaperoned, they believed the picnic would provide the opportunity for the final skirmish, the ultimate quest of spring.

Soon, Bentley learned that every other member of the group was invited to the picnic. They were not as handsome, articulate, or experienced as he, but that night, the other boys adopted a sense of humility foreign to Bentley. They became models of proper behavior except when they went outside to take a drink, undetected even by the watchful eyes of the chaperones. Still, one chaperone, Jean Deaton, the youngest, knew well what was going on. Wisely, she said nothing.

Bentley remembered another occasion some time ago when Ron Sutton had offered, "You know what your problem is, Bentley? You talk about yourself too much. You don't know how to treat a girl."

After staying to the end of the dance, Bentley strolled down the long driveway alone, feeling the cool mountain air. A short time later, he arrived at Miller's Boarding House, where he detected the massive figure of Big Jim Hoggard urinating in the shadows near the front porch steps.

On Sunday morning, the other occupants gone, Big Jim Hoggard, sat on the side of his bed, watching his roommate. "Hey, Bentley. You're not supposed to get dressed up for the picnic. It's casual clothes," he barked.

"I shall not attend the simple and mundane picnic," Bentley answered as he tied a bright yellow tie without looking toward Hoggard.

"You're not going to the picnic? I thought we were *all* going. I thought that was part of the plan," offered the confused giant.

"Several girls asked me. Actually, two of them begged, but I . . . I have better things to do," said the little man.

"Better things to do?" asked Hoggard, a perplexed expression lingering on his face.

"Precisely. Better things to do. Things to do that one cannot do at a picnic. Mature things, my man, intimate things, things that men and women do in privacy," answered Bentley, smiling smugly, as if he believed his own lie.

Later, leaving his suitcase at the boarding house, Bentley meandered outside, turning east, away from Martha Washington College. He strolled aimlessly in the afternoon sun, walking down a steep hill where trees arched above the cobblestone sidewalk. Recognizing some coeds from the night before, he was relieved that he wasn't the only person not going to the picnic. Attempting to dismiss his lonely feeling, he continued walking in the random fashion of one who has nowhere to go. Bentley had no way to know that soon, his life would change irrevocably.

Coming upon a white-framed building with a storefront window, he admired the handsome sign, carved in relief and painted like those of Europe. It read, "G. N. Wertz Photography." As he looked in the studio window, his own reflection first caught his attention, but stepping closer, he saw an array of photographs of all sizes in organized clutter.

Looking at a photograph of Jean Deaton, he felt as if he had seen her before. He soon discovered there were several other pictures of her. Then his eyes fell upon the picture of a beautiful young girl who appeared to be in her early teens. Her eyes drew him in, gazing beyond the photograph in a mystical way. She sat in unaffected dignity, without the exaggerated effort of some others. As Bentley gazed at the picture, it occurred to him that a chicken sat on her right hand, a toy feathered prop. Quickly, he realized there were many photographs of the girl, some showing her a few years older; yet, in all she projected the same demeanor. The symmetry of her face held perfect balance with a Grecian nose supported by high cheekbones and gently defined lips above her slightly dimpled chin. Her full hair, pulled back in a soft, flowing way, appeared to be brown in the black-and-white photograph.

Bentley stood several minutes before turning to walk to the other showroom window opposite the front door. He heard the creaking of the screen door opening; the form behind it appeared murky and difficult to discern as the doorway filled with the silhouette of a young woman looking back into the studio. Still behind the screen, the form turned, but plunged suddenly into the afternoon sunlight, an off-white blur, falling toward the cobblestone walk. Second later, knees cushioned by a dress and full petticoat, the girl rolled gracefully into a sitting position, looking down as if she were surveying for damage. Medium brown hair, long and thick, falling around her face showed highlights of auburn in the afternoon sunlight.

Moving quickly, Bentley instinctively fell to one knee. Without speaking, he extended his hand, gently touching her upper arm. To his surprise, she looked up slowly, calmly. Her hair, falling to the sides, revealed the face in the countless photographs as pale green eyes met his. No longer confided to a gold-leaf frame, the girl continued looking at him without speaking. Taken aback by her calm demeanor, he stammered, "Are you all right?"

"Yes, I think so," she answered.

"Are you sure you're okay?" he asked again, feeling the need to say something.

"I'm fine. I was walking toward the door, looking back at my father, talking to him. Somehow I tripped. I guess it made me miss the first step. I hope I didn't scare you."

"No, uh. No, no. You didn't scare me," Bentley stammered.

"Were you coming to the studio?" she asked.

"Actually, I was just strolling by and, ah, I saw . . . Aren't there pictures of you in the window?" he uttered, pointing toward the first window.

"Oh, yes. I'm there lots, in both windows. At times it gets embarrassing," she answered. "My father is G. N. Wertz," she explained, noting Bentley's lack of recognition. "The photographer," she continued, looking up at the sign bearing his name.

"Oh, I see," Bentley responded, smiling broadly for the first time. Still a bit unsettled, he blurted, "Were you at the dance at Martha last night?"

"No, I wasn't there. I go to Stonewall, but sometimes I go to the Martha dances. I wasn't there last night 'cause we had something at our school," she explained.

Knowing that Stonewall Academy for Women was a nursing school, he responded, "Oh, so you're gonna be a nurse?"

"I hope so. I'm just finishing my first year," she answered.

Bentley mused to himself that she must be eighteen or nineteen and announced, "I go to King."

"What's your major?" she asked.

"I'm an accounting major," he responded, eager to change the subject. Continuing quickly, he ventured, "I, uh, I don't mean to be forward, but, you see, I'm just taking a walk before I have to catch the train. And I wonder, uh, would you like to have a soda? I think there's a drugstore up the hill. Isn't there?"

"Yes, it's across from the courthouse. Well . . . sure. That would be nice. I'll go ask Daddy," she answered, stepping back inside.

In the back of the studio, her father, George N. Wertz, tinkered about in the clutter among his cherished photographs. Glancing up, he saw the treasure of his life approaching.

With a daughter's charm, she girlishly sought permission. "Daddy, I'm going up to the courthouse for a soda. Okay?"

"Yah, it's okay. Be careful," came a resonate voice with a distinctive German accent.

Walking back to the door, she wondered if the young man outside were too old for her. He appeared more mature, more worldly, than the boys she knew. "Yes," she called from the steps, "I can go."

At the moment they stood across from St. Thomas Episcopal Church, where her German immigrant father and her pretty mother, a local girl, had presented her as an infant to God and to the congregation in Holy Baptism. It was there that her parents and those assembled were asked, "Do you renounce Satan and all the spiritual forces of wickedness that rebel against God?" There they had answered in her behalf, "I renounce them."

Still not knowing each other's names, Bentley and the girl walked toward the courthouse. Bentley, normally polite and courtly, had failed to introduce himself, but neither thought about it at the moment. Talking easily, they climbed the hill in the bright sunlight of the spring afternoon. Bentley would eventually come to learn the girl's name - Georgia Wertz.

As they entered the drugstore, Georgia's first cousin, Jean Deaton, and her friend, Eliza Horn, were walking out. Jean immediately recognized Bentley, but he did not remember her except in a vague way, although such handsome good looks normally registered with him.

After the girls greeted each other, Georgia turned to Bentley, realizing she did not know his name. Stepping forward, nodding slightly at each girl, he announced, "Ladies, I'm Bentley Thompson, from King College."

Jean and Eliza introduced themselves, but following Jean's lead, they did not linger to indulge in the small talk that invariably followed introductions. Walking away, Eliza spoke first, "Jean, he's handsome even if a bit short."

"Yes, he's handsome. I don't know how Georgia met him," Jean answered reflectively.

"So you know him?" Eliza questioned.

"I saw him around Martha for two or three years when I was there," she explained.

"So, what's the problem?" pressed Eliza.

"There's no problem really. He's older than she is; he's near our age." She chose to say no more about Bentley Thompson to Eliza, but Jean felt a primal feminine alert, visceral and inchoate. Jean and Georgia possessed a bond deeper than most friendships, an abiding love, that began as a feminine gift between two children who had grown together into two young women. Now they loved each other deeply, like sisters but without the coincidence of being born to the same parents.

Meanwhile Georgia and Bentley talked easily over ice cream sodas. They were too young to offer synoptic versions of their short lives. Bentley, drawn to her every word, spoke a great deal less than usual, much less than the night before. So soon the couple was walking back to the studio. When they reached the foot of the hill, neither could remember the walk. It seemed as if they were magically lifted from the drugstore and deposited in front of St. Thomas Episcopal Church. They said good-bye, and soon Bentley found himself on the train returning home.

Spring, always feminine in her adornment and life-giving essence, seemed unseasonably bold and warm the weekend the King boys went to the Martha dance, the time Bentley Thompson met Georgia Wertz. Then spring slipped away quietly, allowing for the slow and sensuous march of summer.

Love, like the seasons, comes in several ways, but invariably, romantic love, the spring of loves, at least for a while, overtakes all the others. When it flows, especially the first time, the lovers are held in the grip of its illusion and madness and joy. Who can say why two fall in love or do not fall in love? Who can say why, sadly, sometimes one falls in love and the object of that love does not love in return? Love has its own mystery, one never solved. Georgia Wertz and Bentley Thompson would soon put their own unique stamp on first love. That love would bring them to the defining moments of their lives.

Chapter 2

Georgia Wertz was the only child to bless the union of George N. Wertz, a German immigrant from the mountains of Bavaria, and the former Frances Fuller, a local girl of the Blue Ridge. At the time Georgia was born, life was good, almost prosperous, for her parents, but a problem persisted: Her father was losing his hearing. Through the years several doctors confirmed that although they did not know the reason, he should ultimately be prepared to deal with total deafness. That diagnosis changed the plans of Frances and George Wertz, and the baby planned as the first became the only child.

George Wertz, assuming his first child would be a boy, never considered a name other than his own; but by necessity, the baby was named Georgia. She would transform his life and remind him in many ways of his mother a continent away in the forests of Bavaria.

George was born a few kilometers from the Austrian border, in the beautiful valley of Fussen, Germany, where his father died when he was an infant. Like many sons deprived of a father, he assumed the role of his mother's protector at an early age. But Anna, a strong woman, planned for her son's leaving home from the beginning. She had gently repeated her point, over and over, until he accepted it without question, so, early on, she released her only son to the world.

On a trip to Berlin at seventeen, George discovered photography, changing his life forever. He was drawn to the technology and to the art form. Captivated by photographs in Munich and Frankfurt, he returned home to tell his mother he wanted to study photography. Smiling sheepishly because he had come to understand, he had told her that he would go to Munich to study.

Finally, inevitably, the two had stood clinging to each other, fighting back tears, experiencing for the first time the devastation that comes with irrevocable good-byes. Then he was gone.

George began apprenticeship in the studio of an old photographer, a picture taker as demanding and precise as the ground lenses of his cameras. George found the study intense and challenging, but his dignified manner and dedicated work ethic captured the heart and affection of his cranky old mentor. George lived frugally, harboring the unrealistic goal of saving enough money to buy a used camera and equipment after his apprenticeship. After two years, his work and study over, his teacher offered full-time employment, but George possessed a vision that did not include staying at the studio.

The old man's eyes were misty when the day came for George to leave. Without speaking, the aging photographer looked into the young, handsome face and motioned with long, pale fingers for George to follow as he walked to a camera case. With a faltering voice, the old man said softly, "Here, my son, it is for you. It is yours." George was shocked to find an older but expensive camera and tripod. He protested, saying it was too much for his teacher to give. "You are too young to understand now, George. It is not just I who has given to you, but you who have given to me in a greater way. In the wisdom of later years, you will learn to receive with grace. This is the last lesson I shall teach you: Receive my gift gracefully, and use it not just to capture images, but also to capture imagination; if you are as talented as I believe you are, you will capture souls. Now, be gone, my boy, before my eyes cry as much as my heart does."

Complying with those bittersweet instructions, George Wertz was gone again.

He was a tall man for his day and blessed with a wiry leanness that he would keep for life. Thick and wavy chestnut brown hair with highlights of auburn and a full mustache made him appear slightly taller and older than his twenty-three years. High cheekbones and a strong chin along with an angular nose suggested Germanic aristocracy for one who came from humble origins. He could have been dashing, but he wasn't. His pervasive nature, contrary to his lineage, was peaceful and kind; yet always when George was tested for courage and pressed into the ageless masculine conflicts that masquerade for honor, he persevered physically. He would come to follow the life of a gentle and sensitive artist, one who created with lenses and sight and instinct and soul.

Nothing captivated his imagination like the stories of the new world that beckoned. George could not precisely understand the attraction, but like the moon and the tides, it existed, and he had to flow with it. After several months his arrangements were made, and he returned to Fussen for what would be the last time.

George had meager savings, but the amount was more than he had anticipated because of the gift from the old man who passed through his life and graced it. Now he brought a portion of his money to give to his mother; but before he presented it to her, she approached him with her own gift, secret funds she had saved for years. Since he was a boy, she had prepared the gift for the day he would leave, the day they now shared.

Anna had no idea that her only son would depart for another continent, another world; yet, the day of his leaving ultimately found its way to them as those kinds of days eventually find their way into all lives from time to time. Regardless of all she had taught him about the necessity to leave her and the lovely Bavarian valley, George felt painful slivers of guilt and dread. Looking into his mother's smiling face, he saw her pale green eyes betray her as tears flowed; but, as always, she maintained a dignified sense of inner strength, one of quiet resignation and calmness in the face of profound loss and pain. When she presented her gift, George, engulfed in the emotions of the moment, instinctively blurted, "Mother, I cannot take it."

Without speaking, Anna smiled and placed the heavy wool sock with the currency in his shaking hands. Then she clasped her hands over his, whispering, "Yes, you can, George. This is for you, for your future."

In a flooding rush of recall, George heard the words of his old mentor, *Learn to receive with grace.* Then he said the right thing, "Thank you, Mother. Thank you so much. You always—"

"You are welcome," she interrupted softly.

Wracked by the bittersweet moment, they faced the awful truth, that likely they would never see each other again. Being held by her son for what would be the last time, Anna shook against his chest, sobbing. Suddenly to George she seemed so much smaller, so vulnerable, this strong woman, now more like a little girl clinging to him. Anna felt pieces of her soul cracking and falling in painful shards of anguish as she gave way to the unfathomable pain of loss. Suddenly, George's quiet composure began to collapse, attacked by emotions he had buried as a boy while pretending to be a man. His sobs demanded release, and as the little boy cried, the man could do nothing.

With more money than he ever possessed, yet still under funded, George traveled to London where he set sail for New York. Two aspects about the young George Wertz drew others to him: his status as a budding photographer and his rudimentary knowledge of English.

An older Berliner suggested that he photograph the United States Navy ships and crews. He told George of a German photographer in London who made a good living by taking pictures of Her Majesty's Navy. The sailors loved to have their pictures taken to send home. He suggested that George move near an American Navy port in the new country.

Finally, the skyline of New York City stood in the distance. Stark and menacing, it did not look like a safe haven of opportunity after the seemingly endless crossing. Once they disembarked and George was finally reunited with his friends from the crossing, they moved together into the sprawling and exciting streets of New York.

George had visited many of the major European cities, but none had the vitality, the aggressive, almost combative, nature of New York City. The pressure seemed relentless as they marched forward, hearing more languages being shouted on those streets than he had encountered anywhere else. An exuberant but threatening place, the city seemed out of control. With information from their own network, George and the others moved to a neighborhood called Little Berlin.

Quickly George realized the Germans competed not only with each other but also with the Irish, Italian, French, Scotts, Brits, and others. Jobs were available, but if one could not speak English well, the jobs were in manual labor. In a twist of fate that seemed more like betrayal than irony, many people found themselves facing greater hardships in America than the hardships they had left behind.

George was hired at a construction site because of his ability to speak English. His constant companion was a worn and tattered German–English dictionary bought years before in a musty bookstore in Fussen. Soon he was giving English lessons in the evenings and on weekends. Because of the demand for his humble skills, he quickly built a budding cottage business.

After six months it became apparent that he was making no progress. All his money was spent for food and shelter, and the outlook for the future was no more promising. Stories spread in his community about those who had lost their lives in accidents or through violent crime. Many opined that the police were not concerned over the death of faceless immigrants.

After escaping an attempted robbery after payday one Friday evening, George made a life-changing decision. He would linger no longer on what he had come to view as the mean streets of New York. He understood that his search in the new world was not over. It was just beginning.

George properly gave his employer two weeks' notice. The last Friday night after work, he pulled out a dog-eared sheet showing the amounts owed him by his English students. As his students came to say good-bye and pay their bills, George forgave every debt. That night, sitting with friends at the New World Beer Garden, he could not pay for a pint himself. For the first time George relaxed enough to look more closely at the pretty German waitresses who flirted and encouraged the young men to spend their hard earned money.

The next day, wracked by a brutal beer-garden headache, George said his good-byes as he boarded a train for Norfolk, Virginia, where he hoped to photograph sailors of the United States Navy.

In Norfolk he found vitality and excitement, but the relentless New York competition simply to survive was no longer a part of his existence. He realized that the immigrants here attempted to blend into the community rather than exist in ethnic pockets.

The first week in Norfolk George met Hans Metz, a successful German photographer, who offered him a job in a profession where there was little competition. George was assigned menial tasks at first; but early on he impressed Mr. Metz by taking very good photographs. The wise old master in Munich taught George how to capture the intimate essence of people. Soon George accompanied Mr. Metz to weddings and other special occasions, where they set up two cameras. George was unaware that he created a great deal of attention among the young ladies.

Living in a boardinghouse beside a tidal marsh, George felt happy in a vague way; yet, like many young men, he looked through the days at hand concentrating instead on his tomorrows, on the future, where his hopes and dreams resided, where promise and success and independence beckoned.

One Sunday afternoon walking toward the harbor in search of a scene to capture, he met a young woman, Nancy Adams, who took him home for dinner. Her father, a prominent doctor, liked the dignified and handsome young man of apparent intelligence and promise.

The weeks passed as a romance budded tentatively between the immigrant and the doctor's daughter, his first woman of summer. Eventually, he kissed her good night as she held him tightly in their momentary embraces.

Soon George grew restless again, realizing there was little hope he could gather even a small portion of the business in the area. With that realization, the dream which drew him to Tidewater faded.

On one of the last hot evenings of summer, George sat with Nancy Adams on her front porch, describing the cool mountain breezes of his home, more soothing in his memory than in reality. Dr. Adams joined the conversation, noting that Virginia had her own mountains in Southwest Virginia, the highest in the state. *Mountains in Virginia!* George thought, unaware until then of their existence.

Nancy sat silent as George questioned her father about the presence of photographers in the highlands of Virginia. Dr. Adams doubted that any skilled photographers lived in the region. Yes, he believed that one could make a living there. A professional photographer should, he noted, choose a community with a college, which would provide a continuing market for a studio. He knew of one such town in faraway Southwest Virginia.

George N. Wertz, immigrant photographer, said good-bye to Nancy Adams, who had tears in her eyes, one who would remember him all her life. He would recall her fondly through the years but never with regret or longing. He kissed her on the platform, then boarded a Norfolk and Western train with a one-way ticket to Abingdon, Virginia, where there were two schools for young ladies, both in the same small town.

Soon, a devastated Nancy Adams slowly made her way home as George gazed intently out the window of his coach at the passing of lovely expanses of wetlands. Their majestic stretches of salt water, some gleaming in the sunlight, sent spiking shards of light from bright pockets of reflection. He watched, too, as the canals passed, their dark brown waters dismal and still.

The next day, in a moment of astounding perception, he saw it for the first time, the color of the Blue Ridge Mountains. He gazed, fascinated, as the train chugged into forests of dogwood and laurel and lilac as drifting summer fog glided silently at ground level and his soul took flight! George was too young to understand that in some convoluted way, awareness usually follows what the soul already knows.

Stepping from the train in Abingdon with all his possessions, George rented a room at the Hotel Abingdon. That first night in the town where he would spend the rest of his life, George wrote to his mother in her mountain village a continent away, explaining he felt at home again.

The second day George moved into a room in a boardinghouse and began a search for a suitable place for a photography studio. Walking up the hill toward the courthouse, he came upon the newspaper office of *The Virginian*. The mammoth press was operating wildly, the entire building shaking and vibrating as the massive black contraption thundered and jerked, pressing black words onto blank white paper. All the while the press spewed the jet-black specks of printer's ink, coating the office in literary soot. Peering cautiously through the open door, George could not hear the voice behind him. Turning, he saw the moving lips of an intense-looking older man.

Mr. Harold Kane, editor of *The Virginian*, eventually announced that he needed help in his newspaper office, which plunged George into his first business negotiation. When it concluded, he felt triumphant. As part of the agreement, George could use the vacant rooms in the back of the building as his studio. The actual salary would be miniscule, but Mr. Kane would barter the rooms for part-time labor.

Soon George's studio was sparsely furnished. When he found an attractive wooden love seat that cleaned up well, George decided it was a favorable sign from God that he should be there. It would be perfect for portraits.

Harold Kane, having an insight for selling papers, wrote a feature story about the young German photographer, which helped sell papers. Right away the community was drawn to the story.

From the beginning George produced extraordinary pictures at fair prices, quickly generating good business, and soon, the G. N. Wertz Photography Studio became well known. Many of the young ladies of the town found the handsome German more interesting than his pictures.

Two years later George moved to a new studio that fronted onto Main Street in a hollow near the creek at the foot of Courthouse Hill and sat across the dusty road from St. Thomas Episcopal Church. He had no way to know then that four generations of his bloodline would come to their knees and worship there. Business went well, and soon, he maintained a running ad in *The Virginian*.

George, a well-known and respected young professional, ultimately came to attend St. Thomas, where, at age thirty-five he met Frances Fuller, ten years younger. For whatever reason, the mystery of love that failed to come with Nancy Adams came with Frances Fuller. She was a sturdy yet curvaceous Scotch-Irish girl with regal carriage whose thick brown hair framed a pretty face. Her parents, like so many others, liked George from the beginning, captivated by his German accent, demeanor, and artistic profession.

Soon after their marriage, George joined the Episcopal church. Two years slipped by quickly, and Frances presented him a daughter, Georgia, born one year after his mother died on another continent.

Chapter 3

Bentley Thompson never reflected about what might have happened to his life had a pretty Martha girl invited him to the spring picnic or if he had not taken that Sunday-morning stroll or had missed seeing the blur of Georgia Wertz stumbling to the sidewalk. He did not ponder the universe and its cosmic order and the profound consequences in life of random events or nonevents dictated simply by chance. As he returned weekly to visit Georgia, their chance encounter of spring blossomed into a summer romance.

George Wertz scrutinized Bentley Thompson closely the day Georgia brought him to the studio. George's fatherly desire to protect his daughter from the advances of any male did not come into play. He did not realize that nestled comfortably in a part of his soul was an extraordinary sense of gratitude toward the kind men in his life; subconsciously, he prepared to repay the kindness.

Frances Wertz was charmed by Bentley's handsome looks and courtly manners, yet she realized Georgia was rushing head-on, into the blindness of first love, the love of loves, the love that can sustain one for a lifetime. She knew that there would be little use to remind Georgia that those first vast rushes of romantic love inevitably fade, unable to sustain themselves in their sheer, blinding passion. She knew too that her daughter was locked in the cosmic pull of glory and exhilaration, of illusion and madness. Watching lovingly and quietly from a distance, Frances dismissed her first warning signals, a distant feminine alert. Any mother, she realized, felt conflict, being both pleased and saddened to see her daughter captivated by a young man.

The fickle and unpredictable chill of June disappeared as a blazing July fell upon the mountains. As if captivated by the same changing magic, Georgia and Bentley, like shiny new magnets, were drawn to see each other every weekend.

Working each Saturday, Bentley routinely rushed to catch the last train for Abingdon at six-thirty. Georgia waited for him at the railroad station and, later, outside the Belmont Hotel, where Bentley, a consummate deal maker, managed to get a reduced rate.

They strolled endlessly in the evenings, moving through dusk into the darkness of summer nights decorated by the sporadic incandescence of fireflies and the screechy chirping of crickets. Once while strolling, Bentley told Georgia of his parents in Johnson City, where his father worked "in the printing business," failing to explain that his father was a print setter. He confided that he got his personality from his gregarious mother.

An intuitive man, Bentley came to understand and appreciate Georgia's personality, which she presented as an uncomplicated and uninhibited gift. Captivated and intoxicated by the soaring magic, Bentley held her apart, as an untouchable, pristine model of womanhood. Soon he felt more, much more, as he became driven by a physical desire that threatened, it seemed, to engulf him. Further fanning his raging hormones, Georgia herself raced head-on with abandon in her own desires; yet, magically, she always wrestled herself back into control. While that restraint came with great reluctance, it came nevertheless with strong resolve. Eventually both grew accustomed to the rhythms of their mating ritual, an elementary dance of desire. Each time she brought the passionate flow to its abrupt, unsettling halt, she did so with a gentle sweetness that dissipated Bentley's anger, if not his frustration. He, too, was in his own throes of first love.

In August a carnival created the highlight of the summer. At twilight on a Saturday evening, the young couple walked on the sawdust street of the exciting, brightly lit midway. Bentley sported a fashionable outfit, while Georgia wore a white cotton dress, modestly low in the front and tight around her small waist. Strolling past the rides and sideshows, they received many admiring glances.

Quickly drawn to the melodic notes of the carrousel, she bolted forward, crying, "Bentley! Let's ride!" Childlike, she gazed upon magnificently carved horses, commercially artistic gems, as they flowed past, each frozen in dramatic racing poses with terrified expressions, menacing eyes, and flared nostrils. Their look of madness was strange contrasted to the sweet refrains of the organ music and the gentle rising and falling of the animals in their endless circular race.

Georgia ran toward a black stallion, his eyes glaring insanely under a full, wildly chiseled mane. Deciding to sit sidesaddle in her flowing dress, she called, "Lift me up, Bentley, please," He eased her into the saddle and started to speak, but the carrousel jerked forward. "Hurry, Bentley!" she shouted as if he were in danger of being left behind. Mounting the inside horse, a caramel-colored mare, poised in the lowest position, Bentley began to rise as Georgia's mount fell beside him.

As the carrousel surged underway, Bentley touched the knot of his red tie and adjusted the linen handkerchief in his breast pocket, oblivious of Georgia for the moment. "Bentley!" cried the girl on the stallion beside him.

"Yeah?" he responded, chin still buried in his chest, looking down at the handkerchief.

"I love this night, and I love you!" yelled the Blue Ridge girl as her stallion fell to the low point of his circular crusade. Bentley, at a momentary zenith, turned to her, but before he could speak, he had fallen and she had risen above him, so he did not respond.

"Bent-ley!" she called again, drawing out his name to a rising lilt.

"What is it? What do you want?" he yelled, frustrated.

"It was nothing, Bentley, nothing really important. I was just being silly," she confessed, hesitant to reveal her disappointment. Gazing outward, away from Bentley, she thought, *After all, he is a man.* He was not, she told herself, expected to get excited over such a childish pleasure, but her feminine intuition would not be denied. Georgia realized that Bentley did not understand the magic of the moment, her simple childish joy. Forgetting the silly incident, she forgave his maleness.

The next afternoon they watched the transitory and ephemeral prize of color and excitement that had decorated the landscape for the previous week being stripped of its magic. In a remote way, she sensed that lives were enriched by the facade of illusion.

All around them, the carnival collapsed in frenzied, controlled chaos. Those who had beckoned relentlessly to the town folks during the week now shouted harsh orders sprinkled with profanity and vulgarity, ignoring the bystanders.

"Oh, Bentley! This is awful," she whispered, clutching his arm tightly.

"What is, sweetheart?" he asked remotely.

"This was magical; now it's coming apart. It was so beautiful before, and the animals, they're pitiful."

"Yeah, it's sad to see 'em locked up that way," he answered, attempting to convey concern he did not possess. "Want some iced tea?" he asked.

"That would be nice. Let's go home so we can have some time together before you have to leave."

That Sunday night at the end of summer, Bentley went home, the carnival left town, and Georgia, in passing, thought of the carrousel.

* * * * *

Fall crept to the Blue Ridge, masquerading as Indian summer; but, like first love, it could not sustain its own glory, its own passion. The hue began to fade from the mountains as Georgia returned to her second year at Stonewall Academy of Nursing. She was surprised to learn Bentley was not taking courses at King. He needed to concentrate, he said, on the demands of his new position as assistant manager. She was proud of his promotion, confident that eventually he would get his accounting degree.

Frances continued to monitor Georgia and Bentley, wanting to maximize Georgia's happiness within reason. That accounted for her decision to allow Georgia to visit in Bristol with her Aunt Kate and her family. Frances's sister, Kate Benson, seven years older, was a hardy woman of keen intellect and quick wit. She and her husband, Jim, had three children—two sons and a daughter—all of whom looked to Georgia as a sister. She had spent a week each summer with the Bensons since she was twelve years old. Georgia, the only child, craved the familial relationship and the exciting and hectic family life of her cousins.

Georgia loved each of her cousins, secretly favoring Newton, two years older and a King College student. Slightly shorter than Bentley, Newton possessed a spirited, fiery personality and a zest for life. Sarah, an attractive young woman a year older than Georgia, was not graced with the haunting beauty of her cousin. Georgia's oldest cousin, John, twenty-two, was her older surrogate brother. Returning from pharmacy school, he insisted on paying for his room at home until he got his own place.

For reasons of chemistry more than bloodline, Georgia and the Bensons shared a deep familial bond. As the cousins grew into young adults, Newton and John became as protective of Georgia as of their sister, Sarah.

The Bensons knew Bentley in the superficial way family members come to know the boy who arrives on the doorstep to escort a girl from their midst. Kate and Sarah were impressed with his looks and manners. John saw him occasionally in the men's shop, but he gave little thought one way or the other.

Newton was different: He disliked Bentley Thompson from the beginning. Bentley, sensing Newton's negative feelings, chose to ignore him, considering him to be just "another minion" as he once remarked to Georgia. Georgia's quick defense of Newt was so protective that Bentley promised himself to never broach the subject again.

On a Sunday afternoon John found himself in a heated discussion with his brother about Bentley Thompson. "Yes, goddamn it, I'll admit that I don't like him. I *hate* it when that little son of a bitch sees me and says, 'There's little Newt!' He has about a quarter of an inch on me!" fumed Newton.

"Okay, okay, Newt. I'll admit it, I'm not particularly fond of him either," confessed John, his voice falling lower as he continued, "But listen: Georgia may be in love with him; and if she is, there is nothing you or anybody else can do about it. If you go against Bentley, it will be going against her. Attack him, and you'll be attacking her. I know you don't want to hurt Georgia."

"No, I don't," admitted Newton, "but, on the other hand, I don't want *him* to hurt her. What am I supposed to do? Just pretend that I think he's a great guy?"

"That's all you can do right now," answered John.

At that moment, Bentley Thompson walked toward the front porch, where Georgia and Sarah sat swinging in the fall breeze. Carrying a small pot of chrysanthemums, he announced, "Good afternoon, ladies," looking at Sarah before meeting Georgia's admiring gaze. Extending the flowers toward her, he announced, "These are for you, Sarah."

"Bentley. How thoughtful! Let me go put them inside," Sarah responded, excusing herself quickly.

As Bentley eased onto the swing, Georgia leaned forward, kissing him on the cheek. He resisted slightly, a bit uncomfortable on the open porch. Bentley knew that he was under the scrutiny of the Benson brothers, especially Newton.

Bentley Thompson was not the only young man with a date that afternoon. At that moment suited with a bright red tie, Newt opened the front screen door and stepped onto the porch. Focused on his own romantic quest, he was slightly startled when Bentley called, "Well, there's Newt!"

"Oh . . . Hello, Bentley," Newt intoned with traces of sarcasm, remembering his brother's admonition. "See you later, Georgia," he said, skipping down the steps.

A short time later Georgia and Bentley walked to a single-horse surrey, which he had borrowed for the special day. Riding aimlessly around a small lake in the fading golden glow of the Sunday afternoon, they passed other couples dressed in their Sunday best, strolling arm in arm as if the very act of walking were an art form.

Georgia nestled closer to Bentley and asked softly, "Bentley, I just remembered. You said you had a surprise. Is this it? Is it the buggy?"

"No, sweetheart, it's something else," answered Bentley. "It's a place, somewhere you've never been before," he answered, turning for the first time to look into her pale eyes.

"The shop! You're taking me to the shop! But Bentley, it's closed today isn't it?" she asked, perplexed.

"Don't forget, I'm the assistant manager now. I have a key," he intoned proudly.

Twilight was fading as Bentley turned the key in the back door of J. S. Simpson's Clothing Shop. The last pale light of day brightened the windows enough to cause a slight glare as she stepped inside. Assaulted by a mixture of masculine odors, she paused to get her bearings. The smell of fine leather and wax on hardwood floors merged with the musky scent of stacked fabric and the distinctive, slightly sweet aroma of fading pipe tobacco. She recognized the scents of Bay Rum and Lilac Vegetal because her father used both.

Without speaking, Bentley took her hand and led her toward a leather couch. A rough-hewn coffee table with magazines and a walnut cigar box sat in front of the sofa, suggesting carefully constructed masculine casualness. Georgia sat down and extended her arms open wide as Bentley moved to her and pressed his lips gently on hers. Quickly they were lost to another dimension as he kissed her neck at the cradle of her shoulders. Georgia moved her hands to his upper arms, gently pushing him away as Bentley, breathing heavily, stared up in surprise. He pulled her urgently, closing for another kiss, yearning desperately to renew the blinding race toward oblivion. He did not see the pale green eyes that gazed upon his face, but he heard the soft, gentle drawl of the Blue Ridge as she whispered, "No, Bentley. No, my love."

"Why not?" he asked, voice thick and heavy. "We love each other, we want each other, and we're alone for the first time!"

"We have to wait," she whispered as if to keep a secret.

Bentley said nothing when she suggested it was time to leave. Driving home, he was distant. She sat close, clutching his arm, remembering that he was a man, knowing that the physical frustration had to be greater for him. Again, like the night at the carnival, she forgave his remoteness. At least this time she could understand.

The next morning Georgia awoke to find an anemic, drizzling rain, a dismal Monday. After breakfast, Aunt Kate and John accompanied her to the station, where she boarded the train for Abingdon.

The passing countryside, dripping wet in the gray fall rain, moved by in a blur as she thought of her time in the park and in the shop with Bentley. As her reverie drifted further back to the carnival, she was unaware the train was slowing to a stop. Reality returned when she saw the erect figure of her father holding a black umbrella on the station platform. He stood poised, smiling slightly, as he watched and waited to escort her to the safety of his carriage.

Chapter 4

On a brilliant Saturday at the end of October, Jeanette Moore, a handsome woman of thirty-eight, made a strange discovery. As she walked from the back door of her rented carriage house toward her clothesline, the beauty of the splendid day did not escape her. Indian summer, adorned in a magnificent autumn garb, first arrived dragging with it the sensuous heat of August, but now this lovely cool day of fall was in perfect balance with the season of the Blue Ridge.

Jeanette's attractive face had large features, suggesting traces of Eastern European peasantry. Her full black hair matched jet-black eyes the color of the coal her father and brothers still wrenched from the dark mines of West Virginia.

Pausing to study the gauzy clouds overhead, Jeanette drifted in thought back to West Virginia. Like most people removed from the place of their childhoods, hers would reside in her soul forever; but she remembered the home of the little girl, home before she came to learn how little they possessed, before she came to know they lived an impoverished existence. As those fleeting recollections came to Jeanette, she was unaware that her soul gleefully played tricks on her conscious mind, making her believe that home was better and kinder and happier than it ever really had been. She did not realize that selective memory came as a gift from that soul, allowing her to forget the cruel and painful part of growing up; ironically, though, the soul never forgets, and one of its dimensions is the pain it suffers and endures.

At eighteen Jeanette fled from a muddy hollow in West Virginia to seek an education, something that had eluded the rest of her pathetic family trapped for generations in poverty. As a young girl, she worked where she could find a job. Later she became the nanny to a young coal executive and his wife who eventually relocated to Abingdon. When invited to move with her employers, Jeanette accepted happily. Staying with the kind and affluent family a few years, she learned social graces and acquired tastes unknown to her clan at home, yet Jeanette had a dream of getting an education, so, with meager savings, she left the family and enrolled in a bookkeeping course, pursuing a profession that belonged at the time to males only. Eventually she received a certificate as a certified bookkeeper.

Thirteen years had passed since she was hired by the most prosperous accountant in town who, after recognizing her talent, began using her to make compliance reviews as part of his pre-audit procedure. Being sent to businesses around town, Jeanette grew in poise and self-confidence. Some clients were impressed with her looks, looks that grew on a man. Such recognition, however, did not motivate her employer to pay her as much as he would have paid a man doing the same job, which was one of the reasons Jeanette also worked as a waitress on weekends at Kit's Café near Depot Square.

Jeanette met several young professionals through her audit work, but always, they eventually drifted away to marry local women from families of wealth and position. Over the years she selectively took a lover or two, but none of the affairs moved past infatuation. She was still not too old, she hoped, to fall in love. Then, three years ago, it happened, Jeanette Moore fell in love when she was sent to perform a pre-audit at the Express Office of the Norfolk and Western Railroad Station. The aloof station master, a pale, thin man in his mid-sixties, was overtly disdainful of a woman in a position to review any aspect of his operation. When she was introduced to Will West, the assistant station master, his handsome looks attracted her right away, but, more than looks, his kindness drew her in, touching her deeply. She cherished his respect for her position as a professional.

Will had thick black hair and a swarthy complexion, giving dark looks to a face chiseled with attractive features. His dark eyes sparkled when he talked to Jeanette, making her feel as if she were the only person present for miles. In short, he seemed too good to be true. He was; he was married. Jeanette learned that Will, married to a remote woman from a wealthy family, was one of the promising young men of the community.

Standing in the backyard in the morning sunlight, Jeanette dismissed thoughts of Will West as she approached her clothesline. Later, while sorting her laundry, she found that a pair of black silk panties was missing. Always on a strict budget, she knew well each item of her clothing, but she assumed she was mistaken, that they were in her lingerie drawer.

Not far away on Valley Street, Georgia Wertz sat in the sunshine on her back porch steps with her first cousin, Jean Deaton, and their friend, Eliza Horn, who requested, "Okay, explain it for me, Jean."

"Well," Jean sighed, "everybody in admissions at Martha knows about it. Anyway, a pair of Natalie White's panties was missing from the clothesline, so Mr. White called Sheriff Woodward to report the missing underpants!"

Neither the sheriff nor the underwear victims knew that for several months, many women had discovered underwear missing from their clotheslines although some thefts had gone undetected. Some suggested that it was a college prank, perhaps part of a fraternity initiation. Only one person knew the truth.

* * * * *

The Indian summer, mellow with smoky twilight evenings, drew to an end as the days began to lose their luster, like tarnished copper plates in the Wertz Studio. Soon, those days gave way to cold nights as winter approached the Blue Ridge. Georgia was moving into two seasons: the spring in the essence of her being, and the less complicated, natural season of winter.

* * * * *

On a sunny Friday afternoon near the end of October, Frances insisted that Georgia call Bentley to tell him not to come for the weekend because she had the flu. Georgia was in no shape to receive any visitor, even Bentley Thompson.

At seven o'clock on Saturday evening Bentley rang the doorbell at the Wertz residence. Frances responded, telling her daughter's suitor that Georgia was in bed asleep. "Could I visit with her just a moment, Mrs. Wertz?" he asked.

"Bentley, please understand. She's *sick,* in *bed,* and she's *sleeping,*" Frances stressed in a loud whisper to emphasize her words.

"Oh, yeah, okay. I'm sorry, Mrs. Wertz, of course. I hope she'll be better tomorrow. I hope you and Mr. Wertz have a nice night," he responded, backing toward the steps.

As he turned away, the front porch light went off while a dark figure watched from across the street. As Bentley walked downtown, he and the figure paralleled each other on opposite sides of Valley Street until, heading to Kit's Café, Bentley turned south to Main Street. Usually, some of the old gang without dates hung out there drinking beer on Saturday nights.

At that moment, Helen Hanson, a shy, twenty-one-year- old waitress at Kit's Café walked toward the long table of King College men. A thin girl with unremarkable features, Helen had short, straw-colored hair, which was pulled back severely on the sides. Thin and wearing no makeup, Helen was easy to overlook. As she approached the two tables pulled end-to-end, she was afraid of the boisterous young men who had been drinking beer for hours. Trembling, she made her way through the smoke-filled room. Overhead the fans of summer still turned slowly moving the heavy air, rank with the competing odor of fried food, smoke, and spilled beer.

Each time Helen approached the table, she was startled by the brazen way the young men tried to grope her as she squeezed between close chairs. The most menacing of locals, the dark and dirty mountain men, never did that. Helen was thankful her best friend, Jeanette Moore, was working that night. Jeanette didn't get that treatment from the group because she had a presence the younger and timid Helen did not possess.

A bottle of Tennessee whiskey, passed under the table throughout the night, was taking its toll. Helen was frightened, but she knew Kit liked the way the college men spent money and regularly gave them more leeway than the local customers. This night, though, Kit was out of town, making Helen feel even more insecure.

Approaching Big Jim Hoggard sitting at one end of the table, Helen had no way to know of his metamorphosis, that he had changed from a docile sweet boy to an angry, aggressive man. His sheer size intimidated the locals, who were thoroughly disgusted with the group.

Holding a large pitcher of draft beer by both hands, Helen stopped next to Hoggard. "Who gets this pitcher?" she asked faintly, vainly attempting to hide her fright.

"Right here, little darlin'. You put it down right here," came a response from across the wide table.

Helen's intuition warned her not to weave her way to the other side of the table, where she might be trapped. She decided instead to lean across the table. With both arms extended, holding the full pitcher, she reached across to her left. As she stretched forward, her trailing right leg rose slightly from the floor, as she precariously balanced on her left foot. Off balance, she was horrified when Hoggard's massive sweaty palm slid under her dress up her thigh. She bolted forward across the table before running frantically into the arms of Jeanette Moore.

"It's okay, baby. You don't have to go back over there again."

As Bentley fell into an empty chair next to the grinning Hoggard, a full glass of beer was shoved in front of him. Taking a quick sip, he glanced up to see Hoggard smiling at him.

"Bent!" slurred the giant in a guttural voice, "You're the best. You know that?"

"Thank you, Hog Man," responded Bentley, hoping he would not be the brunt of taunts from the table.

Entering the front door, Will West sensed the elevated tempo, even for a Saturday night. Jeanette made her way toward Will with a draft beer. Will noticed her concerned expression. "Hi. Anything wrong?" he asked.

"Everything's wrong," she answered, glancing toward the table of college boys.

"What is it?"

"We're short of help. Kit's gone. Those King boys are out of control, and you know Kit doesn't allow us to call the law," she said, her husky voice quivering uncharacteristically.

"I heard them when I came in. What have they done?" asked Will, his eyes locked on hers.

After Jeanette quickly told him about Helen's abuse, Will asked, "Have you been back to the table since it happened?"

"No, we're afraid to," she answered.

"Which one put his hand under her dress?" asked a deadly serious Will West.

"The big son of a bitch, the monster," Jeanette answered, arms folded across her chest.

"Y'all should never be subject to that," Will muttered with disgust. "Let me see if I can appeal to their reason."

"Where's he going?" asked Helen.

"Over to your table," Jeanette answered. "Said he was going to appeal to their reason, but it's too late for that."

At that moment, all the students were shaken to hear Hoggard announce, "I think it's Niagara Falls time!" As he reached to unbutton his pants, all knew he was ready to urinate under the table so they turned to the only person capable of influencing him. Taking the clue quickly, Bentley stood up, saying, "Hog Man, listen! Are you listening?" Hoggard, bemused by Bentley, allowed his massive hand to leave his fly and return to the tabletop. Bentley, desperate to keep him diverted, started to speak but was interrupted.

"Talk about something besides yourself, Bentley," chided Ron Sutton.

"Ron, you know what? You're not worthy to lick the sweat off my balls!" retorted The Bent.

In a flash, Sutton sucker-punched Bentley, driving him backward into the approaching Will West, knocking him to the floor. As several of the boys restrained Sutton, two more helped Bentley to his feet, but nobody made an effort to assist the townie in the khaki work clothes. The conflict was diffused by quick apologies from the combatants, neither of whom wanted to fight.

As Will returned to the cash register, a tearful Jeanette asked, "Will, are you all right? I couldn't believe it."

"Yeah, I'm okay . . ." he answered detachedly. "Do you have any rolls of half dollars?"

"Sure, there's several rolls in the cash drawer," she answered, pointing toward the massive brown cash register.

"Let me have two. I'll give them back in a minute," he requested.

"What in the world . . ." she began slowly.

"Just give me two rolls, please," Will repeated gravely.

As Jeanette took two rolls of half dollars from the cash drawer, Will pulled a red railroad bandana from his rear pocket and enclosed the heavy coins, drawing the cloth tightly around them. He tied a hard knot at the base of the coins, leaving the rest of the cloth as a grip for the homemade blackjack. The locals gazed silently as Will again made his way toward the table. This time, several people moved the chairs to make a path, but the college boys failed to notice.

Will walked toward Bentley, still sitting next to Hoggard. "Excuse me," Will said to Bentley.

"It's a local townie staking out his territory like a dog pissin' in the yard," came a voice from the opposite end of the table, causing nervous laughter. Bentley ventured a snicker because, after all, he had the giant for protection, and the giant was *in the zone.*

Will, ignoring the insult, addressed Bentley. "You knocked me down a few minutes ago, and you didn't say a word. Didn't your parents teach you manners?"

Bentley stammered, but before he could answer, Hoggard stirred. "Well, what the hell's goin on here?" he barked, standing up, knocking his chair to the floor. Will instinctively took a step backward as the massive man rose, towering over him. Keeping his eyes on the giant's face, Will saw the man's massive hand grip an empty beer mug. "What's your problem?" Hoggard shouted again.

"My problem's not with you. It's with this man," answered Will, canting his head toward Bentley without taking his eyes off the giant.

"You don't understand," bellowed Hoggard, "You don't have a problem with *him*! You have the problem with *me*!"

Will responded in a low voice, "I don't have a problem with you."

Hoggard grabbed a mug of beer, taking several gulps before spewing a stream through his teeth onto the floor toward Will. Still standing, Hoggard jerked his head back toward the ceiling as he bellowed a deep laugh that reverberated around the room. Will's right fist embedded itself deeply into Hoggard's flabby gut. Hoggard's huge body involuntarily contracted downward as he crashed to the floor, but rolling quickly to his knees, he looked up just in time to see the blurred object as the bandana delivered the coins through his wild mane into the hard bone of his skull. Flashing a bewildered look, Hoggard's eyes rolled upward under their lids as he fell to the floor, unconscious.

Bentley stood ashen and wobbly as Will moved toward him. "Now," began Will, "let's start all over. You knocked me down, and you didn't say a word."

Bentley, feeling faint, started feebly, "Sir, I knew I bumped against somebody, but when I looked around, I didn't see you. I apologize. I'm sorry. It was inexcusable."

"I accept your apology," Will responded, turning toward Mark Smith as he ordered, "You! Get over here!" Smith, a tall, thin lad stumbled toward Will, his lower lip trembling in terror, tears in his eyes.

"Yes, sir," Smith said weakly, drawing near the man with the bloody bandana.

"I heard what you said," Will began calmly, "about the dog and the territory."

"Sir, I'm sorry! It was stupid! I didn't mean it! I'm sorry, truly sorry!" gushed a terrified Smith.

"Thank you. I accept your apology, too," Will responded, glancing down at the unconscious body of the giant.

"Now, I want to talk to you," Will ordered.

After he spoke quietly, the students walked in a single file toward Helen and Jeanette. There, each one stepped forward, apologizing first to Helen, then to Jeanette. All eyes stayed on Will as he directed the boys to pull Hoggard to the door. "I'll pay for a taxi, and I'll call Doc Smith and tell him you're coming," said Will as an order.

"Yes, sir!" responded Hugh Carrington.

Relieved to see Hoggard regaining consciousness, Will whispered, "What I did wasn't right, Jeanette. And it's not over yet. If the big boy files charges, I'll need a good lawyer."

"Do you really think so?" she asked, instinctively touching his forearm.

"I know so," he answered gravely.

He quickly kissed Jeanette and Helen on their cheeks, and then walked home.

It was near midnight when Jeanette saw the familiar silhouette of Sheriff John Woodward fill the front door. Walking toward the counter, the sheriff removed his gray western-style hat. At fifty-two years old, the sheriff still moved in a way that suggested the controlled energy of a younger man. He wore a dark three-quarter–length coat, dress pants, and cowboy boots. His pearl-handled .38-caliber revolver hung from his right hip at hand level. His swarthy face was mildly handsome, with few lines, brown eyes, square jawbones, and a full mustache. Placing his hat on the counter, he straddled a stool and sat down as Jeanette approached, heart pounding.

"Evening, Sheriff. Can I get you a cup of coffee?" asked Jeanette.

"Good evening, Jeanette. Yes, thank you, I think I will have a cup," replied the sheriff of Washington County. As Jeanette walked away, John Woodward casually surveyed the room, noticing that eyes diverted as he looked about. He saw it clearly; he saw corporate guilt.

As Jeanette placed a cup of steaming hot coffee on the counter, she asked, "Can I get you something to eat, Sheriff?"

"No thanks, Jeanette. Coffee's enough," he answered, looking directly in her eyes. "Is everything all right?"

"Sure, Sheriff. Everything's fine," she answered, too quickly.

"I understand there was a problem over here earlier," he responded, holding his gaze intensely.

"Oh that," she began with a quick smile, "Yeah, there was a little problem with, you know, the college crowd, but everything's okay now."

"Well, that's good to hear," he responded, taking his first sip of coffee.

Jeanette sensed correctly that the sheriff knew precisely what had happened earlier. "Sure I can't get you something to eat?" she asked, afraid the sheriff might question her about Will.

Sheriff Woodward answered by pushing a nickel and his coffee mug toward her side of the counter as he stood with his hat in hand. "No, I appreciate your offer, but I've had a long day. Got to get home. Good night, Jeanette."

"Good night, Sheriff," Jeanette answered as she watched him pass through the door into the night.

All eyes followed the sheriff through the door, including the eyes of one who scrutinized the sheriff very closely, instinctively viewing him as the enemy. That person had no way to know that eventually, their paths would cross and change the course of several lives.

Later that night, Sheriff John Woodward lay awake beside his sleeping wife, thinking about the assistant station master. Will West wasn't the only person concerned that a complaint might be filed by the college boy.

As Will West and John Woodward lay in their respective beds, the shadowy figure that had walked for a while alongside Bentley still moved about the town, eventually passing both their homes.

No one from the white side of town knew Jamie's last name, but many saw the thin, sinewy black man every day, walking incessantly, as if some invisible cosmic energy set him in motion, never to rest. Most people assumed correctly that the journey itself, with the seemingly random routes, was the central part of his existence. Like a soldier in an endless march, Jamie crisscrossed the town, day and night.

No one knew his age, but most assumed he was in his late twenties. A small, dark-complexioned man, Jamie kept a stubble of sparse black beard around his smiling face, which exuded a simple sweetness. He was a shy man, unable to look one directly in the eyes. Like a human puppet dangling from an invisible string, Jamie leaned backward from his waist and canted slightly to his right. Resembling a comic strip character, his backward cant made his feet and legs appear in front of the rest of his body.

Jamie's people lived on the south side of town. There, in his community, he and his family were well known. "Jamie can't keep no job," they acknowledged with resignation. "Walkin', he ain't able to do nothing but walkin'." On the other side of town, he remained a mystery, traversing between the two worlds.

Chapter 5

Georgia returned to her second year of nursing studies at Stonewall while Bentley excelled in his job. They wrote letters during the week, and he traveled to Abingdon each weekend. Always eager to be alone, they continued evening walks as they had in summer. Neither was aware that they were the secret focus of another's deep interest.

Georgia continued to talk to Jean about Bentley, but for the first time in her life, Jean was not candid with her cousin, deciding to be circumspect about Bentley. As a result, Jean withheld even veiled criticism of the man. *After all,* she told herself, *if Georgia's in love with him, he must have good qualities. And, too, everything she says about him makes him seem very nice.* Still, she could not dismiss a pervasive distrust of the dapper and articulate Bentley Thompson.

Jean had other things on her mind; she was being pursued by thirty-three-year-old William Webb, a doctor with a budding practice. William, an angular man with dark hair, was widely known as a disheveled, egocentric maverick. His intense eyes suggested an intelligence often masked by reckless behavior. His education and prominent family background did not dispel the rumors alleging that he used codeine and drank alcohol to excess. Perhaps his dimension of madness attracted the fiercely independent Jean, whose youth made her believe she could change the course of his self-destructive behavior.

Georgia had never seen Jean touched by a man, but she didn't articulate her apprehension about the doctor; thus, the two who could share the same thoughts without speaking chose to silence their respective concerns.

The turning season moved toward winter when the tobacco market opened, and the town's pace quickened as farmers streamed into the warehouses, their wagons laden with flat baskets stacked high with the golden dried leaves. The Norfolk and Western trains kept the town in touch with the ever-expanding outside world. All in all things were going well for the hamlet in Southwestern Virginia until a Martha girl went missing.

Sheriff John Woodward, having been called at eleven o'clock on a Sunday night, rode to the campus of Martha Washington College. The president, Dr. Sidney Clarke, a Richmond native, was still dressed in a suit and tie. In his mid-sixties with silver-gray hair, a trim build, and gold-rimmed glasses, Dr. Clarke *looked* like the president of Martha Washington College. Smiling nervously, he opened the door and ushered John into his well-appointed office. Although the president could raise disdain to an art form, he always showed deference to the sheriff. John suspected that it was because they both attended St. Thomas Episcopal Church, but in his own right, the sheriff was a popular community leader. Now the president of Martha Washington College desperately needed John Woodward. "John, please sit down," he requested.

"Thank you," John responded, sitting in front of the massive walnut desk as Dr. Clarke paused. Taking the cue, John asked, "Dr. Clarke, please tell me everything you know at this point. Begin, if you would, at the time you were first notified the girl was missing."

John took notes as Dr. Clarke related that a sophomore from Roanoke, Anna Marie Holmes, was last seen walking on campus near dusk. He described her as a pretty girl who quietly pursued her studies "and did not break rules; apparently, she did not *think* about breaking rules. And that, Sheriff, is one of the things that distresses me. It's unlike her not to return to her room for curfew. Her roommate said that she doesn't have a boyfriend so she shouldn't be delayed for that reason, especially until this late hour."

Anna Marie was last seen in a garden on the west side of the main building near the arboretum, an area separated from the tracks of the Norfolk and Western Railway by a fence, honeysuckle, and unattended undergrowth. Dr. Clarke explained that he sent a party of male professors to search the area but they had found nothing out of the ordinary. Anna Marie's roommate, Sue Harper, reported her missing when she failed to return to the room at the eight o'clock curfew. Hours later, after much debate and checking and rechecking by faculty members, Dr. Clarke directed a professor to call the sheriff.

Dr. Clarke's secretary tapped lightly and, stepping inside, informed John that his deputies were downstairs in the main parlor with the professors who conducted the search. All were standing by, awaiting orders from the sheriff or the president. Dr. Clarke looked at John with pleading eyes.

John Woodward had handled hundreds of investigations in his career, some major, but most routine. With this complaint, he sensed he was embarking on a major journey, a long voyage into uncharted waters. "Did you speak with Sue Harper?" he asked Dr. Clarke.

"No, one of the professors talked to her. Dr. Brown, I believe."

"Who talked to the girls who saw Anna Marie last?"

"Sheriff," began Dr. Clarke tensely, "I have no idea who talked to each of the girls. My secretary provided me with the details of the inquiry."

"Would you join me for a conference with your professors and my deputies? I'll make assignments, but I would appreciate your being present."

"Of course."

John met with the deputies and the professors in a classroom in which Anna Marie Holmes had sat two days earlier. He assigned one of his deputies to assist the professors in another search of the campus. This time, the search would be conducted systematically by defined quadrants.

John asked Dr. Clarke to have every room checked to ensure that Miss Holmes was not present and to ask each occupant if she had seen Anna Marie during the past twenty-four hours. John noted that he wanted to interview any person who had seen Anna Marie during the day. He hesitated before he said, "Anna Marie," choosing not to use the phrase "the victim" at that time.

As the men silently filed from the room, Sidney Clarke asked, "I am prepared to call her parents, John. Would you concur with that action at this point?"

"Sidney," John began, "she's been missing for over six hours. Now that you've officially reported her missing, I would have to notify them if you don't. So, I think you'll have to do it tonight."

"I'll call them right away," responded Dr. Clarke, walking briskly from the room.

John, his deputies, and the volunteers worked well into the morning without developing new information. At two-thirty the men gathered in the classroom again. Because Dr. Clarke was absent, John thanked the men in behalf of the president. All said good night and walked from the room in a reverent silence, like monks leaving a darkened chapel.

The next morning at daybreak John and his deputies searched the campus again, but there was no trace of Anna Marie Holmes.

* * * * *

The Wednesday before Thanksgiving Georgia stepped from the train in Bristol to see Bentley walking briskly toward her.

"Georgia, I'm sorry I'm late! Had trouble getting off in time to meet you," he called, leaning forward, kissing her quickly on the cheek and reaching for her bag.

Walking toward a taxi carriage, Georgia asked, "What time will you pick me up for the dance tonight?"

"I'll be there by seven-thirty."

"If you can get to Aunt Kate's in time, we could ride with Sarah and her date," Georgia offered.

"I have my own rig tonight," Bentley revealed, helping her into the taxi carriage. "I'll get there as soon as I can. Bye," he called, raising his hand to wave. Soon, Georgia reached the Benson home, where Aunt Kate moved the curtains to peep out just as the taxi stopped.

After Bentley arrived, he charmed Aunt Kate while John looked on, bemused and apart. After polite conversation and good-byes, Bentley and Georgia left, arriving soon at the hotel. As they danced, sipped punch, and occasionally talked with others, Bentley was pleased knowing Georgia drew the attention of many. Soon he told her that they could be alone in the shop again if she were willing to leave early. Relieved, he saw her subtle smile, one that conveyed their secret; they had a place to go!

The shop was cozy, pleasant against the chill of the night. Sitting on the leather sofa in the center of the room, they were again surrounded by mounds of stacked fabrics while a single light burned in the center of the store. The streetlights outside shined dimly through the front windows. "I'm glad they banked the fire," Bentley said as he looked toward the potbelly stove still glowing orange inside. "It'll be nice and warm in here for a long time," he said, getting up.

"Where are you going?" she asked.

"I have a little surprise. I'll be right back." Georgia heard his footsteps descending the basement steps. Minutes later Bentley returned with a small bottle of champagne and two glasses. He poured Georgia's first without speaking and handed it to her. After he filled his glass, he saw that she held hers at eye level toward the pale glow of the stove. She said nothing, staring at the straw-colored effervescence.

"Georgia?" he said softly, still standing, "Here's to us."

"To us," she said, raising her glass slightly.

After they both took a sip, he spoke her name again. "Georgia?"

"Yes?" she answered, looking up.

"Will you marry me?"

Closing her eyes, Georgia slowly leaned her head backward against the sofa, her chin elevated, her long elegant neck extended. Then leaning forward, away from the sofa, she slowly ran extended fingers through her thick hair. She turned slowly, deliberately, as she reached for his hands and whispered, "Yes. Yes, Bentley. I will marry you." The kiss that followed was gentle, soothing. When they pulled apart, Georgia looked into his eyes and smiled.

"Are you ready to go?" he asked softly.

"Yes," she whispered.

Driving toward Aunt Kate's, neither discussed his proposal and her acceptance. His question and her response defined the night. There was no more to say, nothing to ask and no answers to provide. They gave no thought to the fact that a proposal and an acceptance always bring profound consequences. Theirs would be no exception.

Before the holiday ended, they agreed that Georgia would finish nursing school and attempt to get a job in Bristol, where Bentley would pursue his successful career. At her insistence, he promised to continue taking accounting courses toward his degree. Those general plans were enough, enough to carry them forward into a new season of their lives. They agreed that for the present, they would keep their engagement a secret.

The amber glow of the Thanksgiving harvest celebration faded as a crisp December brought snow flakes and the approaching Christmas season. The glow in Georgia's soul flowed with the Advent season. Georgia told only one about her engagement, and Jean listened quietly, revealing only surprise and happiness. They would share the secret.

George and Frances Wertz noted Georgia's outward glow and her pensive moments. They knew, as parents often come to know, that she was no longer theirs exclusively. Now Georgia loved a man, another man besides her father. They understood with a bittersweet happiness in their hearts that Bentley, the object of her love, possessed a part of her now, and with that realization, they fully accepted Bentley Thompson. Wisely, they understood they could do little about the relationship anyway.

* * * * *

The highlight of the season was the Christmas Eve candlelight service at St. Thomas Episcopal Church, a yearly ritual since Jean and Georgia were children. William declined to accompany Jean, but because that did not surprise her, she was not disappointed. For Georgia the service would not be complete without her Bentley. She was relieved on Christmas Eve when he knocked on her door in the late afternoon.

From the center aisle Georgia and Bentley entered the pew occupied by her mother and father along with Jean and her parents. The glowing reflection of candlelight sent dancing patterns on the arched ceiling of the nave as drafts from the door teased the flames. Burning wicks sent a faint trail of black smoke curling upward as the melting tallow emitted an aroma that blended perfectly with the scent of fresh pine. Georgia's eyes were drawn to the simple but elegant altar bathed in candlelight.

Kneeling beside Bentley, she turned to whisper as her warm, moist lips touched his ear, causing rumblings in him vastly inappropriate for the service. "This time next year everybody will know we're engaged, and we'll be getting married in a few months."

"That's right," he whispered back, gazing toward the altar.

Kneeling at the altar rail for Holy Communion, Georgia's euphoria blended with the mystery of the enchanting night. She was shaking slightly as they walked back to their pew, the envy and admiration of many. She had no way to know that this night would become a reference point in their lives for many members of the congregation.

In the early morning hours of Christmas day Georgia and Bentley sat cuddled in front of a softly glowing fire. She presented Bentley with Bay Rum and a shiny black fountain pen—one with a broad point, the kind he liked best—and a small bottle of ink. She had made payments on the pen for months as it was clearly more than she could afford. Bentley gave her a fourteen-carat gold chain and cross, which she would wear for the rest of her life; although Bentley appreciated the pen, he would soon lose it during the intensity of work at his shop.

Chapter 6

On a bright cold morning in late March, a Norfolk and Western handcart pulled slowly from the station in Abingdon. Operated by two railroad men, it gained speed, traveling toward White Top Mountain. Being payday Friday, it was a good day to inspect the rails. The assignment offered the freedom of being away from the station and the supervision of Will West, whom they both liked and respected. There was a slight upgrade going out, but the two veterans understood the technique to achieve maximum thrust with minimum effort. They knew, too, that coming home would be a breeze. Facing each other as they rhythmically pumped up and down with equal, measured thrust, they looked remarkably alike: middle-aged, generally the same portly size, and wearing the railroad garb of blue denim and engineer caps.

When they stopped for lunch at a picturesque rise, they could see the middle fork of the Holston River snaking around the foot of steep leafless knobs. At the moment both were focused on the cold bottles of beer stashed on the cart, a special treat to wash down lunch carried in matching black lunch pails.

Later, through with work for the day and feeling no compulsion to rush back to the station, they descended slowly down the grade as the dropping temperature forced them back into their jackets. To fight against the chill of the breeze, they began to sip from a pint of Tennessee whiskey. Moving slowly on the silver parallel rails behind Martha Washington College, they stopped the cart and dismounted without speaking to take the last break of the day.

"No reason to git to the depot afore quittin' time," announced the first to the second, removing the bottle from his jacket pocket.

"Yeah, might as well have us one," replied the second, sitting on a tangle of bare honeysuckle vines on top of a mound of dirt separating the tracks from the south property line of Martha Washington College. He watched as his partner unceremoniously pulled a deep swig from the dark brown bottleneck.

"Whew!" he wheezed, wiping his mouth and nose on the sleeve of his dirty denim coat, "I sure took a good 'un!" Screwing the cap back on, traces of a smile formed seconds before he tossed the bottle without warning toward his friend. Caught off guard, the other man lunged forward to catch it, but the bottle deflected off his rigid outstretched fingertips, falling behind him in the brown undergrowth. "What in the hell do you think you're a doing?" he cried at his partner.

"You hunt it! You missed it!" laughed the bottle thrower gleefully.

"You beat any damn thang I ever seen, any damn thang!" the second muttered as he pulled on his work gloves and scrambled into the matted, dormant undergrowth. In the falling darkness, the railroad man crawled, sweeping the ground with his hands, searching for the brown bottle he could not see. Inching forward into a depression, he felt loose earth and thought he glimpsed something white. Was it his imagination? No, there it was, something white, but what was it? He crawled closer, then, sitting back on his heels, removed his gloves to touch the white object with his bare hands. It was a piece of cloth, but as he tugged gently, he felt resistance. *What in the hell?* he thought. As he yanked forcefully with both hands, the upper torso and decayed face of Anna Marie Holmes popped upward toward him from her shallow grave.

"Ahhh!" he screamed, lunging backward into the dead honeysuckle as the other man fought his way through the tangled undergrowth.

"Oh, goddamn! Oh, goddamn!" he screamed, bumping into his kneeling partner.

Silent and ashen faced, they pumped furiously toward the Norfolk and Western Railroad Station. Relieved to see Will West, they jumped from the cart and ran toward him. Moments later, the assistant station master called Sheriff John Woodward.

By seven-thirty several windows were filled with young faces as Martha girls saw a cluster of bright railroad lanterns just west of the campus near the railroad tracks. They could detect several men moving about, but they could not discern what was going on behind the strange illumination.

Shards of light streaked out between the men at the scene, penetrating the darkness with incandescent spikes rotating from time to time like illuminated bicycle spokes. As time passed, the coeds became quieter, sensing that whatever was going on below was ominous. They were puzzled by bright bursts of illumination that seemed to explode from time to time within the bright glow of the railroad lanterns.

Standing at a distance, undetected in darkness on the other side of the tracks, Jamie recognized most of the men moving about in the lights. He saw Will West standing back, more observer than participant. He saw Sheriff John Woodward, clearly in charge, who spoke often with Dr. Smith, the county coroner. Standing to the side, away from the other men, was the solitary figure of Dr. Sidney Clarke, president of Martha Washington College. Jamie watched with interest as George Wertz moved his tripod from time to time. In each new position Mr. Wertz ignited black powder, flashing illumination for his photographs. Jamie understood what was going on; he did not have to be told. He knew that the men stood around the body of the missing Martha girl.

A small crowd of town people gathered a short distance from the arc of railroad lanterns, speaking in hushed voices. One, who stood in silence, took great interest in the operation.

Later in the evening, Dr. Clarke confirmed to faculty and students that a body had been found. The next day Dr. Smith, the coroner, confirmed it was the body of Anna Marie Holmes, which revealed few secrets because it was well on its way to becoming the dust from which the Bible says it came, the dust to which the Bible says it shall return. But a great deal more than dust was placed there months before when someone pushed dirt over a pretty face with glazed eyes. The dirt fell into wavy brown hair pulled to the back of her head with a sterling silver barrette given to her when she graduated from high school. The dirt fell on a simple, one-piece linen dress with thick petticoats underneath. The vile predator had not placed a metaphor in the shallow grave; he laid the body of a young and gentle person in the dark soil. It was the body of a vibrant young woman who had yet to intimately know a man, who would never get to explore fully her own being and her own femininity. She was a promise left unfulfilled.

Just after dawn on Sunday morning John Woodward stood leaning against the top of the fence, holding a coffee cup as his horse trotted toward him. The handsome animal snorted and grinned, exposing his large white teeth. Thunder, a large horse for his breed, stood over sixteen hands tall, but otherwise looked like a typical Appaloosa with a roan coat, along with black spots splashed on the patch of gray on his crop. Trotting to John, the horse nudged his chest with his soft, velvety nose, which John had kissed countless times. "Whoa, boy! Whoa! You're gonna spill my coffee!" John cried, laughing as he fell backward, off balance, extending the hot cup of coffee away from his body. Thunder then stood still, allowing John to stroke the warm coat of his muscular neck and drift back to the first time he saw the horse.

Dr. Preston Smith, a small man in his early sixties with white hair and a handsome, intelligent face, was John's best friend and the county coroner. One night five years earlier Press called to tell John that Chuck Perkins, a wealthy and eccentric farmer, was found dead in his barn. John accompanied his friend in case of foul play. Perkins, dressed in British equestrian attire, still lay sprawled where he had fallen on the barn floor, a riding crop at his side. Press ultimately determined that the man, only forty-four years old, had died of a massive heart attack.

A few feet from the body, moving about nervously in a stall, stood the unusual Appaloosa horse, a breed rarely seen in Southwest Virginia. The wealthy farmer purchased the horse in Richmond along with a costly English riding saddle for a horse whose breed originated in Spain and got a foothold in the West with American Indian tribes. With the twinkle that often danced about in his dark blue eyes, Doc mused,

"Well, that's Chuck for you. He bought a wild west horse and put an English saddle on him!"

Several days later Mrs. Perkins called John, explaining that she could not bring herself to look at the strange horse or the English saddle hanging in the tack room. She asked if he could find a buyer for the horse, noting that the price would include the saddle. Because John was in the market for another horse, he took the timing and circumstance to be "one of those things that are just supposed to happen," so he bought the horse, to the great relief of Mrs. Perkins.

From the moment he looked into the dark eyes of the horse, John felt a kinship, but the feeling wasn't mutual at first, as the animal was skittish and unapproachable. Katherine Woodward watched from the porch as the horse ran to the far end of the pasture and stood looking defiantly toward his new master, ears plastered to his head. "John, this is absurd. That crazy horse will kill you!" Katherine exclaimed.

"It'll take some time, but he'll be a fine horse. He's real pretty," John mused, disregarding his wife's strong feelings. "Look at his crop and hind quarters. Looks like black raindrops on a gray sky," John declared.

"Doesn't remind me of raindrops. Reminds me more of a thunderstorm," Katherine replied dryly.

"Thank you," he said, turning toward her, smiling broadly.

"For what?" she asked incredulously.

"You've just named him, Thunder! A great name!" he answered, kissing her cheek as he walked away.

John patiently allowed the horse to warm up to him on the animal's own terms, and after countless hours, when the barrier was finally broken, Thunder was a one man horse. As if he carried a heart bursting with latent affection, Thunder poured it out on John as each took delight in the other.

Intelligent and eager to please, the spirited horse was easy to train, John found. Because the animal had a natural affinity to do it any way, John taught Thunder to walk beside him without being led by the reins and to stay in place when he dismounted, leaving the reins crossed over the horse's neck or hanging toward the ground. The horse always galloped to John when he whistled, which was every time he approached the pasture.

Later John sat beside Katherine, trying to concentrate on the Sunday sermon, but his mind was occupied by the murder. On Saturday morning at daylight he returned to the scene with his deputies and methodically searched again, beginning at the grave site and moving outward. As the radius expanded, they found trash and debris thrown from trains or dropped by people walking along the tracks. In the dead honeysuckle very close to the grave, his chief deputy found a pint bottle of Tennessee whiskey. It was half full, and the fresh, label showed that it was was thrown away recently. They decided not to classify it as evidence, and by ten o'clock they began the interviews of the Martha girls.

John returned to the grave site in the late afternoon and knelt, studying the shallow depression. As he reflected, he felt guilt for not recovering the body shortly after the girl was reported missing. Why, in the name of God, hadn't they found her then? John didn't have blood hounds at his disposal, but he could get them from the next county. The hounds may have been able to do what the men could not do: Find the sweet scent of the girl who lay dead, hidden from the rest of the world only feet from where they had searched.

Scooping loosened black earth in his hands, John placed each mound on a white cloth. Dirt, pebbles, and twigs - nothing more - appeared to be on his ground cloth, until his eyes caught the light color in the dirt. John reached forward to delicately retrieve a white, nondescript button. It looked like those put on common shirts the laborers and farmers wore. He could not connect it to the killer of Anna Marie, yet it was in the ground where her body was abandoned like so much rubbish. Another hour of searching failed to reveal any other items of possible evidence. He told no one about the button, which he secured in his safe.

"I know you're worried, but there was nothing you could have done about the girl. There is no way you could have prevented her death," offered Katherine as John left for a meeting with Press Smith, which would be followed by another at Martha Washington College.

"Maybe not," he answered vaguely, still looking into the distance, "but I should have found her. That's one thing I could have done. Found her, so she could have a proper burial at the time, so we would have more evidence, so her parents wouldn't have to go through everything twice, so . . ."

Press answered the door and ushered John into the study, a comfortable room, a safe haven, but today John was tense to learn the autopsy findings.

John and Press were best friends for many reasons. They possessed the same sense of humor, often laced with irony, and they shared fundamental principles and beliefs about life, yet there was something else, an inexplicable, deep and abiding friendship, a unique masculine affection. Although neither focused consciously upon the relationship, it was a gift that decorated and enhanced their lives. Like the love of a woman, it offered an intimacy that flowed naturally, unaffected, and went unexamined.

Neither had a way to know the winds of change were stirring. They did not realize that the depth of their friendship would be drawn upon to support them on a journey now underway.

John reached for his writing pad, and said, "Let's do it, Press. What can you tell me?"

Eyes narrowed, the coroner began, "Unfortunately, not much, John. There wasn't much to work with."

Fountain pen poised, John looked intently into the doctor's eyes, asking, "Cause of death?"

"I can't tell you, John."

"You don't know how she died?" John pressed.

"No."

John felt incredulous, having watched Doc work miracles with the living and pry secrets from the dead.

"Not the exact cause, John. You saw her. Her body was badly decomposed. There was no soft tissue, so I can't tell you how she died."

"What will you say? How will the cause of death be listed officially?"

"Unknown criminal causes," the coroner answered as if he were on a witness stand.

"Press, remember the stocking. One of her stockings was removed, lying beside her. I thought surely you'd find that it had been used as a ligature," offered John.

"That's a possibility, but again, with her condition, there's no way to tell, and too, the stocking itself was deteriorating and brittle. I can tell you her neck was not broken."

"But Press, it wouldn't necessarily take enough force to snap her neck. She could easily have been choked without suffering a broken neck. Right?" asked the sheriff, urging confirmation.

"Yeah, right."

Leaning forward in his chair, elbows pressing into the top of hard thighs, the sheriff asked, "What about her clothes? Were they cut or torn?"

"Again, the clothes, as you saw, had begun to disintegrate, but I looked as best I could, and I didn't detect their being cut or torn." Pausing a moment, he looked at John, then continued, "I do have something though. Nobody, of course, knows this but my assistant, and now I'm telling you. The victim's underwear was removed and shoved up between her thighs."

John prepared to address the yet unspoken issue. They both knew from years of experience that the unexplained death of any woman, especially a young woman, carried with it the distinct suggestion of criminal sexuality. The fact that the killer was a man was not a point of discussion. Breaking the silence, John offered, "She must have been raped, Press. That's what we're dealing with."

Press paused, then began cautiously, "Not necessarily, John. First, we don't *know* she was raped. I'll grant that rape is a distinct possibility, but still, that's an assumption. And I don't have to tell you that assumptions and probabilities are not evidence."

"But—"

"Wait, John. Let me finish," Press interrupted gently. "Even if we make the assumption that she was raped, we should not consider sex as the sole motivation of the killer."

"Now you're saying that even if we assume that she was raped, we should *not* consider sex as the motive?" John asked earnestly.

"No, that's not it exactly," Press continued patiently. "I said we shouldn't consider sex as the *only* motive. I'm suggesting that if you incorrectly assume the motive for the murder is sex, you'll probably overlook the real motive, the underlying motive. The real motivation for rape is not sexuality. The crime, the assault, is acted out sexually, of course, but the real motivations, the root causes, are anger, power, and control. If rape were driven solely by strong libidos, raging sexual urges, hormonal juices flowing, and the like, you'd be investigating a hell of a lot more rapes."

"All right, Doc," John began earnestly, still deeply focused. "This is what we've come to: We have agreed that we don't know how this girl died, but we will classify her death as unknown criminal causes. We do not know if she were raped. If, however, we make the assumption that, in all likelihood, she was raped, we must do so with the caveat that sex was not the primary motive, possibly not the motive at all."

"Right."

John left for Martha a few minutes later without remembering to mention the small white button, but there would be plenty of time to do that later.

Chapter 7

Thunder walked slowly, rhythmically, as if he understood that his master had ample time to reach Martha Washington College for his three-thirty meeting, while a thought haunted John: If the girl had died in an accident or because of illness, there would have been some explanation, some reason, some rationale. If that were the case, the parents would not have to wrestle with the senselessness of it all and with the unknown. John could not remember another case when his emotions had threatened to interfere with his professional detachment.

Earlier in the afternoon, Dr. Clarke, the Reverend Joe Dunn, rector of St. Thomas Episcopal Church, and Will West met the Holmeses coming from Roanoke to take their only child, what was left of her, home. After brief introductions, the Holmeses went to Hotel Abingdon.

It was Joe's idea to have John join them later, knowing the sheriff would have perfect instincts in the delicate situation. While Clarke's stilted and formal manner worried Joe, John's natural kindness and grace should counterbalance the aloof Clarke.

The Holmeses were forced to accept what they could not understand. In diffused resignation that defeated them, they pondered the inexplicable, the senselessness of it all. They were compelled, forced, to acknowledge that Anna Marie had faced a dark, unfathomable evil, a terror that took her life and changed theirs forever. Later they would come to pray that when their daughter faced the darkness that devoured her, she had gone quickly, with little pain.

Dr. Clarke and Father Dunn stood as the Holmeses were ushered into the president's suite, Mrs. Holmes walking several paces in front of her husband. Joe Dunn moved toward her with both hands extended to grasp hers. His broad smile and boyish appearance made him very approachable, especially in contrast to the president, who happily deferred to the young priest. From the night the girl went missing, Clarke's primary concern was the college's liability. On Saturday morning after the body was found he spent an hour with Brett Grant, counsel for Martha Washington College. Brett cautioned Dr. Clarke, "Be very circumspect; admit no liability."

Hanna Holmes was a handsome woman in her early forties. Her intelligent face revealed profound grief, yet her dignified presence and bearing suggested a remarkably strong inner strength. Her husband was another matter. William Holmes, a fifty-year-old banker, was broken, defeated. Hanna Holmes quickly sensed that Joe Dunn was a sensitive and compassionate man. She was about to meet another.

John walked into the room holding his tan western-style hat with both hands as Sidney Clarke stood, relieved to see the sheriff of Washington County. Smiling broadly, Joe Dunn walked to John and, with his hand in the middle of the lawman's back, moved with him toward the Holmeses.

"Mr. and Mrs. Holmes, I would like to introduce you to our sheriff, John Woodward," offered Joe. Hanna Holmes extended her hand, which John grasped momentarily, saying only, "Mrs. Holmes." Turning and leaning behind her, he extended his hand to William Holmes.

"Please everyone, be seated," intoned Dr. Clarke, as all sat down where they were standing, leaving John sitting on one side of Hanna while her husband sat on the other.

Dr. Clarke rose, offering a litany in dispassionate language of the initial efforts of college personnel to find the girl. Glancing sideways at Hanna Holmes, Joe saw eyes fixed on the president. Knowing that anger is a part of grief, he saw it building within her. Within her grief, her ego, like an old friend, was moving to rescue her from the jagged edges of oblivion.

Finally, Dr. Clarke concluded, "I hope that provides a reasonable understanding of what we have done, of what we have been up against."

Eyes flashing but expression unchanged otherwise, Hanna Holmes began in a steady voice, lowered an octave, "Dr. Clarke, we sent Anna Marie to you with the assumption you would ensure her safety while she was in your care, custody, and control."

Care, custody, and control, the words struck at the president's heart. They had a legal connotation! The Holmes must have talked with a lawyer! Clarke regretted that he had not invited Brett Grant to the meeting. *He would know how to handle this woman!*

Hanna Holmes continued, "What did you do *before,* not *after* our daughter's disappearance, to safeguard her and the rest of the girls from such a danger?"

"Mrs. Holmes . . ." Dr. Clarke began, then paused, looking toward the ceiling, not accustomed to offering explanations about any phase of his professional or private life. Masking his irritation, he continued, "Indeed it may be difficult for you to understand the depths of our profound grief over the loss of your daughter. It was an event, however, that occurred within a system, an environment, that we believe to be perfectly safe and legally secure for all our young ladies."

William Holmes did not move his fixed gaze toward the floor as Hanna jumped to her feet, her purse falling to the floor. "Those words are mechanical and so cold! Where is your sense of loss, of remorse?" Hanna Holmes gasped before she sank, sobbing, as John touched her upper arm, gently directing her toward the sofa.

Dr. Clarke walked away from the group to the windows, where he gazed outside at the fading afternoon light. His secretary entered and extended a glass of cold water, which Hanna took in both hands before the older woman walked briskly from the room.

As Clark approached, Hanna looked up, still remarkably kempt and offered, "I regret the outburst."

"But of course. It's understandable that you're grieved and under stress," the president responded. "A final matter, Mr. and Mrs. Holmes," Dr. Clarke began, as Joe and John bristled into tenseness once again. "As you know, with your permission, Dr. Preston Smith performed the autopsy." Although John kept his eyes on the president, he felt Hanna Holmes jerk involuntarily. "It would not be proper, of course, for me to have access to that information. I'm confident, however, that I can arrange to have Dr. Smith meet with you tomorrow to advise you of his findings."

"Dr. Clarke, are you telling me that we will have to wait for tomorrow, go through another endless night, before we find how our daughter died?" she asked, looking up through swollen eyes.

God! This is turning into a nightmare! thought John as he quickly stood. "Excuse me, Dr. Clarke," interrupted John. "Before I came here, I met with Dr. Smith. He informed me of his findings."

Turning to Hanna, John explained softly, "I am an officer of the court, Mrs. Holmes, and entitled to that information as part of the investigative process." Hanna focused intently on John's face, nodding slightly.

"I shall excuse myself then," intoned the president as he walked from the room.

"Father Dunn," Hanna said weakly, touching the man's black sleeve, "please stay." "Please, sheriff, tell us," she pleaded moments later.

"Mrs. Holmes . . . and uh, Mr. Holmes too, well, both of you," John stuttered. Now, holding the broad rim of his hat with both hands, and his shoulders stooped as if he were apologetic for having to address the awful subject, he continued, "Dr. Smith did the autopsy, but unfortunately he was unable to determine the cause of your daughter's death."

"*What!*" gasped Hanna Holmes in disbelief, glancing at her husband, whose wide eyes conveyed his dismay.

"I'm very sorry, but it was impossible for him to determine the cause of death because you see . . . her body was too badly decomposed," John admitted softly.

Still in disbelief, Hanna looked at John with pleading eyes. "You mean there's no way to tell if she were . . . if she were . . ."

"No, ma'am, no way to tell about that either," he answered softly, knowing she referred to rape.

"And her body, it was . . ." she whispered, barely audible.

"Yes, ma'am, it was too far gone." He spoke softly.

"I should have known . . ." she began in a monotone of resignation but didn't finish. John wasn't sure what to say, so wisely, he remained silent. Hanna began again like a student grasping a difficult concept, "Of course, it had to be . . . so, we'll never know, never ever know. How did they find her?" she continued, clutching her hands together, her knuckles blanching white.

John began slowly again, "Do you mean . . ."

"I mean how was she found in the ground?" Hanna uttered as if to expel the words from her mouth as quickly as possible.

"Your daughter was lying on her back, fully clothed, and there was no sign of struggle," answered John.

"And what will you do now, Sheriff?"

"I'll do everything I can to identify who murdered your daughter," John answered softly, Joe Dunn still looking on in silence.

Hanna moved a step closer to John, putting her hand on his forearm as she looked up into his intense brown eyes. "Please do. Please find who killed Anna Marie. Please do that for us, for *her*."

"I'll do everything I can. I promise you that," he whispered as she moved closer, her chin rising and her face turning slightly, exposing her moist cheek. Hanna Holmes moved to receive a kiss from the man who was a total stranger minutes ago. His lips gently touched her flushed cheek as her hand rested lightly on his forearm. The two of them didn't understand it fully, but Joe Dunn understood what he saw - a rare moment of grace. He watched an intimate act of compassion, an extension of love from one stranger to another. He saw a gift given and received in a fleeting, circumstantial moment. It was a moment that the two men would eventually forget. Hanna Holmes would *never* forget it. Mr. Holmes in his suffering failed to notice.

The Holmeses watched as John Woodward disappeared through the tall double doors. Without speaking, Hanna Holmes and Joe Dunn sat down again. He wished desperately that they were not in the opulent office of the president but in a more intimate setting. Joe reminded himself that, regardless of the reasons, God had seen fit to put the two of them together at that time and in that place. *Please, Lord, please, give me the grace and insight to say the right thing, to say what you would have me say!* he prayed frantically, waiting for Hanna to speak.

"Father Dunn," she began after taking a deep breath, "tell me, please, why our daughter died? What could the reason *possibly* be? She never hurt anyone; she was such a good girl, such a good person. I need to know why, to understand why." For the first time in the afternoon William Holmes looked up, staring at Joe Dunn.

"I wish I could tell you why," Joe began honestly. "It is one of the greatest mysteries of life—why innocent people suffer, why innocent people sometimes die at the hands of evildoers. Remember Jesus himself said to his disciples, 'I am sending you out like lambs in the midst of wolves.' I have to tell you that the answer to your question is *not* in the

Bible. When I meet God face-to-face, I plan to ask Him that question. The Bible in the book of Job tells of the suffering of a good and decent man who does not lose his faith. The Psalmists bewail man's suffering, and the prophet Jeremiah asks God, 'Why does the way of the guilty prosper? Why do all who are treacherous thrive?' God seems to make no promises about suffering. He tells us that He will always be with us, but He never says we will not suffer at the hands of others. If He had chosen, He could have created a world without evil, devoid of suffering, but He chose otherwise and gave us freedom of choice. He chose to allow us to love Him, or not to love Him; to behave lovingly or to commit evil acts, sometimes vile, despicable acts. Therein lies part of the mystery of life. There will always be an ambiguity to life, depths of uncertainty we cannot fathom. Due to our very limited nature and God's vast and infinite quality, we can never understand Him fully. Once we assign human characteristics to God and demand human answers on our own terms, we are looking through the glass darkly."

Joe Dunn paused, worrying he had offered too much verbiage, that he sounded too preachy.

"Then you're telling me, Father, that there is no answer to my question, the *only* question I'll have for the rest of my life?"

Joe began again slowly. "Mrs. Holmes, you and I and most of us are blessed by the love we have in our lives . . ."

"Love? I don't feel any love at the moment, especially from God."

"I assure you that God loves you, particularly at this moment, but, actually, I was thinking in terms of our earthly love in its several forms."

Hanna Holmes was used to a fundamental preacher, one who was never in doubt, one who could and routinely did answer any question by a literal interpretation of the Bible. Joe's honesty made him seem vulnerable.

"When I said love, I meant all the types of love which grace our lives. You know them all. We have love for our fellow man, love for our family, erotic love, and, finally, agape love, unconditional love that asks nothing in return. As I see it, along with the pain and suffering and the wrongs and the evils and the mystery of life, love, in any of its forms, ultimately pulls us through. This is especially true of the love, for example, that you had for Anna Marie and the love she had for you. Our own earthly love is the prism through which we can glimpse but a flicker of God's infinite love for us. God did not intervene to save His own son in the face of monstrous evil. Having forsaken force, even to save His only son, God does not seem to intervene to prevent the evil we commit against each other. He therefore, it seems to me, grieves with us when we grieve."

Joe felt that he had rambled on far too long. He worried too that he had been too churchy and too scattered in his answer—the most difficult he or any other man of the cloth would have to address.

Hanna sat in silence for a few moments, staring vacantly into the distance toward the president's windows. Finally she turned toward Joe, responding softly and slowly, "The problem, Father Dunn, is that right now I don't *feel* a lot of love. It is as if all my love died." Her voice trailed off as she looked away from Joe, away from the symbol of love, something from which she was estranged.

Responding with total candor, he confessed, "I don't blame you. I would feel the same way."

"*You would?*" she asked, shocked, thinking again of her preacher.

"Yes, I would because it's part of human nature. God not only gave us choice but also blessed us with logic and reasoning. You are a cognitive, reasoning person because God made you that way. He also gave you anger, and he understands your anger now. Of course you have a right to question. It is perfectly justifiable that you don't understand. You have a right to ask Him why."

"I do?" she gasped.

"Of course. I can only tell you that Anna Marie no longer suffers and will never feel pain again. While your loss and suffering is profound, beyond words, she is bathed in the light and love of God."

"In your heart of hearts, do you believe that?" Hanna pressed.

"*Especially* at such times, I believe that," he answered softly.

Exhausted, she stood, saying softly, "Thank you, Father Dunn, thank you very much," before she stepped forward, embracing him. William Holmes stepped forward, clinging to the priest much more tightly than his wife, yet still saying nothing. Joe knew that he was hardly living.

Dr. Clarke and the Reverend Dunn rode to the station with the Holmeses. Stepping from the carriage, Hanna looked up into the face of John Woodward. He stood beside Will West, who had made arrangements to have the remains of their daughter taken home for the last time. John nodded and brushed the brim of his hat with his fingers. Hanna nodded back slightly. As the Holmeses boarded the train, Hanna turned for a final moment in the doorway. Scanning the group, her eyes caught John's for only a split second, but he noticed. Then she disappeared from sight.

The spring, fickle like the inhabitants of the town, turned abruptly back to winter as the temperature dropped, and the wind picked up, blowing on Thunder's spotted rump and against the back of John's neck as he rode home in the darkness.

Chapter 8

Saturday morning two weeks later arrived sunny and warm, a sign that spring had not forgotten the Blue Ridge. High winds, not felt on the earth below, pushed the gauzy clouds toward White Top Mountain as they stretched like streams of sparse, flowing cotton candy at the August fair.

The past two weekly editions of *The Virginian* had presented bold front- page stories about the murder of Anna Marie Holmes. Like Eden, harshly stripped of its innocence, the little town became aware of its deadly threat; but the threat had no face, no image, and no name.

In one of their regular talks Press warned John that the threat, if not resolved, would grip the community in panic, causing the town leaders to become unreasonable in their demands for a solution. Press himself felt the harsh sting of criticism for failing to find the cause of the girl's death.

Harold Kane snatched questions about the sheriff from hushed whispers on the street and splashed them boldly in print for public consumption. John knew well that as a law enforcement officer he would always be under intense scrutiny, yet some of the questions posed in the paper were the very questions John asked himself. Why, for example, had he and his deputies failed to locate the body of Anna Marie?

John, always optimistic, realized that the critical articles did bring an advantage— enhanced community awareness, not only of the danger, but also for the need to help him and his deputies.

John was bemused when Eugene Johnson's name first surfaced. The twenty-four-year-old Johnson had delivered for Colley Brothers' Grocery for several years. Upon reflection, however, John realized that he knew nothing about the lanky, introverted Johnson or about Jamie, likewise suggested as a suspect. Several opined that the strange Negro who roamed the town *could* have committed the awful act. After all, they said, he seemed to be *everywhere all the time.* John heard the same thing about Johnson, the white boy. He was described as "strange" and "weird," a grown man who still lived with his parents, another who "goes *everywhere.*"

John developed a viable list of suspects based on substance such as notification from other law enforcement authorities and violent criminal history, including sexual assault. He was interested in several who worked at the livestock market, a place which attracted a rough and crude element, many causing problems for John and his deputies weekly. Other suspects were developed because of their connection to the Martha campus.

John and his deputies conducted more than a hundred interviews, many generating more leads. He pointed out to his deputies that with the effort they were putting into the investigation, they needed only one more thing—a break, a bit of luck. When he mentioned that to Press, the doctor responded, "That's exactly right, John. Luck is something you have to create for yourself." Then he added, smiling warily, "You know what Lady Luck is, John? She's a fickle and illusive imposter of achievement. But she gets the same results!"

The sun continued to skirt in and out of the clouds as Eugene Johnson, low-ranked suspect in the Martha murder, expertly moved the red Colley Brothers delivery bicycle through the alley toward the Wertz home. He was well over six feet tall, pencil thin, with jet-black hair combed straight back with no part. His elongated head produced an oval face with dark, deep-set eyes. A weak chin failed to support his wide mouth and thick lips. His ruddy face, often flushed crimson, still carried severe acne scars, one of the cruelties of adolescence. Eugene looked like a tall, gangly bird perched on the delivery bicycle.

At eleven-thirty the sun still hiding, Eugene rode from the alley into the Wertz backyard. The bright morning sun reappeared suddenly as he approached the screen door. Sitting around the kitchen table, Georgia, Jean and Eliza were engrossed in quiet, almost reverent, conversation about the murder of the Martha girl. It was awful, a nightmare, especially when they attempted to visualize the inexplicable horror Anna Marie had faced. Death itself was to them a mystery beyond comprehension, yet they were drawn to the dark but fascinating subject, as if they had no choice in the matter. Like a painful tooth that they could not help pressing, they returned again and again to discuss the tragic murder.

Georgia recognized Eugene's slap at the frame of the screen door while he still managed to clutch the groceries in his arms. Running to hold the door open as the young man stepped inside, Georgia spoke casually, "Hello, Gene."

"Hi," he answered without looking up. Neither Jean nor Eliza had heard him utter a word. Unknown to anybody, Eugene Johnson was attracted to women and drawn deeply to the beautiful Georgia Wertz. His attraction, however, greatly exceeded any knowledge or intuitive sense of how to respond to them; consequently, he felt tension around all women.

Standing at the counter close to Eugene, Georgia asked easily, "Have you heard anything new about the Martha girl?"

"The one that got murdered, you mean?" he questioned, still not looking up from his task.

"Yes, the Holmes girl," she answered patiently.

"They don't know what killed her!" he blurted, voice rising as the three girls exchanged surprised glances.

"Didn't the paper say that, Jean?" asked Eliza, as Eugene, uncharacteristically, looked intently at Jean.

Jean began slowly, reflectively, "No, not exactly. What it said was that Dr. Smith and Sheriff Woodward won't make the autopsy findings public."

"They can't tell what killed her because she was rotted," exclaimed Johnson emphatically, moving toward the door.

The three girls stared in awe at the strange, bird-like Johnson poised at the door as if ready to take flight. After several seconds Georgia tentatively began again, "You saw her?"

"Yeah, I saw lights in the back lot of Martha, and I saw the sheriff and all of 'em. And I saw 'em lift her from the grave. She had a white dress; I saw that!" Now Eugene's dark eyes darted quickly from Georgia to the two at the table.

"That's awful! I don't want to hear about it!" exclaimed Eliza as she slowly shook her large head in the negative.

"I do! Tell us about it," countermanded Jean.

"Well, Miss Georgia, *you* should know everything. Your father was there with Doc Smith," Eugene began.

"What?" cried Georgia incredulously. "He didn't tell me anything about that! Why . . . Daddy?" asked Georgia meekly.

"To take pictures of the body," explained Eugene, confidence building in his voice.

Jean wondered why her uncle had not revealed his presence at the scene to Georgia. All the Martha girls and many town people were drawn to the site. The tangled patch of undergrowth, now showing signs of the budding spring, had become a local shrine. Many considered the spot to be a sacred place draped in holy mystery. Some, especially one, came there more than once.

Jean felt anger and resentment mounting toward Eugene. Suddenly, with clarity of insight, she realized why. She was repulsed because the recovery of the innocent girl was presented so callously by this unattractive and bizarre man. He was a person who would never get near Anna Marie in her life, yet in her death, he intruded. Now he was part of her story. There was, Jean believed, an obscenity about the discovery of the girl, whose dignity and privacy were taken along with her life. Her decaying form should not have been laid bare for onlookers like the dark bird to gaze upon. Jean also noted with interest Johnson's use of certain words, words that she did not expect to come from a delivery boy. Eugene Johnson, she decided, although uneducated, had a degree of intelligence, even if he were a social misfit. That made him sinister to her.

As if feeling the negative energy, the stork stepped through the door and was gone.

51

The girls drifted into their own thoughts, each feeling a sliver of guilt, relieved that it was Anna Marie Holmes who now lay buried in Roanoke, Anna Marie who faced the monstrous horror of death.

A short time later Georgia suggested that they go have their pictures made in her father's studio, something they had done countless times before, always to the delight of George Wertz. He took several pictures of the three girls that afternoon, pictures of them in their first cotton dresses of spring. Their faces would gaze out from the photographs through the years, images of perpetual youth and loveliness. Some of the pictures, tossed around by the winds of chance, would be preserved for several generations. Finally, like the girls themselves, the names on the backs would fade, and those images captured, the three girls of summer, would be unknown to the beholders. In future generations, viewers would wonder what had happened in the lives of the girls after their images were captured so many years before.

* * * * *

Georgia, although blessed with the keen eyes of an artist like father, heard another voice whispering to her soul, calling her to be a nurse. Her course was set, and she held it steady toward a destination that now seemed faintly visible on the horizon. Georgia had difficulty articulating her motives, but her soul understood and was in harmony with the changes that transformed her from a pretty girl into a handsome and striking young woman. Her love for Bentley Thompson surged into the strongest force in her life, but it did not diminish her commitment to become a healer.

Bentley still managed to visit most weekends. They flowed in the social circle of the small town, attending spring dances at Stonewall and Martha, where Bentley waltzed her gracefully and dramatically. To their delight, the phrase "Miss Georgia Wertz escorted by Mr. Bentley Thompson," appeared from time to time in a social column of *The Virginian.* They were the envy of many of her friends; and to some older observers, especially several aging widows, their conspicuous love, revealed while strolling along Valley Street, evoked memories of past loves and lost youth.

Their evening walks continued, but at the first signs of dusk, they instinctively turned toward the dim glow of her front porch light, deprived of the innocence they had possessed before the murder. Neither was aware that they were often watched with interest by one from a distance.

In early March, Georgia detected a subtle difference in Bentley. He became more attentive and less aggressive in his relentless pursuit of physical intimacy, now an ingrained part of their unconsummated courting ritual. They still discussed marriage regularly, but always in general terms. Then one Sunday night in late April as he was leaving, Bentley dropped a teaser: He had something important to talk to her about next weekend.

On the next Saturday night, they went to a dance at the Stonewall Academy. Georgia's latest grading period had ended with excellent marks, so her spirits soared as she wondered if Bentley planned to present an engagement ring. Their secret plan and the dreams it evoked carried its own intimacy, one that would be lost with public knowledge of engagement. Like all in love, Georgia and Bentley thrived on secrets and what they believed was their uniqueness.

Near the end of the night, walking from the dance floor, Bentley gently directed her toward an empty parlor. Making their way to a fireplace at the far end of the deserted rectangular room, they could hear refrains of music and subdued laugher floating from the hall. The small flickering fire had consumed itself, leaving only a bed of glowing chunks of coal on which low wispy flames darted and danced about in the drafts. As they sat facing the warm grate, Bentley reached inside his pocket and removed a small, silver plated flask. Eyes wide, Georgia whispered frantically, "Bentley, *what* are you doing? You know I'd be dismissed if they catch us with alcohol."

Glancing furtively over his shoulder before taking a long swig from the shiny flask, he wheezed, "It's only brandy."

"Bentley, brandy is alcohol!" she cautioned sternly, her posture rigid.

"Gosh, Georgia, sorry. The brandy was for a special occasion," he uttered softly.

"Special occasion?" she asked, feeling a deep, undefined dread.

"Yes," he whispered into her thick hair. When she failed to respond, he continued, "Georgia, you've said you will marry me. Right?"

"Yes, Bentley," she answered as he moved to face her as John Woodward had moved to face Hanna Holmes.

"Georgia, I want to do it soon! I love you more every day. I don't want to wait any longer!" he whispered, grasping her upper arms.

"I don't understand," she said faintly. "How could we get married now? You know Stonewall girls can't be married, and Momma and Daddy wouldn't allow it now. And you said you had to wait until you're promoted and—"

"Georgia! Georgia! I know all that, but wait a minute," he interrupted. "Let me ask you: Do you love me?"

She waited a few moments before replying, "You know I do."

"And I love you too. Do you know that?" he asked Georgia, who nodded her head slowly. "Then there is a way," he said, leaning forward and kissing her warm crimson cheek.

"How?" she asked again in a hollow voice devoid of inflection.

Taking a slight breath, he answered softly, "We can get married secretly."

"Secretly married?" she gasped.

"Yes! A lot of people do it, especially college students like us," he began, disregarding the fact that he was no longer enrolled at King. "I know a lot of couples who are secretly married right now. There's a bunch at Emory and King too. They're all like us—all in love, all waiting to get through school . . ."

"But Bentley," she began like a child pleading to a parent.

"Let me finish, sweetheart," he interrupted, touching her dry lips with his index finger. "It's the perfect thing for us! It would relieve the stress we have because of the distance and the time we're apart and the separate paths we're on right now. Remember, Georgia, it's usually *guys* who don't want to get married! *I* want to marry *you*, Georgia! Soon! Then we'll both know beyond a doubt that we'll belong to each other forever."

"I already know that, Bentley," she countered softly.

"And I do too, Georgia," he assured her quickly, understanding the nuances of first refusal. He continued his pitch in a softer voice. "But this way, we'll be more relaxed. We'll enjoy everything more, and we'll have a special secret we can keep forever! When we're old, we'll laugh about it! When you graduate, we'll simply have a public wedding!"

"The vows are for God, Bentley—*not* the public," she responded solemnly.

"Of course they are! They're for God! And as long as we make them, that's all that counts. But God won't care if you want to go through another public ceremony to make your parents feel good. That's all I meant," he countered quickly.

"I don't know if I'd *ever* feel good about it," she responded meekly, turning once again from him to stare remotely at the fading coals.

Bentley began again. "Georgia, it's the perfect answer! Nobody will ever come between us, and you and I will have each other for ever." He leaned forward once again and kissed her softly on the lips. Opening his eyes, he found hers welled with tears. He touched her hair, wet with perspiration, near her temples. In the silence of the moment, waiting for her answer, he removed his handkerchief and wiped his own moist forehead. For once he could think of nothing more to say.

Finally with a detached sense of resignation, she asked, "How . . . when?"

"We'll talk about that later, sweetheart," he answered, closing his deal quickly as he leaned forward to kiss her cheek again.

Riding home in a taxi carriage from Stonewall, both sat in reflective silence. They said good night quickly while the carriage waited to take Bentley to the Belmont Hotel.

* * * * *

The following Thursday afternoon Sheriff John Woodward read the headlines of *The Virginian* in amazement. *Why didn't they tell me? How could this be?* he questioned, his mind racing madly. He still possessed the core confidence of a seasoned professional, but that confidence was challenged as he read the headlines again: **$1,000 REWARD OFFERED IN MARTHA MURDER CASE!**

The story explained that the reward was for "information leading to the arrest and conviction of the godless person or persons who murdered the innocent and lovely Anna Marie Holmes in the sweetness and promise of youth."

John quickly learned that William Holmes' bank offered $500.00, which was matched by Martha Washington College. Only two people, Brett Grant and Sidney Clarke, knew that the recommendation for the college participation came in the form of expert legal counsel from Grant, who suggested that the contribution could diffuse criticism of the college and possibly prevent a lawsuit. The board of visitors was consulted privately, and each member commended Dr. Clarke for his excellent idea, his concern and sensitivity. The board directed Arthur White, a well-known local banker, to hold the funds in an escrow account. "Try," Sidney whispered to his old friend, "to avoid talking to the mother. She's very emotional and difficult to deal with rationally."

Arthur White winked knowingly, nodded, and said, "Thanks, I'll call *him.*"

When Press Smith learned that his friend had not been informed of the reward, he offered to John, "This is some of Sidney Clarke's effort to control public opinion. He's trying to cover his ass!"

The mayor and city council followed the case closely, highly sensitive after newspapers from Richmond to Knoxville carried sensational stories, several headlined **Murder at Martha!** The mayor knew that John and his deputies had interviewed hundreds and sent telegrams to every sheriff in Southwest Virginia and East Tennessee only to find that none had similar unsolved cases or logical suspects to suggest. He knew, too, that John Woodward had eliminated all viable suspects. In a closed session of the council, he told the members, "Nothing is going on in the case."

Below the reward headline *The Virginian* carried a photograph of the victim taken in the Wertz Studio. Anna Marie gazed out from the front page with a winsome and dreamy look. Later in the week the same face appeared on reward posters printed at *The Virginian.* Eager volunteers and the deputy sheriffs hurriedly distributed the posters throughout town.

Not distracted, John continued to respond to the needs of the community. Was it his imagination, he pondered, or was there a subtle change in the way some of the town merchants greeted him? Wisely, John sought to forget his insecurities. He wished he could dismiss them entirely, but that was impossible.

Now all three, the sheriff and the two town travelers, were viewed critically. People asked, "When will the sheriff do something?" Others were concerned about the Negro walker and the strange skinny stork. Soon the unique triumvirate, thrown together by circumstance and chance, were joined by another on the stage of community awareness as the face of Anna Marie adorned reward posters *everywhere,* including the lobby of the Belmont Hotel, where she gave Bentley Thompson a queasy feeling.

Chapter 9

With Easter approaching, Bentley formulated his plan—an age-old ruse, one to be perpetrated upon parents, a scheme to free lovers to be alone. But the plan had a greater depth and breadth than spending the Easter weekend with Georgia in Johnson City.

The Blue Ridge stayed gripped in the persistent chill of the new spring. Strangely, inexplicably, Georgia felt a sense of relief, as if an emotional burden had been taken from her, after she agreed to the secret marriage. Later Jean would opine that Bentley's immense charm overwhelmed Georgia's school-girl judgment. Georgia assured herself it was but a temporary situation. In a little more than a year, they would remarry at St. Thomas Episcopal Church.

What, she asked herself, *could be wrong with being in love? What could be wrong with being happy?* She would do this for Bentley, and she would do it for the sake of love and for herself. Georgia viewed her first love like grace, as a priceless gift, unearned, a treasure she would cherish forever; yet, for the first time in her life, Georgia Wertz felt a sharp spike of guilt in her young breast. She pressed ahead anyway, fortified by the delusions of love, and hope, and by the blind optimism of youth. She announced to her parents that Bentley had invited her to be a guest in his home in Johnson City for the Easter weekend. That was the first step, and it was done. Like a Garden of Evil reversal, Georgia was surprised at the ease with which she took Bentley's apple.

Frances and George, instinctively hesitant to let her go, finally agreed, but Frances insisted that Georgia could not go until Mrs. Thompson called to formerly invite her. Suddenly Georgia, facing the reality of the complex betrayal, was shocked to realize how easily her parents accepted Bentley's illusion as truth because of the trust they had for her. Unsure what to do, she called Bentley. His calm voice reassured her, "Sweetheart, it's no problem, no problem. Tell your mother she'll get the call tomorrow."

"Get the call tomorrow?" Georgia questioned.

"Sure, she'll get the call tomorrow. Don't worry about it," he responded calmly.

"Mrs. Thompson will call you tomorrow, Momma," Georgia said, surprised at her own nonchalant words, as if they were spoken by another person.

It was done. Georgia passed through veil of deceit. She was no longer an observer, a passive onlooker. Now she was part of the drama itself. She left her seat, walked slowly down the dark shadowy aisle, and climbed the steps to take her place beside Bentley Thompson on the dim and murky stage of illusion and betrayal.

"I'm really surprised," confided Jean when Georgia told her about Bentley's invitation, the same version she told her parents. "What did Aunt Frances say about her talk with Mrs. Thompson?" asked Jean softly.

"Momma said she was surprised at how young Mrs. Thompson sounded. Said she sounded like a young girl, but she liked her a lot. Said she seemed very nice," confided Georgia, relating truthfully what her mother said.

* * * * *

"From dust thy came, and to dust thy shall return," Father Joe Dunn whispered almost forty days before, on Ash Wednesday, as he traced the form of a stubby black cross on Georgia's pale forehead. Now it was Good Friday and he placed a wafer in her palm and said, "The body of Christ."

"Amen," she whispered, barely audible, as Joe moved to her parents kneeling beside her at the communion rail. Georgia wanted to focus on Easter, not Good Friday. It was not death she dreamed about at the moment, but her life with Bentley. That very night they would seal their relationship, their enduring love for each other, but the seal would not be an outward and visible sign like the mark of Ash Wednesday; theirs would be a secret seal that no eyes would see, that no lips would reveal . . . at least for a while.

Georgia stood on the platform at the railroad station with her parents. The mid afternoon sun was unseasonably warm, but in the west, toward Johnson City, skies threatened rain, perhaps a storm. She felt as if she were suspended in a surrealistic moment, overwhelmed with the notion that *only she knew* the truth. With that knowledge came a desperate feeling of isolation.

"I'm glad you brought your umbrella, Georgia. It looks like you might need it," remarked her mother, looking westward toward the dark horizon as George viewed the sky in silence.

The massive black coal-burning monster bore down frighteningly toward the Norfolk and Western platform. Georgia watched the cloudy puffs of steam belch upward out of the stack, blowing backward, sweeping over the railway cars before fading into a thin vapor trail. The high oval headlight, only moments ago a glimmering speck in the distance, now shined with a brilliant incandescence for a few seconds before passing in a rush of wind and sound. After she had waited so long, everything exploded on Georgia's senses at once. She winced at the back draft, turning away and trying to avoid flying cinders. Even with her back turned and eyes clinched tightly closed, she could not escape the cacophonous mixture of competing sounds, the clanging of the heavy bell, the screeching of steel on steel as enormous wheels locked on the shiny parallels, and the hissing of steam spewing downward toward the tracks.

Georgia kissed her mother quickly, starting to pull away, but Frances held the embrace a moment longer whispering, "'Bye, baby."

"'Bye, Momma," she answered.

The train began to move again a bit later as Georgia looked out at the people on the platform, who were framed by her window like a Wertz photograph. She saw Frances clinging to George's arm, waving slowly, languidly, with her free hand. Then they were gone.

The locomotive chugged westward like a giant ebony monster belching steam and spewing burning cinders. The obedient, trailing cars merged each into the other until the caboose became a distant speck before vanishing from the horizon. As if reluctant to part with the fading marvel of the time, most onlookers lingered, looking at the horizon. One who had traveled in more than one dimension of life watched with interest from a respectable distance but went unnoticed.

At that moment Bentley was making his way to the train station in Bristol where he called his mother to tell her that he was leaving for Abingdon and that he would miss being with her and his father for Easter. She reminded him that it was the first Easter he would not be home, but his own anxiety made him miss the sadness and the vacant sound in her voice. It did not occur to him that two households would be void of their only children this Easter because of his plan.

Bentley took a short breath when he saw Georgia's classic face looking out the window of the coach as it passed him on the platform. After climbing aboard, he paused and looked at Georgia gazing intently out the window. Upon seeing Bentley Georgia burst into a broad smile as, leaning across the empty seat, he kissed her lightly rouged cheek.

Bentley secured his suitcase in the overhead rack before falling onto the seat and leaning toward her to brush a glancing kiss across her flushed cheek. He was startled when she showed no response so he gently pushed his face into her hair, his lips touching her ear as he whispered, "What's the matter, sweetheart?"

Georgia tilted her head toward the window, disengaging his face from her hair before she turned to look at him and whisper, "I'm afraid, Bentley. I'm afraid."

"Of what, sweetheart?" he asked, moving his hand to cover hers, which were clinched together with chalk-white knuckles.

"I'm frightened, afraid we're making a mistake, doing the wrong thing . . ." she began softly.

The consummate salesman looked down at his hands covering hers and began, "Georgia, I know you're feeling guilt and you're afraid, and that's natural. But I don't feel guilt, because what we're doing is an expression of love, a fragile love we're preserving against all the challenges of life. We're memorializing our love, protecting it. How could we ever regret that, even if we have to tell a few white lies for a short time? We'll look back on this as the time we saved our love, ensured that we would protect it for the rest of our lives."

"That was lovely, Bentley," she began softly, then looking directly into his eyes, added emphatically, "but our love isn't fragile or I wouldn't be here."

"Of course you wouldn't, Georgia. Neither would I! That was a poor choice of words. Here, I've got something to show you," he offered quickly, opening the straps of his briefcase. Reaching inside, he removed a white, legal-size sheet of paper. "This is our marriage license, sweetheart," he explained, smiling broadly as he laid the document on the outside of the briefcase resting on his knees.

Following his instructions, Georgia took his large black fountain pen, her Christmas gift, and in trembling letters penned her name. "Is that okay?" she asked, looking up at Bentley.

"That's fine, perfect," he answered.

Throughout the day, her soul was washed in waves of fear, but each time, like the receding tide, fear subsided, and she was able to continue by focusing her thoughts on something else. Laying her head back on the padded seat, she closed her eyes, attempting to deal with the distant voice of a battered conscience. Georgia's eyes popped open when the engineer cut back on the throttle and began an elongated stop that would take several miles. In the dusky falling darkness she could see the gray and bleak buildings of the city near the depot. Suddenly she was aware that Bentley had slipped from the seat to remove their suitcases.

"This is it, sweetheart!" he said, lifting both suitcases. "Let's go!"

A short time later they walked with other passengers looking for taxi carriages under the dim streetlights as she squeezed his arm, exclaiming, "Bentley! Look how strange and dark the sky is! I can smell rain. I think we're going to get a storm!"

"Yeah, it looks like it, but don't worry. Here's a taxi now," he answered. As the driver dismounted from the high seat to get the bags, Bentley yelled, "Hotel Jeb Stuart."

Once inside the carriage Bentley related that he had arranged for an Episcopal priest to marry them in a private ceremony. Because of a Good Friday evening service at seven-thirty, they were supposed to be at the church at nine o'clock. That arrangement, he explained, should give them time to check into the hotel and have dinner. She was startled when he mentioned that two witnesses would meet them at the church.

"Witnesses?" she asked vaguely.

"Yes, Georgia. We have to have witnesses. It's required by law," he answered in clipped words, making her realize for the first time that Bentley was nervous too.

He told her he had obtained the services of "two old and trusted friends," but he didn't offer their names, and Georgia didn't ask.

As the carriage stopped, both looked out through the isinglass windows into a watery blur of lights and moving forms in front of Hotel Jeb Stuart. "Stay inside for a minute, Georgia," Bentley said as he slipped from the carriage, darting under the canopy. She lost sight of him as a hotel doorman approached the carriage. The doorman wore a red uniform and had a neatly trimmed white beard. Smiling, he held a large umbrella in one hand, extended the other to Georgia, and said, "Ma'am." She held his arm tightly as he tipped his umbrella against the blowing rain and escorted her into the hotel.

"Oh, good, you're here," Bentley said, turning and extending his arm as they followed the bellman moving ahead with the luggage. Both were taken aback by the opulence and splendor of the elegantly appointed lobby and the noisy crowd of fashionably dressed people. As they threaded their way toward the registration desk, her relentlessly pressing conscience sent a reminder: *This is Good Friday.*

Bentley guided her into an empty leather wing chair. "Sit here while I go to register," he requested before moving nervously into the registration line. When his turn came, he stepped forward and announced, "Mr. and Mrs. Bentley Thompson." Quickly, the process was over, and he handed the key to the bellman. "Please take the luggage to the room while Mrs. Thompson and I go to dinner. I'll get the key after that."

Moments later Bentley and Georgia entered the elegant dining room, where they were shown to a small round table near an upright piano played by a man in a tuxedo. The table was intimate and adorned with linen, crystal, and silver. Moments later, a black waiter lighted the single candle between them and nodded respectfully without speaking. His name tag identified him as "Price."

When Price returned, Georgia asked Bentley to order first. He chose a steak dinner and a glass of red wine. She asked for a cup of cream of tomato soup and a baked potato. Price smiled and nodded with approval, slipping away as if to apologize for his interruption.

They watched in silence as Price served them with a simple, matter-of-fact gracefulness. Soon, they concentrated on their dinners, relieved, if only for a moment, from the intensity of their covert journey. Georgia finished the small cup of soup, eating sparingly of the baked potato. Price eased beside her and deftly removed her soup cup and plate, asking, "May I get the lady anything else?"

"Yes. I'll have a glass of white wine," she answered, surprising Bentley.

"Yes, ma'am," answered Price, nodding.

"I'll have another red," Bentley called out. Price paused without turning, then continued walking away.

Georgia sat in silence until the waiter returned with the glasses of wine. Price nodded graciously and quickly left the table. "To us, Georgia," Bentley offered, raising his glass.

"To us," she replied softly.

Bentley removed a gold pocket watch from his vest pocket to check the time before leaning across the table and saying, "This is for you, sweetheart." In his hand rested a small gift-wrapped box, unmistakable in size. She slowly removed the silver tissue and lifted the small hinged top, revealing a gold wedding band. He recognized the same demeanor, the mood, he had seen as they sat by the fire at Stonewall, the night he proposed the secret journey - the night that brought them to this night.

The muffled report of distant, rolling thunder was barely discernible in the cushioned atmosphere of the dining room as Bentley leaned forward again, smiling nervously. Georgia sat oblivious to the rest of the room, her eyes fixed on the golden wedding band. She stared at it through a veil of tears as Price made his way toward their table. As he approached, he saw the beautiful young woman holding the box and the handsome gentleman leaning across the table. He turned with a grace and casualness that brought no attention. In touch with his soul, he innately withdrew from the drama playing out at his table.

"Do you want me to put it on your finger?" Bentley asked softly, still leaning across the table.

"No, my love. That would be bad luck. You may put in on my finger at the altar," she whispered, still looking at the circle of gold.

"That won't be long, darlin'," he said, reaching for the box still in her outstretched palm. When they walked out moments later, Bentley didn't notice that her wine glass sat full on the linen tabletop.

When Georgia returned from the room, where she changed clothes, Bentley was again taken by her appearance. Wearing a gray silk dress, Georgia looked timely and fashionable. She wore a small corsage of delicate white roses pinned to her coat lapel, which she had found waiting in the room along with a bottle of chilled French champagne.

"Our carriage should be waiting. The driver will take us to the church not far away. Then he'll bring us back," Bentley explained with a renewed sense of confidence.

As they approached a new black carriage at the end of the canopy, the driver yelled, "Thompson?"

"Yeah! That's us," called the groom as the driver jumped from the steel rim of a front wheel to the wet pavement. Moving quickly to open the carriage door, the driver looked at Georgia, but the dripping wide brim of his hat obscured his face. She saw only his dark eyes and what appeared to be a swarthy, middle-aged face as she climbed into the carriage. Bentley dashed from the canopy and bounded through the open door, falling into the seat beside her. They laughed nervously, resettled themselves, then snuggled together in silence as the carriage made its way in the night through the steady spring rain.

Through the water-smeared carriage windows, the landscape remained as obscure as the driver's face. After fifteen minutes, the coach jerked to an abrupt stop. "This is it, sir!" the driver called down as Bentley opened the door to look outside. Georgia could make out a white frame church, but there were no lights inside.

"Wait here. I'll go see if everything is set," ordered Bentley without looking back as he slid from the coach, darting toward the church and leaving Georgia alone and afraid. Several minutes later, she gasped as the carriage door was yanked open and Bentley frantically called, "This is it. Let's go." Huddled together awkwardly under an umbrella, they slowly moved through the rain toward the front door of the dark church.

Chapter 10

At nine o'clock Frances Wertz stood in the dimly lit sitting room where her husband lay sleeping on a daybed. *This hard rain,* she thought, *caused him to fall asleep.* Suddenly, George's green eyes popped open, but his countenance was vague and confused as he looked up at Frances. "I dreamed Georgia was calling me," he said, taking Frances's hands in his own.

"Calling you?" she asked, still looking down at him.

"I could hear her calling me, and I knew she was wet from the rain," he related earnestly, looking up into his wife's sympathetic face.

"I know why you dreamed of Georgia—you miss her. And I know why you dreamed of the rain. Listen. It's still pouring down. We need to go to bed."

As they slowly climbed the front stairs, George pulled at the banister and said, "Her voice sounded so natural, so real."

"Dreams are like that sometimes," whispered Frances as she clasped her arm around his lean back.

* * * * *

Bentley moved into the dimly lit vestibule, Georgia clinging tightly to his arm. Seeing two dark figures moving toward them, she squeezed herself against Bentley as the silhouettes became discernable in the dim light. The two young men, both dressed in dark suits and ties, appeared remarkably similar like the two railroad men who had disturbed the eternal rest of Anna Marie Holmes. About Bentley's height and general size, they looked slightly younger as they stood looking at him as if she were not present.

Bentley touched her elbow, leaned forward, nodded to the figure closest to her, and whispered, "Georgia, this is Jim Nelson."

Nelson nodded slightly without smiling and said, "Ma'am."

"And this is Tom Fugate, Georgia," Bentley explained, as Fugate only nodded and turned toward Nelson, with the trace of a dark smile.

"Everything's set," Nelson said softly to Bentley.

"Okay," Bentley answered in a clipped voice.

Seeing the nave only faintly illumined by candles and a single pale light on the altar, Georgia whispered, "Bentley! Why is it so dark?"

"It's a candlelight service, Georgia," he whispered.

Like a child pleading with a parent to protect her from the horrors of darkness, she stood immobile, staring at him. When he turned, he realized he was losing her. He understood that her intense eyes were pleading to him, *Bentley, please . . . no! We can turn back!* He was on the rim of the abyss, his last chance to change course. He could still do it, they both could turn back! They could change their minds and leave it all undone! He smiled reassuringly and took a step forward.

She surprised him by moving beside him as they began walking down the aisle toward the pale illumination of the sanctuary.

Bentley felt Georgia's strong grip loosening as she threatened to collapse. He heard her breaths, now coming quickly in short, shallow gasps, so he stopped their slow procession and whispered, "You can make it! You're gonna be all right! I promise." Relieved, he saw that his words had a calming effect as she took a breath and looked away from him toward the front of the church.

Nearing the sanctuary, Georgia realized that three obscure figures waited on opposite sides of the communion rail. The witnesses, like two murky apparitions, stood to the right while on the left loomed another form, the blackened silhouette a stocky clergyman dressed in a black robe. Georgia clutched Bentley's arm more tightly as they approached the mysterious, faceless priest.

The priest wore only a full-length black cassock, which blended into the shadows of the sanctuary. Stopping at the communion rail, Georgia was shocked seeing his face. He appeared to be in his mid-twenties; so young, she thought, to be a priest. He was slightly taller than Bentley, but heavier. His chubby face had smooth, rosy cheeks and heavy jowls that melted into a thick neck. A full mane of blond tussled hair, poorly combed, contributed to his extraordinarily youthful appearance. *He must look younger than he is!* she thought.

The portly priest smiled mechanically and nodded to Bentley. Georgia saw that the *Episcopal Book of Common Prayer* shook slightly in his hands. *He's very inexperienced,* she assumed. The priest began to read the form of Solemnization of Matrimony, but Georgia sensed right away that the reading was rote and flat, lacking the rhythmic cadence, the accompanying tonal quality and the expressive inflection she was used to hearing from Joe Dunn at St. Thomas.

"Dearly beloved, we are gathered together here in the sight of God, and in the face of this company, to join together this man and woman in holy matrimony which is commended of Saint Paul to be honorable among all men and therefore is not by any to be entered into unadvisedly or lightly but reverently, discreetly, advisedly, soberly, and in the fear of God. Into this holy estate, these two persons present come now to be joined. If any man can show just cause why they may not lawfully be joined together, let him now speak, or else hereafter forever hold his peace."

The only dearly beloved gathered with them stood like granite as the priest continued reading.

"I require and charge you both, as ye will answer at the dreadful day of judgment when the secrets of all hearts shall be disclosed, that if either of you know any impediment why ye may not be lawfully joined in matrimony, ye do now confess it. For be ye well assured, that if any persons are joined together otherwise than as God's Word doth allow, their marriage is not lawful."

For the first time, the priest paused, looking up from the prayer book at Bentley, before continuing, "Bentley, wilt thou have this woman to be thy wedded wife, to live together after God's ordinance in the holy estate of matrimony? Wilt thou love her, comfort her, honor, and keep her in sickness and in health and, forsaking all others, keep thee only unto her, as long as ye both shall live?"

Before answering, Bentley looked into the ashen face of Georgia Wertz and answered solemnly, "I will."

"Georgia, wilt thou have this man to thy wedded husband, to live together after God's ordinance in the holy estate of matrimony? Wilt thou obey him, and serve him, love, honor, and keep him in sickness and in health and, forsaking all others, keep only unto him, as long as ye both shall live?"

Staring ahead as if in a trance, she answered softly, "I will."

"Who giveth this woman to be married to this man?" read the priest before he realized that the question was unnecessary. Forgetting to ensure that Bentley took Georgia's right hand in his right hand, the priest began to intone phrases that Bentley repeated. "I, Bentley, take thee, Georgia, to my wedded wife, to have and to hold from this day forward, till death us do part, according to God's holy ordinance; and thereto I plight thee my troth."

In a soft voice that echoed the winds of the Bavarian forests, Georgia repeated, "I, Georgia, take thee, Bentley, to my wedded husband, to have and to hold from this day forward, for better or for worse, for richer or for poorer, in sickness and in health, to love, cherish, and to obey, till death us do part, according to God's holy ordinance; and thereto I give thee my troth."

"The ring please," intoned the priest. Georgia could feel Bentley's hands shaking as he easily glided the golden band onto her slender finger. She sensed immediately that the ring was much too large as the priest led Bentley again, saying, "With this ring, I thee wed, and with all my worldly goods I thee endow: In the Name of the Father, and of the Son, and of the Holy Ghost. Amen."

Georgia gazed at her ring as she, Bentley, and the priest repeated the Lord's Prayer. The priest then continued "O eternal God, Creator and Preserver of all mankind, Giver of all spiritual grace, the Author of everlasting life, send thy blessing upon these thy servants, this man and this woman, whom we bless in Thy Name, that, as Isaac and Rebecca lived faithfully together, so these persons may surely perform and keep the vow and covenant betwixt them made, whereof this ring given and received is a token and pledge, and may ever remain in perfect love and peace together, and live according to thy laws; through Jesus Christ our Lord. Amen. Those whom God hath joined together, let no man put asunder."

Mr. and Mrs. Bentley Thompson turned quickly to recess from the soft lights at the altar toward the faint glow in the back of the church. At that moment the priest realized that he forgot to read the pronouncement. With a shrug of his broad shoulders, he stepped through the rail and disappeared into the darkness. If the words from the prayer book had been spoken by the priest on that stormy spring night in East Tennessee, they would have been, "Forasmuch as Bentley and Georgia have consented together in holy wedlock, and have witnessed the same before God and this company, and thereto have given and pledged their troth, each to the other, and have declared the same by giving and receiving a ring, and by joining hands, I pronounce that they are man and wife, in the Name of the Father, and of the Son, and of the Holy Ghost, Amen."

As Mr. and Mrs. Bentley Thompson were denied the pronouncement, they likewise missed the blessing. They did not hear because the priest did not read, "God the Father, God the Son, God the Holy Ghost, bless, preserve, and keep you; the Lord mercifully look with his favor upon you and fill you with all spiritual benediction and grace, that ye may so live together in this life, that in the world to come ye may have life everlasting. Amen."

Reaching the dim vestibule, Georgia was confronted by another dark, faceless form. Gasping, she bolted backward into Bentley as she heard, "Ready, Mr. Thompson?" from the driver, who stood dripping rain from his black slicker.

Climbing into the carriage the newlyweds' emotions took flight like two white pigeons rising in soft winds toward home. Georgia cried tears of relief and happiness as, huddled together, they eased into a quiet reverie after their prolonged ordeal. Bentley stared straight ahead into the darkness before closing his eyes.

Georgia's soul would no longer be denied as the enormity of their act which pressed upon her. She reflected upon the journey that had led her to become Mrs. Bentley Thompson. It was piecemeal, incremental, made up of bits and pieces, shards of life that formed a mosaic in which she eventually came to simply whisper, "Yes."

So, it was over. And what was done was done, she told herself. They were husband and wife just as certainly and surely as if they had been married in St. Thomas Episcopal Church. Looking at Bentley's handsome profile, Georgia realized how deeply she loved him. With bittersweet pangs of remorse that she could not share the joyous fact of their marriage with others she loved, especially her father, she willed herself to be happy, to be free to flow with her husband for the short time they had together.

Soon Bentley walked to the front desk, where a polite desk clerk smiled and handed him the key. Glancing in a hallway mirror, Bentley was surprised to see how fatigued and haggard he looked. The events of the long, arduous day had taken their toll on him. Now they were facing the next challenge, the lovely dread, and the first night together, the night Bentley had fantasized about for longer than he could remember.

Georgia, drained emotionally and physically from the surrealistic and frightening events of her long day, was quietly stoical. Holding hands the couple moved slowly down the hall toward the bridal suit. Surprising herself by her calmness, Georgia worried because she felt no excitement, no yearning anticipation. At the door Bentley paused and in a raspy voice said, "Well, this is it, sweetheart."

After he opened the door to the bridal suite, they stood facing a massive mahogany bed with a full backboard rising six feet to a canopy extending outward in a semicircle over the upper half of the bed. Champagne sat chilled in a silver-plated wine bucket.

Georgia hung her coat in the mahogany wardrobe, unassisted by Bentley, who walked toward the champagne. Then she cautiously entered the bathroom, where she was shocked at the face gazing back at her. It appeared older, drawn and worried, with black rings under tired eyes. Unable to escape her own image, she walked back into the large bedroom, lifting an errant strand of hair that dropped across her forehead.

Bentley, coat and tie removed, entered the bathroom, where he ran a comb through his neatly trimmed hair. Standing there in the pale light of the doorway, he looked darkly handsome, as handsome as a groom should be.

"I was so scared. Were you?" she asked as he moved toward the bed.

"Well, I was nervous," he admitted, sitting beside her, "but I wasn't afraid. I could feel you shaking though. I was worried about you for a while."

"Well, Bentley, it was so strange, everything so strange! The terrible storm, the dark church, and the priest . . . . He seemed so young, and he was nervous too. What was his name?"

"Father Dwight Osborne," he answered softly. "And you're right; he's young. This is his first parish as an assistant priest. I don't know him personally," he explained in clipped words as he slid off the bed and stood beside her. He kissed her gently on her forehead, then moved to her lips, which were parted and warm. "That's enough talk tonight, Georgia, about everything else and everybody else but us. I just want to talk about us."

She reached out and, stroking the side of his temple, whispered, "I do too, love. I just want to talk about us in the time we have left."

Bentley pulled her fingers to his lips and kissed them. Still holding them close to his lips, he tried to reassure her, "We have tonight, tomorrow, tomorrow night, and part of Sunday, sweetheart." When again she sat in silence, gazing demurely into his face, he asked, "And we have the rest of our life, don't forget about that . . . . Shall I open the champagne?"

"Yes, love," she answered, leaning forward, kissing him on the cheek, "and I'll get ready for bed." Always fascinated by her, he watched Georgia move to the wardrobe and then into the bathroom carrying a nightgown and her small leather vanity case.

After opening the champagne, Bentley stood in his silk undershorts, pouring a glass of champagne. Without waiting for his bride, he gulped a sip of the sparkling, straw-colored champagne.

Georgia stepped from the bathroom in a white silk nightgown. As she turned, he realized that her thick brown hair, upswept all day, was now falling toward her shoulders. As she was walking toward the bed, an illuminating flash silhouetted her pale form.

As Georgia sat on the bed, back against the headboard, Bentley passed her a glass of champagne in trembling hands. Seeing that his glass was almost empty, she brought hers to her lips without the pretense of a toast. She took a sip, then extended her hand, revealing a sizable wad of medical tape on the underside of her ring. "I had to put it on to keep from losing it," she said calmly.

"Where'd you get the tape?" he asked, anxious to conclude the small talk so he could begin the conquest he had pursued for so long. It did not occur to Bentley Thompson that the conquest would elude him once again this night because he would encounter surrender.

Bentley poured himself another glass and moved back to his bride. After a few moments of silence, Bentley rolled onto his shoulder to look into her eyes, and they both smiled a common smile, a knowing smile. The time had come.

The ritual begun so many times before, the secret song of lovers, the symphony commenced but never concluded, began again, but this time both knew it would be played differently, unlike any time before. They had learned the first movements well, knew that the swell of the music would come as they kissed slowly, gently, with no urgency. Soon, they flowed toward the major movement. Theirs was a melody with no composition, free-flowing music that maintained itself through its soulful movement. The well-known refrains and themes begun so often in the past came flowing again, this time to the end.

As they lay entwined in each other's arms and legs, Bentley soon fell asleep. Later, she slipped away, disengaging herself from his grasp and extinguishing the candles. She stood for a few moments looking at the blackness behind the watery window panes. Then she eased back in bed with her husband without waking him. Soon she and Bentley lay sleeping the sleep of spent lovers.

Chapter 11

The pale morning sun cast a faint tint on the large wet panes, not yet illuminating the lingering murky light in the room. Like all new lovers, Bentley and Georgia were gloriously entangled, legs and arms like fleshy Lincoln Logs.

When Bentley opened his eyes he could see inside of the gloomy room, lighted by an anemic sun hidden behind the dismal overcast of blue-gray storm clouds. Easing an arm from under Georgia's sleeping form, he slipped from the bed and checked his gold pocket watch. It was eight o'clock as he walked into the bathroom and quietly closed the door.

Emerging a short time later, groomed to perfection, he could not see Georgia's face as the Tennessee winds pushed gun-barrel–blue clouds high above in an easterly direction. The sun ventured out slightly as its gauzed, diffused glow softly brightened the earth below.

As he stood watching her sleeping form, his soul allowed him to grasp a concept: Understanding the extraordinary uniqueness of the moment, he was aware that of all the people and places on the earth, and of all the time that had ever been and would ever be, the two of them had arrived together at that specific place and that singular point in time. Somehow, for reasons he could not fathom, that awareness, whether simple or complex, took on an undefined and unexplained importance; but, not one to ruminate, he closed the door softly and went to get breakfast.

Georgia awoke abruptly, startled by her strange surroundings. Reaching for Bentley quickly, she found herself alone and frightened in the massive, canopied bed. *Where is he?* she thought, fighting back her fear of abandonment. She did not have to look for Bentley. She could *feel* his absence. Then it came, searing and painful, almost overpowering. Her heart was wracked deeply, to the core of her soul with the vast and barren pain of remorse and abject guilt.

She saw his face clearly, as if he were present in the room, but it was not the face of Bentley Thompson. It was the face of George Wertz, to her the face of goodness, of trust and of love. It was the vision of a face her soul allowed her to glimpse, a face with no trace of judgment, no threat. It seemed to be smiling the way she remembered it as a little girl. As if being pulled helplessly by the retracting surf and a strong rip-tide, she felt herself slipping into madness. Burying her face in the heavy down pillows, she muffled primal screams of hopelessness.

Exhausted, lying in a state of semi consciousness, she heard somebody knocking! Drawing the covers to her chin, she bolted up and stared, wide-eyed, at the door, unable to answer, unable to move, gripped in blind, debilitating panic.

"Georgia! Open the door," Bentley yelled.

"I'm coming!" she gasped, crawling across the wide bed and stumbling to the floor. With shaking hands, she managed to open the door slightly, to see Bentley standing outside holding a tray. Stepping back slowly, she held the door open as he entered quickly.

"I had to knock with my foot, holding this tray! I thought for a minute you'd left the room. Are you okay?" he asked hurriedly.

"No!" she gasped, falling against his chest, her face pressing on his freshly starched shirt and her arms tightly wrapped around him. "Just hold me for a minute," she whispered. With waves of remorse and fear rolling over her again, she started to cry silently. Bentley wanted to speak, to do something, but he sensed her tears would have to run their course, and again he had no inkling of what to say.

Stepping back, holding him at arm's length, she looked through swollen, puffy eyes, as if she had not seen him clearly before. "You're all dressed up! You look so good, so in control! Look at me, I'm a wreck, and I look awful!"

"I'm dressed up for you, sweetheart," he said, "dressed up for my wife. I'm just happy, Georgia. That's what you see—happiness, because I'm with you, and because you're my wife, my wife forever, for as long as we live." She moved back into his arms, and stood holding him again in silence. When Bentley felt her body relax a bit, he scooped her into his arms. Moving to the broad bed he gently put her down and sat beside her. Georgia rolled to her side, facing the wall. The panes were darker now as the filtered sun faded again behind heavier clouds. Soon he realized she was asleep.

An hour later, Bentley sat sipping a cup of coffee. He felt slight relief simply because the sun brightened slightly, threatening to display itself fully in the Tennessee sky. Mile-high zephyrs blew the gray storm clouds eastward toward the Blue Ridge. He had no way to know that, like the handsome prince who kissed Sleeping Beauty, he had awakened a part of Georgia's soul, a part of her consciousness that had slumbered soundly before. He would, he decided, take his cue from her, rather than reach forth blindly in some vain attempt to comfort her.

"Bentley," she began in a steady voice, "I want you to know that I'm all right now. I won't do that any more to you, or to me for that matter. I won't fall apart again, I promise. I'm okay now. What we did, we did together. What's done is done. It was a decision we both made; if it were wrong, we have no control over it now. We can do nothing about the past and really nothing about the future. I realize we have only the here and now. We simply have to do the best we can, make the best of our decision, until we can announce our marriage. I want you to know, Bentley, that I love you at this moment as deeply, as profoundly, as I can. That will *never* change for as long as I live. I promise you, my love."

Later, after a breakfast of hard biscuits and lukewarm coffee, they took a bubble bath in the large tub. Afterward, laughing and happy, they strolled the streets aimlessly, browsing the shops near the hotel.

The second night fell as they entered another realm of enchantment. They moved easily, joyfully, into the magical dimension, one that lovers chart again and again, one of sweet discovery and exciting exploration.

* * * * *

At four-thirty on Monday afternoon, when the eastbound Norfolk and Western train stopped in Bristol, Bentley slid from the seat beside her and pulled his suitcase from the overhead rack. Looking down he met her intense gaze. "I love you," he whispered.

"And I you," she answered as Bentley kissed her on the forehead.

Then he walked away without looking back, with her ring in his coat pocket. He promised to have it resized and back to her quickly because she wanted to cherish it secretly.

Georgia did not remember the ride to Abingdon as the train jerked to her final stop, hissing and spewing rising clouds of steam in the late afternoon air. She stood to remove her suitcase just as the middle-aged conductor approached and retrieved it for her.

Moments later Georgia saw her father walking toward her alone as she ran into his outstretched arms. As they stood holding each other tightly, twisting slowly back and forth, she asked, "Where's Momma?"

"She's at home. . ." he began.

"What's wrong? Is she sick?" Georgia interrupted.

"She has one of her bad headaches. Hasn't had one in years, but last Friday night it struck her. On Saturday Dr. Smith came and gave her medication, but she didn't get relief until today so we didn't go to church yesterday," he continued in a tired voice.

"Oh, Daddy, I'm so sorry!" she exclaimed.

"You're a good daughter, always concerned for us. So, tell me now, how about you? Are you all right?" he asked, looking down at his only child.

"I'm just fine, Daddy," she offered, gazing straight ahead, hoping the tears gushing into her eyes would not spill over to her cheeks, hoping that he did not see them.

"Good, let's go home," said the man from the dark forests of Bavaria.

The next day after nursing school Georgia went to the studio and asked to have her picture taken. She was wearing her best gray dress trimmed in white. In some pictures she held a black, broad-brimmed hat on her lap. Delighted, George Wertz took many shots of the crown jewel of his life, never thinking to ask why she was so dressed. Later he would choose the shot he liked best and display it in his studio on a table next to a photograph of Anna Wertz.

Chapter 12

Georgia, a daughter of the Blue Ridge, watched with delight as winter's drab garb slipped from the flowing mountain ranges. Her first inkling that the season had relented came on the Saturday afternoon in Johnson City. Now feeling spring at home, it seemed the perfect time for Georgia Thompson.

Now in her second spring with Bentley, Georgia realized that a year before, she had no way to know that her journey would take a daring turn, an irrevocable change in course, one that would profoundly alter her life. Now she came face-to-face with the shadow of her soul, a dark dimension of her spirit, one that she had not known existed, one that allowed her to deceive ones who loved her.

Georgia decided that she *could not* further weave her dark cloak of deception through another wedding. She resolved that when the time came, she would summon all her personal strength, pray hard to the God she believed in, and tell her parents the truth. She would beg their forgiveness for her cruel deception. That would be hard, but it would be a better course for all concerned. Her parents would probably place an announcement in the paper about the marriage. Perhaps, she thought, they would have a reception at the church. Then, Georgia prayed, she and Bentley would move on with their life together.

Georgia Thompson was not the only person awakened to the renewal of spring heightened by abiding romantic love. Some were blessed to experience the many dimensions of mature and seasoned love, while others, like Georgia, raced with abandon into their first loves. In Georgia's exuberance and celebration of the season, it did not occur to her that some were forced to accept a station in life in which romantic love would elude them forever. Most of those lonely souls managed somehow to resign themselves to an existence of exclusion, observing from a distance what appeared to be the feast of life to which they were not invited. Georgia could not know that some of the disenfranchised, feeling isolated and unloved, veer off the path of lonely resignation in a twisted journey of anger and rage. One dark person with a fragmented soul watched Georgia and other young women from a distance through his veil of distorted perception. Once he moved closer than observation. Once he went to the feast uninvited, participating in his dark dance, his version of pursuing love.

* * * * *

Although the sight was familiar to the Martha girls, they always paid attention to the sheriff of Washington County, who, on a warm Friday afternoon in late spring, watched the coeds moving about campus. He wanted his presence to remind them of their lost sister, realizing that youthful minds do not grasp the concept of vulnerability, much less mortality. Yet, tragically, the Martha girls learned unequivocally that death knows no seasons, follows no rules, and leaves no explanations.

Watching the pleasant afternoon draw toward its end, John reflected as always about the case. All of the initial suspects, some of whom had appeared viable at first, had been eliminated for one reason or another. A canvass of other sheriff's offices in Southwest Virginia and East Tennessee had generated leads but eventually all fizzled out. There were murders in the other jurisdictions, but all were cases in which one drunken family member killed another or in which violent men killed other violent men under the influence of whiskey and surging testosterone. In all the murder cases John worked over the years, it was eventually determined that the victim knew the killer. *Maybe*, he thought, *just maybe, Anna Marie knew her killer*; yet, his intuition suggested otherwise - she had *not* known the last evil presence she had seen in her life.

His experience with rape cases was similar. Most victims knew or had some association with their attackers; but again, he remembered Doc Smith's admonition that they could not assume the Holmes girl was raped.

"Sheriff?" called a young woman, abruptly wrenching John from his reflections. Standing beside Thunder, cradling several heavy textbooks, she squinted up into the fading afternoon sunlight.

He had failed to see or sense her approach, something rare for John. "Yes, miss?" he answered, bending at the waist toward her.

"You still haven't found who killed Anna Marie?" she asked in a frail voice as John dismounted.

"No, miss, not yet," he answered, removing his felt hat. Her demeanor touched him, one that suggested vulnerability, the kind he had come to envision for Anna Marie Holmes.

"She was my friend. I wish I could help you," the girl said resolutely.

"I wish you could too," he answered softly, smiling slightly.

"There's something I've already done to try to help you, Sheriff," she said.

"There is?" John responded, stepping toward her in an effort to hear her soft voice.

"Yes. I've prayed for you. Prayed that you'd catch the person who killed Anna Marie," she answered, her young face devoid of expression.

"That's very kind of you. I hope you'll keep me in your prayers," responded the sheriff of Washington County.

"I will," she promised, turning, "and I still pray for Anna Marie too."

Later as John walked into Kit's Café, his last stop before going home, several friends nodded when he made his way toward the stool beside Will West. Sitting down, he and Will exchanged greetings in the easy-flowing way men do when they have affection for each other.

Once John was settled, Will asked, "Anything new?" He did not have to frame the question further.

"No, I wish there were. Two possibilities exist. She was killed by a drifter, a person she didn't know, who moved on, or she was killed by some local, somebody she may or may not have known, a person who could still be in town," John explained, feeling relieved just to have said the words to somebody besides Doc Smith and President Clarke.

"I've done what you asked, watched men, all kinds, get on and off the trains, but I haven't seen anybody who looked suspicious. And lately we've had no hobos around here. I think they're afraid to stop, afraid they might be considered murder suspects."

"You might be right," John mused pensively.

"By the way," Will began, turning on the stool toward his friend, "last year I was sent to a two-week training course in Roanoke with the Railroad Police. It was part of the Norfolk and Western management program. I've been around firearms all my life, and I bird hunt; but anyway, I was trained in the use of the revolver and the shotgun. So if you ever need to deputize civilians, I'm volunteering now."

"Will," John began as he stood up, dropping two nickels next to his half-full cup of coffee, "if I *ever* have to, you'll be the first person I call."

"That would be my honor, John," responded Will, looking up into the eyes of the sheriff of Washington County. Neither man had a way to know that their exchange would have profound consequences in their lives.

"You haven't touched that beer. Do you want a fresh one?" Helen asked Will, pressing her thin hips against her side of the counter.

"No, Helen, this one's fine."

"Did you know that you have a friend who misses seeing you?"

"Who?"

"You know who, Will. Jeanette. Jeanette Moore? Remember her?" teased Helen, smiling down at Will.

"Since I haven't worked on the weekends lately, I haven't seen her when she's here," he explained.

"She'll be in a little later on, Will," Helen offered. "This is Friday night. Remember?"

"I do, Helen, but I have to go. We've got company coming for dinner. Tell Jeanette I'll make a point to see her soon and tell her that I've missed seeing her too," Will added.

"She *will* be thrilled, I'm sure. I'll tell her," Helen answered. Moments later she held Will in her gaze until he disappeared into the spring night. Jeanette Moore wasn't the only woman who had a crush on Will West.

Several nights later John Woodward entered the Smith home for the weekly meeting with Press. John tossed his hat on the coffee table as he sat down in one of the leather wing chairs. Press set two glasses of red wine on the mahogany table between the chairs. The men sat in silence for a while, until John told Press about his experience with the young Martha girl who had prayed for him. "That's something," Press mused, "really something."

"Press," John began, "do you think we're out of the woods yet? It's been almost eight months."

"I think we are, John. Eight months is a long time. What happened had to be some isolated case. You and I both know that there are countless unsolved, random killings in this country every year. This is going to be one of them. There'll be a problem with closure; people will be unsettled for a while. But hell, people forget; they get over things. Unfortunately, Harold Kane is unable to disabuse himself from the theory that death lurks around every corner. But, hey, he hasn't had an article in the paper in . . . let's see—"

"Three weeks," John interjected quickly, continuing, "but, Press, I really don't mind those pieces. We have to keep people aware of the threat."

"I don't think there is a threat any more. His articles are inflammatory. They keep people stirred up, agitated. That threat, whatever it was, *whoever* it was, has moved on," Doc Smith ventured emphatically.

"There's one thing that still bothers me though," John began slowly.

"What?"

"I'm still concerned about the stolen underwear. None of the wives reported the thefts, just the husbands, and one father. Arthur White called me to his bank to report that some of his daughter's underclothes were taken. Anyway we thought that it might have been some kids, but we never resolved it."

"Yeah, I remember. Sounds like an Emory and Henry fraternity prank to me," Press offered.

"Remember though some thefts occurred when school wasn't in session, and I believe a lot were never reported so we don't really know the actual number. After the Martha girl went missing, the theft reports stopped too. When we found her body months later, her underwear was pushed up between her legs," John said, staring straight ahead.

"But it seems to me," Press began, turning toward John, "if the thefts had anything to do with the killer, he would have taken the victim's underwear—instead, he left it at the scene."

"I know, I've thought of that too," John said, now looking at Press earnestly, "but I'm still not ready to concede that the thefts and the murder are not connected."

"Well, assuming you are correct," Press began, leaning forward in his chair, "where does that get us?"

"I'm not sure," John responded slowly, "but if the murder and the thefts are connected, we can put the killer in town for quite a while. That would discredit the theory that our victim was murdered by some drifter who happened upon her in a
random encounter."

"I guess we'll just have to wait and see; but, again, I think we're out of the woods,"
Doc answered, looking over to meet John's intense gaze.

* * * * *

Thirty minutes later Natalie White, a day student, left the Martha Washington
College library. It was just after nine as she stepped outside in the clear spring night,
deciding to walk home without giving thought to the matter.

The night was a bit cooler than she expected, but her full-length sweater would be
enough for the walk home. Natalie, an athletic young woman, was not beautiful, but
she projected a sleek feline aura.

After walking for several minutes, she noticed that the sidewalk and road were
deserted. She quickened her pace and squinted to see the small hands on her expensive Swiss wristwatch. The only sound she could hear was the gravel meshing under
her feet as she noticed that most of the houses were dark. Feeling isolated by the eerie
quietness of the deserted street, she suddenly sensed she was being followed. Whirling
around instinctively, she saw nothing but the darkened street. Picking up the pace
again, she passed beneath a line of slender, towering elms that cast deep shadows on
the uneven cobblestone pathway. The image of Anna Marie Holmes, the soft, wistful
face on countless posters, entered her consciousness.

Natalie tried to convince herself that her intuition was false, simply a childhood
flashback of insecurity at night. As Natalie pulled her sweater closer together, the sig-
nal, instinctual and primal, telegraphing danger flooded over her again. The first time
she had *sensed* she was being followed; now she *knew* she was being followed. Desperate to control her panic, she realized she could not run to her home without stopping. Whirling around suddenly, she caught a glimpse of a large dark figure as it
darted behind one of the trees lining the walkway.

Oh dear God! she thought, slipping into the fight-or-flight syndrome. Impulsively,
like leaping into a cold mountain lake, she glanced furtively over her shoulder. Now
the menacing apparition loomed closer as she realized her heavy book bag was bang-
ing against her knees. Yanking it from her neck and slinging it to the ground, she was
uplifted by a momentary sense of release of the dangling restraint.

Breaking into a full run, she heard a guttural sound, a primal moaning, punctu-
ated by panting breath moving the big body closer. Natalie turned again, seeing not
a face but a black hood as the form pressed toward her. Running faster, she saw him!
She saw the solitary figure emerging from the shadows and moving toward her. He
was leaning backward and canted to the right from the waist up.

"Jamie! Jamie!" she screamed.

Stopping abruptly, Jamie was amazed to see the white girl running toward him and calling his name as he glimpsed something else, a dark figure, behind her, but the girl demanded his attention as she closed upon him quickly, falling hard against his chest and clinging to him, sobbing. Feeling her legs buckle as she started to collapse, Jamie bent his knees to support Natalie White.

"Miz' White! Miz' White! It's okay! You okay now," he said softly in a surprisingly rich baritone. As Jamie helped Natalie to her feet, she looked back, staring into the blackness of the night. Now like a fragile vessel sailing for home port, listing to starboard side, the strange couple made its way through the spring night. Gender and color meant nothing to the souls who walked together in the darkness toward the White home.

Chapter 13

At nine-thirty John Woodward received a call from an excited deputy about Natalie White. "Who? What do you mean?" he demanded.

"That's all I know, Sheriff. Arthur White called and said to tell you that a man tried to assault his daughter. Said he wants you there right away!" explained the deputy soberly.

"Okay, call Doc Smith and tell him what you've told me. Ask him to meet me over there in case he has to examine the victim," directed John. John knew this situation would be extraordinarily delicate. White was difficult under favorable circumstances; this night he could be impossible.

After Thunder warmed up, John let him go to a full run. Loving the late-night race, the horse resisted when John reined him back upon seeing the bright lights on the Whites' porch. Nearing the front steps, John recognized a carriage from Martha Washington College. White, an important member of the Martha board, had apparently called Dr. Clarke before he had called the sheriff of Washington County. John quickly dismounted, leaving Thunder free in the front yard. He knocked lightly on the frame of the door, which opened quickly to expose the stooped form of Mary White looking drawn and grave. "Mrs. White, is your daughter all right?" John asked, unable to wait being told.

"She's all right, Sheriff, but only because of the grace of God," replied Mary White in a monotone that confused, but also relieved, John Woodward. Then she added, "Come in, Sheriff," and John removed his hat and stepped inside. "Wait here, please," she said, then walked down the spacious hallway.

After standing alone for several minutes in the large, richly appointed entry hall, John thought, *Strange. This is very strange.*

When Mary White returned, she managed a faint smile, saying, "They're waiting in the library. It's this way." She would not join the men.

Dr. Sidney Clarke and Arthur White stood in front of an empty fireplace, both wearing perfectly tailored suits with expensive, fashionable ties, each face mirroring the grave look of the other. Arthur White, a short, pudgy man in his mid-fifties, wore large horn-rimmed glasses, magnifying his dark eyes. He was bald except for immaculately trimmed gray hair on the sides of his head.

"Good evening, Arthur," John began as he nodded, walking toward them. Turning to Dr. Clark, he simply said, "Sidney." Clarke nodded slightly but didn't speak.

"Sheriff, you've got a problem!" bellowed White, stepping toward John without offering to shake hands. "Natalie was chased tonight! Actually *chased* by a man! I want to know what you're gonna do about it!"

"Is she all right?" ventured John calmly.

"Hell, I don't know if she's all right or not. She was hysterical when . . . whatever his name is, that Nigra, who walks everywhere, brought her home. And *thank God* for him, Sheriff."

"Jamie?" asked John, confused. "Jamie brought her home?"

"Yeah, she was a wreck, a goddamn mess," reported the agitated banker.

"Arthur, was your daughter assaulted in any way?" interrupted John, his voice calm but firm.

"No, Sheriff! That's my goddamned point. If it weren't for that half-wit, if it weren't for him, my daughter might be raped or dead as we speak. She was chased by a man, and had that Nigra not come along, well, only God knows what might have happened," answered Arthur White, eyes flashing in anger.

"Where is Jamie now?" asked John calmly, patiently.

"He's out on the back porch," responded the banker.

"The back porch?" John repeated in dismay.

"Yeah, we tried to get him to come in, but he wouldn't. I'm not sure he's all there. He doesn't act right to me, but I told him I wanted him to stay here until you got here, Sheriff," related White.

Realizing that Arthur White could take a bad situation and make it worse, John nevertheless sympathized with a frightened father concerned about his only child. "Arthur, is it possible to speak with Natalie?"

"Not tonight; she's had a sedative and gone to bed," replied White.

"A sedative?" John asked incredulously.

"Yeah," began Arthur White sheepishly, "it's some liquid medicine with codeine in it that Dr. Webb gave Mary for her nerves several years ago. I told Mary to give Natalie a good slug of the stuff. She's asleep now. When she wakes up in the morning, the first damn thing I want to know is what in the hell she was thinking about."

At that moment the doorbell emitted a crackling, harsh buzz. "What the hell?" questioned White.

"That's probably Dr. Smith," John stated, looking toward the library door.

"Dr. Smith? Who called him?" demanded White.

"I did, Arthur," John began calmly. "I couldn't tell from the information my deputy received if your daughter, God forbid, had been assaulted. So, not knowing, I sent for Dr. Smith to be on the safe side."

"It may be a good thing, Arthur," offered Sidney Clarke, speaking for the first time. "Perhaps he can look in on Natalie to ensure she is all right."

At that moment Mary White ushered Press into the library. He nodded, speaking cryptically, and then stood holding his black medical bag with a quizzical expression. John explained briefly what he knew. White instructed Mary to escort Press to Natalie's room. It did not escape the doctor that Arthur White failed to *ask* if he would check on Natalie. "I'll be happy to look in on her, Arthur," Press stated, glancing at John rather than Arthur White.

"Sheriff, now that you know what happened, what do you intend to do?" pressed Arthur White again as the doctor left the room.

"The first thing I have to do is find out what happened, Arthur," John began.

"You already know! I just got through telling you, for God's sake. You know enough to go get the son of a bitch," interrupted Arthur White, pointing a stubby cigar butt in the direction of John's face.

Those who knew John Woodward well would have noticed the way his jowls locked and the vein in his neck rose toward the surface. They would have known that he had reached a threshold where he would tolerate no abuse. "Arthur," John began gravely, one eye slightly squinted, "you need to understand something. I'll treat this case *exactly* the way I would treat *any other case.* I'll work it to the best of my ability. Money, power, and influence mean nothing to me as far as victimization goes. *Anybody* who gets hurt has the right to expect that the subject will be brought to justice. My success won't come solely from the effort I put into the investigation; it's also dependent upon the cooperation we get from the community—"

"Christ, Sheriff! All I ask, and I would still like to know, is that now you know what happened, what are you gonna do about it?" interrupted an ashen-faced White.

"I *don't* know what happened, Arthur," John began, his face grave in controlled anger. "You sure as hell wouldn't loan the bank's money knowing as little as I know now. Perhaps you can tell me, though. Tell me about the man who chased your daughter. Did she know him? If not, did he look familiar, remind her of anybody? Was he a white man or a Negro? How would she estimate his age? How tall was he, what kind of build did he have? How much did he weigh? How was he dressed? Did he say anything? If so, did he have a local or regional accent or some other kind? Did she see his face clearly? Can she recognize him again? Will she be able to make a positive identification? Was there anything unique about him? Right now we have absolutely no information about the person we're looking for. You've denied access to your daughter at a critical time; therefore, the best thing I have going is Jamie. So, excuse me, I want to interview him."

"Sheriff, you've made your point," began a more controlled Arthur White. John noticed that his voice lacked contrition as he continued, "Surely, though, as a father, even you could understand the tremendous pressure . . ."

"I do understand, Arthur, and I hope you understand mine. Now, I need to talk to Jamie," said the sheriff, moving toward the door without waiting for a response.

"I'd like to sit in on the interview, John, to hear what he has to say," said White, using the sheriff's name for the first time that evening.

"I'm sorry, Arthur, that won't be possible," said John, pausing to look back at the banker. "This man will be very intimidated by me. Two of us will overwhelm him. You can listen from the next room if you like. I need to bring him into the kitchen, get him off the porch."

At the door to the library, John met Press, who confirmed that Natalie White was sleeping soundly. "I'll wait here until you're through," said Press, realizing the delicate nature of the interview.

After Jamie was coaxed from the back porch to the kitchen table, he sat opposite the sheriff, his eyes rolled up and to the right as if they were gazing at some invisible object. John observed that, as always, Jamie was dressed in bib overalls and a denim shirt, that he had an African black complexion and short cropped hair with flecks of gray. His oval face presented a strong chin and a broad nose. John realized for the first time that the man had a handsome quality.

"It was getting chilly out on the back porch, wasn't it, Jamie?" began John with an easy, casual smile.

Smiling back, Jamie responded, "Naw, suh. Won't chilly to me."

John felt an inner surge of humility as he looked at the small, dignified black man with the sweet and gentle demeanor. John realized that had it not been for this mysterious town walker, he could have been investigating the death of another young woman. So to engage the dark, enigmatic little man, he first talked in generalities, beginning with the weather.

A few feet away Arthur White scowled at the college president and whispered, "Why doesn't he get on with it?"

John learned that Jamie was James Lamont Anderson, age thirty-eight, who possessed a special facility for names and dates. Because of Jamie's limited communication skills, John did not know how much information he could elicit from him.

"Jamie, please tell me everything that happened tonight. Begin, if you will, by explaining exactly where you were and exactly what you first saw in connection with Miss White. Okay?"

"I be walkin' and Miz White come running into me, cryin' and scared, and I be bringin' her home," he answered, gazing over John's head.

"Do you have any idea about the time, Jamie?" John questioned.

"Time it was?" intoned Jamie incredulously. John suspected that Jamie lived in a world of changing lights and hues and temperatures, a world in which he walked devoid of clocks and time.

"Naw, suh," Jamie said finally.

"That's okay, Jamie. That's fine. Tell me exactly where you were when you first saw Miss White," he asked, sitting on the edge of the kitchen chair, leaning across the table toward the slight little man.

Ultimately he interpreted Jamie's explanation to reveal that while Jamie was walking west on Valley Street, he encountered Natalie White running toward him. Moments before she reached him, he saw a dark figure dart behind a tree. Natalie had collapsed against him, and he walked her home. Jamie felt as if there were something familiar about the big man who seemed to move fast for his size. While he hadn't seen the man's face, Jamie thought he could identify him again by his shape and movement.

When the interview concluded, John believed the suspect to be a large white male of unknown age who was a fast runner and taller than John's six feet one inch. John knew that most witnesses exaggerate the size of perpetrators, but he decided the man must be six feet one or two. The sheriff was convinced too that the man must be over two hundred and fifty pounds. He obtained little about the unknown subject's dress; nevertheless, he had some physical description.

It was too dark to properly search Natalie's suspected route home, but John rode along it, finding nothing. Later as John and Press slept exhausted in their beds, Jamie continued to walk into the night.

At the first light of morning John and the deputies traced the route Natalie had walked. *Anything! Anything!* John thought. *If I could find anything the guy dropped last night.* On the first check he saw the oblong denim book bag, lying twisted and dew laden against the base of one of the tall elm trees lining the cobblestone walkway. A cursory search of the contents revealed that the book bag belonged to Natalie White. Although it was of no evidentiary value, it documented in tangible form what had happened—Natalie White had been chased and terrified and, to escape, had thrown the book bag away in panic. John had the bag draped over his right forearm as he knocked on the Whites' front door at nine o'clock that morning.

Although it was Saturday morning, Arthur White was at the bank. Mary appeared more composed and cordial than the night before. "Please, John," she stated graciously, "come in, and I'll get Natalie. She's anxious to talk to you." Not noticing the book bag, Mary White ushered John into the elegant living room, where he sat waiting for Natalie White. When the girl entered the room, John noted her natural feline sexuality, an appeal that most men would detect. His investigative mind raced ahead, thinking, *Could that be the reason? Could it have been her looks, her appeal? Was she chosen because of that, or was she a random pick?* Her demeanor, her aura, carried something fresh and natural yet deeply sensual. John, though, saw Natalie White as a little girl, a frightened child who could easily have lost her life.

Natalie examined her book bag and found nothing missing. She explained that she had given little thought to walking home alone although now she was embarrassed and chagrined. That, she said, was the first thing "Daddy" had spoken to her about this morning. As Natalie related the events of the night before, John sat in intense concentration. He knew from years of experience not to interrupt the stream of consciousness from a witness or victim. When Natalie told of looking back and seeing the hood, however, John couldn't help himself. "Hood? He wore a hood?"

"Yes, sir," Natalie answered. That was the only way she could describe it: "some sort of cloth on his head, a dark hood." She related the rest of her ordeal and the improbable rescue by James Lamont Anderson.

John sat stunned. The information about the mask changed all other possibilities. The attack had been planned! *But was the victim chosen or random? Did Natalie White and Anna Marie Holmes have similar characteristics? Was she singled out because of a projected sexual appeal?* Assuming the two events were connected, was the Martha campus, by virtue of its number of young women, an appealing hunting ground?

John's surprises were not over. When Natalie told him about the guttural sounds, the mixture of breathlessness and moaning, he scooted to the edge of the Victorian horsehair sofa. Later John would discuss the possibilities with Press. Was it, they would come to contemplate, an athletic expression of exertion, or was it a more dark and primal sound, one that signaled a loss of control just before the dark predator closed in for a deadly attack? Finally, at the end of the interview, John asked, "Natalie, is there anything I didn't ask you that you think may be important to me now?"

"Well, I'm not sure . . ." she began reluctantly, tentatively.

"Go ahead," John urged softly.

"Well," she began slowly, "last summer, some clothes were stolen from our line in the back yard. Several pieces of my underwear. . . ." As she related the circumstances, John acquired information he failed to gather from his earlier conversation with her father. Now, John believed, the disappearance of the lingerie, the murder, and Natalie's ordeal were somehow connected.

The strange story of Natalie White raced through the community. Arthur White allowed her to be interviewed by Harold Kane "for the safety of all women in town." Kane did not know of the missing underwear, but he jumped quickly to draw similarities between Anna Marie Holmes and Natalie White. He noted that Anna Marie had disappeared on a Friday night, the same night of the week that Natalie was chased. That point had not escaped John Woodward and Press Smith.

The little town was changing. It had been no better or worse than any other in the Blue Ridge Mountains, or anywhere else, for that matter; yet before the murder of the Martha student, the inhabitants for the most part enjoyed an element of innocence, some pristine sliver of naivety, a fleeting wisp of Eden. Nobody would feel the emotional shift away from that state of mind more than Sheriff John Woodward.

Chapter 14

As a damp June crept into the Blue Ridge, making a rainy transition from spring, the Martha girls were at home pursuing other interests, while Georgia and Bentley found solace in their secret. His trips to Abingdon became less frequent, but Bentley was right. Because of their secret marriage, Georgia was secure in the relationship in his absence. She knew that work prevented his coming sometime; yet, Bentley often seemed preoccupied. When Georgia questioned him, he confided that he had concerns about his job. He had many things on his mind. She understood that; she did, too.

Eliza had a new boyfriend, a young lawyer, while Jean was in love with the maverick doctor, William Webb. On a warm summer afternoon the conversation among the friends did not linger on the loves in their lives. It turned instead to the dark threat, the menacing man who chased Natalie White.

"I don't like for Bentley to walk from our house back down town to the Belmont Hotel," Georgia offered.

"Will he be here in time for the Cotillion Dance tonight?" Jean offered, abruptly changing the mood.

Eliza, not going to the dance, excused herself. Once alone Jean admitted again that she was in love with William Webb. Eventually she confided to her cousin that William had asked her to marry him, but she noted that both sets of parents were strongly and adamantly opposed. *I wonder if they've made love,* Georgia mused.

Georgia, dressed for the dance, waited in the lobby of the Belmont Hotel while Bentley changed clothes in his room. *I hope he brought my ring,* she thought almost as a prayer.

Soon Georgia and Bentley made their way through the ballroom toward Jean and William. As the immaculate Bentley neared, he noticed that Webb's cream-colored suit appeared worn and rumpled. Jean stepped forward, touching Bentley's arm as she said, "William, this is Bentley Thompson from Bristol."

Webb extended his hand, his dark eyes peering down on the shorter man, as he intoned, "Bentley."

"Dr. Webb," Bentley answered, "nice to meet you."

"Hell, don't call me doctor. Call me Will. Otherwise, I'll feel too damn old!" directed Webb with words that sounded friendly yet harsh.

The orchestra played sweetly, allowing the soft music to float out the ballroom windows, as Will West worked across the square in the Norfolk and Western office, finishing a monthly report.

A little later while the drama of the dance played out in the individual lives of those attending, Will West sat at the counter in Kit's Café, sipping a beer and talking easily with Jeanette Moore. For Jeanette, Helen Hanson, and a third waitress, business was slow because of the dance. Now in the quiet, subdued café, Jeanette had the luxury of talking to Will with no interruptions.

The lights reflected a soft glow on the darkly stained wood-paneled walls while the overhead fans buzzed, turning slowly as the music from the hotel ballroom drifted through the open door.

"Do you want anything to eat, Will?" Jeanette asked, pressing against the opposite side of the counter with her upper thighs as Helen had before.

"No thanks, Jeanette. I'm just going to have a beer and talk to you before I go," he answered easily. "Why don't you join me? There's nothing going on here tonight,"

Moments later they moved to a large booth, where Helen put two fresh draft beers on the table. "Here's to you," said Will softly, smiling easily as he raised his cold glass toward Jeanette's.

"To you too, Will," she responded, gently moving her glass toward his and feeling their fingers touch for a moment. Each took a slight sip as silence fell upon them. Speaking first, she asked, "Will, guess who started working here as a cook on the weekends?"

"Who?" he answered vacantly.

"Well, he works for you! That Price guy, Frederick Price. He says he learned to cook in Roanoke. Kit says he's a great fry cook," Jeanette revealed, watching for Will's response.

"Hum, that's strange, but I guess he doesn't have to tell me his business outside of the freight office," responded Will as he thought how little he knew about the big man. Being twenty-six years old and well over six feet tall, Price demonstrated significant muscularity by routinely hauling more freight than his fellow workers. Will knew Price to be a remote loner who had moved to town from Roanoke—or was it Richmond?

Behind Will's façade early on Jeanette perceived a lonely man. As time passed, she realized that the two of them possessed kindred spirits as they laughed frequently, sailing along on a common wave of humor. Beneath the surface each felt the undeniable tug of Eros. This night with the mounting storm and the faint strains of music drifting through the rain, the attraction loomed stronger.

Jeanette, a survivor who escaped the shackles of ignorance and poverty, felt emotional and vulnerable as she surrendered to her pervasive melancholia and confided to Will that she believed she would never marry.

His face took on a softer character, and his gentle eyes conveyed sensitivity. For a while he said nothing, choosing not to prostitute their friendship by offering a superficial statement designed to make her feel better for the moment. After a while he began, "I don't know what to say, Jeanette. You're such a pretty woman, and you're so smart. I know that's not what you want to hear now, but if I were single, I would have fought the others off a long time ago."

At that moment Will West believed he could have fallen in love with her at a different time, in a different place. His large, tanned hand moved to cover hers on the tabletop.

Will West had no way to know on the rainy Saturday night sitting with Jeanette in the deserted café that soon he would make a choice that would affect the course of their respective lives.

Rain, blowing horizontally at times, left drops clinging tenaciously on the front door screen. Those clustered drops glistened in a soft translucent glow from the inside lights. The music stopped down the street, but Jeanette and Will did not know because they could not hear it over the sound of the incessant downpour. Down the street in the ballroom of Hotel Abingdon the summer storm made Georgia Thompson think of her trip to Johnson City, the night her life changed, the night she became Mrs. Bentley Thompson.

The lights in the café dimmed several times, then went out, so Helen lit candles and brought one to Jeanette and Will's booth. She explained that Kit just called to say that he would return later to close so Jeanette could leave. The night beginning like any other changed abruptly; suddenly, it seemed to push them together.

Jeanette gazed across the table into Will's eyes, his face cast softly in the small arc of candlelight. If ever the two would come together, regardless of how much each may have denied the attraction in the past, it would be this night. "What are you thinking?" he asked softly.

"Oh . . ." she began slowly, "many things, but don't worry. I'm not going to feel sorry for myself any more. Actually I was thinking something mundane, about how difficult it'll be to get a taxi tonight with the dance and the storm. I'll bet there's not a taxi carriage in the square."

"I'll take you home," he said easily, comfortably.

"Will, I didn't say that so you'd offer to take me home," she replied honestly.

"I know, but you're right; you'll never get a taxi tonight. Don't worry, I'll get you home," Will assured her, sliding from the booth and walking toward the front door. She saw him break into a run before he left the cover of the canvas awning, running toward the Express Office.

Jeanette was comforted by the fact that neither of them had planned this night yet it was as if they were destined to be together. She wondered if he would come in when they got to her rented cottage. She had no way to know that Will didn't know what he would do if she extended an invitation.

A short time later as Helen watched from the door, Jeanette raced through the sheets of rain until she plunged onto the leather seat, colliding hard with Will's firm body. Will and Jeanette both laughed easily as he said, "Whoa, girl! Are you okay?"

Before starting Will leaned toward her and kissed her cheek gently. Jeanette managed a controlled response, a proper response.

The kiss, a spontaneous act with origins of warmth and compassion, surprised Will himself.

Will glanced at his watch. It was ten thirty-eight, railroad time, and the rain-soaked streets were almost deserted.

Turning the last corner two blocks from the Harris house, he broke the silence by asking, "How are you getting along with the judge?" His question drew them both back to reality from the surrealistic night.

Judge Harold Harris, a short and pudgy sixty-five-year-old alcoholic, had always had an eye for women. His strong urges and dark impulses had not diminished with age, and when the slightest opportunity arose, he acted on it. He had a wild mane of thick gray hair and heavy jowls that hung like pasty, white dumplings. His perpetually watery eyes stared out above a broad nose and full, protruding lips as naturally red as the painted lips of women of the night, many of whom he had known well. The judge drifted along in a world of his own, isolated from the masses except in one dimension—his sexuality, that great equalizer of men.

His reputation as a womanizer existed along with his status as a learned and scholarly jurist. Perhaps he was psychologically compelled, perhaps had no choice in the matter, but his affinity made him part of the brotherhood of crude men like the primitive mountain men who ventured into town on Saturdays. With the dark stubble of beards and the odor of stale sweat, they often stood on the streets in groups of two or three, approaching life from its most primal elements. Their dark sexuality seemed mysterious and mean, especially to women of the town; yet, it was the most notable dimension of their character, the predominant essence they chose to show to the world. The judge snickered at the same ribald jokes and the same coarse senses of humor. Although he was never in their company, a dark sexuality bound them together, the vulgar, illiterate mountain men and the judge.

More than once Judge Harris drifted back to the little cottage behind the "big house" when plied with expensive bourbon, seeking Jeanette's favors through the pretext of slurred nonsensical conversation, but that happened seldom, and to live in the cottage was worth the occasional inconvenience.

Jeanette's cottage home was filled with antiques and tasteful furniture. The judge's wife, Faye, a modestly handsome but plain woman from Tennessee, married the judge late in life. She had given up on her husband ten years earlier, about the time they stopped sleeping together, about the time she rented the cottage to Jeanette. As the two women became close friends, they chose to be silent partners in a dance of dunces, in which both pretended the judge was normal, that he wasn't a mess. Jeanette confided to Faye months before that her underwear was stolen from the line. Each secretly suspected the judge. Jeanette had learned through the years how to handle the man, depending upon his degree of intoxication. She wondered how Faye, a refined woman, tolerated him.

Jeanette's racing mind almost forgot Will's question about the judge. "He hasn't been difficult lately. I've hardly seen him. Faye keeps a close watch on him," she answered, looking straight ahead.

As the carriage moved slowly through the rain toward the Harris home, Will had to make a decision. He thought of his cold and remote wife. Would it make a difference? Would it really make a difference in the total scheme of things if he went home with this very appealing woman? Earlier his reasoning had faltered, falling victim to the drifting music and the storm and the soft face that smiled gently at him in the candlelight.

The cottage sat at the end of a rectangular lot facing the back of the stately brick two-story Georgian home. It was used as an elegant storehouse for treasured and valuable pieces that didn't fit any place else. Jeanette felt good in the house and had come to love its clutter and charm, feeling less alone in its fullness.

They had not yet reached the Harris house when Will surprised himself by asking softly, "May I come in for a while?"

"I'd like that, Will," she whispered, gently squeezing his arm.

"I'll pull the carriage around to the alley," Will said, casually moving past the facade of the brick mansion.

"No, wait!" she said quickly. "The gate to the alley is locked. I'll have to go in from the front so I can unlock it," she said, slipping from the carriage into the rain, which was now a steady drizzle.

Jeanette paused, straining to see through the rain toward the lighted kitchen window. Rising to her soggy toes in the shadows, she saw the stocky form of the judge slumped in a chair at the kitchen table, but she understood what the blurred image revealed. The judge was sipping bourbon and reading. A flash of lightning bathed the wing in a brilliant silvery light as the judge bolted upright, looking toward the window, directly toward Jeanette. Several moments later she saw him amble slowly toward the window. *God,* she thought, *of all nights! Please don't let him see me this night! Please keep him away this night.* When he turned away from the window, she bolted into the rain, sloshing through the wet grass along the fence, hoping the lightning would not reveal her dash toward the alley.

Moments later Jeanette arrived at the gate and unbolted it. She could not yet see the carriage, so she left it standing partially open because there was no handle on the alley side. Inside the cottage she did not turn on the lights, afraid that the judge might see them and attempt to wade through the yard to her. If he were drunk enough and if the demons were calling him loudly, the old fool *might* try it! He had not been that brazen for a long time, but this night was not one she could risk. Quickly, she pulled the heavy fabric drapes across the windows. Moving to the walnut sideboard, still dripping pools of water on the stained hardwood floor, she lit the three candles on small silver candelabra. She was torn emotionally, unsure of her instincts. She wanted to change her drenched clothes, but she was afraid to leave the door, afraid that Will would be confused if she were not there to let him in. She was relieved when she heard the soft knock.

Will stepped inside, rainwater trailing from his clothes and boots. Neither spoke, but in a fluid motion, they came together in a gentle embrace and stood holding each other without kissing. He pulled back gently to look into her eyes, then they kissed softly, standing, rain-soaked and dripping, in a puddle as water drained from their single form. Their souls stirred in unison, and the kiss took a different turn. The lips that first gently touched suddenly melded together pressing hard. Pulling back to see his face, she whispered, "Will, you're soaking, but I don't think I have anything to give you to wear."

"I'm okay. You go get some dry clothes. I'll be all right," he answered softly.

Jeanette moved away silently but stopped at the sideboard and lifted a decanter. "Here, Will. I got this brandy for Christmas two years ago, but I've never tasted a drop." She poured a snifter half full and handed it to him, extending her arm as if she were afraid to draw close before she quickly walked into the shadows toward her bathroom, where she pulled the black waitress dress off then slipped from her soaked underclothes. Jeanette began urgently toweling herself dry. She quickly wrapped herself in a large white terry cloth robe, which carried the faint scent of lilac. Frantic to return to Will, she wore the robe and nothing else.

Will breathed the vapors of the brandy before taking a slight sip. Standing alone in the entry hall while holding the snifter, he was too wet to sit down or move further into the room. Suddenly reality hit forcing him to think about where he was and what he was doing. Feeling no guilt, he was overwhelmed with a deep sense of sadness, of undefined regret. He thought of his distant wife and the good and decent woman at the other end of the darkened cottage. In an instant flash of insight, Will realized that, *regardless* of the reasons, he could not cause either of those women to suffer because of him, because of his selfishness. The clarity of his reasoning seemed as if it came from another person. Somehow the less appealing dimension of reason prevailed. He knew what he must do, what he *would* do.

Emerging from the bathroom, Jeanette walked down the dark hallway toward the front door. She could see Will's silhouette near the entry, faintly illuminated by the sideboard candles. He was looking down at the brandy snifter, which he held in both hands. Drawing near, she could see he had hardly tasted the brandy. Approaching him she pulled the robe together near her neck self-consciously.

Raising his head slowly, Will looked into her eyes, causing her to stop several feet from him.

"You're leaving," she said softly but definitively.

"Yes," he whispered, the single word failing to convey his profound regret.

Moving closer, she lifted the brandy snifter from him, set it aside, then took his hands in hers. The robe fell apart slightly showing the rising suggestion of her breasts. "Will," she began, looking intently into his eyes, "you are a good man. I want you to go because of what you *know* you should do. I wouldn't want a part of you here; and if you stayed, I would have only a part of you, but before you go, I want to tell you something. I will never tell you again, but I want to tell you one time. I love you, Will West. I love you deeply, and I don't see how I can stop for the rest of my life."

Will lifted their entwined hands and moved hers toward his lips. Then he released her hands and stepped back. Looking directly into her eyes, he whispered, "I love you too, Jeanette. I love you too." Turning slowly, tentatively, he opened the front door, and without looking back, he quickly disappeared into the storm.

Chapter 15

*"Do not boast about tomorrow,
for you do not know what a day may bring."*

Proverbs 27:1

Jeanette stood, eyes closed, pressing her back against the door that Will West closed behind him moments before. Her bare feet stood on the wet floor in the puddle created from rain she and Will tracked in, rain that dripped from their clinging bodies. She did not feel rejection, just a deep and abiding loss; and with that loss, Jeanette, like Will, was filled with regret. She regretted her life in general and the fact that Will West was unattainable. *It's a damn shame,* she thought, *a goddamned shame.*

Opening her eyes, she reached for Will's full brandy snifter, and after taking two large gulps, it was gone. The brandy warmed her deeply as the eerie flashes of lightning continued to cast the outside in transitory images like Wertz negatives. As she drifted toward the sideboard, her bathrobe fell open, exposing a firm, well-formed body conditioned by hard work and miles of walking. It was a body that would have responded to a lover this night.

I have to do something for myself, she thought remotely. Deciding to have another drink and take a hot bath, she reached inside the walnut sideboard to remove a bottle of Kentucky bourbon, another unopened Christmas gift. The dark brown liquor splashed into a crystal whiskey glass until the glass was half full. Holding her drink in one hand and gently lifting the candelabra in her other, Jeanette made her way toward the kitchen. Pausing, she peered outside through the drapes and saw that the lights were still on in the big house. The bluish-white illumination from the lightning flashed more often now, and suddenly in a rapid, shutter-quick flash of illumination she thought she caught a glance of a figure standing outside near the kitchen of the big house. Instinctively Jeanette bolted back, away from the window. Setting her glass aside, she quickly drew the robe tightly around her naked body. Tentatively leaning forward again toward the windowpane as the lightning flashed, she saw the back of the house as a fluttering silver image. Nobody was there. *That fool! Surely, he's not standing in the rain. Surely, oh God, surely, he wouldn't . . .* she reasoned with herself. Looking again, she could make out the rotund form of the judge silhouetted in the long window gazing out toward her cottage. *Probably looking for my lights,* she thought. Assigning his identity to any fear soothed her ragged, unsettled nerves. Walking slowly to the back door, she found the deadbolt secure.

Soon she had teakettles with water simmering on top of the black cast-iron stove. Hattie, a black maid in her late sixties who worked for Judge and Mrs. Harris, laid firewood and paper in her stove each afternoon. At night Jeanette had only to light the paper, and soon the stove would be hot. Surprised to see that her glass was empty again, Jeanette realized she was drinking more than usual, too much for one night, especially this empty night; yet, she felt little effect from the alcohol except a dreamy weariness. In that softened state the pain of loneliness and regret began to subside as she fixed another drink.

Walking back into the darkened living room, waiting for the water to heat, Jeanette was overwhelmed with the feeling that she was being watched although the drapes were still drawn. Wrapping the white robe tightly again, she sat down on the Chippendale sofa, where she took a long pull from the bourbon in her glass. As a single woman she forced certain mental disciplines upon herself. One personal resolve was never to allow fear to pervade her thoughts on spooky nights.

Soon she arose to freshen her drink. Approaching the sideboard, Jeanette instinctively glanced straight ahead into the mirror toward her own transitory image; but in the mirror's reflection, to the side, through slightly parted drapes, she thought she saw something move outside. As she crept back to the window, as if on a cue, the yard was lighted again like the day. She saw nothing. *Honest to God, what is the matter with me?* Through her own strong mental resolve and the soothing whiskey, she chose to ignore her primal instincts.

Later the steamy water flowed into the small porcelain tub as Jeanette allowed her robe to drop to the floor. Standing naked in front of the mirror, she watched the shadows dance on her firm body as the candle flames flickered. Her eyes came to rest on her modestly wide hips. *It probably would have been easy for me to have children,* she thought. Moving closer to the mirror, she stared at her face, cast so much younger in the dim light. Thinking of all the dances she had missed as a young girl, her mind drifted in the empty chambers of isolation and pain formed by so much exclusion in her life—as a child and as an adult. *This night was no different,* she mused to herself. *All the dances passed me by.*

But Jeanette, the survivor, refused to succumb to her looming despair, forcing herself to concentrate the image of her handsome body. Raising both arms over her head to form an elegant and graceful arch, she watched her moderate bosoms lift slightly. Turning her right knee a bit, while studying the shape of her upper thighs, she worried that soon they would grow heavy. This night, though, they looked Grecian as she stood, a wounded Venus, cast in the flickering light.

Moving from the mirror, Jeanette slid into the warm tub and closed her eyes. The hot water soothed her tired body as the drinks eased her haunted mind. She quickly drifted into a light sleep, soon easing into a dream.

A violent clash of thunder shook the house, abruptly wrenching her back to consciousness. Bolting forward, she did not hear the front door knob turn slightly. When no resistance came, the knob continued full circle. Jeanette, breathing heavily, finally gathered her senses. Remembering the dream, she sloshed backward against the warm tub. At that moment the front door opened and closed quickly without making a sound.

Pulling herself from the tub, Jeanette began to slowly dry off. Dropping the towel to the floor, she slipped back into her robe. Walking toward the staircase with one of the candles in her hand, she sensed that some of the night, part of the rain, had entered the house. *Of course it has,* she thought wearily, *Will and I brought the rain inside. Holding the candle in one hand* slowly, laboriously, she climbed the stairs. She remembered the other burning candles, but she was too weary to go back. *They'll just burn out anyway,* she thought. That was unlike her, but this night she was exhausted, too spent to return to the candles. Reaching the second landing, she took the few steps down the short hall before turning right into her room, where she put the candle on top of her low chest of drawers. The candle's twisting flame made shadowy traces on the ceiling.

Slowly Jeanette pulled her arms from the robe, allowing it to fall on the floor at her ankles. Stepping across the robe, she reached into the wardrobe and felt the cool silk of her best gown, the one she *might* have worn if Will had stayed this night. The gift from Faye Harris fell easily over her bare body.

Turning slowly toward the double bed, she heard a primal whine, a guttural wheeze. Her frantic eyes darted up toward the black mask closing upon her as her knees buckled before the massive heavy hands violently hit the soft tissue of her neck. Still falling, she clung tenaciously, frantically, to the wrists of the hands now gripping her collapsing throat. The force and intensity caused her soft neck to implode as her nails dug into her attacker's fleshy wrists. His elevated whine pierced the room with a frenzied demonic song of death as her hands fell limply from their last grip. Mercifully, it was not a lack of oxygen in her lungs, but the blocked blood flow to her brain that ushered Jeanette Moore into oblivion.

She was gone; yet the gargantuan dark figure was relentless, continuing to shake his fallen prey in a violent and ritualistic dance of death. Her thick black hair flew wildly, jerking up and down, as if her lifeless head and limp neck gave way to a final submission, conveying an awful affirmation, "Yes! Yes!"

Finally, breathing and wheezing heavily, he stopped, releasing his grip. Once, he had failed to lock his deadly grasp in the underbrush along the railroad tracks, and once, another defenseless prey regained consciousness after he removed her underwear. When she began flailing her long thin arms and kicking with surprising strength, he had pressed her silken undergarment into her gasping mouth and covered her slender form with his massive body until she fell limp again. Then he shoved the underwear between her thighs.

This night Jeanette would not return from oblivion as Anna Marie Holmes had for a few hopeless seconds. Jeanette would never again be conscious in her former world. Freed from her pathetic and painful childhood in West Virginia and her adult loneliness, she was on her way to meet God and discover the secrets of the universe. It made no difference that she had been dispatched by a vile predator, one who chose to play God, a flawed god, a god that did not give life, a false god that wrenched life away. But the Dark One was not finished. His ritual with Jeanette had just begun.

At four-thirty in the morning, the storm moved away eastward toward Roanoke, revealing luxuriant white clouds, bathed by a full moon in the dawn sky. The bright oval planet changed the morning sky from darkness into pale light.

Now the little highland town stood shining, washed hard, scrubbed by the violent summer storm. Nothing really seemed different, but something was different. Jeanette Moore was no longer present. She had inhabited the earth for thirty-eight years until this early summer morning. Now she was gone.

Natalie White, whether by the randomness of the universe or the grace of a benevolent God, lay sleeping less than a mile from the cottage that held the still body vacated by Jeanette Moore's soul.

A little further away, at the west end of town, a good and decent man, troubled deeply by walking away from that woman, tossed fitfully in his sleep. Going against his instincts earlier in the evening, he made a difficult decision, one he *believed* to be right and moral, the best for all concerned. He was unaware of the profound consequences of that "right" decision. Will West would later come to reason that had he made another choice, whether morally right or wrong, the one he had wanted to make, an innocent life *might* have been be saved.

Helen Hanson slept soundly in her unadorned room, unaware that her best friend, her surrogate older sister, her cherished confidante, was gone.

The owner of a mediocre café in a humble mountain town lost his best employee, and a highly regarded and respectable accountant would come to learn that he had not fully valued or compensated his talented and loyal employee.

Now in the fragile and vulnerable time of early dawn, in that dark hour of the soul, no one knew about the terrible loss but one; yet soon the town would come to know about the awful night. Nevertheless, the day moved forward like any other day, like all the other days. Time would not alter the course of life for Jeanette Moore or anybody else.

As the pale dawn faded and the day fell on the town, the judge stirred. He would awake soon after passing through the veil of alcoholic slumber.

Georgia Thompson lay sleeping fitfully in her home on Valley Street, a few blocks away. In this time of breaking dawn, she regularly dreamed about the future. Her husband, Bentley Thompson, lay sleeping alone in his room at Hotel Belmont.

Later some would ask if God himself shuddered and cried when the profound evil followed its course during the stormy night. Some would wonder if God were asleep, unconcerned or unable or unwilling to stop the vile predator who romped freely, taking a good and decent and innocent life.

* * * * *

Several hours later Faye Harris and the judge sat silently, finishing their Sunday luncheon, prepared and served by Hattie Brown, a large, dignified black woman who had worked for them for twenty years.

"Hattie, we have so much left over. You take some home," urged Faye who loved the woman as a member of her own family.

"No, ma'am. Not today. Today's the day I fix the big supper at home, but I bet Miss Jeanette would like some of it," suggested one who cared for Jeanette Moore as much as Faye.

"That's a good idea. I'll finish clearing the table. Why don't you walk back and ask her if she wants some lunch?"

"I'll do that, Miss Faye," confirmed Hattie enthusiastically as she placed two rolls in a linen napkin planning to return for more food if Jeanette accepted the offer for luncheon leftovers.

I'm sho gonna ruin my good shoes, thought Hattie as she made her way across the soggy lawn toward the little house. She and Jeanette were dear friends, brought together initially by their common dependence upon the Harrises. In a sense they were a lot alike, but, independent of circumstance, background, and all else, they simply enjoyed a genuine affection. Secretly Hattie and Jeanette sometimes laughed about the judge behind Faye's back.

Puzzled when Jeanette failed to respond to her knocks, Hattie found the front door unlocked. Inside the opulently furnished house, she found the drapes and curtains drawn, leaving the room in darkness. Shafts of harsh sunlight slashed through the front door cracked open behind her.

"Miss Jeanette! Miss Jeanette, you here?" she called cautiously as, inexplicably, she shuddered from a sudden chill, jerking involuntarily. The dark little house felt damp inside, but there was something more, a feeling she could not discern. Hattie walked slowly past the kitchen, ambling to the bathroom. *How odd,* she thought, seeing the tub filled with water and candles burned to their holders. Deep within her soul, Hattie felt a remote and inchoate warning, a primal feminine alert. Walking slowly to the stairs, she spoke aloud in a low voice, "Well, I've come this far, I may as well go all the way." Pausing for a moment, she looked up the stairs and called loudly, "Miss Jeanette! Miss Jeanette, you up there? Are you all right?"

Pulling herself up by the stair rail, pausing on each creaking step, she reached the bedroom door, where she called, "Miss Jeanette! You in there?" Taking a deep breath, she thrust the door open.

Instantly, in cosmic awareness, she perceived the enormity of the horror, the awful reality assaulting her eyes. Jeanette Moore's nude body, cast in an ashen hue, lay displayed on the bed. Her head was propped upright against the headboard as veiled, vacant eyes stared into the next world while her arms were extended from each side, white palms turned upward as if waiting for a lover. Her legs were crudely spread apart. Pillows, placed under each knee to keep them bent upright, heightened the vulgarity in mocking shame. Her marble-white body, now rigid, lay posed in a raw position of suggested sexuality. Her sheer silk nightgown was wadded and thrust between her legs.

Hattie stood paralyzed by the scene as if she were an earthly visitor at hell's door. She was. The visceral and primal scream began in the depths of her being before it exploded into the quiet Sunday afternoon as she wailed, "Oh my God! Oh sweet, precious Jesus! Oh, my God! This child! This child! Oh, God no! No! No! No!"

Her paralysis abated as she whirled herself past the first step, plunging down the steep stairs, frantically trying to grab the banister before her heavy body plummeted downward, collapsing into an unconscious heap at the foot of the stairs.

Approaching the cottage at the same moment, Faye dropped a covered basket and broke into a run. Bounding through the front door, she *knew* the origin of the scream was an unspeakably tragic event, and she *knew* it was deadly as she raced toward the stairs, stumbling into the unconscious body of Hattie Brown. "Hattie! Oh, my God! Hattie!" she gasped, dropping to her knees. Lifting the large woman's head, Faye frantically watched Hattie's eyes open and then roll upward toward the top of the stairs.

Jerking herself forward by the banister, Faye bounded up the steps. Breathing heavily, she walked cautiously toward the open door. Stepping tentatively inside, she too was assaulted by the abhorrent scene of death and mutilation. Gazing at the ravaged body of her fallen sister, Faye felt her profound shock manifest itself in a serene calmness. Bringing a nurturing response as if she were a mother tending her child, a deep and abiding instinct emerged. Disregarding the carefully staged display of deviant sexuality, Faye moved slowly to the side of the bed, looking into Jeanette's partially open eyes gazing outward in a distant stare of resignation. Faye had never seen the vacant eyes of death, but abruptly, her intellect took charge, telling her that she should touch nothing so she turned and moved slowly down the steps to care for Hattie.

The two women approached the big house, Faye struggling to support the massive frame of Hattie Brown, still faint and disoriented. When the judge saw their faces, he tossed his book aside, sensing that they looked somehow changed forever. They were. Faye's somber voice carried a tone he never heard as she forbade him to go to the cottage. Then she stated simply, "Jeanette's dead."

"I'll call Press and John Woodward," he responded quickly, without asking for more information.

Confused as he raced Thunder toward the stately Harris residence, John remembered the judge's cryptic words, "John, Jeanette's dead! Get over here quickly!"

John's immediate response gushed out in a single word, "Murdered?"

The judge answered softly, almost apologetically, "I don't know."

As he pulled Thunder back from a full gallop, John was surprised to see a buckboard. It belonged to Dr. Webb. *Webb! Why Webb?* he asked himself as he banged harder than he intended with the large brass door knocker from England. Mrs. Margaret Dutton, a next-door neighbor whom John knew well, opened the door. A pleasant woman in her late seventies, Mrs. Dutton projected somberness and loss. He did not see the judge or Faye Harris as Mrs. Dutton walked him through the house toward the back door. "I'll take you back, Sheriff," was all she said, but her expression of bereavement and her hollow, resigned tone were all too familiar.

Stepping inside the darkened living room of the cottage, John saw the form of Dr. Webb at the foot of the stairs. As John approached, the thin and disheveled doctor spoke first. "Sheriff, the Moore woman is upstairs. I've confirmed she's dead, but I didn't touch anything in the room." When the young doctor saw John's confused expression, he volunteered, "Press wasn't at home so they called me."

Entering Jeanette Moore's room, John involuntarily gasped. He had seen many crime scenes through the years, but never one like that before him as Jeanette stared from her obscene position.

It was as if he were standing in an ancient temple where sexuality and death were fused in a deadly pagan ritual. Scanning the room quickly, he noticed a bathrobe, two bread rolls, and a linen napkin lying between the door and the bed. "Can you estimate how long she's been dead?" he asked softly, as if Jeanette were sleeping.

"I'd estimate about eight to ten hours," Webb's voice boomed.

As John entered his protective zone, his dismay and shock abated. His demeanor now, like the doctor's, was one of professional detachment. His single focus was to acquire all the information possible. Years of experience dictated that he *must* move slowly and cautiously gathering all the available evidence and destroying none in the process. Certain things in life cannot be rushed, and John knew well the task before him was one of them. *We'll learn so much more than with the Holmes girl,* he thought; yet, with so much evidence before his eyes, he could not understand most of it. Turning again to

Dr. Webb, he asked, "How about the cause of death? Could you make any guesses at this point?"

Again Webb's voice bellowed in the small room, "Based upon the discoloration and apparent trauma to the neck, I would think Preston will find that she was strangled."

"Dr. Webb, thanks for coming, and thank you for preserving the crime scene. I don't want to do any more in here until I can get George Wertz to take pictures. By that time Press will be here, I hope," said John honestly.

"That's fine with me, Sheriff. I'm finished here. I sure as hell wouldn't want your job, though. I'd say you have a psychotic on your hands, a mad dog! It makes no difference *what* makes a dog mad, Sheriff. A mad dog is a mad dog! You need to kill the mad dog!"

John stiffened taking a deep breath. He knew well that the fear and anger of the town would eventually be directed to him, but he had not realized how quickly it would come. *My God, I'm being attacked by a professional who can surely see the depth and dimension of the madness before his eyes.* He realized at that moment that it would not be the awful loss of life, but his response, that would become part of the critical focus of the town.

A brazen voice called from the foot of the steps, "Sheriff? I'm coming up!" Before John could respond, Harold Kane appeared outside the doorway, reporter's pad held in a bony hand. John lunged toward the door with both arms extended to prevent Kane from seeing Jeanette's nude and ravaged body. He was overwhelmed with the thought, *God, she would be humiliated!* Kane, an older man, but a persistent older man, surged forward again, visibly shaken. John broke the man's momentum forcefully, causing the newspaper editor to fall backwards a couple of steps, an event he would not soon forget.

"They have a right to know! Everybody's in danger! You can't hide the danger, Sheriff!" Kane yelled as John pushed him gently through the front door into the yard, where bystanders stared at the commotion.

Now the newspaper man entered *his* zone, at the moment hating the sheriff. He was a respected, powerful man used to getting his way. With age and preferential treatment, he had become the brat of the town nursery. *I'll fix that bastard;* he thought bitterly. *I'll fix him good!*

Looking toward the big house, John was relieved to see Press and two deputies walking toward him. He needed the help.

John and Press talked downstairs in the cluttered, ornately furnished living room in hushed voices. The older doctor's demeanor was in stark contrast to Webb's. As Press talked, his tone conveyed a heavy sense of resignation and regret. Their discussion was soft and terse, seemingly appropriate in the face of unspeakable loss. Then they fell silent, each in his own thoughts, awaiting the arrival of George Wertz.

Soon the aging photographer was ushered into the room. His Germanic face was grave and eyes intense as he looked at John Woodward. "I am so sorry," he said softly to the sheriff as if he were a bereaved family member.

As George Wertz viewed the scene, he winced noticeably and then went to work methodically and objectively, saying nothing but clearly perceiving the ritualism of the horrid display. *The poor thing has been displayed for others to find,* he thought. The little room became stuffy from the heat of the afternoon, but his hands were cold and clammy like Jeanette's. The revolting obscenity did not repel him as much as the senseless loss of life.

"I believe that's it, John. Can you think of any more photographs you need?" George asked in a voice revealing his fatigue and fragile emotions.

"Do you think we need any more, Press?" asked John.

"We might need a few more," answered the doctor. "We should turn her over to see if there are any marks on her backside." He and John removed the pillows and rolled the stiff body over. All were relieved to see that there were no marks; yet, each felt a sense of shame at the task he had to perform. Soon they filed out of the room in silence.

Robert Bradley, the middle-aged undertaker, dressed in black on the summer afternoon, waited downstairs. He was tall, lean, and appropriately somber. Press explained to Robert that the body could not go to the funeral home from the house. He would have to get permission from Jeanette's nearest of kin to perform an autopsy. Robert could pick the body up from the morgue after the autopsy.

Chapter 16

*"You hide your face, and they are terrified; you take away their breath,
and they die and return to their dust."*

Psalm 104:30

D riven by anger and exuberance to sell newspapers, Harold Kane's pencil
scribbled with such fury that later, the typesetters could hardly decipher
his words. Nevertheless, *The Virginian* published a special edition providing all the information available about the tragic death of Jeanette Moore. What
was unknown about the facts of the murder was made up for in sensationalism and
sentimentality. Getting this story had been more difficult than the editor anticipated.
First he attempted to interview Faye Harris, well-known to him and others in the community for her charitable projects, but the judge's wife responded with cautious,
guarded answers and remote detachment. When it became apparent he would *never*
acquire significant information from her, Kane assumed that John Woodward
instructed the woman not to reveal anything to him. *That bastard!* Kane thought bitterly.

Pressing Faye to make Hattie Brown available for interview, Kane spoke as if he
were talking to the parent of a child. "Hattie's a grown woman. She can make up her
mind," Faye answered indignantly. Her tone conveyed an air of finality, suggesting
that she would not discuss the issue further. Faye knew Hattie could handle herself
with Mr. Kane. It might be uncomfortable, but it would be better, Faye thought, for
both of them to submit to his questions. Hattie's status in life dictated that she
could not refuse the request of Harold Kane, the prominent and powerful newspaper
editor; yet she knew how to handle the situation. Having learned as a girl that there are
degrees of cooperation, she sat in the judge's library as Howard Kane pressed for the
details of the murder scene. To his credit the editor sensed her legitimate, lingering
grief and attempted to be gentle, but compassion and empathy often faded in the wake
of racing excitement for a sensational story. Hattie hated his patronizing tone as she
had all the other times in her life when enduring an affront to her dignity. As a coping technique, she answered to a limited extent, then she fell into silence as if she possessed no more information. Hattie revealed only what she thought appropriate and

honorable. Like Faye she refused to describe the awful scene of the death room. When pressed by Mr. Kane again and again, she simply clasped her large, chocolate-colored hands in her lap, and while gazing down, she slowly shook her head in the negative.

Walking back to his office, Harold Kane decided to turn his attention to Jeanette Moore's life. He wanted to know about her reputation, her friends, "what made her tick" as he would come to ask.

Later he began to canvass his many sources, telling each, "I want to know anything good she did if she did anything good, and vice versa. And I want to know if she whored around," he stated, conveying his male mentality, postulating that any sexuality expressed by a woman meant "she whored around," as if there were but one, a feminine side, to the sexual equation. Harold Kane maintained some credible sources of high status in the community, powerful and educated persons. He also had other sources of lesser status, merchants and tradesmen, some of whom he paid for information from time to time. It would be up to them to help him explore the life and the mystery of Jeanette Moore.

One such informant who often frequented Kit's Café suggested that he ask Will West for comments about the murder of Jeanette Moore. The source believed that Will and Jeanette were "tight." *Interesting, very interesting,* Kane thought, *this married man, this promising young town leader and a barmaid.*

Harold Kane called on Will West early Monday morning, a day before the special edition was on the street. When the older man asked Will about the murder victim, pencil poised, he acknowledged that he had known Jeanette for several years. He explained how they met, and he said that he saw her regularly at Kit's Café. His voice grew reticent when he spoke of the murder, describing it as "unbelievable, awful, something that only a sick man, a goddamn coward, would do."

Kane quickly realized he sat with an angry man, and he understood that anger is an element of grief. He was not surprised shortly thereafter when Will West concluded, "That's it, Mr. Kane—all I know." While ushering the newspaper man out, Will explained that he was leaving for Roanoke on the incoming train.

Later Kane pondered his interview with Will West, finding it interesting that West did not ask why he was questioned about the victim. Looking closely at Will, watching his eyes and his body language, Kane believed that West was a bereaved man, a man who had suffered a significant loss. The editor jotted a note to himself: "Crime of passion? West: Lover or killer—neither or both?" Will West was not mentioned in the special edition; there would be plenty of time later.

The Sheriff of Washington County, however, was featured prominently as "uncooperative in providing timely and gravely important information for the safety of the stricken and endangered citizens of this good community."

Being unable to discuss the details of *any* pending case, John could not explain to the wide audience that it was impossible to state *with certainty* that the first and second murders were connected. Harold Kane simply took the premise and treated it as a given, as the truth. "Any reader of this paper would reasonably conclude that both killings were committed by the same sick and depraved person," he wrote.

On Tuesday morning John arrived at the Harris residence to tell Faye he was through processing the cottage, asking her to be alert for anything that did not appear to belong to Jeanette. He confided that a telegram had arrived from West Virginia stating that Jeanette's family did not have the money to come to Virginia for the funeral and burial and likewise they were unable to handle her final arrangements. Parishioners from her church, he said, were taking up a collection to help defray the burial expenses. Making no comment, Faye thought, *Harold will pay for everything if he has to, if it comes to that. I will see to it.*

Faye and Hattie could not bring themselves to enter the cottage for several days. Now they walked slowly, arms entwined, back to the little structure for the first time since their awful discovery. Their shared experience, their journey into abject horror and loss, produced a greater intimacy between them. Somehow it fused deeply within their womanhood and their femininity as they undertook the final task, a task usually left to women: They had to gather together Jeanette's possessions, sort through the remnants of a life suddenly swept away.

Soon it was over. They quickly erased the traces of a woman who left no living memorials to her life, no husband and no children. Except for the few who carried her essence in their memories, and their love for her in their hearts, Jeanette Moore was gone from the face of the earth.

Lingering in the cluttered living room, Faye casually lifted the cover of a lap secretary sitting on a library table. "Hattie! Look!" she exclaimed, holding up a savings passbook from the Bank of Washington County. Later in the day it was examined by Arthur White, who confirmed that Jeanette Moore had a savings account in the amount of $1,574.32. It was more than enough to pay for her funeral and burial. The balance would be wired to her mother.

The funeral was held Thursday afternoon, two hours before the regular edition of *The Virginian* was spit from the soot-spewing press. The preacher, dressed in black, grim and erect, climbed into the pulpit. With somber demeanor, his purpose was not to comfort the sad flock, but rather to warn sinners of the wrath of God. At first, to the relief of many present, he reminded the mourners that Jeanette no longer felt pain. She was, he pointed out, now in the arms of Jesus. He stated that the Lord often moves in mysterious ways. Ways, he said, that should not be questioned even though they were not always understood. The purpose in life of those present, he preached, was to accept what happened as "God's will." Some, however, pondered why God would have such a dark and terrible will. From time to time several men affirmed the preacher's words with their own: "Amen, brother," and "Yes, Lord."

The Thursday edition of *The Virginian* sold out quickly, documenting the intense interest in the Moore story. A picture of a demure Anna Marie Holmes mystically looked out again from the front page along with a handsome picture of Jeanette Moore from a Wertz portrait. Hattie Brown was quoted saying, "I looked with horror on the body of poor Miss Jeanette on that bed." Hattie had not uttered such words, but Kane wrote them, thinking, *If she had said anything, that's what it would have been.* He knew well he would not be challenged by Hattie Brown, who went about her job in silence and hidden rage while Faye suspected what happened.

The editorial examined "the inexplicable and prolonged failure of the sheriff to solve the Holmes murder and to identify the man who chased Natalie White." Several of Mr. Kane's close friends suggested privately that he came down too hard on John Woodward. Meeting those comments with disdain, the editor replied parentally, "I'm doing this for your wives and daughters. If you can't understand that, I can't help you."

John Woodward at first dismissed the articles, confident that his long record of serving the people of the county would keep his reputation intact; yet he was drawn back to the harsh, accusatory words of William Webb at the cottage. As John reflected upon them, he braced himself for worst to come. John was too busy to concentrate on the paper. Unlike the Holmes case, leads were coming in daily by the dozens as he and his deputies worked from daylight into the night.

John reasoned that with so many leads there *must* be one or two of value. He found it interesting that several times the name of Will West surfaced. John decided to interview Helen Hanson first.

Helen related that she last saw Jeanette alive when she ran from the café into the storm. Helen assumed that Will was waiting outside to take her home in a carriage. The next day the sheriff learned that Will West had taken the train to Roanoke.

On Saturday night Eugene Johnson rode his bicycle past the office of Dr. Preston Smith. The strange-looking Appaloosa stood outside, the reins hanging toward the ground. The dim light inside told Johnson that Sheriff Woodward and the coroner were meeting. Eugene, taking interest, rode by slowly with a bouquet of wild white roses in the bottom of his delivery basket. The flowers would be discovered the following day on the fresh grave of Jeanette Moore. While passing, the stork had no way to know that this was the first meeting between the sheriff and the doctor since Press Smith had completed the autopsy on Jeanette Moore.

After both men settled in comfortably, Press asked about any physical evidence gathered outside the cottage. John patiently explained that with the rain, and later the onlookers, any footprints of possible value, including those at the gate, had been obliterated. The killer *could* have crept through the gate from the alley, but it would have to have been opened from the inside first.

Anxious for Press to relate his autopsy findings, John finally had to ask his friend for the information. Press appeared tired as he began slowly, "This, as you know, is a strange one, a real bizarre case." Press had determined that Jeanette Moore had not been raped and had not had sex the night she was murdered. He found evidence of some vaginal penetration, but he believed it came from an inanimate object. As John knew, there were bite marks on each of Jeanette's thighs. Even without rape, the attack was, of course, sexual in nature. Jeanette Moore died from strangulation. She fell unconscious in twenty-five to thirty seconds, possibly sooner, from the time the killer's hands brutally closed around her throat. Press found alcohol in her system, concluding that she was moderately intoxicated at the time of death. There was evidence that she had eaten a light meal earlier in the evening. She was a well-defined, non-obese, and healthy woman free from any abnormal pathology.

Press paused and then told John that he found semen stains on Jeanette's right calf. He did not, however, believe the killer had a premature ejaculation as he attempted sex with his unconscious or dead victim. The murderer masturbated at the scene, he theorized. "I figure he stood over the body while it was still on the floor. Later he moved it to the bed."

John made no comment about the semen. After seeing the crime scene, he was beyond shock and past surprise.

* * * * *

What a beauty! What grace! thought the sheriff the next afternoon, watching Thunder perform under the blue August sky. John's short whistle, as always, brought the Appaloosa racing to his side. Bolting backward several feet, Thunder reared skyward quickly, jerking his head up and down. John had no way to know that it was the same quick way Jeanette Moore's head had jerked up and down during her last seconds of life. "Whoa, old boy. We've got to go to town," said John, walking across the pasture to the barn. The handsome animal followed at his heels like a well-trained dog, nudging his back. Mary Woodward watched from the kitchen window, praying her husband would somehow survive the case, the ordeal. She knew he would need all her prayers before it was over.

John restrained the spirited horse as they made their way on Main Street toward the Express Office. During the pleasant ride, he felt for a short time as if things were the way they used to be, as if he were not facing the greatest crisis of his career. Entering the Norfolk and Western Express Office, the enormity of the case returned.

"I was wondering when you would come to see me, John," Will began after they settled down, each with a glass of iced tea and mint pulled from the dark earth beside the Norfolk and Western tracks.

"Why is that, Will?" asked John without guile, confident that the interview would not be a cat-and-mouse exchange.

"'Cause I think I was *next*-to-the-last person to see Jeanette alive," he confided candidly, looking directly into John's intense eyes. "If you hadn't called today, I planned to call you. I've been out of town on company business. I heard you'd been by here when I was out."

"Tell me about it," asked John.

"Okay, John, I'll tell you everything I know," responded Will West leaning across his desk, both elbows resting on the green ink blotter. He talked openly, making no excuses, sparing no details and not asking for confidentiality. He described how they met, that they became friends first and later were attracted to each other. He related candidly that the attraction was never acted upon until the last night he saw her alive. Will explained that he took her home and decided to come inside. When Will related that he had reluctantly decided to leave, John believed him. John, having had years of experience interviewing men and women from all walks of life, believed Will West.

Will had seen nothing suspicious as he parked the carriage in the alley. Jeanette had opened the gate so he simply walked through to her front door. When the congenial interview drew to a close, John asked Will to call him if he remembered anything else that might be pertinent.

Standing by while John mounted Thunder, Will squinted up at the sheriff in the late afternoon sunlight like the girl on the Martha campus, as he confessed, "John, I wish I had stayed now."

"I wish you had stayed too, Will. I wish like hell you'd stayed," responded John in the soft voice of resignation. Turning without saying more, Will walked back into the Express Office. *But if he had stayed,* John thought grimly, *perhaps some other woman would be dead today. But, again, maybe not; maybe Jeanette was chosen well before she died.*

Riding slowly from the railroad station, John suddenly remembered the autopsy findings. Jeanette Moore had not had sex the night she died. That critically important fact had not occurred to John as Will related his story. *Of course he told the truth.* Turning toward Main Street, John was surprised to see one of his deputies approaching at a fast gallop. "Doc Smith wants to see you, Sheriff," the deputy called urgently.

"Did he say why?" yelled John.

"No! Just called to say he needs to see you right away," responded the deputy.

Soon in Press' office John asked, "He said what?"

"Webb said he could *probably*, and note I said 'probably,' get information that might help solve the murders," answered Press.

What bothered them most about Dr. Webb was his dangerous recklessness. The mood of the town demanded great sensitivity, care that Webb might violate. Both regretted that the young doctor arrived on the scene before Press and saw how Jeanette was left, broken and posed like an obscene puppet. Both worried about Webb talking, especially to Harold Kane. If evidentiary information known only to the killer were released, the case would be compromised.

Press explained that Webb would soon travel to the University of Virginia, his medical school alma mater, where a distinguished psychiatrist from Vienna was a visiting scholar. The learned man from Austria, he said, specializes in criminal behavior, deviant sexual behavior and psychological pathologies that manifest themselves in violence and murder. Webb claimed that the Austrian doctor studied the cases of Jack the Ripper in London and hundreds of others throughout Europe. This doctor had interviewed many violent men who committed murders, some multiple murders. Why not, Webb asked, present the two cases to the doctor? Webb said that he would gladly take the material to Charlottesville.

"What do you think, Press?" asked John, staring intently into his eyes.

Press paused and began in earnest, "Well, if it were *anybody* but Webb, I'd say it might be a good idea. As far as I'm concerned, there's no scientific proof about this field of psychiatry. Freud himself can not scientifically prove any of his hypotheses. This whole thing could turn out to be a monumental waste of time and send us on a witch hunt."

"But Press, what if it helped?" questioned the desperate sheriff. The older doctor pointed out that legally, Webb was not privileged to see the confidential autopsy report or the photographs. John countered that he could be deputized as an officer of the court.

Relenting a bit, Press asked, "Let me check with my sources at UVA to find out who this *doctor* really is. Then we can decide. How's that?"

"That's great, Press, but do it today," John responded quickly.

"Today? Today's Sunday," answered Press, surprised at John's request. "I can't call up there on Sunday."

"You'll have to, Press; it can't wait."

* * * * *

Except for the pall hanging over the highland town, the humid August could not be distinguished from others. Vegetables and fruit grew abundant in mature, lush gardens and lined the well-stocked bins at markets. Cold watermelons and grapes graced most tables at lunch and dinner. Tobacco was being cut to hang in barns to yellow and cure for the market in November. The schools prepared for the coming fall enrollments. The people of Washington County moved through the hot, sensuous season responding to the demands and events in their own lives; yet the grizzly, unsolved murders pressed hard on the somber community consciousness.

Bentley visited Georgia less frequently and occasionally missed coming several weeks in a row. Their secret marriage gave her security if not contentment. During the week she wrote letters, often quoting short Bible passages. It was a game, her secret strategy to draw him toward the church or at least stir some latent interest in spirituality. Trying to pique his interest, she sent questions in the form of a riddle with a reference to a biblical passage that would unravel the mystery. She was persistent, urging him, "Just try it, Bentley. It's just like a crossword puzzle." Once she wrote, "If you want to know the relationship I will have with your mother, see Ruth, Chapter 1, v. 16." That he read with interest, "your people shall be my people." Georgia wisely knew that she could not press her faith upon him. She found frustration in that fact, feeling as if she possessed a gift that she could not give to her beloved.

One important issue lingered—Georgia did not have her wedding ring. She finally stopped asking, coming to realize that, for whatever the reasons, Bentley seemed unconcerned. He casually reminded her that she would have a lifetime to display the ring to the world, and now she couldn't wear it anyway. The jeweler, Bentley explained, would resize the ring free. For that reason it would take time, longer than usual—after jobs were finished for paying customers.

Georgia and Bentley were not the only ones with a secret. Jean and William were formulating their own plot. Jean decided not to tell Georgia her plans to spare her cousin the inevitable furor that would follow. She knew well what would happen after both families learned of her elopement with William Webb. Jean, forever independent and proud, was unconcerned with the opinions of anybody else except her parents. She knew, though, that they would never approve of her marriage to William because of his reputation. His prominent family, oblivious to that negative legend, expected him to marry a girl educated at a prestigious school and supported by a wealthy family. Both sets of parents assumed that the attraction between Jean and William would wane with time, but like many parents when judging their children, they overlooked an important fact. They failed to perceive that, regardless of the reasons and the rationale, regardless of the diverse nature of their backgrounds, Jean and William had fallen in love.

In a day Press determined that Dr. Juergen Dietrich was a renowned medical doctor and a legitimate visiting professor of psychiatry at UVA. Meanwhile John covered all remaining leads, exhausting the possibility of developing a viable suspect.

On a Saturday night after the Smiths enjoyed dinner at the Woodward home, Press and John excused themselves to the back porch, where, occasionally, they could hear Thunder whimper and whine for John's attention. When the conversation turned to Dr. Webb's offer, together they agreed to decline it. "John, I can tell you myself," Press began emphatically, "we're looking for a sexual deviate who hates women. He's gonna be a large and powerful man, and one who, for whatever the reasons, doesn't have sex with his victims. I doubt that we'd get more than that from Dietrich."

"You're right, Press. I was wrong. I hadn't thought it through when I said we should use the foreign doctor.

Chapter 17

At that moment Dr. Dan Hurt, pastor of the Presbyterian church, searched his parsonage for a book. Finally he decided to walk the single block to the church to look for it in his study. Emerging minutes later, book in hand, the preacher noticed a light in the parish hall kitchen. Surprised, he discovered that the double doors were unlocked. Once inside he walked rapidly through the darkened meeting hall toward the dim glow of the single low-watt bulb. Dr. Hurt quickly pulled the cord, casting the room into darkness, but turning he was startled to see a sliver of light shining through the pantry door. "Strange," he muttered, half audibly as he squinted to discern what appeared to be something white in the background. *Do I have to do everything?* he thought in frustration, yanking the door open wide.

She stared at him with veiled eyes cast forever toward the open door. Bathed in the stark light, she was propped against the opposite wall in the sitting position. Trim, youthful legs were spread apart with her knees bent upward, each supported by a flour sack. A white blouse, ripped and torn, revealed youthful, modestly formed breasts. Pale white arms lay outstretched and limp at her sides with the palms upward. She was nude from the waist down, but her underclothes covered the area between her legs. Froth and blood still foamed from her slightly parted lips. Purple bite marks were visible on firm, young thighs. In death her expression conveyed a message of resigned bewilderment.

Plunging deeply into shock, Dr. Hurt fell against the wall opposite the body of Vivian Grant, his attractive, twenty-one-year-old office helper. The color of her thick, tangled mane was full-blown red. In the harsh pantry light her hair looked strangely theatrical, contrasting eerily against her chalk-white face. But it wasn't all white; the left side was swollen and puffy, covered with purple bruises. Kneeling before the battered body, Dr. Hurt's first instinct was to pray, but the prayer that emanated from the learned man of deep religious conviction was a mantra like the one uttered by Hattie Brown weeks before. *"Oh my God! Oh my God in heaven! Please God, please,"* Dr. Hurt chanted again and again, lost in his primal lament.

The ring startled John, sending him running barefooted to the wall phone. Richard Smith, an elder of the Presbyterian church, summoned him to the parish hall. No, he said in a somber voice, he could not say why the sheriff was summoned. He related that Mrs. Hurt called him to ask that the sheriff come as soon as possible.

"John, she told me not to go inside. Said to meet you at the door but not to go inside," Smith explained, bewilderment in his voice.

"Where's Dr. Hurt?" John yelled into the mouth piece. Smith said Dr. Hurt was ill, that Press Smith had been called to the parsonage.

John asked Richard to remain outside as he entered the dark parish hall. Several minutes went by before the sheriff returned to the front door. His ashen face looked pained and hurt.

"You'll be here to help us tonight, Richard, so you need to know this. It's the Grant girl, Vivian Grant . . ." He paused, unable to continue for a moment.

"Vivian Grant?" Green asked, his voice rising. "You mean . . . that she's, she's . . ."

John nodded his head as he removed his hat and ran his hand through his dark hair. Then he looked directly into the other man's eyes. Richard reached out, touching John's forearm gently as he uttered, "God have mercy on her soul."

John and Richard waited for only five minutes before Press Smith stepped inside. With his jaw set, looking directly into John's eyes, he nodded without speaking. Even in his own fragile state, John was touched that his friend looked so tired and older than earlier in the evening. Doc Smith made his way slowly, wearily, behind John who walked toward the pantry.

Moments later George Wertz nodded politely as a deputy escorted him to the kitchen.

Together again for another morbid mission, the three men set about their work. George Wertz took pictures as John entered written notations in the photography log. No one commented about the pitiful and ritualistic spectacle before their eyes. Their voices stayed low, speaking only about the task at hand.

Although it was near midnight, a crowd gathered outside the parish hall. Expecting another tragedy, the onlookers were subdued. The sheriff gave his deputies specific orders not to allow Mr. Kane to breach the security and get inside the building.

Earlier the assistant pastor and an elder were dispatched to the Grant residence, while two other elders were sent to the home of their son, Brett Grant, well-known throughout the region as a young, but successful, defense attorney. When he arrived at the parish hall on a lathered horse, a low murmur erupted from the group of onlookers.

Quickly Brett Grant became a force that had to be addressed. He *demanded* to see the body of his sister "right now!" Pale and trembling, his shock manifesting itself in rage, he waved his fist near John Woodward's face. "You *cannot* deny me the right to see my sister, Sheriff! We're on public property, church grounds! I want to see her! I want to see her *right now.*" Lunging past Press toward the kitchen, John grabbed Brett's arm as the driving momentum spun them both around in the opposite direction.

"Brett! Wait a minute!" John pleaded, clutching both of Grant's upper arms. Without releasing his grip, he looked toward Press, who nodded his head slowly and closed his eyes, conveying *Go ahead, let him see.*

"Give us a minute then. Just a minute. We'll have to get Mr. Wertz out," John began quietly.

"George Wertz?" Brett shouted, clearly confused.

"Yes," answered John gravely, "he's finishing taking pictures of the scene for evidence. I'm sorry."

A few minutes later John moved slowly toward the pantry with Grant behind him and the doctor following. Pausing, John put his hand on Brett Grant's forearm. "Brett, you don't want to see her like this."

"I want in *now*, Sheriff," Grant demanded, voice shrill.

John opened the door slowly and held it as Grant stepped inside the pantry. The sight assaulting him was more than he could comprehend, more than he could bear. Falling backward against the wall, he collapsed as Dr. Hurt had hours before. The young man eased toward the floor into unconsciousness until he sat, his back against the wall, knees raised. He and his sister, like children in a nursery, sat in an eerie replication of body language.

Outside, the mood of the people was dark. George Wertz, who came out of the parish hall first, winced when he heard mean-spirited shouts from the crowd directed at the sheriff. A few moments later the crowd grew quiet as John stepped outside, assisting Brett Grant to a waiting carriage. Suddenly a man shouted, "What are ya gonna do *now*, Sheriff? How many more gotta die?" Shocked, John stopped suddenly, spinning around toward the voice and finding the group standing in absolute silence, motionless, as if chiseled in a stone carving. One solitary figure caught John's eye. Smoking a cigar as if bemused, William Webb, loomed behind the group of citizens.

Press Smith stepped out last as his assistants removed the remains of Vivian Grant to the morgue. There he would pry into the secrets of the body that hours ago was a vibrant, healthy young woman. Press glanced up, seeing a young boy bolt from the group and slap the Appaloosa on his hindquarter. Thunder, high strung and sensing the excitement, danced around in a half circle, kicking outward several times, but he held his position to await John. *Oh God!* Press thought to himself.

Press watched John walking toward him, leading a jittery Thunder.

"I don't know what we're gonna do, John."

"I know one thing we can do," John stated gravely.

"What's that?" asked his friend in the same somber tone.

"Tell Webb we need that foreign doctor," answered John, his jaw clenched tightly.

"I'll call him in the morning, John," Press answered, traces of resignation in his voice.

"You don't have to wait that long. He's standing over there under the tree behind the crowd," said the sheriff of Washington County.

Chapter 18

"The one who first states a case seems right,
until the other comes and cross examines."

Proverbs 18:17

B y Sunday afternoon word of the murder of Vivian Grant had spread through-out the shocked hamlet of the Blue Ridge. The details of the vile sexual muti-lation were not known, but the response to yet another senseless murder brought a common sentiment: Most assumed the three victims had been raped, allowing that motive to become the hook on which many people hung their cloaks of reason.

Howard Kane wrote, "How many more victims will have to die at the hands of the sex maniac?" That question, posed often among friends and family members, left hus-bands and fathers asking how to protect wives. Many, as usual, went about armed.

A special joint meeting of the town council and the county board of supervisors was quickly scheduled "to allow Sheriff John Woodward to brief the citizens on the sta-tus of the investigation of the murders and to advise what people could do to keep safe." The mayor asked Dr. Smith as the coroner to be present too, but clearly the focus and the pressure fell on John.

The sheriff and the coroner, leaving nothing to chance on their side of the equa-tion, could reveal only information already known to the public. They would do so, however, in an official way, and their confirmation, they hoped, would make it appear they were providing new information. Most people assumed that the victims were raped, and, unless pressed about that fact, John and Press would not address it. If asked, they would neither confirm nor deny it. That neither of the last two victims had been raped remained a critical fact, known only to them and the killer, so that information needed to be protected.

The killer's dark and twisted autoeroticism and the careful arrangement of the bodies had to be the perverted creation of the same demented person, the same sick and dangerous *man*. John realized that both murder scenes were staged to shock, offend, and cruelly tease whoever would find the body. Press believed the killer was "taunting" authority figures. "Hell, John, he's probably watching us now," Press offered, deadly serious.

With the murder of young Vivian Grant, John felt profoundly inadequate, blaming himself for not taking the killer off the streets. He could no longer deny it—he was desperate. They agreed that it would be useless to state that they could not with certainty connect the first murder with the second and third. To hold that position would make them appear defensive and guarded and possibly inflame ragged emotions.

John reluctantly decided to tell the citizens about the renowned psychiatrist from Vienna, and he solicited the support of Mayor Tom Wilson. The mayor, already under fire himself, jumped at the possibility of help from *anybody*, especially one as prominent as the Viennese doctor.

At six-thirty the two friends stood in Judge Harold Harris' chambers, while the judges sat outside in the jury box with the mayor and members of the town council. Mayor Wilson decided to remain apart from the sheriff. If John Woodward did well, if he were able to stem the negative tide rising against him, the mayor could always join him. The courtroom, filled past normal capacity, grew stuffy as the harsh volume of mixed voices elevated. Taking a deep breath, John grew more erect and stepped toward the door. Press touched his forearm, offering, "John, one more thing."

"What?" asked John, his inflection higher than usual.

"Remember, the killer could be in the audience."

The courtroom fell silent as John walked to the front of the bench and began, "Good evening." No corporate response followed as chiseled faces, solemn and grave, stared at him in cold silence. John's eyes fell on Brett Grant sitting in the second row with his law partner behind the county supervisors. He could not bring himself to look at his own wife, knowing she felt the mounting tension as much as he. Scanning the audience to establish a sense of rapport, John began, "I have always approached my job and the confidence you have placed in me not only with commitment to the county, but also with what I hope could be described as competence and honor. Tonight I will tell you what I can about the murders. The many lawyers and jurists present know that to tell you *all* I know could cause a legal prejudice that we might not be able to overcome in court. So if I am unable to answer a question, please understand it has nothing to do with power or arrogance or unneeded secrecy; rather, it is simply in the best interest of the investigation, in the best interest of the citizens of this town and county. I will offer an overview of our investigation to date, and, as I have always done, I will seek your help. My associate, Dr. Preston Smith, the county coroner, will also answer questions that are in his realm of expertise and responsibility. Finally allow me to state that the responsibility of this case rests squarely upon my shoulders, nobody else's. I deeply regret the situation that brings us together this night, yet I am honored to appear before the citizens of this town and county. Now, in the first tragic case at Martha . . . "

As the sheriff spoke, it was clear to even the most callous observer that John Woodward was candid and deeply committed. As he offered a litany of the efforts made to solve the cases, the crowd changed from high anxiety into a reflective state.

Finally John moved to the psychiatrist, identifying the renowned Dr. Juergen Dietrich. Silence fell for several moments after John asked if there were any questions. At that point Mayor Wilson eased from the jury box and moved to stand beside John and Press.

Herman Wise, the law partner of Brett Grant, rose, paused, slowly removed his glasses, and pointing them toward John, stated, "Sheriff, I know I speak for the good citizens of this town and county when I say that we are not so much interested in the scope of your inquiry as we are in the *results* of those efforts. By your own admission, those results are nil, yet we continue to see innocent girls, women, dying. Now you say you are bringing in an expert . . . From where? Was it Vienna, Austria? Anyway, that may be all well and good, but what we want, Sheriff, is not the views of a European academician; what we want is a safe community, one in which the perpetrator is identified, arrested, and brought to the bar of justice. My question, then, is this: What are you doing to protect the citizens of the town, right now, at this point in time?"

Don't be defensive. Be honest, John cautioned himself. "Thank you, Mr. Wise; that is an excellent question," he responded. Speaking calmly in a fatherly manner, he noted that he had synopsized his efforts to solve the cases; reminded all citizens, men and women, about personal safety; and revealed that he had increased patrols. Moving to the subject of Dr. Dietrich, John explained that the Austrian was not solely an academician but also a medical doctor with additional training as a psychiatrist with many years of experience, specializing in criminal, deviant behavior.

Harold Kane had planned several questions, but the old man knew how to read a crowd and sensed the mood of this one, so he said nothing. Press Smith did not speak, but his presence was important, reassuring to the audience, as the natural dignity and honesty of the sheriff prevailed. Kathleen Woodward sat in the back of the crowded courtroom with tears in her eyes and a prayer of thanks in her heart. John had just purchased a little more time.

The next day the funeral of Vivian Grant was held in the church only yards from where she had died. Like the service of Jeanette Moore, it grew into a community event. Dr. Hurt solicited another pastor to handle the service, his emotions remaining too fragile for him to officiate. He realized he needed a shepherd for strength and renewal himself. He did not demand an answer from God. He simply grieved.

Two weeks after Vivian's funeral Joe Dunn, vicar of St. Thomas Episcopal Church, sat in his study, fielding questions from an angry Brett Grant. Joe remembered the meeting with the bereaved parents of Anna Marie Holmes, finding irony in the fact that for the second time, he was attempting to answer the unanswerable because of the dark force he could not fathom. Brett Grant had more than once successfully represented drunken mountain men who had committed murder in the passion of fleeting moments, but he considered his law practice simply as an intellectual challenge. The Constitution granted every man the right to a fair trial, to be presumed innocent until proven guilty. Their innocence or guilt meant nothing to him. He remained above it all, never reflecting upon the fact that most of his clients were predators preying upon their fellow men; yet, the reality of violence and brutality was invariably lost in nuances of procedure and the stilted protocol and decorum of the courtroom. Fortunately for Brett and his clients, the dignity of the hallowed courtroom sanitized the humiliation and pain of victimization. Sometimes the victims were not present because his clients had dispatched them to the next life. Brett was adept at establishing reasonable doubt. That's all it took, a speck of doubt, which he could easily mold into a mass of reasonable doubt. He did not view the process as the pursuit of the truth; he saw it simply as a game, a profession.

Brett Grant who sat in front of Father Joe Dunn was a man without arrogance, a man destroyed by bereavement. His abject grief, however, was expressing itself in fiery anger. Turning the conversation inward, Brett confessed that as the days passed, he became more distraught over the death of his sister, his only sibling. He considered himself a good and decent man, a religious man. Now, though, he said, his faith was shaken to the core. He felt anger at the "vile, sick son of a bitch who wiped Vivian from the face of the earth." And, he said honestly, he was "mad as hell at God."

Joe Dunn, himself a bright and scholarly man, knew that he did not always understand God either. Patiently the priest allowed the young man to vent. Finally Grant said, "So that's it, Father Dunn. I'm mad as hell at this *alleged* just and loving God."

"How do you think you should feel, Brett?" asked the older man softly.

"Look, Father Dunn, please don't patronize me. We both know I'm here asking for help, but I'll answer your question. Assuming God gave man intellect and reasoning as well as anger, I'd be a damn fool not to feel anger. My problem is that my anger doesn't seem to dissipate. It seems to grow. Finally let me ask you this: How would *you* feel under the same circumstances?"

And so the meeting went for over an hour with the angry young lawyer demanding answers from the priest. Distraught, but used to being in confrontational situations, Brett Grant hammered away, once interrupting the priest with, "I'm sorry, I don't have your piety."

"It's not piety, Brett—" the priest began softly.

"Okay," Brett interrupted again, "it's not piety. Perhaps it's faith. I'll stipulate the fact that while you exercise faith, mine is clearly crumbling, but I don't want to address the faith issue right now either. I want to ask you this: Where was God when this miserable, low-life example of the vilest form of scum killed my innocent sister? Where was He . . ." Brett's voice faltered, choking into a sob. Joe Dunn saw it coming, realizing the young man was too emotionally vulnerable to sustain his intense passion indefinitely.

Moments later he began again, "Father Dunn, once again: Why did God allow my sister to die, and why did He allow her to die broken and humiliated?"

"Brett, son, let me remind you that Christianity teaches that God sent His son into the world to save it for all mankind including you and me. God did not intervene to prevent the death of His *own* son who, while divine, was also fully human. *Some* believe that when God, whose very nature we will never understand completely, gave us free will, He *in a sense* stopped intervening in major ways."

"Then why do we pray?" demanded the young man.

"We pray, Bret, I believe, for intervention in our personal lives and the lives of loved ones."

"Well," Bret began, "I cannot bring myself to worship a God who would first create humanity, then not like his creation because of man's behavior, then inexplicably send his own son to die a horrible, excruciatingly painful death because of those humans who turned against Him. I can never understand that! I can tell you, I never will! Never!"

Father Dunn, facing the Atonement, a question with which he always wrestled emotionally, spiritually, and intellectually, continued, "Bret, your question is legitimate. Indeed, that question has been asked since Christianity came to be; but allow me to say that you envision an anthropomorphic God. That is, quite naturally, you, like most people, think of God in terms of our human characteristics. This is quite natural from our understanding and perspective; however, God, by His very nature is infinite and incomprehensible. Therefore, when we attempt to view or understand God in our human terms and demand answers, we are in a sense arrogant; we have no standing. Consequently we fail to achieve understanding."

"For the last time, Father Dunn, please tell me not only why God allowed Vivian to die, but why He allowed her to die in such a vile, cruel way."

"Brett, son, I don't know."

* * * * *

September eased into the mountains, disguising herself as summer, but cool evenings hinted that the warm season would soon pass. It was just as well. There was little joy as Indian summer, its hue the color of tarnished brass, crept across the mountains, easing into the hollows. Its smoky mist muted the magnificent colors of fall, bringing a somber mood of melancholia. This year the tobacco festival would be held against the backdrop of inexplicable death as a corporate age of childlike innocence passed. Harold Kane read the mood of the people well as usual, writing again that, symbolically, the Dark One had driven the town "from the lushness of the garden to a dark and empty place east of Eden."

But other journeys, natural passages, continued as they always do because lives are not lived corporately; they are lived personally. The murders did not change that, so those outside the immediate circle of loss went on living more or less as usual.

The strange courtship between Jean and William Webb continued as Bentley visited less than in the spring. Georgia returned to her third year of nursing at Stonewall as her parents worried over her remote detachment, assuming that the awful events of the summer had taken an emotional toll.

Bentley arrived late one Saturday night in October after having missed the previous two weekends. Georgia had for some time sensed a change, an abrupt modification in his emotional course. Arriving at her home, he explained that he had not had time to eat after work so he grabbed a bite at Kit's Café before coming from downtown. She could smell beer on his breath, but she said nothing, knowing that Bentley knew well that she would have prepared his dinner. They sat on the front porch, but the chill of the mountain night drove them inside to the dimly lit parlor where they talked softly. Bentley was different in another way: He was no longer able to sustain boundless energy predicated by desire. Georgia had changed too. Her passion no longer took flight as before.

Bentley asked *her* if anything were wrong. She told him no, silently feeling the bittersweet sting of irony from his question. She did not reveal that it was he who had cast her somber mood, sensing the dimension of remoteness in him. She cupped his face in the palms of her hands and softly kissed his lips. He did not make more of the kiss, but it was just as well. She knew it was time they had a talk. She had things to tell him.

At that moment Frank Deaton, Jean's father, walked into his kitchen for a glass of water after awaking from a restless sleep. When he turned the light on, he found the note Jean thought he would read the next morning. Written in black ink in her precise, controlled script, it stated that she and William had gone to Greendale to get married. She asked for her parents' blessings, explaining that she and the young doctor decided that elopement was the best for all concerned.

Frank called William Webb's father to quickly discuss their options. There was no disagreement; both parents wanted to stop the couple before they could get married. Asking for a court order preventing the justice of the peace from performing the ceremony, William Webb, Sr. called his friend Judge Harris. The judge, drunk, nevertheless realized that the two adults could do what they chose. All they needed was a proper marriage license. "Hell," he slurred, "I'll just call Hank Hines and tell him he *can't* goddamn marry them. If he does, he won't be a justice of the peace tomorrow!" Then the judge called John Woodward and ordered him to stop the elopement.

John realized the folly of the situation, but the judge's drunken order could not be ignored, so he sent two deputies after the lovers, cautioning they could only tell Miss Deaton and Dr. Webb that their parents asked them to return to town. They could not, he warned, interdict the couple, regardless of the order from the judge.

Greendale Justice of the Peace Hank Hines stood illuminated under his front porch light, expression grim and jaw set. Hank Hines could tell that Judge Harris had been feeling no pain when he called, but he had no way to know that the young doctor approaching was well fortified with expensive whiskey himself. Mr. Hines quickly announced that he *could not* perform the ceremony. Webb stared at him, clearly astonished, Jean clinging to his arm. Seconds later the two lawmen arrived on lathered horses. The chief deputy announced that both sets of parents requested that the couple return home. Jean was shaken and embarrassed, as Webb fell into uncontrollable rage, screaming that the deputies had no authority to intervene. They both assured him that he was correct and said again that they were simply conveying a message from his own parents and from the Deatons. Assuming that Hank Hines had betrayed his confidence, William Webb sprang from his wagon and ran, mane flying, eyes wild, toward the startled Hines on the porch steps, knocking the older man back against the door. Before either could move, the deputies pulled the young doctor off the porch. "You son of a bitch! You no-good, chicken-shit son of a bitch!" William yelled, waving his fist in the air toward the shaken justice of the peace before he jerked away from the deputies and bounded back onto his carriage. The justice raised both palms toward the deputies and shook his head in the negative, conveying he would not press charges. All he wanted was for the wild man to leave his property.

Sitting beside her enraged lover on the leather seat of the expensive carriage, Jean urged him to leave, begging him to stop yelling at the deputies and the frightened Hines. It was a reasonable request, but he would never forgive her for making it. He screamed at her on the way back to town as he continued to take long pulls from a whiskey bottle. Ashamed and intimidated, the parental intervention made Jean feel like a child; but William's explosive, violent temper, fueled by alcohol, shocked her to her depths. Seeing him out of control overwhelmed the strong-willed woman. The romantic beginning became a shattering, abrupt ending. Reaching the Deaton home, Webb deposited Jean at the boxwood bushes in front, dropped her small suitcase off on the brick sidewalk, and drove away without speaking. Jean stood defeated and humiliated as she turned toward her parents standing on the porch looking down at her on the walk.

When William refused to see Jean, which hurt her badly, she was able to reexamine her feelings for him. Her emotions, like kaleidoscopic shards of broken crystal, threatened to shatter her soul as she slipped quickly from the illusive grip of romantic love for the wild William Webb. She would always remember, and at times long for, the lanky, rumpled maverick who managed to charm and infatuate her; but with the abruptly shattered relationship, she felt betrayed. She realized she had fallen in love with a man who did not exist except in her own mind's eye; now she realized her own vision was flawed, as she had chosen to view him as she wanted him to be, not the way he was. She was left with a lingering sense of mourning over the ordeal, partly from embarrassment and partly from a personal sense of failure.

Jean had no way to know that she would never marry, that her mad and reckless lover would live but a few more years. She suspected correctly that he would never forgive her, forever blaming her for writing the note to her parents. Jean Deaton became a woman of summer, and for whatever the reasons, in romantic love, she would not live the full four seasons of the year.

The Deatons were surprised when Jean agreed to accept their offer to visit relatives in Florida, hoping she would "get over William." Jean, always before a strong and independent young woman, was tentative and fragile when she met with Georgia to say good-bye. They talked for hours, and when they finished, there were no secrets between them.

Chapter 19

A week later Press called John, telling him the report came from UVA. "I'll be there at five," John responded, hanging up quickly. At the end of the day he stood waiting outside the office as Press, a bit bowed in the shoulders, appeared at the door and motioned to his friend. The fall wind shifted suddenly putting a chill in the air as John stepped away from Thunder. As he walked toward the office, the horse followed closely at his heels. Stopping at the steps, John turned back to the Appaloosa, encircled the large head in his arms, and kissed him just below his left eye. "You wait here, old boy. I'll be back," he said in a low voice with a tinge of resignation.

John was surprised to see Press appear in the doorway again, this time wearing a coat. "You ready to go, John?" he called.

"Go where? I thought we'd go over the report," answered the sheriff, his brow furrowed.

"We will, but Dietrich sent the damn thing to William Webb," said Press, stepping from the porch, unable to hide his consternation. "I didn't mention it to you on the phone since there was nothing you could do but stew about it all day. I asked for the report to be sent to me, but, remember, Webb transmitted the request. He and Pat Malloy are waiting for us over at Martha."

Dr. Patrick S. Malloy, chairman of the psychology department at Martha Washington College, was considered by both men to be a trusted friend. Both were unaware that the counsel sought from the foreign doctor had been revealed to Harold Kane by William Webb when he was interviewed about his trip to UVA. Kane, pursuing a routine story, had no idea he would walk away with such a nugget.

Before the report was received, plans were in place to restrict its access. Judge Harris was briefed regarding the dissemination to the doctor. Tom Wilson, the mayor, was also informed, which was risky, but they had no choice. Wilson sat in their camp, at least for the moment. The mayor was very concerned about Kane, who maintained the community had a right to know.

It was Press' idea to recruit assistance from his close friend Pat Malloy, who was receptive and encouraging from the beginning. Moreover he had heard of Dr. Juergen Dietrich, which was an additional validation for Press and John. Bringing Malloy into their camp was one thing, but getting Webb out would be quite another. Press knew of no civil way to subtract Webb from the equation.

Pat Malloy greeted Press and John warmly as they walked into his office. Both men liked the professor, a short and stocky Irishman with streaks of gray in his reddish hair and a ruddy, weathered face. His quick intelligence was always evident, but a twinkle in his eyes made one feel that Pat never took life completely seriously. His warm and friendly demeanor was in total contrast to the rumpled and intense Webb, who stood at the end of a conference table looking down at the package in front of him as if it were a sacred object. Webb cut the package open, removing the report from a leather folder. "Well, who wants to read it out loud?" he asked, looking down at the document.

"Pat, how about you?" suggested Press, gently nudging the elbow of his friend. John leaned forward with eyes fixed intently on the bound leather cover of the report. They all exchanged quick glances as Pat stepped forward, responding, "Sure, I'll be happy to, Press."

He opened the report as the other men settled in their seats nervously. John glanced up at Press and William Webb, both sitting with eyes fixed on the professor. Wiping moist palms on his trousers, suddenly it occurred to John that he had been holding his breath slightly for several moments, so, taking a deep sigh, he settled into his seat and waited.

As Pat Malloy opened the report, the conference room door opened without a knock, as Dr. Sidney Clarke strode in. John was shocked, unprepared for the intrusion and stunned that the circle of access to the sensitive information was quickly expanding. He knew well that Clarke was a political animal, which could cause grave consequences.

Clarke walked to a chair at the conference table closest to Malloy as the others watched in silence. After sitting down, he nodded, speaking the single word, "Gentlemen." Both elbows of his expensive suit rested on the shiny mahogany tabletop as he folded his hands together and looked over his glasses toward Malloy. Pat explained that he was just about to start reading the report from the Austrian psychiatrist.

Initially the doctor issued a caveat to emphasize that the field of psychiatry was yet to be considered exact science. Next Dr. Dietrich set forth a litany of his academic credentials, his publications in medical journals and elsewhere, and his experience in the field of forensic psychiatry. The latter included his studies of the so-called Jack the Ripper murders in East London in the 1880s. He stated that his paper was written in a synopsis style with opinions informed by his credentials and experience but without scholarly footnotes and documentation. He acknowledged assistance from associates at UVA in both the departments of psychiatry and English. He wrote as follows:

While the autopsy evidence suggests that rape was not a factor in the second two cases, and cannot be determined in the first, the assaults were sexual in nature. Except for the inadequacy of the killer, he would have committed rape. Rape is motivated by anger and rage and acted out sexually; therefore, the attempted crime of rape should be considered in these cases vis-à-vis suspect development. Yet, the case should not be viewed solely as a sexual crime. Rape is not predicated by the perpetrator's overt sexual drive but by hostility and the desire for power, control, dominance and status. The act is aggressive, violent, debasing and humiliating. There are different types of rapists driven by several psychological pathologies. For the purposes of this report, please note that the three I have identified in laymen's terms are Anger Rapists, Power Rapists and Sadistic Rapists. Not all rapists, however, can be categorized with precision into a single classification.

I believe your subject, a Caucasian male, to be predominately a Power Rapist who attacks viciously and kills quickly; however, he displays behavior characteristics of another type of predator, the Sadistic Rapist. His bites to the body of his victims, and his ritualized death scenes show traits of the Sadistic Rapist. His is driven to compensate for substantial and pervasive feelings of inadequacy. His desire is to capture, to control and to possess, which allow him to express issues of mastery, strength, authority, identity and capability. His intent is to assert his competency and validate his masculinity. His sadistic behavior, unlike the typical Sadistic Rapist, is acted out postmortem.

Usually Sadistic Rapists, and indeed your subject, focus on a specific area of the body for abuse. He achieves great satisfaction from the intentional maltreatment of his victim, and takes pleasure from her torment, anguish, distress, helplessness, pain and suffering. Your subject, however, kills quickly. He finds gratification to act out what he fantasizes as infliction of pain on the body/corpse of the victim/deceased. Since his abuse of the body is postmortem, your subject's behavior is more fetish than sadistic and deals with the fantasy of possession. Like the typical Sadistic Rapist, your subject, after the second and third murder, participated in ritualistic acts.

The killer positioned the bodies in cases two and three. Taunting is evident, especially in the position of the body of the last victim. The perpetrator is becoming more accomplished and gaining confidence. He believes he is more intelligent than his pursuers.

You are dealing with a multiple killer, and he will kill again. Your subject is acting out his sexual fantasies. Unlike normal sexual fantasies of young males, his were infused with violence as an adolescent and will remain constant throughout his life. He cannot separate sexuality from violence and death. To him sexuality, violence and death are merged into a single state; thus, he will act them out again and again until he is apprehended. His sexual urges are escalating. His excitement intensifies during each act of killing. His gratification likewise grows during his ritualistic behavior and autoeroticism after death. It is quite likely that he is drawn to the publicity upon which he will thrive.

In any crime scene an effort should be made to isolate any singularity which is evident. The singularity should be concentrated upon in the second and third cases where the crime scenes were preserved. All decedents were Caucasian females, attractive, and young. Underwear was between the legs of all victims. The killer may have taken other articles from his victims as trophies. (See below.)

Regarding the singularity of the murderer himself: If one wants to understand the artist, he must look at the work of art. All artists, sculptors, painters, poets, writers, and composers leave their signatures on their works. Your multiple killer will be no different. If you want to understand your killer, you must look for his signature at the crime scene. The most important part of the crime scene is the body of the victim. While his modus operandi is fluid and subject to change, elements of his signature will remain the same.

Your killer chooses similar victims, kills on Friday or Saturday nights, and leaves highly ritualistic crime scenes. He may wear a mask if the account of Miss White is accurate and if she were, in fact chased by the killer of victims two and three. He bites the flesh of his victims. His bites are isolated to the inside of the thighs. He overkills. He crushed the esophagus and larynx of the second and third victims. In all likelihood the first victim was killed in the same way.

This subject is autoerotic at the scene. This activity is highly symbolic to him for unique, personal reasons. He is incapable of having sex with women who are alive. This is due to vast feelings of sexual inferiority and inadequacy in concert with his anger and high impulsivity rather than necrophilia.

While the killer is inadequate sexually, he is very aggressive. If confronted, he is likely to be <u>extremely dangerous</u>.

Psychiatry normally examines a person and attempts to forecast how he or she will react to some given situation. In an analysis of multiple murderers one must reverse the process and attempt to identify the murderer from his acts. The process is more inductive than deductive. Thus, again, the most important piece of evidence is the body of the victim.

In the multiple murder cases I have studied, escalation becomes apparent in all. Your case is no exception. Ten months passed from the first to the second murder. The interim between the second and the third, however, was only seven and a half weeks. This can be accounted for by excitement and possibly stressors in the life of the killer. (See below.) Therefore, as noted above, your subject will murder again. I base this opinion upon significant statistical data I have gathered through years of research.

Often indicators of potential criminal pathologies are evident at an early age. As one matures he may be cruel to subordinates and peers. An obsession with pornography seems to be a life-long condition of these sexual, multiple killers. In the background of suspects look for the homicidal triad: Cruelty to animals; enuresis (bed wetting past the normal growth and developmental stage) and setting fires.

Multiple murderers often take a trophy from their victims. Through the trophies the killer can achieve stimulation and excitement and renew mental domination and control long after the actual killing. (See below.) Consider what may have been taken from the murder scenes.

Multiple killers can be placed in two categories which I have classified for laymen as Organized and Disorganized. No multiple murderer can be absolutely placed in one category or the other. That is, all possess some of the characteristics of the other group. Most, however, can be placed in one of these two groups.

The Organized Multiple Killer will have a psychopathic personality. He will plan his crimes. He will be manipulative. Usually he will have adequate, sometimes very good, verbal skills. Control is a main element of his modus operandi. His victims are personalized. He will adapt his behavior to his environment during the commission of the crime. He will be mobile, and he will achieve greater expertise in the efficiency of his murders as he continues to kill. The Organized Killer will bring his own weapon. Normally he hides bodies to prevent early detection. Occasionally, when driven by a strong ego, he will flaunt the bodies rather than conceal them. He will often take items from the victims as trophies through which he will relive the excitement of his crime. He will have an adequate personality. Compared to the disorganized killer, he will be outgoing; yet, he may cause confrontations in his workplace. He feels superior and more intelligent than others. He will be unable to sustain long-term relationships, especially with women. He may, however, have sexual female companionship and perform at least adequately as a sex partner. He will be angry in general and hoard enormous hostility toward women.

The Disorganized Multiple Killer will suffer grave psychological patholo-gies. His mental disorders will not allow him to choose victims logically; con-sequently, his random victims may be high risk to the Disorganized Killer himself. He does not personalize his victims. He does not plan his attacks which are opportunistic and seemingly often devoid of logic. His personal appearance will be unkempt as will be his dwelling place. He is *not* likely to live with a woman. He will exist in a confused state, and the crime scene will reflect that confusion. He may attempt, but he usually does not complete the sex act with his victim. He will kill her quickly. He will be withdrawn from society generally and have a poor self-image. He will have a menial job if he has a job at all. He is likely to go from one failed relationship and one job to the next.

Multiple killers are often activated by stressors in their personal lives. As noted above, heightening sexuality infused with delusions and fantasies of vio-lence and death will be precursors to the first a violent act. Look for stressors that could activate the inadequate personality into violence. This is a charac-teristic common to both types of multiple killers. Look for one who has lost his spouse, girl friend or mother; look for one who has lost his job.

You should look for a Caucasian male between twenty-three and twenty-eight years old. He will in all likelihood be younger than twenty-eight.

There have been no known cases where multiple murderers were other than Caucasian males. Caucasian multiple murderers always kill victims of the same race.

The victim's personal, social and business background should be exam-ined to determine if she were a high risk or a low risk victim. Such a risk analysis of the victim will assist in determining the type of killer. One must ask <u>why</u> this victim was selected from all other choices and how she was mur-dered. Then ask <u>who</u> committed the murders.

Your killer is likely to return to the murder scene or visit the grave sites of his victims. Such visits are likely to occur on the anniversaries of the deaths or burials. Such memorialized days can be the anniversary of the day of the week or the month or year of the killing. This enables the murdered to relive the sexual fantasies many times.

Unlike the Trait School of Psychology where it is postulated that traits can be used to predict behavior (i.e. personality can predict behavior), in this endeavor we must start with behavior at the crime scene and attempt to predict personality from that perspective.

Psychotics (those who have lost touch with reality) rarely commit murders; psychopaths/sociopaths often commit murders.

Invariably, multiple killers come from dysfunctional family backgrounds. Most have suffered physical, mental or sexual abuse as children. Often alcohol or drugs were prevalent in their homes. This is not to suggest that all those who come from such backgrounds become multiple killers. I postulate, however, that all multiple killers will have suffered some of those problems in their backgrounds.

In your particular cases, I respectfully offer observations and opinions as follows:

Your subject is an <u>Organized Killer</u>. He is a Caucasian male from twenty-three to twenty-eight years of age. He is most likely to be under twenty-eight of age. He will live within a few miles (probably two or less) of where at least one of the victims lived. He is more apt to live closer to where the first victim was killed than the others. (I have no information regarding the locations of the residences of the victims in relationship to each other or other data concerning distances.)

Your killer has great feelings of sexual inadequacy. These inferior feelings in part fuel his rage. He is incapable of maintaining normal romantic heterosexual relationships. It is likely that he has never married. If he has been married, it is highly probable that the marriage failed early. He has never had a significant relationship with a woman other than his mother. While she may think otherwise, his relationship with her is the basis of his anger. Ironically, he may live at home with his parents. He will be a loner. His upper body strength is sufficient to carry out a brutal attack against women.

Your killer may attempt to interject himself into the investigation. He will closely follow the case. <u>He may have been interviewed</u>. It is likely that he has completed high school, but he will have been a poor student. He is an Organized Killer who plans his attacks and selects his victims. Since he kills his victims, the mask, if indeed one was worn during the murders, suggests that he harbors a sense of shame. It can also indicate a ritualistic quality to his attacks. When you find your subject, you will find trophies from his victims. His mask shows he was organized in his planning. He may know his victims. His shame is superficial, and the mask, if worn, is more for ritual than concealment. Because the subject is a sociopath, he is incapable of normal feelings of guilt.

Your subject will be a manipulative person. At first he may be truthful to some limited extent; however, the information he provides will not be incriminating. He will initially appear cooperative because he will feel some exhilaration from the attention. Later, however, he will become defensive and withdrawn and become uncooperative. He believes he is of greater intellect than law enforcement officials. He will be somewhat narcissistic and egocentric.

In the interest of brevity and clarity, the above information has been offered without qualifications, caveats or disclaimers. While I fully believe most of the analysis will be proven to be correct, some aspects will be incorrect. I assume no academic, professional or legal liability for this diagnostic report. It is offered as a professional courtesy. It is subject to the agreements and conditions as set forth in the document captioned, "Memorandum of Understanding," signed by Dr. William C. Webb and me, dated September 8, 1909. Respectfully submitted this tenth day of October in the year of our Lord 1909 at Charlottesville, Virginia, U.S.A.

The group sat in silence after Dr. Malloy finished reading. Dr. Sidney Clarke broke the silence with a prolonged, "Well?" The word with its inflection was directed at his subordinate, Pat Malloy, but Dr. Webb stood and spoke first.
"Gentlemen, I don't claim to be schooled in psychology or psychiatry; therefore, I cannot unequivocally support this paper. Conversely, however, I am likewise not qualified to take exception to any part of it or to the document as a whole."
"Pat?" asked Clarke.
Pat rose and began slowly. "Dr. Dietrich is a well-known international expert in his field of forensic psychiatry. He's pioneered a discipline of which few of us have any knowledge. His propositions are fascinating. Frankly, I need to digest the paper. Reading it once is not enough. And, of course, I am not a clinician. Always, Sidney, as you know, there can be debate about scholarly theories. I will say this about psychology: It is not an exact science. It is, I think, part of an academic discipline not yet fully developed and not likely to be developed in our lifetime. It is also part art form. Sometimes, and some psychologists or psychiatrists may take exception to this, it requires one to draw from his heart and his soul, his spirit—not just his cognition, his mind. Anyway, there is one simple test for any type of psychological instrument that measures something or provides information. The test is this: Ask yourself if having it, whatever it is, is better than not having

it? In other words, does it help in *any* way by having it? If the answer is yes to either question, it has some value. I recommend that John and Press try to exploit the information toward the solution of the case. I'll be happy to assist them, as they know. None of us is qualified to attempt an analysis of Dr. Dietrich's findings. We either must accept or reject them."

Dr. Clarke broke the silence stating, "Well then, Pat, I am sure you and the other gentlemen have a lot of work to do. Good night."

Dr. Webb nodded to the others without speaking, following Clarke out of the room.

Press and John paused on Main Street just outside the gates of the college. "This report made me realize something," John said, interrupting their silent thoughts.

"What?" asked Press turning to look in John's face.

"The underwear," answered John, gazing into the distance with eyes narrowed.

"The underwear between their legs?" Press asked, still looking intently.

"No, the underwear stolen off the clotheslines in summer. I believe those thefts were connected to our case," John mused, still gazing toward the west.

"I'm not sure I follow you," responded Press quizzically.

"Well," John began slowly, "those trophies the doctor wrote about. I think the stolen underwear were trophies to our killer. Only this sick guy began taking the trophies *before* he killed anybody."

"You may be right, John," sighed the doctor slowly, his voice revealing deep fatigue.

"If I am right, we know something else, Press," continued John remotely. "We know this guy is *here*. He doesn't come and go."

"If your theory is correct, John, the doctor's paper has already helped you," Press mused softly.

* * * * *

Two days later in the fading afternoon, John left the Martha Washington College campus, turning his spirited Thunder right toward the residence of Judge Harold Harris. When Harris learned that the paper arrived from Charlottesville, he requested a personal briefing. Harold Kane also called the sheriff's office, but John did not talk to the editor, wondering if he knew about the report too. At the moment he had to concentrate on the judge, and he had grave concerns.

Because Judge Harris would hear the case if and when the killer were brought to trial, John knew it was inappropriate for him to learn the details of the report. What would John do if he were questioned on the witness stand about who gained access to the report? He did not want the judge to develop prejudice against any aspect of the case the commonwealth might build. Harris acted unpredictable in the courtroom; his moods swung wildly from one extreme to the other. More than once his antics on the bench caused reversals by the Virginia Supreme Court in significant criminal cases. He often defied the Court, challenging it to reverse his rulings. Law-and-order types especially liked his criticism of the "liberal" high court; however, once those challenges were memorialized in the record, the appellate court often acted to validate his predictions, which delighted every defense attorney who walked into his courtroom. Judge Harris' impulsiveness kept John and others forever off balance. One never knew how he would react to any issue, legal or otherwise.

Before picking up the report, John stopped to see Herbert P. Mitchell, the Commonwealth's Attorney, to seek his advice and counsel regarding Harris' order to be briefed. Mitchell, a middle-aged man with prematurely white hair and matching mustache, listened intently. Then he shook his head and sighed deeply. "Jesus Christ! The smartest legal mind in Southwest Virginia can do the dumbest fucking things!" he lamented. "Well, John, handle it the best you can," he said, deep resignation in his voice

"Herb," John said, looking at his friend, "I thought you might call the judge and advise him against the briefing."

"John," Mitchell began slowly, "you remember my predecessor in this job, Mike Pitt. Well, Pitt was an honorable guy. He was a graduate of VMI and wouldn't compromise on anything that involved honor. As you may know, he tried pulling that shit on the judge. Pitt actually confronted Harris when he saw the judge do things that, at least in his eyes, were, if not illegal, improper and unethical. You know where it got him. The next election the judge pulled the support of the Democratic Party, and poor old Mike didn't stand a chance of getting reelected. If that hadn't happened, I wouldn't hold this office today. You might say that there wouldn't be a Herbert P. Mitchell if there hadn't been a Mike Pitt. He's undoubtedly making a lot more money since joining a law firm. The point is I don't have a law office to go to, so, John, you can offer your opinion to Judge Harris, but before you do, you'd better have another job waiting come election time."

Just after five-thirty Faye Harris answered the front door as a tentative smile crept across her face. John interpreted the smile to be an apology for her husband waiting in the library.

John entered the room, finding the judge slumped in a blue wing chair which made his pudgy, flushed face appear to be resting on his chest. Glancing up through watery eyes without moving his head, the judge asked, "How about a drink, John?"

"Well, it's five–forty-five; I may as well have a short one," answered the sheriff, knowing he would insult Harris by refusing. The judge motioned toward a bottle of Tennessee whiskey sitting on a silver tray with an ice bucket, glasses, and a pitcher containing cold mountain spring water. John poured a drink and walked back to the sofa. "Judge, I'm not a lawyer," John began, like a man approaching a copperhead, "but I have some concerns that portions of the information in this report might cause problems for you later down the road . . ."

"Problems? What kind of problems, John?" asked the judge, raising his large head slightly.

"Well, sir," John began slowly, hesitantly, "it seems to me that I would be doing you a disservice if I were to present information that you would later view as prejudicial against some future defendant, and I . . ."

"John, you were right about one thing. You're not a lawyer, so I'll determine what is appropriate and what isn't. So, let's go, old boy, what've you got?" asked Harris, raising his glass slightly, pointing toward the report in John's hands.

"Perhaps you'd like to read the report, Judge," John offered tentatively.

Wiping his mouth carefully with a linen handkerchief, Harris said emphatically, "I don't want to read it. Tell me what's in it."

"Judge, it's very complicated. I've only heard it read once. I'm afraid there's no way I could adequately brief you on it," John stated, his own voice resolute.

The judge paused as if he were taking John's words under advisement. Finally he said, "Hell, that's fine. Go ahead and read it. I've got all night. First, let me refresh my drink." Laughing sardonically he ambled toward the tray. Returning, he collapsed in his seat, his drink deftly extended to the side to prevent spillage. Now, finally ready, he waived a pasty hand in the air as if he were directing a servant to start a task.

As John read the report, it was clear the judge's mood was turning dark as he let his head rest against the back of the wing chair. John had seen him do the same thing in the courtroom where he never missed a word, notwithstanding jokes to the contrary behind his back. When John finished reading, the judge's eyes opened quickly as the two sat in silence.

Breaking the silence, John asked gently, "What do you think, Judge?" as if he were now prodding the snake with a stick.

The judge looked up as if John's question startled him, "I'll tell you what I think, Sheriff. I think it's bullshit! I *know* it's bullshit. You show me one opinion of the so-called expert that can be proven in a court of law. If this goddamned *doctor* were any good, why in the hell wouldn't he be practicing traditional medicine, *real* medicine? I'll tell you why: Because he found a way to make more money easier than working his ass off at some hospital."

John was shaken, knowing that while Harris was a mess, his mind was sound. Clearly he missed the point, but John was not about to attempt to explain that the report was not intended to be evidence but simply an investigative tool. John viewed the judge as a learned jurist and an extraordinary thinker, one who just dismissed the findings out of hand. John emotionally embraced the document because it could be a tool that might solve the case. This attack after the staid reaction of the other professionals caught the sheriff off guard, shaking a confidence already very fragile.

"Judge, maybe you should keep this copy and read it yourself," he offered hesitantly.

"Spare me, please! Hell, I don't need to read that shit!" Harris snapped. "It's drivel, unadulterated crap! I'm a good listener, John; that's what I get paid to do. Except there's one thing: Those I usually listen to, even the half-ass lawyers, know at least a little bit of what they're talking about!"

Stung by the harsh, caustic words, John could not escape their meaning: They were not only directed at the Austrian psychiatrist, but at him as well; yet the judge was right about one matter as far as John was concerned. Clearly he was out of his league. He really didn't understand the paper.

Looking up into the sheriff's face through narrowed eyes, he continued, "I'll tell you this, John, it won't replace good police work, and it won't replace good lawyer'in'. If I were you, I'd forget about the magic and sorcery, the goddamn smoke and mirrors. I'd go out and try to solve this case before any more innocent women die!"

John stood up, report in his hand, as he reached for his hat on the sofa. Understanding his subordinate position to the judge, he nevertheless had passed a threshold; now he would refuse to take more abuse from the judge. As the sheriff walked toward the door without speaking, the judge collapsed again into his chair and called, "John!"

The sheriff stopped. Without turning, he responded, "Yes?"

"Thanks for your time, John." Harris spoke as if they had finished a warm conversation. "One more thing: Don't let those comic book fantasies get out to the public. It could taint a goddamn jury!" He slowly leaned forward, smiling darkly as he reached for his glass, noticing for the first time that John's glass sat untouched.

John paused at the front steps, oblivious to Thunder's soft nose pressing against his chest, as he reflected upon the harsh rebuke of the judge.

"Sheriff," Faye Harris called from the front door, "Mr. West wants to speak to you on the phone."

With the receiver pressed to his ear, the sheriff answered, "Yes, Will?"

"John, we just received an important telegraph for you. I'll carry it to your office and meet you there if you want me to," West clipped quickly with an urgent tone.

"That's fine. What's it about?" asked John, still pressing the receiver harder against his ear.

"The murders," answered West.

John allowed Thunder to break from a gallop into a spirited run the last two hundred yards before pulling back on the reins, bringing the horse to trot before they reached the office.

Press spoke first without greeting his friend. "I ran into Will, and when he told me what he had, I wanted to be here, John."

"Sure, that's fine. What have we got, Will?" John asked, pitch elevated, as West handed a telegram to John, who read it slowly then handed it to Press. Press slowly read each line from the Sheriff of Sullivan County, Tennessee.

Chapter 20

The next day, a gray, overcast Saturday, the midmorning light remained as pale as dawn, as John Woodward sat gazing out the window of a Norfolk and Western coach. His soul felt the tinge of sadness that comes with the fading fall in the Virginia highlands, but his mind focused on the telegram from the Sheriff of Sullivan County.

As the train carried the sheriff westward, Eugene Johnson, driving the horse-drawn rig, approached the back door of Kit's Café after backing the Colley Brothers wagon to the loading dock. As he opened the back door with some grocery items in his arms, Frederick Price turned from a hot grill laden with sausage patties and bacon strips sizzling in their own natural grease. The odor of sage and pepper from the seasoned meat and fat cooking was pungent to Eugene coming inside from the crisp morning air.

"Put 'em over there by the icebox," Price ordered harshly, turning slightly to eye the stork with a pained countenance, as if he were disgusted at what he saw. At six feet tall, he weighed two hundred twenty pounds that were supported by short, stocky legs that appeared out of proportion with his massive upper body. Price cooked in a gray undershirt revealing muscular biceps above hairy forearms decorated with crude homemade tattoos. Thin black hair lay damp, glistening with perspiration, matted to the top of his large balding head. His dark, deep-set eyes looked black beneath heavy, bushy eyebrows. Frederick Price, unkempt and overweight, called himself Frederick. Will West hired Price as a freight handler shortly after he came to town from Richmond a year earlier. His coworkers at the Express Office were afraid of him as the big man's explosive temper and obvious physical strength were two elements that nobody wanted to test. Will West assigned Price to the freight delivery wagon, where he worked alone most of the time. Frederick, a hard worker, never asked for help, even when he needed it for heavy sheets of razor-sharp roofing or long rolls of unmanageable barbed wire. He wasn't always reliable about coming to work or arriving on time, but when he was there, he often performed the labor of two men, so Will managed to strike a proper balance between control and confrontation to keep him on the job.

When Kit ran an ad for a fry cook for the weekends, Frederick Price applied, astounding the owner with his deftness cooking on the grill, a trade he said he had learned in Richmond. Kit quickly hired the big man.

Frederick wiped his sweaty brow on a large hairy forearm as he eyed the lanky Eugene Johnson walking back outside. Tossing the long spatula to the side of the grill with a clang, he rubbed his large greasy hands on his apron with no concern that flecks of raw sausage clung tenaciously to it. He strode outside like a rotund bantam cock as Eugene worked in the wagon gathering another load of groceries, his back turned toward the dock.

"We get all this shit?" Price yelled from the elevated platform.

Startled, Eugene jerked around, answering, "Naw, not all of it. From those two boxes there," he answered, pointing toward the middle of the narrow wagon. "The rest goes to Martha," he added as the fry cook ambled toward the wagon, where he scooped up two fifty-pound sacks of potatoes with ease before strutting back toward the kitchen, easily carrying a sack under each arm. Johnson made more trips without speaking to the big cook. Finally he was through, waiting with the invoice in his hand as he called tentatively, "You wanna check the items off? They always check the invoice." Price turned and dropped a short, stubby cigar stump to the floor before moving forward and snatching the invoice from Eugene as if annoyed by the interruption.

"Let's see here," he said slowly, gazing intently at the bill. Beginning methodically at the top, he mumbled, "Okay, today is the tenth." Glancing up at Eugene, he grunted, "This is the tenth, ain't it, kid?"

"Yeah, it's the tenth of November, four months since Jeanette Moore was murdered," answered Johnson, gazing upward toward the high greasy ceiling.

"What the fuck d'you say?" barked Price, startling the delivery boy.

"I said it's the tenth," Johnson answered meekly.

"Not that, you little asshole! What'd you say about Moore?" Price demanded, taking a quick step toward Eugene.

"Jeanette Moore!" he gasped, taking a slight step backward away from the menacing Price. "She worked right here," he added quickly.

"I know that, goddamn it! But what'd you just say about her?" Price growled, his black eyes narrowed.

The stork stepped back again, eyes wide, clearly threatened. He seldom spoke, much less volunteered information; now he deeply regretted his comment, stammering, "I just said Miss Moore was killed four months ago today."

"Now, how in the hell would *you* just *happen* to know that?" Price demanded, rubbing a clinched fist against the bloodstained apron tied around his considerable girth. His elbows were extended, making him look, for the moment, like a large beefy butterfly.

"Well, *The Virginian* had an article about her the day before yesterday. It said that the tenth would be four months since she was murdered, and nobody knows who did it, and the sheriff can't seem to find out, that's all I know," recited Johnson as fast as he had ever spoken.

Quickly Price uttered, "Oh, yeah, *that*. I saw that shit too. Forgot about that." Walking back toward the grill, he tossed the invoice on the large chopping block next to a meat cleaver imbedded near the edge. Eugene could see grease smudges from Price's fat, stubby fingers. Without turning Price yelled, "Shit's here. You can have the goddamn bill." Eugene had no intention in requesting his signature. He would rather explain to Mr. Colley than take the chance of incurring the wrath of the threatening Price.

As Eugene closed the door, the fry cook was leaning forward, peering through the order window into the restaurant. He watched with interest as Will West, his boss from the railway station, sat down at the end of the counter near the cash register, the same section where the sheriff usually sat. *Taking his mornin' break,* Price thought to himself. Helen Hanson, as usual, walked toward Will with a fresh mug of steaming hot coffee. Price took the scene in and smiled faintly as if he were privy to an intimate secret. He liked one aspect of his vantage point. He could get a good view of the waitresses from behind as they tended to the counter or stood waiting for customers, but the best part of his job was their dependence upon him to fill the orders.

John Woodward was oblivious to the rhythmic clatter until heavy slick wheels banged repeatedly crossing rail joints; yet his thoughts remained on his conversation with Press the night before. His friend said he was surprised Dr. Dietrich had not developed a time line regarding the murders. Press ventured forth with his own frightening forecast. He pointed out that Anna Marie Holmes disappeared on the night of October 12, 1908. Her body was discovered the following March. Jeanette Moore, he noted, was murdered on July 10, 1909, and Vivian Grant on October 13, 1909. The time between the last two murders was approximately three months. At that rate Press forecasted grimly, they could expect another woman dead by January 1910. John was making a conscious effort to control the hope that now lifted his spirit and teased his mind.

Maybe . . . just maybe it's all over, John thought as he pulled the telegram from his coat pocket. He began to read once again the message of the Sheriff of Sullivan County, Tennessee once again.

"This date William Houser Grimes arrested for assault and rape stop Victim's condition critical stop Subject admits the assault of this victim and the three murders in Abingdon stop He has been there in past stop Contact me for details stop Thompson S. Brown, Sheriff of Sullivan County Tennessee stop"

John stepped onto the platform, where he met Sheriff Tom Brown, who was generally the same age. Brown wore a western-style hat too; and, like his associate, he was dressed in a dark suit with his badge pinned to his lapel. They shook hands and went straight to the office, where Tom Brown closed the door, poured John a cup of coffee, and began briefing him about William Houser Grimes.

The woman assaulted, Brown related, was a prostitute, whom he had arrested several times in the past. He noted that only because she was rescued by chance had she survived the brutal attack. She was almost choked to death and was unconscious when she reached the hospital. It required five men to take Grimes into custody, and that was accomplished only after he was knocked into oblivion by a billy club.

"Tell me about Grimes," John asked when Brown finished the summary of the case.

"He's forty-five years old. Admitted he served time in Richmond for murder once before for killing a guy in a barroom brawl. Says he was convicted of manslaughter on a plea bargain. I've sent a wire to Richmond to get his record. Down here he worked for a lumber company, but he says he used to hire out on a farm outside Abingdon. Said he worked for a guy named Charles Perkins who's dead now." Brown laid his file down and looked over his glasses at John.

"That part is right," said John. "There was a man, Chuck Perkins, and he died of a heart attack in his barn."

"Since it was your case, I didn't attempt to interview him about the murders. I just took his background. He was a little vague about some of it. You ready?"

"Just a couple of questions first," said John, thinking about the UVA report. He wanted desperately for the suspect to fall within the parameters of Dr. Dietrich's profile, so he asked a series of questions to an impatient and confused Sheriff Brown. Finally John asked, "Did he say why he assaulted her?"

"No, but that reminds me of an interesting point. He volunteered that he did your murders. Offered to talk about 'em, but in passing it seems like he doesn't want to discuss assaulting this whore. He wanted to talk to me about your cases. Didn't seem to like the idea of waiting for you. You ready to interview him now?" asked Tom Brown, pausing to get on with the task at hand.

"Let's do it," said John, loosening his gun belt and handing it to Tom. Brown removed his own sidearm and gave both to a waiting deputy, as no weapons were allowed in the jail.

As they walked down a narrow hallway, Brown paused and turned back to John. "Oh, yeah. I almost forgot to mention an important part of what Grimes said. He claims that he used to work at Martha Washington College in the stables. So we know he's been up there, and we know he's killed before. You've got your man, John. Congratulations."

"I hope so," ventured John tentatively, possessing none of Brown's confidence. Turning to Brown, John posed a final question, "Tom, why do you think he wants to talk about the murders when he won't talk about your rape and assault?"

Brown began in a low voice, "I think we'll find that he's wanted somewhere else. Possibly here in Tennessee, probably for other murders. He may figure that he's less likely to hang in Virginia. Probably thinks he can get a plea bargain up there. If this whore dies, we'll hang him real quick down here. He'd rather do life in Virginia than hang down here."

When the prisoner was escorted into the interview room by two deputies, John sensed immediately that chemistry would be bad between them, something that rarely happened to him in such situations. As a professional his sole purpose was to gather the *truth*. But this time it was different; his visceral reaction was negative toward the prisoner. Nevertheless, John knew that he could overcome his secret prejudice. He was surprised by the prisoner's casual demeanor as well as the lack of security. Grimes entered, accompanied by two deputies, with leg shackles but no handcuffs.

He looked every bit of his forty-five years. Too old, John believed, if Dietrich was right about the killer's age. The prisoner was a tall, muscular man with heavy arms. His black hair was peppered with gray, matching his beard stubble of several days. After Brown nodded, his deputies left the room as one said, "We'll be right outside the door, Sheriff."

Now the three sat alone, better for the interview John realized, feeling an undefined apprehension.

Brown began unceremoniously, "Okay, Grimes. This here's Sheriff Woodward from Washington County, Virginia. He wants to ask you some questions."

"Yeah?" Grimes responded, unable to hide the trace of a sneer. Clearly he knew how important the questions would be to the Sheriff of Washington County.

John Woodward began the most important interview of his career by asking easy questions at first about Grimes' background in part to establish a flow of communication. When he took a detailed physical description, he asked Grimes to display all his scars and marks including crude tattoos that John recognized as prison vintage. The prisoner seemed to enjoy the attention and answered all the questions fluidly. The longer they talked, the more at ease he appeared. Maybe Grimes would tell the truth, yet his underlying arrogance bothered John as he spoke freely about his time in prison in Richmond for murder.

The questions continued at length until John said, "Okay, please tell me in your own words about the murders in Abingdon." He believed this man to be a streetwise and worthy opponent who had read about the crimes, so he didn't want to reveal any information to Grimes.

"Sure, Sheriff. What do you wanna know?" answered Grimes. John studied his eyes, black as onyx. They were sinister. *A killer, a real killer*, he thought. Then again he sensed a primal alert telegraphing danger. Even though Grimes was in custody, he possessed a menacing, deadly quality.

"Begin, please, by telling me about the murder of the Martha girl," he requested in a monotone.

"What do you want to know?" asked Grimes, now starting his own probing with the interrogator. John knew Grimes was asking for specific questions, an indication that he might not know about the murders. Tom Brown could not understand why John didn't ask the prisoner specific questions right away.

"Anything you want to tell me. Just tell me in your own words. I'll ask questions later when you're through," answered John.

"Ain't that much to tell, Sheriff," began the big man slowly, sensing the control he possessed of the two lawmen, relishing his position at the moment. Smiling darkly before he spoke, the prisoner started again, "I was down by the tracks not far from the depot. Drinking and all when I seen this girl walkin' by herself on the college side of the fence. You know, that low wire fence with the honeysuckle and shit growing around it. Anyhow I seen she looked ripe, so I grabbed her and pulled her into the brush. That's about it. But I'll tell ye one thing, buddy, that little bitch was a real hellion, that one was!" Smiling darkly, in a manner that incensed John, the prisoner fell silent, waiting to be coaxed for more explanation.

"Go ahead, give me the details," John requested patiently.

"Well, the little bitch hit me cross the face and tried to scratch me. No damn woman's ever done that and gotten away with it, so I hit her a good 'un in her face! The next thing I knowed, she's limp," offered Grimes, expecting both men to be sympathetic to hitting a woman under such circumstances.

"Did you rape her?" asked John easily, hiding his revulsion.

"Rape her? Hell no, I didn't rape that little bitch. She was out. If she'd been awake, though, I'd had my way with her. I'd stuck her real good. Hell, I'd made her like it a lot! I'd made her squeal a little too. You know what I mean, Sheriff?" Grimes asked, grinning darkly, peering through squinted eyes at John.

Ignoring the question of his repulsive adversary, John asked, "Did you remove any of her clothes?"

"Remove any of her clothes?" repeated Grimes slowly, in obvious contemplation. "Let's see; no, I didn't. Left her just the way you found her," volunteered the suspect.

"The way we found her?" asked John, leaning slightly forward with his eyes locked on Grimes.

"Yeah, you know, I know how I left her, and you found her later," stated the prisoner, his voice assured.

John decided to move on to the other cases. He could always come back and fill in the gaps once he established that the prisoner was telling the truth.

"Why did you choose the Moore woman?" he asked, shifting away from the first line of questioning.

"'Cause she lived by herself I guess. Shit, I ain't for sure," Grimes shot back quickly.

"How do you know she lived alone?" John prodded.

"'Cause she fuckin' *told* me. *That's* how, Sheriff. 'Cause that bitch told me!" he answered boldly.

Sensing that Grimes knew Jeanette Moore in some way, John probed, "When did she tell you she lived alone?"

"When I was in Kit's, she told me that *there*," Grimes answered in a taunting way.

John now believed Grimes was lying. He sensed that the violent man before him, for whatever dark reason, wanted to confess to murders he had not committed. He continued to craft questions solely to show whether or not this base and disgusting man could be the murderer.

"All right, William. We'll get the details later, but let me ask you this: Why did you bash her head in?" asked the Sheriff of Washington County.

"Why'd I bash her head in? So she wouldn't holler," Grimes answered without hesitation. Clearly he was enjoying the interview.

"What did you hit her with?" asked the sheriff.

"A brick."

"Where did you get it?"

"Outside her house in the yard."

"What did you do with it?"

"Threw it in a creek."

"Which creek?"

"I don't know *which* creek, Sheriff, just some fuckin' creek."

"Okay, now the last girl. I want to ask you about her. Why did you remove all her clothes and leave her stark naked in the pantry?" asked John, not realizing his own eyes were narrowed. Sheriff Brown sensed John's growing intensity and assumed the answers were incriminating Grimes.

"Well now, Sheriff, I'll jes' tell ya. I 'speck you know anyhow. I jes' wanted to see that pretty little thang's body."

"Why did you rape her?" said John evenly, patiently.

"Well, I stuck her a little bit," answered Grimes, a dark smirk cast across his sweaty face.

"Okay. Tom, I need to speak to you outside," said John, turning to his associate for the first time. Brown opened the door and ordered the deputies to guard the prisoner so he and Sheriff Woodward could leave the room. John stepped outside and told Tom Brown that Grimes was lying about the murders, attempting to give answers to facts suggested that were incorrect.

"Are you sure, John? Jesus Christ! This guy could clear your cases," Tom stated, placing his hand on John's forearm as if to plead with him.

"I'm sure," answered John resolutely.

They stepped back into the small interview room. The deputies, standing behind the prisoner, did not leave this time.

John remained standing as he asked, "Why do you waste my time, Grimes?"

"What the fuck you talking about, *Sheriff?*" barked Grimes, boldly drawing out the title to demonstrate it was distasteful to speak the word.

"You're lying to me. I don't have any more time for you. I suggest you tell Sheriff Brown about the woman down here. Tell him how a big man like you likes to hit women! But don't waste any more of my time," John stated, revealing his contempt as he looked down, reaching for his notepad on the table.

For a tall man Grimes moved with fluid, lightning speed. John, off guard, was totally unprepared for the crushing blow to his left temple by Grimes' large flashing fist coming quickly and powerfully, plunging John into unconsciousness before he hit the floor. Sheriff Brown and the deputies lunged toward the prisoner. Going down himself, Grimes managed a violent kick with the toe of his heavy black boot into John's rib cage. Although he appeared lifeless, John gasped involuntarily as the air was knocked from his lungs. Later it was determined that the kick cracked two ribs.

Tom Brown rode Grimes to the floor, but with powerful arms, the prisoner tossed the Tennessee sheriff off like a rag doll. As Grimes turned his head toward the door, a deputy swung his lead-filled night stick with full force, following through like a major leaguer at Wrigley Field. The blow smashed into the temple of William Houser Grimes as blood spurted from his ear. The big man, now with a punctured ear drum and major concussion, was violently knocked sideways. Then his heavy body collapsed in a heap, his front teeth shattering from the impact as his face smashed into the floor. Blood shot, projectile like, from his lips and tongue, both bitten deeply by broken, jagged teeth. Now he, too, lay unconscious and bloody beside John Woodward, each floating in his personal state of unconsciousness.

The doctor who responded to the sheriff's office found John semiconscious. He could tell right away that the sheriff suffered a concussion, cracked or broken ribs, and possibly a fractured forearm.

Within the hour Sheriff Brown filed four charges against Grimes for assaulting a peace officer; attempted murder of a peace officer; assault with intent to kill; and attempted escape. Counts were filed against the prisoner for both sheriffs and both deputies, but that complaint was of little consequence. The next morning word came that the woman Grimes had assaulted died during the night. She passed away in the same hospital one floor above the ward where her attacker and the Sheriff from Washington County lay in their respective beds.

Although John insisted otherwise, the doctors kept him in the hospital for two days. On Tuesday afternoon Press arrived to meet with his doctor and to accompany his friend home the next morning. Press soon learned that Harold Kane had arrived in town the day before, but he did not go to the hospital to see John; he was there for the other part of the story, to learn about the suspect in the murders. Kent interviewed the Sheriff of Sullivan County about the assault and appeared most sympathetic about John Woodward, according to Sheriff Brown. Press and John winced when they visualized what Kent might write.

Grimes remained in the hospital, suffering a serious concussion, tingling in his legs, and pain in his lower back. His mouth, a mess, would never be the same, and he would have double vision for months. Upon reflection, in his crafty, streetwise way, he could not understand a sheriff who did not jump to save his own ass, but he had misjudged John Woodward. Before his interview, while boasting of his plot, Grimes bragged to his cell mates that he would get a well-known defense attorney, Brett Grant, to represent him. One prisoner recognized the name as the lawyer any guilty man should retain to craft a defense based on their lies to him and the doubt he would create. With Grant in their corner many guilty predators arrogantly walked away from the Washington County Courthouse as free men before celebrating across the street in the toughest tavern in town, The Knot Hole. Neither Grimes nor his cell mates had a way to know that not enough money existed on earth to retain Brett Grant as a defense attorney again.

On the ride home John, still suffering from a searing headache, briefed Press about his interview with William Houser Grimes. His left arm would be in a sling for three weeks, and his ribs bound tightly for a month. Usually John Woodward visualized himself as a much younger man. This gray November afternoon and his battered condition made him feel every bit of his fifty-two years. As the N&W train glided into the station at Abingdon, he leaned toward the window. The first person he saw was Kathleen Woodward standing on the platform. Holding her hand above her brow to keep the cinders out of her eyes, she leaned eagerly toward the train. As he looked at the figure caught inadvertently in a sweet salute, a welcome home, he felt a sliver of shame. How could he have thought so little for so long about the one person who meant the most in the world to him? For the moment John forgot his headache and the case.

The Thursday edition of *The Virginian* attacked the sheriff and mayor for not keeping the town advised of developments in the case. Mayor Wilson quickly left the sheriff's camp as John and Press admitted they were wrong not to advise him of the trip, explaining it was inadvertent on their part.

In *The Virginian* the sheriff was not treated sympathetically; rather, he was portrayed as an incompetent, bumbling fool who was attacked by a prisoner in jail because of his failure to ensure that he had adequate and proper security. The tone was mean-spirited, and those who inherently disliked law enforcement took delight in the treatment.

Murph Murphy, the owner of the Knot Hole, seldom read anything, but when he was told about the piece, he quickly bought a paper. Murphy, a criminal himself, laughed as he passed the paper among patrons. "Shit," he bellowed gleefully, "what kind of pussy sheriff do we got, anyway? He goes in the fuckin' jail, and the goddamn prisoner kicks *his* ass!" Murphy had no way to know that soon, he would have the opportunity to test the sheriff himself.

Chapter 21

Will West told his Western Union operator he would handle it himself, wondering why such information was not conveyed by a quick telephone call. Assuming that Georgia Wertz would be in nursing school, Will decided to call George to tell him about Georgia's telegram.

Frances Wertz gazed pensively out the studio window at the leafless trees standing stripped and barren, the substance of their true and elegant beauty silhouetted against the winter sky. Tomorrow would be her favorite holiday, Thanksgiving.

Moments before George announced, "Georgia has a telegraph from Bentley saying he can't come tomorrow, but don't let Georgia know we know. Will told me so we wouldn't worry until she opened the Western Union herself. I don't know why the boy didn't call her. The telegraph complicates much."

"Why do you suppose he's not coming?" she asked, draping her arms around him.

"I am not sure."

Standing in the fading afternoon light like two young lovers, George drifted back to Norfolk and Nancy Adams, a good and decent girl with whom he had not fallen in love. Was his soul warning him, alerting him that Georgia was to Bentley what Nancy Adams had been to him?

Later, after reading the telegram, Georgia folded it and said nothing as her mother watched her from a respectful distance. Taking Georgia in her arms, Frances whispered, "It's okay, honey. We'll still have a nice Thanksgiving," she said softly.

"How do you know what it said, Momma?" asked Georgia remotely, looking over her mother's shoulder out the studio window.

"Your face told me that Bentley can't come tomorrow," answered Frances, not compromising her husband and Will West.

"It has to do with his work the next day," Georgia volunteered in a hollow voice.

"I'm sure it does, baby," responded the mother-in-law of Bentley Thompson.

* * * * *

When Bentley did not return until the second week of December, Georgia wrote to him several times. He responded with a single letter, explaining in flowing script that he had to work late the day before Thanksgiving and the day after; thus, he couldn't come. That was reasonable, yet her soul sensed Bentley drifting away. Her conscious mind told her Bentley's behavior was normal. He was, after all, her husband, and nothing would change that fact. Men had to make a living, she told herself.

Turning to her only confidante, Georgia wrote to Jean in Florida, unaware that her soul—not her brain—took control of the letters. She thought her words did not reveal she was frightened; yet, like single stones in a mosaic, they came together, forming a pattern that Jean quickly discerned. Georgia realized that now, since Jean knew all her secrets, she would not be critical of Bentley.

When Bentley arrived, Georgia was edgy with a single focus: They had no choice in the matter—at Christmas they would announce their secret marriage. Bentley agreed they should wait no longer.

Often as Georgia lay in light sleep in the dark hours just before the dawn, ghosts entered, parading—uninvited, but they arrived anyway. Some, the ghosts of her carefree past, came mocking and taunting. They laughed, knowing all her secrets now and how she had changed. Some unfolded the vast expanse of loneliness before her, ushering her forward, gleefully it seemed, further into darkness. Who were the new spirits? Were they from the future, smiling darkly as if they had a secret she would not learn from them, at least not yet?

During those fearful times, Georgia took refuge from the ghosts by thinking about her Grandmother Anna. Anna and Georgia had not inhabited the planet together for a single day, yet Georgia felt her love and the breath of her closeness. Taking on larger-than-life proportions in Georgia's mind, Anna gave her the comfort she could not seek from her mother. In her secret world of coping Georgia could bury her face in the mystical breast of Anna. Visualizing her grandmother she was not alone; and, too, Jean should be home soon.

* * * * *

A week before Christmas, Bentley had another idea. "Georgia, I've never asked a lot of you," he began, looking intently into the eyes of a girl who had allowed him to change her life. "But I have to ask you just one thing now. Just wait until New Year's Day to make the announcement. We can tell your parents on New Year's Eve, and, after all, we're only talking about a week longer."

"Wait another week, Bentley! Why? I can't wait another week!" she responded frantically.

"Here's why," the ultimate salesman began slowly, "we should wait just *one more week*. Beginning New Year's I get a week off. After we make the announcement, I should be by your side for the next several days. I can't do that after Christmas. I have to work the next day, but I can be with you on New Year's Eve and the following week. This is a time when we should be *together*. You shouldn't be alone. I *want* to be with you. Can't we wait one week?" Bentley did not remember his last proposition made at Stonewall the night they had sat beside before the fire, the night he had revealed his plan. Like that night, Georgia softly whispered, "Yes."

The next afternoon, Sunday, the day of good-byes, Bentley stood in the hallway of the Wertz home at the front door, poised before stepping outside into the cold December afternoon. Georgia wrapped her arms around his fashionable black overcoat and put her warm cheek against his. She turned slightly from her waist, twisting gently right, then left, as if rocking a child to sleep in the faint refrain of a distant lullaby. Pulling away to look into his eyes, she whispered, "Now I have to have it, Bentley."

"I'll bring the ring. I promise," he whispered.

Taking a step backward, she turned the collar of his overcoat up and pulled the lapels closer together. "Keep bundled up, my love. It's so cold outside. I hope you'll have time to warm up in the depot. The train will be so cold," she said softly, looking up through misty eyes.

"I'm okay. I'm fine, Georgia," answered Bentley Thompson, leaning forward to kiss his wife.

He withdrew slowly from the soft lingering kiss, but she pulled him back, whispering, "One more." They kissed again softly. Then he was gone.

* * * * *

On Christmas Eve Georgia asked her father to drive to St. Thomas for the service, breaking the family tradition of walking. Disregarding their ritual, her father readily agreed to drive, appreciating the fact that Georgia asserted herself enough to ask him because lately she acted apathetic about everything.

Perhaps it was her imagination, but walking toward their pew in St. Thomas, Georgia felt that all eyes fell upon her. Jean's parents, their own daughter absent, sat waiting. The church, as was traditional, was lighted only by ivory-colored candles. She gazed at the red poinsettias adorning both sides of the elegant altar, bathed in soft candlelight. Long green garlands with sticky brown pine cones, draped throughout the church, emitted the subtle aroma of white pine.

As the procession moved slowly down the aisle, she saw the night not for what it was, but for what it could have been. It was not shaped by those around her, but by those absent. It was cast not by what she had come to be, but by what she *used* to be. She remembered the same night the year before, that happy, elegant night when she, Bentley, and Jean sat on the same pew, kneeled on the same kneeler, and took Holy Communion from the same cup. Now both were absent. A year had passed, a year profound in the changes it ushered in, but like the sound of the bell once tolled, she could not bring it back. If she had learned anything, it was that time cannot be captured and reshaped by what is understood after its passing.

Georgia was relieved when Father Dunn took the pulpit and began his sermon, weaving it around the theme of the Christ child. God, he said, chose to move not through force, but through the humility and the love of a child, a baby born in a stable. He noted that every person in the church was blessed by having earthly parents. Then he asked all present, especially the parents, if they could imagine a gift greater than the love they possessed for their children, suggesting that through such love, they could but glimpse the love God had for them. That God, he reminded them, is the same God who allowed His own son to be sacrificed for their sins. Imagine such a sacrifice if you possibly could, he asked.

Georgia, unable to absorb any more, involuntarily entered a state where she simply existed in a void with no conscious thought, moving through the rest of the service emotionally detached until she knelt for Holy Communion. Then she prayed desperately for forgiveness and for renewal. She asked for strength, and she asked to be uplifted. Rising from her knees like an older woman, she grasped the communion rail to pull herself up. Now she walked back to her pew alone, remembering vividly how proud she was last year when she left the same communion rail on the arm of the handsome and dashing Bentley Thompson. She wondered how many in the church would come to understand, accept, and forgive what she had done. She had no way to know then that all of them, every single one, would come to know, but few would understand.

Chapter 22

As the year turned from 1909 into 1910, Jean devoured every word in *The Virginian*, mailed each week. She searched through the new 1910 edition for the announcement of Georgia's marriage to Bentley Thompson, finding nothing. By mid-January Jean had not heard from her cousin since before New Year's. While waiting frantically for any word of the marriage announcement, she could not write to her own parents to ask. Jean's well-paying job at a fashionable hotel was conditioned upon her staying until the end of April when the tourist season subsided; so with deep concern, she wrote Georgia, explaining that she could not come home until April. When that letter went unanswered, Jean sensed that something was dreadfully wrong, but what could have happened? Surely Jean's parents would tell her if they knew anything. If the announcement were *not* made, Georgia must be frantic! Jean could not imagine how that could be possible.

Remarkably the sojourn had done for Jean precisely what her parents wished: She was over William Webb and had come to realize that what she thought of as love was but a flawed infatuation and misdirected passion. She realized too that she was living an illusion, a prolonged vacation in a fairyland that was not her home, not the place she was destined to inhabit, at least at that time. Jean could not bring herself to feel anything for any of the young men, even those with handsome looks from families with wealth.

More than any other emotion, she felt grave concern about Georgia. It was not like her to leave Jean out of anything. Jean prayed that Georgia was all right. She wasn't.

* * * * *

Bentley did not come on New Year's Eve, and he failed to call or write. Georgia, stunned, unable to grasp the reality of the situation, was humiliated; but nevertheless, she mustered the courage and called his shop, asking to speak to him in a quivering voice. Bentley was off for several days, explained a man revealing nothing more. Her message was simple: "Please tell Bentley to call Georgia right away." She considered calling her cousins in Bristol to ask if they could find Bentley, but she could not bring herself to ask, so she wrote a letter to her husband. Letters were incredibly slow, yet she had no choice. She wrote pleading for him to first call right away, then to come to her as soon as he could get there. When both letters went unanswered, Georgia's fear turned into panic. Frantically she wanted to call his parents, but she had no number for them, and the information operator failed to locate a listing.

Georgia's thoughts raced forth in rapid succession. *Why, my God, why? Why didn't he come? Why doesn't he call?* Something was dreadfully wrong. She loved Bentley deeply, but that love pulled her into the terror of abandonment. Bentley knew the true nature of their relationship, they were husband and wife and more, but that fact no longer consoled her. Lovers might abandon lovers, but husbands should not fail to come to wives in time of need. *Where is my husband? Oh, dear God, what could be wrong?* she asked God and herself over and over, her chant falling into a haunting mantra.

Soon Georgia withdrew to her room and refused to come out.

Her parents, shaken and bewildered by the entire series of events, begged to be let in, but Georgia refused, her faint voice barely audible behind the heavy oak door. Defeated, alone and afraid, she did not open the door except to creep to the bathroom in the middle of the night or the very early morning, avoiding contact with her parents.

Frances became frantic after Georgia remained in her room for two days. She left meals outside the locked door, but little of the food was removed. Only the liquids were gone. She called Stonewall to say that Georgia was ill, that she would return to classes soon.

Desperate, Frances called Press Smith who listened to the story with a mildly quizzical expression. When Frances finished, Press asked not about Georgia, but about Bentley Thompson. When George explained that nobody could reach Bentley, the doctor said, "I think I'd try to find him." Then he offered to examine Georgia, whom he had ushered into the world, if she would allow it.

Frances knocked gently on the door, and getting no response, called, "Georgia, Dr. Smith is here. Will you see him? Will you let Dr. Smith see you?"

Response came in the faint voice of a stranger. "No, Momma," was all that would be heard that day from Georgia Thompson.

Before leaving, Press explained, "These young girls can get very emotional. Sometimes you just have to let them go through whatever is bothering them. I suspect she and her boyfriend have parted ways. That can take a heavy toll on a young girl sometimes, especially if it's the boy's idea. I thought those two would wind up getting married, and they may yet." Pausing at the front door he offered, "Let me know if you need me for anything. I don't think you will. She'll probably come out when she gets hungry enough."

On the way home Press wrestled with a nagging feeling that the situation might be worse than he had portrayed to Frances and George Wertz.

The next day in mid-afternoon Frances removed an untouched plate from Georgia's door. *The glass of ice water must be inside her room*, she assumed. She tapped the door and called softly, "Georgia?" but there was no response.

At five o'clock the winter darkness had already fallen, as Frances, deeply troubled, stood alone, preparing dinner. Her effort was but a ritual, as she knew well that neither she nor George would eat the meal; but, hopefully, she thought, Georgia would take some soup.

The scream, piercing the silence in the darkened house, assaulting her senses, plunged Frances into abject terror. Starting again, with a low, primitive gurgle, the volume soared upward quickly, racing into a high, frenzied octave before falling to silence again. Frances stood, paralyzed in fear, instinctively holding her breath, her heart racing frantically, when another scream erupted, releasing her from her state of paralysis. Bolting from the kitchen she grabbed the banister, jerking herself forward, skipping steps like a young girl.

Reaching the door, she wrenched the knob violently, but it was locked! In her response, instinctual and primal, she stepped back, then lunged forward into the hard oak door with her shoulder and upper arm. As the door burst open, Frances stumbled forward, desperately trying not to fall.

She gazed in horror on the prone body of what appeared to be a stranger as Georgia lay on her back, a gray flannel night gown, soaked with sweat, clinging to her swollen, bloated stomach. Terrified by the explosive entry, she jerked up from the bed with wide fearful eyes fixed on her mother. Her stark white knees were raised toward the ceiling and slightly parted as her heels dug downward into the rumpled sheet. Tangled, matted hair, moist with sweat, framed her face accentuating its sickly pallor.

Unable to fully absorb the incomprehensible sight, Frances fell to the floor on her knees beside the low bed. "My God! Georgia!" she uttered barley audibly.

Georgia, breathing rapidly, hyperventilating and gasping for air, uttered, "The baby! The baby's coming!" as she reached out instinctively toward her mother.

In a speck of infinity Frances grasped it all: the horrible, inexplicable sight of her daughter's swollen stomach, the undeniable shape of pregnancy; but how could that be? An eerie calmness fell upon her, as she leaned forward, asking softly, "Georgia, how is this possible?"

"Married Bentley, Momma, got married at Easter . . . Good Friday . . . Johnson City," gasped Georgia as her eyes slowly closed.

Frances, hardly believing her own ears and eyes, controlled her compulsion to ask her daughter how in the name of God she could have hidden her pregnancy. Leaning forward, she uttered, "I've gotta go call Dr. Smith."

Georgia's eyes closed slowly as if she were starting to relax, after hearing the comforting words spoken by the greatest soother of her life. "Momma," the ancient word came faintly, pushed out again with shallow breath.

"Yes, I'm here, baby!" Frances whispered again.

"Bentley . . ." she faintly uttered through slightly parted lips.

"Yes, yes! What about him?" Frances urged.

"Bentley and I . . . married . . . . Call him . . . . Tell him to come . . . to please come," whispered Georgia slowly as her voice faded into unconsciousness.

Frances raced back downstairs to the phone mounted on the wall in the hallway, where she cranked the code for Dr. Smith. It seemed an eternity until finally the faint greeting of a nurse crackled over the line. Frances's voice telegraphed her fear as she asked to speak with Dr. Smith.

"Hello? This is Press Smith."

"Press! It's Frances Wertz! You've got to come quickly! Georgia's very sick! You can't wait! Oh, Press, please!" Frances pleaded.

"Frances! Hold on a minute! Tell me what's the matter?" Press yelled.

"She's having a baby!" Frances uttered.

"I see. I'll be right there," Press responded in a comforting monotone devoid of surprise.

Frances whirled around from the phone toward the foot of the stairs just as the front door opened to reveal the tall, slender figure of George Wertz. Suddenly she felt the release of overpowering physical and emotional stress as she fell sideways, hitting the wall before she crumbled onto the hallway floor into the oblivion of unconsciousness.

Frances, opening her eyes, found herself in her husband's arms, and with extraordinary clarity, she told him the awful truth. He sat on the floor and gasped. "Pregnant? No! No! It cannot be! How could she . . . She shows nothing! We would have seen! We would have seen!" George stammered, his words faltering out with a noticeable German accent.

Holding his face with both hands as if he were a child whose attention she demanded, she answered, "I don't know either! I must get back upstairs! You wait on Press!"

As Frances climbed the stairs, George stared up, fighting the urge to race to Georgia's side, but he could not do that now. He could have a few minutes ago, but not now. The intimacy of what he was told and the new feminine dimension and mystery of his daughter kept him at bay. Now it was his turn to view her as a stranger - not his little girl, but an unknown woman, an unknown woman who occupied the room upstairs. It had nothing to do with love. He loved her no less. Actually in her state of need, he loved her more. It had to do with her feminine mystique, an enigma to him.

Neither George nor Frances knew that while they had been in church, their Georgia and Bentley explored the sweet essence of their love on Sunday mornings of summer, but now, the drama that began on a rainy night in Lent was about to unfold, and it would wait for no one. When the doorbell rang, Francis cried down, "It's Press!"

Press carried his familiar black bag, the one he used when he treated Georgia for measles and chicken pox and other childhood diseases. Frances ushered him past George up the stairs, where they approached Georgia's open door.

Frances sat silently as Doc Smith examined her daughter who was partially conscious. His expression was serious, his concentration fixed on the form before him. Her temperature, he said, was over one hundred and three. It would have to come down, so he dispatched Frances for cold towels. As Frances bathed Georgia's face and arms, she regained consciousness. Dr. Smith asked Georgia if she had experienced bleeding or pain before. She answered yes to both questions, and when he asked how often, she said for the last two days only.

For the first time Frances noticed two corsets on a chair near the bed. *My God,* she thought, *she used those corsets to hide her shape! She must have been so desperate, so very, very desperate!*

After Doc Smith finished his examination, he gave Georgia a sedative to allow undisturbed sleep. Gathering his instruments, he nodded at Frances. She understood; that motion meant *we've got to talk.*

Frances poured each a cup of coffee as the three sat at the kitchen table bathed in the dim overhead light. The doctor had seen other women hide their pregnancies before, he related, although usually not as long as Georgia. She was close to delivery, and while the baby would be born soon, he did not think it would be this night. Some women remain small during pregnancy and have normal babies. Press was worried because to hide her secret, Georgia had strapped herself with corsets, especially during the latter months. That pushed the baby inward and restricted its movement, which was dangerous for the unborn child and for Georgia. He could hear the baby's heartbeat; it sounded normal, yet he was prudently concerned about Georgia and the baby. She was obviously suffering from anemia and had gone without prenatal care. He told them that some women did not see a doctor at all during their pregnancies. A lot of mountain women, for example, routinely got no prenatal care.

None of his comments made them feel better; yet they were greatly relieved just to get the information, just to *know,* to *understand,* even if remotely. Press cautioned, his voice soft, but unequivocal, that Georgia and the baby were in significant danger. He could not predict how things would go. If her temperature, now dropping, shot up again, they were to bathe her in cold towels and call him immediately. She must stay in bed. They were to allow her to get up only to go to the toilet. He would monitor her closely.

"We can wait," Press said, standing up from the kitchen table, "and we can pray." He believed in the power of prayer, but the suggestion also relieved him of some of the incredible pressure he felt in such cases. He used the suggestion sparingly, only under the appropriate circumstances. This was one.

Reaching the front door, Press stopped and said, "George if I were you, I would get Bentley up here. He needs to be here for several reasons. Foremost, though, he might make Georgia better."

George looked at his friend through Germanic tears, some of which spilled out at the corners, leaving his cheekbones moist and shiny where he had wiped them away with his shirt sleeve. He could not speak, so he nodded.

Speaking for both, Frances responded, "We'll get the boy up here, Press. He'll want to be here when he hears how she is. I know he will. I don't like what he's done, what *they've* done, but he's a good boy. And Press, before you go . . ." she choked, fighting to maintain composure, "we can't thank you enough. I don't know what we would do without you. You brought Georgia into the world . . ."

Putting his hand on hers, Press squeezed it slightly as he nodded and stepped through the door. Frances and George stood in the hallway, clinging to each other with no words to speak.

* * * * *

The faint winter light of dawn shined through Georgia's upstairs bedroom window, bathing it in a patch of soft illumination on the floor in front of her small walnut spool bed. Forms in the room began to take shape as the predawn darkness evaporated in the early morning light. She awakened slowly, opening her eyes to see the ceiling as she lay on her back, the most comfortable position. Her fever was gone. For the first time in days, her head seemed clear. She felt an immense sense of relief. Her parents knew! They finally knew! The deception of more than nine months was over! It was done, the truth was revealed, a great part of her emotional ordeal was over; but, as she lay there thinking, her temporary relief was fleeting. *Where is Bentley? Why, oh God, why doesn't he come?* she asked herself, again and again.

Sensing another presence close to her, Georgia slowly turned her head to the side to find her mother asleep in a rocking chair beside the bed. She sensed that her mother spent the night in the chair and that she must be deeply and profoundly troubled.

Frances slowly opened her eyes, looking directly into Georgia's gaze. Without speaking, she moved to the bed, cradling her daughter in her arms. Neither spoke as both drifted in and out of sleep.

Later when Frances got up to fix breakfast for her daughter, she found George, shoulders stooping, at the kitchen table, staring into a cup of black coffee. She gently touched his arm then quietly suggested that it would be a good time for him to go up and be with Georgia alone.

When he knocked gently with the knuckle of one finger, she answered, "Come in, Daddy." George walked in slowly, hesitantly, now feeling awkward, as if he were entering a sacred place, a sanctuary reserved for the mysteries of womanhood. Frances's words had not prepared him for what he encountered. He was deeply shocked seeing the drawn, pale figure, the love of his life. Her stomach, hidden under the covers nevertheless had the form he recognized from so long ago.

Reaching the bed, he leaned forward and kissed her forehead. She reached outward, touching his arms gently with her long, slender fingers. In that act, in that graceful moment with its simple elegance, they reunited. Their hearts and their souls spoke. In that act they transcended the awful fear, the need to ask for forgiveness, and the act of granting it as George sat down in the rocker.

She spoke first as he sat silent, listening intently, holding her warm hand. In a voice surprisingly confident for the circumstances, Georgia told him everything, beginning with the rationale for getting married. She could not, however, explain Bentley's absence; yet, confident in his love, she believed there must be a reasonable explanation. As a matter of fact she was very worried about Bentley and had been praying for him and his safety.

As Georgia lay silently, her mother entered with a tray of hot oatmeal and cream, Georgia's favorite childhood breakfast. Standing up, George looked into Frances' eyes as she attempted a tearful smile, conveying that she understood. Leaving the women to be alone together, he walked silently from the room.

Georgia could not look at the breakfast until she talked with her mother again to provide details of her marriage. Like George had, Frances sat in silence, listening intently without interruption. Georgia told the story to her mother differently, relating how she had fallen deeply in love with the handsome and charming Bentley Thompson. She described vividly the night he proposed, the shop where Bentley worked and where for the first time she first said yes.

Frances saw Georgia growing weaker, but she could not bring herself to interrupt, as Georgia related the night by the fire when Bentley first presented his plan for their secret marriage. Burning with shame, she told about the deception of the trip to visit Bentley's parents, and provided details of the marriage ceremony. Georgia pointed out that they had waited until they were man and wife before they were intimate. Her face grew flushed as she continued, noting she must have gotten pregnant on her honeymoon. Assuming that her turbulent emotional state had caused her to miss her periods, she discounted them at first.

Georgia did not mention the marriage license, but she spoke about the ring Bentley would bring. She could not articulate the indescribable conflict, feeling torn between her obligation to her husband, who had begged her to keep the secret until the last minute, and her desire to tell her parents. Frances understood Georgia's deference to her husband, something a married woman should do.

Press arrived a short while later, finding Georgia's blood pressure dangerously low, her pulse rate elevated, and her fever well past one hundred and two. He told Frances and George their daughter should get all the rest possible, noting he would return at lunchtime.

At nine o'clock George insisted upon calling Bentley's shop in Bristol himself. Frances understood that he was *compelled* to do *something—anything!* With surprising clarity, George heard the man answer the phone, "Simpson's Clothiers."

"Bentley Thompson, please," George yelled, his heart beating wildly.

"He'll be in this afternoon," was the response in a pleasant voice.

"Be there when?" shouted George.

"At one. At one o'clock this afternoon," the man answered.

"When he comes, please tell him to call Georgia Wertz in Abingdon. Tell him it's an emergency!" pleaded Bentley's father-in-law.

"Wait a minute. Georgia . . . Wertz . . ." the voice on the phone responded slowly as if he were writing the message. "Okay, I got it. I'll tell him."

"Thank you! Thank you very much," George yelled with obvious relief, at least for the moment.

George turned to Frances, explaining, "He'll be in at one this afternoon."

Turning to him, revealing her fright, Frances proposed, "Why don't we have Kate's boys go by the shop to tell him to get up here as fast as he can?"

"Yes," he agreed.

Frances called Kate Benson as George pressed close to hear one side of the conversation. Kate would arrange everything.

Later Frances notified her other sister so Jean's parents knew the surreal situation. Unconsciously the focus of familial concern was shifting from Georgia Thompson to Bentley Thompson, but no one consciously perceived that transition. No one realized that Bentley, not Georgia, was taking center stage. Georgia had no way to know or understand the bitter irony of it all, as she once again deferred to her Bentley.

Chapter 23

"Where has your beloved gone, of fairest among women?
Which way has your beloved turned, that we may seek him with you?"

Song of Solomon 6:1

P ress Smith arrived a little past noon the next day to find Georgia's condition unchanged as she drifted in and out of sleep. He explained that it was critical for her to get rest and be immobile. He suspected there was but one thing to help her fragile emotional state—the presence of her husband, Bentley Thompson. He told her frantic parents he would stop later in the afternoon on his way home.

Frances, with swollen, red eyes, announced that she would make the call to the shop in Bristol at one o'clock even though her sister Kate was working on the other end.

A peasant male voice answered, "Simpson's."

"May I speak to Bentley Thompson, please," she asked.

"This is Bentley."

"Bentley!" Frances gasped.

"Yes, ma'am," he answered.

"Bentley! This is Mrs. Wertz. We know everything! We know you all are married! It's all right. Now, you've got to come because Georgia needs you. She's very, very sick, and she'll have the baby any moment! You must come!" she pleaded. When she paused, there was silence on the other end. "Bentley, are you there?" she cried.

"Yes, ma'am. I'll take the train this afternoon. Gets up there about six," he responded soberly.

"Oh, thank God! A little after six," breathed the desperate mother.

"Yes, ma'am, I'll be there a little after six," Bentley confirmed, then added, "Good-bye, Mrs. Wertz."

"Good-bye, Bentley," Frances breathed into the black mouthpiece, but Bentley Thompson didn't hear her because he had already hung up. "He'll be here on the train at six," she said, looking into George's eyes, which were locked intently on hers.

Sitting by Georgia's bed all afternoon, Frances watched her daughter move from the groggy fogs of half sleep and meandering words into moments of clarity. In mid-afternoon, Georgia stirred and whispered, "Momma," faintly.

"Yes, baby," Frances answered, springing from the rocker to the side of the small spool bed.

"If the baby is a boy, we'll name him Bentley . . . . If she's a girl, we'll name her Christy,"

"What a beautiful name, Georgia," whispered her mother. "Where did you get the name Christy?" But her question went unanswered as Georgia fell back onto the abyss of medication and fatigue.

Doc Smith called around three to say that he would be delayed. He was told that Bentley would be in at six o'clock. "Glad to hear it. He needs to be here," said the doctor tersely.

After speaking to George Wertz, Press called John Woodward to tell him that Bentley would arrive on the six o'clock train.

The sheriff paused several moments, then spoke, "There's something I don't like about this."

"What is it?" Press asked.

"I don't know exactly, but something's not right," John Woodward confided to his friend.

"Do me a favor. Meet Bentley at the station to get him to George's house as quickly as possible?"

"Sure. Be glad to," John answered, but after reflection, he decided meeting Bentley at the station and escorting him to the Wertz residence would be heavy handed. John decided to ask Will West to meet Bentley and take him to the Wertz home. That plan should deliver Bentley Thompson to his wife the quickest way but with little fanfare.

At three minutes until six, railroad time, Number Forty-Two roared into Abingdon ahead of schedule. Will and John moved in unison like two dancers on the cold, windswept platform, both turning, each clutching the brim of his hat. The passenger coaches came to a halt in front of the platform as Frederick Price ran past them with several other haulers pulling empty freight wagons. While the other workers noticed the sheriff and their boss, Price took the most interest, pondering, *Now just what are they up to?* Assuming John Woodward would make an arrest, Price was confused when they watched the coaches unload and then walked away. He did not know that they were there to meet Bentley Thompson who did not arrive on Number Forty-Two.

Fifteen minutes later John stood in the January darkness on the front porch, telling George Wertz that Bentley was not on Forty-Two. They fell into silence for a few moments as if George were having difficulty absorbing the message. As if to remind him of the penetrating coldness, John reached out his leather glove, gently touching George's long arm. The photographer nodded slightly, acknowledging the subtle gesture of affection, and moved slowly back inside.

They did not know they were watched from across the street by Jamie, who wondered why the sheriff and Mr. Wertz stood talking under the front porch light. Walking back inside to tell Frances, it occurred to George for the first time that all in the town would come to know about their daughter. All, though, would learn that she married before she got pregnant; after that fleeting thought, only Georgia occupied his mind.

In late afternoon, Frances could not wake Georgia from her lingering sleep long enough to get her to take soup. Earlier Georgia asked several times about Bentley. "*When?*" she whispered, "When will he get here?"

"Soon, soon, baby," Frances answered each time.

At eight o'clock, just before Doc Smith came, she asked her mother, "Momma, is Bentley here?"

"Not yet, Georgia. Not yet, baby. He's coming, though," Frances whispered again to her daughter.

"Momma?" she uttered softly, eyes closed.

"Yes, Georgia?" answered Frances, leaning forward.

"When he gets here, will you tell me before he walks upstairs so I can comb my hair?" she asked faintly.

"I will, Georgia. I'll tell you," promised Frances, her heart heavy with doubt.

The previous night at five o'clock, Kate had told her sons about their cousin. They were stunned, speechless. All were in a state of denial that Georgia was pregnant and sick, dismayed that Bentley was not at her side.

Minutes later the brothers entered Simpson's Clothiers as John cautioned, "If Bentley's here, don't say a word until we get him aside. We don't want to talk to him in front of anybody."

John explained to Mr. Simpson that they were there because of a family emergency. Mr. Simpson related that Bentley left the store just after one o'clock due to illness in *his* family. Bentley told him that he had to go to Johnson City and that he would call on Monday to advise when he would return to work.

Thirty minutes later Newt knocked loudly several times on the dark front porch of the home where Bentley rented a room. Finally the front porch light flashed on as a stooped, gray-haired woman cracked her door open. Appearing to be in her mid-eighties, she was relieved to see two nicely dressed young men. John stepped forward to introduce the two of them. "Well, yes, I see, it's nice to know you boys," she responded. She explained she had not seen Bentley since earlier in the afternoon, when he left with a suitcase. When John asked if they could see his room, the old woman was a bit confused. "See his room?" she repeated slowly.

"Yes, ma'am, he's our cousin. We need to check to see if he left something there for us," blurted Newt.

"Left something?" she said, still befuddled.

"Yes, ma'am. He was supposed to leave something there for us!" answered Newt again.

"What was it?" she asked, staring into Newt's intense eyes.

"A Bible," he answered confidently, as John glanced at him in surprise.

"A Bible! Well, I guess that's all right then. Come on in," answered the woman, opening the door. "Bentley's such a nice boy," she muttered.

"Yes, ma'am, he is," agreed John, stepping inside the dark house where both were assaulted with the musky smell of old age, dust, and mildew. They followed the old woman dressed in a heavy felt robe as she slowly climbed the stairs.

Opening the door and ambling into the middle of the darkened room, she raised a weathered hand in the direction of a cord hanging from the ceiling light. With a unique deftness, the humped figure made a graceful, sweeping ark in the dark until her hand met the cord, jerking the room into harsh illumination.

It was bare; Bentley had fled. Newt and John walked about, desperately looking for any clue to his whereabouts. Newt opened each drawer in a tall mahogany chest-of-drawers as John looked in the nightstand. Newt yanked open a trunk, then moved the large walnut wardrobe, which was empty.

Bentley's bed, rumpled and unmade, was the way he had left it that morning. In a gesture of frustration, Newton tossed the top quilt to the side. Both saw it at the same time, and both glanced toward the old woman! Luckily, she was poking in the closet. Newt snatched the envelope, slipping it into his overcoat pocket.

John thanked the old woman and patiently followed her downstairs, where they said good-bye. Reaching the streetlight, John extended an open hand toward Newt, who, with no protest, obediently handed the letter to his older brother. The envelope bore Bentley's name clearly penned in Georgia's script. John read the single-page letter and handed it to Newt. Newt read it twice as if trying to comprehend the words, then returned it to John. "We gonna tell anybody?" Newt asked almost apologetically.

"Not yet," John stated emphatically.

"What about Momma?" Newt pressed.

"Not gonna tell her either. Not gonna tell anybody yet," said John firmly. Uncharacteristically Newt fell silent as both realized there was no more they could do that night. Tomorrow they would take the train to Johnson City to search for Bentley.

After ten o'clock Press Smith wearily pulled himself up by the banister rail toward Frances Wertz standing on the landing. Stooped with age and fatigue, the doctor lumbered slowly into Georgia's room, disappointed at what he found. Her vital signs were weak, and although he had stopped the medication, she still drifted in and out of consciousness. There was little he could do at the moment. Press, understanding his limitations, exhausted from delivering a baby in the country, said wearily that he would return tomorrow.

During the night Frances dozed in the rocker. Her sister, Martha Deaton, present all day, urged her to go to bed for a while, but Frances refused. Martha understood and chose simply to stay nearby, always available. George slept in his clothes downstairs on the day bed. Frank Deaton went home for the night.

"Momma?" came the weak voice in the darkness at three in the morning.

"Yes baby," whispered Frances quickly, springing forward from her chair in the dim glow of a nightlight on the dresser.

"Bentley hasn't come yet." Georgia spoke with a clarity she had not possessed all day.

"No, Georgia, he's not here yet," whispered her mother, leaning across the bed again.

"When he gets here, get my ring from Bentley if I'm asleep," Georgia requested, asking her mother to slip the ring on her finger. She wanted to wear the ring when her baby arrived. This early morning there would be no ghosts to visit Georgia, no dark spirits to parade, and taunt, and beckon her forward. When she fell asleep again, her lips held the traces of a smile. Frances stroked her hair for a few moments before she fell into the rocker exhausted.

As daylight seeped through the window, Frances slept fitfully in the rocker but was awakened suddenly when Georgia bolted upright, eyes flashing wide and looking into hers. "Momma, I'm so wet!"

"It's okay, Georgia!" cried her mother, lifting the cover to look into the soaking bed. "Your water's broken! It will be over soon!"

Martha, hearing the excited voices, appeared behind Frances. "Shall I call Doc Smith?" she asked softly.

"Yes, yes, please. I'll stay with Georgia. Call Kate too. Tell her to come this morning!"

Examining Georgia, Press was pleasantly surprised to find she looked better than the night before. He said the baby would come soon, but not right away. He would summon Mrs. Pokey Hartley, the midwife, who would wait with them. Gently patting Georgia's long delicate hand, he assured her, "We're gonna get this thing over with today, little girl!" Georgia responded with a weak smile. There was, of course, no choice in this matter; her body had to give up the life it carried, and when that happened, Georgia would discard the singularity of her former being and take on a duality of woman and mother. She had no way to know that what was beginning would take more than a day.

Helen Thompson was a wiry woman of fifty-five whose thick graying hair framed a face that could still carry traces of youth and beauty if she were smiling; but she wasn't. Her face was wrenched into a scowl as she walked to her door at eleven o'clock in the morning in response to Newt's loud knocking. The curtain parted slightly as she peered out to see the two well-dressed young men standing on her front porch. Both watched as the door cracked slightly, but she did not speak.

Stepping forward, John asked, "Mrs. Thompson?"

"Yes. Who are you?"

"Mrs. Thompson, I'm John Benson, and this is my brother, Newton. We're friends of Bentley. Georgia Wertz from Abingdon —I know you have heard of her through Bentley —she's our cousin. We're looking for Bentley. It's very important that we talk to him as soon as possible," he explained in a tone that pleaded for cooperation.

"Bentley's not here," she said quickly, offering no more explanation.

"Where is he, Mrs. Thompson?" responded John.

"*Gone*, to Knoxville," she answered, emphasizing the first word.

"Knoxville? Where in Knoxville?" he asked, unable to hide bitter disappointment.

"All I know is that he has a college friend there who is very sick. It's his best friend. He was in an accident I think. Anyway, Bentley left for Knoxville. Said that he would let me know in a few days what was going on. I have no idea where he is or how to contact him."

There was no choice, so John Benson told Mrs. Thompson that he did not want to shock her, but she needed to know that Bentley had secretly married their cousin and was about to be a father. It was imperative, he explained, that they locate Bentley as soon as possible.

Her predictable response insisted there was a terrible mistake. Her Bentley would have told her everything, but, in any event, she had no way to reach him. She suggested that they contact his shop in Bristol, where Bentley was likely to turn up first. The door closed quickly, the deadbolt slamming into place.

Feeling helpless, each hoping the other had an answer, something that would renew their search for Bentley Thompson, the brothers stood on the porch in the January wind. Finally, resigned, John said, "Let's go. There's nothing more we can do here. We won't get any more from that woman. She probably doesn't know where he is herself."

Georgia's contractions started after lunch, growing more severe and frequent throughout the afternoon. Press Smith arrived and gave her a mild medication, hoping to induce labor. They could do nothing else, he said, but wait. At four-thirty a phone call came for Kate Benson. John related their experience with Bentley's mother. She relayed the story to Frances and Doc Smith outside of Georgia's hearing. As soon as she was through, Press called John Woodward, asking him to come to the Wertz home as soon as possible.

When John arrived, he and the doctor stood on the front porch as Press explained the situation to him. "The mother's lying," John quickly responded.

"You think so? What else can they do? What can they do to find Bentley?" asked the weary doctor.

"Remember, Press, she's lying," John began slowly. "If she said he went to Knoxville, then figure he went the other way. He probably came right through *here*. He probably went the opposite way, toward Richmond—not Knoxville. We should check the train station."

"The train station? Hundreds of people move through that station in Johnson City," said Press, looking up in the porch light toward John's grave face.

"Bentley didn't leave from Johnson City; I think he left from Bristol. He's been coming and going from Bristol for over two years now. They all probably know him there. I'll notify Tom Brown. He'll check for us as a courtesy."

Will West called John at the sheriff's office at seven-thirty, advising a telegram arrived from the Sheriff of Sullivan County, Tennessee. Will read the Western Union language: "Contacted N&W ticket agent today stop Ticket agent knows Thompson well stop Yesterday agent sold Thompson a one-way ticket to St. Augustine Florida stop Thompson left on Forty-two which passed through Abingdon at six PM. stop Train continued to Richmond where Thompson would have transferred south to Florida stop Advise if more assistance desired stop Thomas H. Brown, Jr., Sheriff, Sullivan County, Tennessee."

Arriving at the Wertz residence, John read the telegram to Press on the porch.

Looking up into the January night sky, Press lamented, "That's it, John. Bentley Thompson has run away."

"That's not all, Press," said his friend gravely.

"What do you mean?" asked the doctor, turning back toward his friend.

"He never married her, Press. We're gonna find that he never married Georgia," John uttered softly with a sigh of resignation in his voice.

"But they have a license! And there was a ceremony! And Georgia had a ring! They've told me! *Georgia* herself has told me . . ." blurted his friend.

"Press, the ceremony was a sham . . ." John began.

"What?" Press exclaimed.

"We've had a few around here, but in other areas there have been a rash of mock weddings. The *bride* thinks she married, but the whole thing is a sham, it's a mock wedding, not the real thing! They are usually performed as secret marriages for reasons you can imagine. The so-called bride is the victim," explained the sheriff.

"I can't believe it," whispered Press Smith, leaning his brow against his forearm, resting now on the side of the door.

"Press, think about it. If they were legally married, why would Bentley Thompson run away? I don't understand how he could run away from that sweet girl under any circumstances, but if he has, it's because the marriage was a mock ceremony!" opined the sheriff of Washington County.

Facing another unexpected burden, neither spoke. John would have marriage records checked, and he would attempt to identify the church, based on the description Georgia gave her mother.

As night fell Georgia grew weaker. Now in labor more than eight hours, she could not muster the strength to press the baby out, and her vital signs were dropping. Knowing she needed a break, Press asked Frances to leave the room. He would work with the midwife, who had delivered hundreds of babies.

Pokey Hartley, a portly and matronly woman of fifty-five, wore black. Her gray hair was wrenched back severely into a bun clearly exposing a plain face with small eyes, thin lips, and a tight little mouth. Frances perceived that the woman carried a judgmental air. Was she some fundamentalist who saw the world in clear terms of black and white, of good and evil? Was she prejudiced against Georgia? Had she decided that Georgia was sinful and that was that? Later when Frances asked Press about the midwife's faith, he answered, "Holy Roller. But she's a damn good midwife, the best in Washington County."

At four Georgia shrieked out again as she had several hours before. The sound turned from screaming to moaning. It wasn't the voice of a woman they heard now, but that of a little girl as Georgia uttered, "Oh God . . . oh God . . . please . . . please . . . help me . . . help me, God, ohhhhhh . . . please . . . please . . . "

Then, again, the early morning darkness fell silent.

When the sisters heard the faint cry of a baby a little after five, they were confused because they had not heard Georgia for over an hour. As the three exchanged glances, Martha clung to one of Frances' arms while Kate held the other.

As the door opened, the three sisters stepped forward to see the tired pale face of Press Smith. Rumpled and disheveled, his bloodstained white smock frightened them. His tired look was nevertheless intense as he spoke in a flat voice. "Frances, you have a baby granddaughter. I think the baby's gonna be okay." Frances stared into his face, her hands clasped tightly, knuckles white, sisters still holding her arms, as the doctor continued wearily, "Georgia had a real tough time. The baby didn't want to come, so she used all the energy she had, then some. There was bleeding, too much." Frances gasped, her sisters pressing into her from both sides. "I have to tell you," Doc continued, "her vital signs are very weak. It could go either way."

"You mean . . ." Frances whispered, unable to speak the words.

"I mean she's in danger," he said quietly.

"Of . . . of . . ." stammered Frances, eyes wide again, breath shallow.

"Yes, of dying," Press answered, forced to speak the unspeakable. "You can come in, after Pokey cleans up."

When the door next opened, a softer, gentler Pokey Hartley extended a bundle of blankets toward Frances, exposing the small, wrinkled, face of Christy Wertz Thompson with eyes squinted closed and a tiny clinched fist pressed against her crimson cheek.

Stepping back, looking into the demure face of the midwife as if she were seeing another person, Frances whispered, "Is she all right?"

"She's all right, she's fine. She's gonna be a healthy girl," said Pokey, handing Christy to her grandmother. Torn between seeing the baby, the miracle of her own flesh and blood, and going to Georgia, Frances stared at the tiny face. Then she turned, handing the baby to Kate before stepping inside the room.

Martha, relieved that Kate had the baby, ran downstairs to telephone Frank, who slept soundly but answered in a crisp voice as dawn broke. Martha spoke rapidly, "The baby's come! It's a girl. She's okay. But Georgia's bad. Go to Western Union. Send for Jean. She needs to get here as soon as she can!"

* * * * *

Doc Smith left the Wertz residence exhausted. He was getting too old for two difficult deliveries back to back, especially a dangerously prolonged process like Georgia's. When he got home, falling onto the bed with his clothes on, he was asleep in seconds.

Throughout the morning Georgia lapsed in and out of consciousness as Frances refused to leave her bed. George stood by the window, his back toward the distant Blue Ridge Mountains, now seemingly unremarkable with their hue gone and the ranges faded into browns and grays. Kate took charge of Christy. Telling her husband to gather their children and come to Abingdon on the afternoon train, she had called home. Their cousin, she said, "is mighty bad."

At three-thirty a rested Doc Smith examined Georgia. She remained unconscious, her ashen face lifeless. Press had difficulty finding a pulse, and Georgia's blood pressure was dangerously low. He did not have to tell George and Frances; they could see their daughter, and they saw his deeply troubled face. Standing slowly, looking first to Frances, then to George, Press said nothing as he slowly ambled toward the door. When he reached it, he turned, speaking softly, "I'll be downstairs. I'm not leaving until she comes out of this. Call me if you need anything." Frances nodded, attempting a weak smile of gratitude. George stared vacantly at the ashen face of his daughter.

Dusk was falling when Georgia stirred, and Frances moved quickly to the bedside. As she bent forward, turning her ear to daughter's dry lips, George put his hand on his wife's back.

Georgia's eyes stayed closed as she whispered, "Momma?"

"Yes, baby. I'm here," Frances said into Georgia's hair directly over her ear.

"Is Bentley here?" she asked faintly.

Frances, eyes flashing wide, knew George hadn't heard. Pressing her lips against Georgia's hot ear, she whispered, "Yes, he's here, baby! He's downstairs in the kitchen!" The only response was Georgia's faint breathing through her mouth. *Did she hear? Oh, dear God, did she hear my lie?* Francis pondered frantically.

As if to answer Frances's thoughts, Georgia uttered, "I knew he would come . . . and I have my ring."

Forty-Two arrived on schedule again, this time bringing Kate's family. When the doorbell rang at the Wertz residence, Joe Benson stood grim-faced. Beside him his daughter, Sarah, once a passing interest of Bentley Thompson, clung tightly to his arm. Behind his father and sister, Newton stood beside John, both staring blankly ahead. Across the street outside the glow of the streetlight, the black sentinel maintained his solitary post. He was not walking much this night. He knew Georgia was gravely ill, and so did most of the people of the town. When he saw the Bensons filing onto the front porch, pausing at the door, he assumed they were family, thinking, *Miss Georgia must be mighty bad.*

After eight o'clock in the evening, Frances was back in the rocker as George sat nearby leaning forward, his forearms resting on long, angular thighs. The rest of the family, respecting the intimacy of the vigil, remained at a proper distance. George stared blankly toward the foot of the bed, thinking how quickly things changed. Frances rested her head on the back of the rocker with her eyes shut. Suddenly she stirred, and her eyes popped open wide as she leaped to the side of the bed. Stretching across the frail body to touch Georgia's face, she uttered, "Georgia?" Detecting no breathing, she screamed, "Geor-gia!"

Running into the room, Press first lifted Georgia's pale wrist, checking her pulse. Eyes vacant, expression noncommittal, he released her wrist and leaned forward with a cold stethoscope, searching for her heartbeat. He moved to her long delicate neck that wore the necklaces of summer, pressing his fingers below her ear. Frances clutched her hands tightly, pushing both hard against her lips, as George, standing behind, squeezed her upper arms. Finally, Press stood, looking into the two frantic faces staring back in terrified disbelief. He shook his head slowly, placing his warm hand on Frances' arm.

"She's gone," he whispered. Turning wearily he closed her eyelids, which had drifted open for the last time.

* * * * *

No one in the house remembered it was a month from Christmas Day, January 25, 1910. George and Frances retreated, broken and defeated, to their room. Jean was moving north at the moment on a train toward Richmond, where she would transfer and travel into the Blue Ridge Mountains of Southwest Virginia.

Christy's delicate foothold in her new world could not be ignored in the face of devastating grief. Checking her a final time, Press looked up at Kate and smiled wearily. The baby was all right, at least for the moment.

As the day changed again, family members found their way to spaces where they would pass the remainder of the night. Sarah went home with Martha and Frank because there was not enough room for her to sleep at the Wertz house.

At one-thirty in the morning John Benson walked into the kitchen with the envelope from Bentley's room in his hand. He studied the controlled, flowing letters Georgia had penned on the envelope, staring at her name on the return address, "Georgia Wertz Thompson." Moving slowly to the stove, he lifted the round iron eye, exposing softly glowing lumps of coal, partially laden with grayish white ashes. "I'm going to read it one last time for you, Georgia," he spoke, barely audible. Slowly he unfolded the letter and read

1/19/10

My Dearest Bentley,

    I know now that you will not come to me, that I will never again see your beloved face. I do not know why you have deserted me, but never doubt that I forgive you. I still love you with all that is me. I release you, my Love. Always remember my messages. Look at Psalm 87, v. 7. I will love you forever.

Your Georgia

John returned the letter to its envelope, then slipped it through the hole in the oven, where it fell on the smoldering coals face up. For a few moments nothing happened, but soon the sides began to crinkle and turn brown as a flame came to life on the right side, the side opposite the script forming the name Georgia Wertz Thompson. As the envelope's corners turned inward, the flame danced across its face, engulfing the honest, flowing letters that formed "Mr. Bentley Thompson" and raced toward "Georgia Wertz Thompson."

A small flame erupted. Then it was gone.

Soon John found a Bible and opened it under the dim arc of the kitchen light. Sitting where the whole mystery had begun to unravel for Frances Wertz days before, he turned the pages to Psalm 87, Verse 7:

*"Singers and dancers alike will say,
'All my springs are in you.'"*

John turned the light out and found his way to the day bed in the parlor where Newton lay sleeping on the floor. Soon John fell asleep without thinking how the world had changed. He did not look out to see it, none of them did, but the faint outline of a pale new moon could be seen in the eastern sky as dawn faded and gave way to the new day.

165

Chapter 24

Awakening the next morning as the crushing pain and lingering disbelief buffeted her consciousness like March winds whipping the Blue Ridge, Frances instinctively felt for George. He was gone. *Where could he be?* she thought. It was seven, but the house was quiet. Opening their bedroom door, she smelled strong, rich coffee, so she knew Kate was up. Frances paused at Georgia's door, consumed with dread as she entered slowly.

George sat in the rocker beside the bed where Georgia lay on her back. Their daughter's face was peaceful but now grayish white. George gazed toward the window, his vacant eyes seeing nothing. He stood as Frances moved into his arms. "How long have you been up here?" she whispered.

"All night. I didn't want her to be by herself," he whispered.

* * * * *

The gunmetal-gray day was bitterly cold as the winds of the Blue Ridge gathered strength, gliding across the icy crystals of the snow-capped peaks of White Top and Mount Rogers. Shrieking and whistling, they whirled themselves earthward through barren, leafless forests, toward the tiny hamlet of Damascus below. Rushing above the beds of trout streams, the draft blew froth from the tumbling, frigid water onto ice-encrusted banks. The intensity of the winds was relentless as they hit the hollows, wailing before emerging from the steep hills of the knobs, moving across fallow fields and bare meadows toward the middle fork of the Holston River. Reaching Abingdon, they carried the crisp pure smell of the mountains, but none of the inhabitants noticed. For the few brave souls who ventured outside, it was impossible to think of anything but getting relief from the bitter cold and the relentless assault of the wailing wind.

The driver and his helper were no exceptions as they sat high on the seat atop the black funeral hearse, bundled in heavy coats and hats. Coming for Georgia, the handsome team of powerful black horses, draped with shiny black harnesses with polished brass, dipping their heads low into the gale, pulled the hearse up Valley Street toward the Wertz residence.

As the men entered the house and climbed the steps, Frances fought to control herself. She didn't want them to touch Georgia! She didn't want these two men, these strangers, to take her baby away. Even now, after all that had passed, even in death, Georgia seemed vulnerable. George and Kate held Frances as she cried too deeply, too profoundly, to be heard. Then it was done. Georgia was gone. Putting her in the ground would be easier than releasing her from the house this last time.

The world had changed again. This was the first day in twenty-one years that Georgia Wertz Thompson did not inhabit the earth; but that fact, unknown to most, affected only a few broken souls. For the rest of mankind, except for others who had lost love ones, life went on as usual. One man, now tasked with a significant and delicate responsibility, was only a few blocks away.

The Reverend Joe Dunn sat in the office of St. Thomas Episcopal Church planning the sermon he would deliver at Georgia's funeral the following day. He had preached difficult sermons, but this strange and unexpected death, this bewildering tragedy, called for a delicate approach—especially against the background of the inexplicable murders. Joe realized Georgia's death as well as her life would have to be addressed in an honest way as he prayed for insight and for grace to pull it off.

After reflecting about the tragic murders of the other young women, he focused on the subject of loss. In those cases unspeakable evil wrenched lives away in a dreadful way. This death was different. It occurred to him that the others died quickly. Georgia, however, had suffered longer. She must have lived those last several months in her own agony, isolated, humiliated, and afraid, and her physical suffering, her labor, lasted more than a day. He kept returning to the same unavoidable conclusion: In the end, Georgia and the young women were alike—dead, wrenched from this life, each because of the actions of a man. The murder victims died at the hands of an unknown predator. Georgia died because of an act in which she knowingly and actively participated; yet she was betrayed in an evil way, and that betrayal resulted in her death just as the vile actions of the unknown killer caused the deaths of his victims.

Bentley Thompson, knowing Georgia's condition, had not come to her. Surely, Joe concluded, Bentley would have come *if* they were actually married. So the priest, knowing about the prevalence of mock marriages, made an assumption: The marriage was a sham; otherwise, why would Bentley desert her? Georgia's youthful judgment was flawed by the blindness of first love, but her act of creating the child, based upon what she believed, was without sin. Bentley, the enigma, through acts of commission and omission, gave Joe reason to contemplate.

* * * * *

When a deputy told Sheriff Tom Brown that Sheriff Woodward had called, he quickly thought, *My God, I hope John hasn't had another murder!*

When they spoke, Tom was relieved to learn no murder had occurred, but he was astounded that John called about the death of yet another young woman. John asked for an informal investigation in Johnson City as a personal favor because no criminal charges had been filed. He admitted prosecution was unlikely. After Tom agreed to assist in any way, John tasked his colleague with three important investigative leads. He asked to send the summarized results by Western Union. John wanted an official record. Oral communications would not suffice in this matter even if no case were ever opened, no prosecution ever undertaken.

Tom assured John he would commence that morning. A deputy would handle the assignment at the Court of Sullivan County, Tennessee. Tom would personally pursue the other two leads.

At six o'clock in the afternoon Will West called John, advising that a telegram had arrived from the Tennessee sheriff. Ten minutes later John stood near the potbelly stove, carefully reading the telegram. Again he placed the telegraph operator under strict orders not to reveal the message's contents. Now John knew that his suspicions, informed by experience, were well founded. No marriage license was on file in the county clerk's office for Bentley Thompson and Georgia Wertz.

Tom Brown found the church based upon the information John relayed, but it was not an Episcopal church; rather, it was a Lutheran church on the outskirts of the downtown area.

The priest, Father Wendell Warfield, remembered making the church available for a wedding rehearsal late on Good Friday. He had been told the wedding party from out of town could not get together at any other time; the actual ceremony was to be the next day at an Episcopal church that was unavailable for rehearsal. No, the Lutheran priest had not met the Episcopal priest from out of town. Father Warfield was positive that no ceremony took place because he would have required the names of those involved to be entered into his parish records.

The priest could not remember the name of the wedding party, and his calendar, filled with commitments, had no notation. Checking his daily journal, however, he found the last entry that date, scribbled quickly in pencil and barely legible: Thompson rehearsal party 9 P.M.

John, impressed with the response from his associate, was still disappointed to learn that no information was developed on the witnesses and the alleged priest. Because no official investigation had been initiated, John could not ask his friend to conduct further inquiry.

* * * * *

Sheriff John Woodward had no way to know that in the passing of years the truth would be revealed. Twenty-two years later the nervous young man who had portrayed the priest would come forward at age forty-two. He would have a daughter, and his journey would be in the stormy, turbulent waters of midlife, where he concluded that his voyage could go no further without a major midlife course correction and only the truth would free him to make the correction.

Deeply shamed, he would admit his part in the dark deception of Georgia Wertz. He would make no excuses, yet he would describe himself at that time as "another person, somebody I no longer know." He would identify the other two men as King College friends of Bentley Thompson. One, he would explain, ultimately died on the fields of France during the World War. The other he had not known before the stormy Good Friday night. He had seen the man a few times in passing but never to speak to him after that dark night in the spring storm of Johnson City.

Since that day, he would say, he had never again laid eyes on Bentley Thompson. When the repentant man would come forward, it would be without fanfare. He would not go to the authorities to set the record straight; rather, he would quietly and humbly seek out a beautiful young woman of twenty-one, one whose lineage went back to the Black Forest of Bavaria. He would tell her that he had participated in the charade, the simulated marriage ceremony of her mother and Bentley Thompson. Like her mother, Christy Wertz Thompson would be a beautiful young woman who would hold the man in her gaze with pale green eyes; unlike Georgia, however, Christy would receive the message angrily and defiantly. "I hope old Bentley Thompson rots in hell," Christy would say in flashing anger, a mantra she would repeat throughout her life.

* * * * *

At the moment, January 26, 1910, John had enough information to confirm that Bentley Thompson deceived Georgia Wertz into believing she legally married him. He would inform Press and Father Dunn. Later, at the right time, he would gently inform George and Frances. With their permission, he would later go to Harold Kane. Kane would devour the facts, seemingly unbelievable, but facts nevertheless, and the story was one that should be told.

At three-thirty Robert Bradley, the grim-faced undertaker rang the bell at the Wertz residence, bringing Georgia home for the last time. Frances and George hovered near as Bradley arranged the coffin in the parlor. Stepping forward hesitantly as the lid was opened, they saw their daughter's face appear. Although they now looked at her in death, they saw that she had regained some of her girlish beauty, appearing peaceful at last. Clinging to each other, they remained alone with her for a time. Their deep and abiding intimacy along with their faith provided the strength to get them through the nightmare.

The endless stream of visitors continued until after dark, when Jean arrived, escorted by Will West in the Norfolk and Western carriage. As Jean and Frances embraced tears burst forth from a deep well Frances had thought was dry. Moving to his niece with outstretched arms, George's mind flashed back to the hundreds of photographs he had taken of Georgia and Jean, visually stirring images of understated beauty. Other pictures were spontaneous and frivolous, like the picture of Georgia with the chicken, the first image Bentley Thompson saw of Georgia Wertz. Only Bentley would have remembered that it was on a Sunday afternoon in a spring that now seemed so long ago.

After Jean asked to be alone with Georgia, she stood in the dimly lit room where Georgia's face in death only suggested the beauty she had radiated in life. Drawing closer, Jean leaned over the casket to kiss Georgia's cold, white cheek adorned with an oval of pink rouge. Jean, incapable and intolerant of sentimentality, rubbed her cousin's cheeks, softening and spreading the color. After all, it was she who first applied lip tint and rouge years before for a grinning, girlish Georgia.

Now, feeling only relief for her cousin, Jean reached into her overcoat pocket to find the small box. She removed the gold wedding band and pressed it to her slightly parted lips. It was the wedding ring the wild William Webb gave her that summer night she would remember for the rest of her life. She had never tried it on, but it easily slid onto her finger. After a few seconds, Jean pulled the ring from her own finger and reached into the coffin to lift Georgia's cold hand. It was a perfect fit for Georgia's slender finger, as if it were made for her. Knowing that she was gone with the essence that was Georgia, soon Jean walked away from the body. She went to find Frances to ask to see Christy Wertz Thompson.

Moments later Jamie watched from across the street as Kathleen and John Woodward stepped from the front porch and walked to their carriage. Remembering Press's prediction as they rode home, John reminded Kathleen that the doctor had speculated that another young woman would be dead by the end of January if the pattern of the unknown killer did not change. "But who would have thought this? Who would have dreamed that Georgia Wertz would die?" John asked his wife.

* * * * *

The next morning at eleven o'clock the St. Thomas Episcopal Church overflowed, so many people gathered outside in the bright January sunlight. The day, unlike the one before, was bright and unseasonably warm.

Bentley knew neither that his sweetheart had passed through the veil of life nor that he had a daughter, Christy Wertz Thompson. He would later learn from his mother, who would send him a clipped article from *The Virginian*, that dying Georgia had called for him. Many close to Georgia would never forgive him, carrying to their graves absolute contempt for Bentley Thompson. So would one who would never lay eyes on him—his daughter, Christy.

Father Joe Dunn, thankful for the elegant *Book of Common Prayer*, knew the inevitable time had come as he climbed into the pulpit and began. "In the book of John in the second chapter we are introduced to Jesus' first public act, his first miracle. Do you remember what it was and where it occurred? It was at a wedding in Cana of Galilee." After recounting the story, he concluded, "Clearly Jesus bestowed his blessing on that marriage and, as well, on the state of matrimony. This simple and happy story endorses God's celebration of the act of love—in this case, romantic love. Jesus blessed the marriage in part by a generous increase of wine. It is noteworthy that he began his ministry by endorsing love and marriage.

"We have heard other scripture read today, and it should bring us comfort although I know clearly that at this moment words alone will not be enough. But please allow me to share from the Apocryphal Book of Solomon: 'The upright, though death comes before expected, will find rest. Length of days is not what makes life meaningful, nor number of years the true measure of life. Understanding, that is the goal of life. A caring life, this is better than ripe old age.'

"Although a young woman, Georgia had a unique understanding and deep caring for others. The poet notes that some leaves first are gold but cannot remain so forever in 'Nothing Gold Can Stay'."

'Nature's first green is gold,
Her hardest hue to hold.
Her early leaf's a flower
But only so an hour.
Then leaf subsides to leaf.
So Eden sank to grief,
So dawn goes down to day.
Nothing gold can stay.'

"I had the privilege to know Georgia Thompson all of her short life. I know her character, and I know her devotion to God, and I know her capacity to love. In her heart of hearts, and in her soul, and in the eyes of God, Georgia was married to Bentley Thompson. Let there be no doubt about that and the fact that at this moment she is in the loving arms of her God.

"This town has suffered losses of young women by wanton and inexplicable acts of violence, and we have all asked, 'Why?' When Georgia passed to the next realm, many again asked, 'Why? How could this happen?'

"I can only say that we are all vulnerable; we are all human; and we are all mortal. This life is not only precious but also fragile. We have no guarantees. We have only this day, this hour perhaps. In such times it is important that we don't lose our faith; rather, we turn to our faith and we pray." Soon Father Dunn finished, "In the name of the Father and of the Son and of the Holy Ghost, Amen."

Thirty minutes later he stood before the open grave of Georgia Wertz Thompson, thankful that Frances and George had a strong family support system. The bright and mild January day was changing; he felt the temperature dropping and braced himself against the rising wind.

Joe Dunn began to recite again from the *Book of Common Prayer*: "'I am the resurrection and the life,' said the Lord. 'He that believeth in me, though he were dead, yet shall he live and whosoever liveth and believeth in me, shall never die.'" After a few more words, he said, "We brought nothing into this world, and it is certain that we can carry nothing out. The Lord gave, and the Lord hath taken away; blessed be the Name of the Lord."

The service for The Burial of the Dead moved swiftly to a conclusion. As it did, the mourners heard the approaching sound of an eastbound train, the one that had so often brought Bentley to Georgia. Soon they heard the high-pitched whistle that moaned and wailed as the train passed through town before fading into the barren and bleak hills of the Blue Ridge.

Chapter 25

When Judge Harold Harris rebuked the editor of *The Virginian* for asking for a copy of the report from UVA, Kane contemplated returning with counsel to argue "the people's right to know." He considered retaining the fiery Brett Grant, having no way to know that Brett Grant was moving into a significant personal journey, a passage accelerated by the brutal murder of his sister, Vivian. Neither did Kane know that Grant and Joe Dunn continued weekly discussions, their meetings no longer adversarial, as Joe gradually became a fatherly mentor to Grant.

Brett, feeling as if he were beginning a recovery, suffered a setback when Georgia Thompson died. It seemed to him and to many others that the Wertz girl, "Thompson" now they all made an effort to say, had been alive and vibrant one day then suddenly the next, like his sister, dead.

The first night Brett discussed Georgia's death, he posed a question to the priest. How, he asked, was her death, in the final analysis, different from the others? After all, he pointed out, a man was responsible for all.

* * * * *

On an early April evening, John sat in his office with Press, opining, "It doesn't make sense to assume they were random victims. He didn't stumble into those women and impulsively attack them. He *had* to know that both were alone! He took his time at both crime scenes. He picked them out. We've agreed we believe he's an Organized Killer, and that's what an Organized Killer would do. That's what he's probably doing now, looking for his next victim."

"All right," responded Press with a sense of resignation, "What are we gonna do?"

After John explained his plan, the coroner, clearly not impressed, uttered, "Well, it can't hurt, John."

The next morning John would carefully make his selections. He would first call on Will West.

Sitting in the office of St. Thomas Episcopal Church, Joe Dunn was delighted as he studied the letter from Noel Eliot, Bishop of Southwest Virginia, who would come for several days to preach and conduct his annual confirmation. Dr. Eliot, a British academician before entering the ministry, thought Southwest Virginia was a bit of heaven.

* * * * *

An ageless enigma of nature is the attraction between the sexes, sometimes between two whose relationship seems to the rest of the world to be most unlikely. Often loneliness, the cousin of despair, weaves the tattered fabrics of two lives together. Loneliness and association explained why Helen Hansen became attracted to Frederick Price while working at Kit's Café. Price cooked only on weekends, and initially she felt intimidated by his coarseness, but Price treated her differently, never harshly like the others. He listened attentively as she talked quietly while waiting for closing time. He offered little about himself except to reveal that he had come to Abingdon from Richmond, where he learned to cook. Helen had never known anybody from as far away as Richmond, and few men, except drunks on Saturday nights, paid any attention to her. Price called himself Frederick, which impressed her. That name conveyed to the girl from the knobs a sense of refinement and taste. No male role models existed in her broken family to enable her to develop discretion, and Frederick Price was the only man in her life.

Helen now had a day job as a maid at Hotel Abingdon. As part of her meager compensation, she was given a room, never used otherwise, on the third floor of the hotel. She managed to save a little money from her two jobs, and, like a member of a diaspora, she often sent money to her impoverished family. Before leaving home, she had known several of the mountain boys intimately. That was three years before, and Helen had yet to be with a man.

One Saturday night after closing, Helen and Frederick climbed the back stairs of Hotel Abingdon carrying two glasses and an ice bucket. After several drinks, courtesy of Kit's Café, the two found their way to her small bed. Helen, embarrassed that Frederick would feel her pounding heart, was immensely relieved when he was gentle if awkward in his attempts to remove her clothes. Finally, she slipped from the bed to let her dress fall to the floor as the moonlight allowed Frederick to see her thin body and translucent underwear.

His large hands were soon exploring her body as she breathed heavily, but Frederick Price could not perform. Helen's fragile self-image insisted it was her fault that she was not desirable enough for the man. Suddenly Frederick yanked her upward, crashing her head into the bed frame so violently that she fell momentarily faint. Jerking her downward, Price rolled on top of her small body as she gasped then held her breath to endure the painful thrusting, but in a few seconds it was over.

Helen lay still, holding back sobs of pain and humiliation. Soon Frederick turned into another man, kissing her softly, breathing apologies, explaining he had not been with a woman for a long time. He ambled to the bathroom, returning with a cold washcloth. Without speaking she took it and pressed it to her forehead. Frederick softly kissed her good night, asking if he could see her again. She whispered yes, and when he was gone, she removed the cold cloth from her forehead and delicately placed it between her thin, bruised thighs.

The next day John Woodward executed his plan. Will West, the first candidate, was quickly recruited. John felt good about him but had reservations about the others. He had no way to know that his decision to solicit the help of Will would bring a pivotal point in both their lives.

Harold Kane wrote a lengthy article about the upcoming visit of Bishop Eliot. The bishop's impressive background was of particular interest to Brett Grant, who contacted Joe Dunn right away, requesting a short meeting with the learned scholar and bishop. Two days later, Brett sat alone with the bishop in the rector's office, explaining his ongoing journey of personal exploration and examination, which was predicated by the murder of his sister. Quickly he moved to what had become his mantra: "I don't think there can be any justification for the suffering and death of innocent people. The victims in the murder cases, and the Thompson girl, not one of them ever hurt anybody; yet they died for no good reason."

Brett paused, waiting for the bishop to respond and, becoming self-conscious, continued, "Let's take it a step further. Let's focus on the suffering and death of little children, innocent little *children*. Tell me, how could a just and loving God allow that? Finally, I'll say this: I believe *there is no justification,* and I don't like the kind of God I've come to believe God is."

"Actually, it does seem that God lets things get in one hell of a mess, as one would say, doesn't it?" began the Bishop of Southwestern Virginia. "I suppose at first one has to consider that he has a choice . . ."

"Excuse me, sir," interrupted Brett, intense eyes flashing, "but I've explored the free will defense of God, and it only takes me so far, then leaves me with yet another question: If He doesn't interfere with our free will, why do we pray?"

Noel Eliot smiled patiently, compassionately, and continued in a soft voice, "You've raised another excellent question, Mr. Grant, a hard question for anybody. I'm not sure I can answer it well, if at all, but actually I wasn't moving to the doctrine of free will. I was going to offer another thought first."

"Thank you, sir. I apologize for interrupting," Brett offered.

"First," the bishop said with a pause, "you have to kill the God of your childhood."

"Sir?"

"I said, first you have to kill the God of your childhood," confirmed the bishop.

"What does that mean?" pressed a confused Brett Grant.

"It means, simply, that one cannot ponder profound questions generated by events, sometimes tragic, in one's adult life, and look for answers from the happy Sunday School God of one's childhood."

* * * * *

On a warm spring night as Press Smith and John Woodward mused about the evolving political storm threatening to remove John from office, Press pointed out that many in the county had little concern for the murders. "If you're far enough down the food chain," he mused, "all you care about is getting by." He did not have to remind John that many inhabitants of the county lived bleak and colorless lives devoted mainly to harsh physical labor that eventually broke their bodies and their spirits. They were suspicious mountain people, many locked in the relentless grip of ignorance and poverty. John had ventured into their lives occasionally, usually because of a murder or a mysterious death; otherwise, few crimes were reported from the knobs. John understood that many suffered from incestuous inbreeding that dispatched erratic and mutated genes to haunt offspring for generation after hopeless generation. It was from that group that Doc Smith received a request.

The request was made by a lean mountain boy dressed in tattered clothes and riding bareback on a skinny black mule. At fifteen the boy was making his first visit to a doctor's office, where, in rudimentary English, he struggled to explain that his mother lay sick. She passed out the day before, he conveyed, but when she woke up she couldn't speak. The boy didn't know her age. Based on that limited information, Press suspected she had suffered a stroke. Finally he ascertained that the family lived in a holler near the north fork of the Holston River. Because he couldn't understand the boy's directions, he told the young man that he would follow him to the house in his buckboard.

An hour later Press drove his horse up a narrow and steep wagon path, moving slowly toward a dilapidated frame house hanging on the side of a nearly vertical hill rising precariously above a muddy, tumbling creek. Pulling his team to a halt, Press looked at a group of dirty, half-dressed children, a ragtag bunch with vacant, hopeless stares. Looking no more than a year apart in age, they appeared to range in age from about six or seven years old to their mid-teens. They gazed at him silently, suspiciously, with dark hollow eyes as Press intruded from the outside world. Stepping off the creaking buckboard, his black medical bag in hand, the doctor smiled at the children, but as he expected, it garnered no response. Approaching the house, Press saw a young woman standing in shadows inside the doorway, both hands defiantly planted on plump, fully rounded hips. Naomi Hess, who looked several years older than the boy, wore a black waitress dress stretched tightly around her stocky body. *She's been eating somewhere besides here,* he thought, knowing that no children of the knobs grew plump. Naomi's oval face, broad nose, and thin lips formed a mean mountain scowl framed by thin brown hair, matted with sweat at her temples. Her English was considerably better than her brother's as she spoke cryptically explaining that her mother was asleep. Doc could tend to her, Naomi said, but she had to go to work in town at the Knot Hole. Press knew well the rough tavern, owned and operated by Murph Murphy, where he regularly stitched torn flesh and set broken bones from barroom brawls.

Naomi stepped into the sunlight, revealing that one eye was puffy and bruised with deep crimson from ruptured blood vessels. A swollen cheek still carried the dark cast left there from the slap of a mean, open hand, but her neck and throat drew his interest. Upon closer scrutiny Press could make out the bruised outline of finger marks. "What in the hell happened to you?" he asked, understanding how to communicate with her.

"Some bastard tried to rape me the other night," she answered boldly.

"Well, *did* he rape you?" he questioned, still studying her bruised neck.

"Hell no, I kicked that son of a bitch in the nuts!" she shot back, dark eyes flashing belligerently.

"Did you report the attack to Sheriff Woodward?" Press asked, stepping closer to study her face and neck.

She eyed the doctor suspiciously with arms folded across her broad, flat chest, suggesting his question was absurd, then answered, "Naw."

"Why not?" asked the doctor.

"'Cause I ain't got no idea who the black bastard was!" she uttered with a mean sneer.

"He was a Negro? Are you sure?" asked Press, leaning forward in disbelief.

"Yeah, from Kings Mountain," she offered with a cynical half laugh.

"Where did the assault take place? Outside the Knot Hole?" Press asked, eyes narrowed subconsciously.

"Yeah," she answered, arms still folded across her broad upper body.

Press knew that no black inhabitants of the town went near the Knot Hole, where drunken mountaineers and other crude and violent men routinely threatened civility and safety. They had their own special places on Kings Mountain to drink and socialize. "You should report the incident to the sheriff," Press urged.

"He don't got time for the likes of me. He's too busy a trying to protect all the *soo ci ety* ladies. Course, he ain't doing that too good!" she laughed dryly. Then, without saying good-bye, Naomi Hess turned toward the main road. As he watched her walk away, he could not see her thick neck, but he knew that neck was recently choked. Normally that would be just another knobs story, but no longer as the shadow of the investigation intruded. Press entered the rickety mountain home realizing he needed to get back to John as soon as possible. The sheriff should know about the assault of Naomi Hess.

* * * * *

Frances and George Wertz found themselves abruptly retracing the steps of their early marriage, frightened once again by the baby in their charge. With sweet irony, they were rescued at least partially from their vast loss by the small bundle of life Georgia left behind. Christy was, after all, the bone of their bones and the flesh of their flesh so the child pushed them on with their lives. Like Georgia, Christy would come to call Frances Momma and George, the only father she would ever know, Poppa. Like Georgia, as she grew up, she and her friends would become the subjects of countless photographs taken in the Wertz Studio, where Christy would replace her mother as the beloved subject of the finely ground lenses of the Wertz cameras.

* * * * *

Before Press returned to town, the sheriff got a visit from Clarence Mitchell, a member of his secret cadre. Beginning with Will West, John carefully selected men he could trust to patrol their own neighborhoods in the evenings, alert for any man they thought did not belong there. Only their wives, who had to know why their husbands left each night, could be told of the secret operation.

Clarence Mitchell reported that he noticed something unusual as he patrolled his area on the west end of town. Frederick Price, he explained, lived with his parents not far from the tobacco warehouse near the railroad tracks. Clarence could not be sure, but he thought Price had taken unusual interest in him several times. In fact, Mitchell said, he believed that on one occasion after dark Price had shadowed him. He admitted apologetically that he could be wrong, but nevertheless he wanted to report it to the sheriff. John decided to talk to Will West, who should know as much as anybody about Frederick Price.

At that moment Will West stood watching passengers leave the train, looking for a professor of English literature from the University of Richmond. A handsome woman moved toward him, her white linen dress bright in the summer afternoon sunlight, which highlighted streaks of gray in her thick chestnut hair. "Dr. Shipley?" Will asked, removing his black western-style hat.

Surprised, she corrected, "I'm *Professor* Shipley, Susan Shipley."

"I'm Will West. I'm the Norfolk and Western station master," he explained easily, using his new title for the first time since his promotion following the retirement of his aging predecessor. "Dr. Clarke had a commitment so he asked me to help you to the hotel."

"Thank you so much," she replied.

Upon reaching the registration desk, Will advised, "Ask the clerk to call me when you're ready to go to the Whites', and I'll send a carriage for you." As Will walked away, the professor smiled slightly, thinking, *Nice touch.*

Walking back to the depot Will reflected. He was never able to convince his rigid predecessor that the operation badly needed an office manager. The old man steadfastly refused, forcing a large portion of the job on Will, which was too much for one man. The Norfolk and Western headquarters had not yet sent him an assistant station master, but Will had moved quickly to recruit an office manager. It was not easy to lure her away from the bank, where she was well paid, especially for a young woman. Eyebrows raised around town when he put a woman in the previously all-male environment. Will thought of Jeanette Moore and how she would have approved, as he convinced his boss that Jean Deaton was the most qualified person for the job.

From the start Jean, a smart and tireless worker, had a critical eye for details overlooked for so long. Because of her organizational skills, employees found their jobs easier as she gained their respect. The proud young woman exercised a no-nonsense temperament, one that tamed the wild William Webb at least for a while.

One railroad man concealed his interest in Jean, but otherwise, the man, Frederick Price, treated her as he treated most people, in a remote and detached way. She had no problem with that, and through her astute observation, Jean viewed Price as the best freight hauler at the depot.

Jean grew to respect Will West, although at first his handsome looks were a distraction, and like many women in the town, Jean was a bit taken by him. He was, she knew, a married man.

At five o'clock Will parked the Norfolk and Western carriage in front of Hotel Abingdon and walked inside, pleasantly surprising Susan Shipley. Moments later Will touched her elbow slightly as Susan climbed aboard to sit on the front seat.

Will held the team to a slow, casual pace as he and Susan spoke in pleasant generalities, the superficial language of newly introduced strangers. He was warm, and his demeanor devoid of flirtation. Will did not wear a wedding band, but she assumed he was married because he *acted* married. She mentioned reading about the murders in *The Virginian* mailed to her home. "Harold Kane hasn't been fair with the sheriff. I would think his articles not only inflame the readers but also divide the community into two camps, those supporting Sheriff Woodward and those against him," she offered as John stopped the carriage in front of the White residence.

During an elegant candlelit dinner the discussion turned to the murders. Natalie White, pleased to be sitting next to Susan, listened politely along with the others as her father pontificated at length, speaking with the authority of one possessing singular and sensitive information. He explained, for the benefit of Susan Shipley, that he and other members of the town council were "*extremely* disappointed in the failure of our sheriff." When he paused, she asked, "Why is the sheriff a failure?"

Arthur White, taken by surprise at Susan's question, smiled as if he were talking to a child. "Well, Susan," White began in a patronizing voice, "the sheriff has failed to solve the case, failed to identify and arrest the killer, failed to rid the community of a menace."

"What has he failed to do that he could have done or should have done?" asked Susan in her naturally pitched-low voice.

Arthur White leaned forward, the sleeves of his expensive jacket touching the white linen table cloth. "A basic tenet of management that I bring to my business and to the town council is the bottom line. In this case the bottom line is minus three: minus three young women now dead and gone." Several guests at the table stirred in their seats as he continued, "You see, Susan, in business, we have strict accountability, the bottom line. We don't care as much about efforts as results. While we want effectiveness and efficiency to be sure, what we demand is success. In this situation we don't want any more young women in the bloom of their lives, like my own Natalie, to lose their lives. That does seem reasonable, don't you think?"

"Of course that's reasonable," Susan responded, "but if the sheriff has done all that *he* reasonably can, and if for no failure on his part, he has not solved the case, are you suggesting that the proverbial baby should be thrown out with the bath water?" Before White could respond, she quickly added, "What if, for example, this killer is dead or what if he has fled to the West Coast? How reasonable, then, is it to get rid of the sheriff if he is a competent professional?"

"Susan may have something there, Arthur," offered a smiling Sidney Clarke. "I'm sure she doesn't know John Woodward from Adam, but her point makes sense. Doesn't it?"

"Of course it does," White began, forcing a tense smile. "Now, I ask that this is not repeated, but some community leaders have begun a recall drive to put the question to the voters. My guess is that John Woodward will not get a vote of confidence; my bet is that he will be recalled from office before summer's end."

At that moment the subject of speculation approached the front door of the Knot Hole. As John dismounted Thunder tossed his head and snorted. "I don't like this place either, old boy. You've got good taste," John said aloud to his beloved companion. Two weathered mountain men entering the tavern looked with furtive glances and overt, lingering sneers. One leaned back to stare befuddled at the highly polished English saddle. He nudged his companion as they laughed under their breaths. Patting Thunder's thick neck, John whispered, "Kick the hell out of anybody who tries to get close to you, old boy."

John was at a loss to understand. When Press told him about Naomi Hess, he intended to find her right away, but before he left his office, Murph Murphy called, asking him to come to the tavern. His previous visits were adversarial, sometimes ending in several arrests. Most citizens believed Murphy was the owner of the tavern, but John sensed that Murph was a front man only. The Knot Hole, he believed, was owned and bankrolled by a secret partnership even if Murphy's name appeared on the ownership papers. John suspected that Arthur White was a secret partner, lending personal money in covert competition with his bank. He also suspected the Honorable Harold Harris, who invariably rendered lenient sentences when Murphy was brought before him. "Live and let live," the judge once remarked after neighbors brought action against Murphy, charging his establishment as a public nuisance.

John had locked Murphy up in the past for selling stolen property out the back door along with bootleg whiskey. Murph had another untaxed income stream, generated from a business as old as the Tigris Euphrates River Valley. Common knowledge held that the "girls" who worked in his tavern were whores. They performed in the upstairs rooms over the saloon where drunken patrons paid for what they thought was pleasure. After continual harsh rebukes from Judge Harris and a string of petty fines, John stopped attempting to police the Murphy Girls.

Murph Murphy, fifty-five, balding, and rotund, resembled an older version of Frederick Price. His gray beard stubble was often moist around his mouth with foam from the warm beer. His small, pig-like eyes darted about, suggesting a quick mind. Vaseline Hair Tonic, used generously on his sparse hair, often washed down the sides of his face in trickling rivers of sweat. Murphy wore undershirts revealing muscular, tattooed arms. He was volatile when drinking, which was most of the time. Regulars knew he kept a pearl-handled .38-caliber revolver and a sawed-off shotgun under the bar but his weapon of choice was a blackjack, which he rendered with lightning speed to quell disturbances in his own way.

Murph had approved months before when he heard that the "high-class railroad feller" took things into his own hands at Kit's Café. The Knot Hole crowd allowed as how the "West feller 'Murphed' the college boys!" Murphy possessed an aversion to "the law," a term referring to any police officer. Murphy realized that John's deputies were afraid to come to the tavern, and when they did, it was always in pairs; but he knew from experience that the sheriff himself would come alone. Although he disliked John for being the law, Murph held a begrudging respect for the man. John had been tested many times, and following each encounter with the tall lawman, it was Murphy who suffered in some way. Now, for the first time, John responded to a complaint from Murph Murphy, fence, bootlegger, pimp, and Abingdon businessman.

After kissing Thunder below his left eye, John walked into the Knot Hole as the horse whined and whimpered. Murphy stood in a veil of cigar smoke behind the long wooden bar that ran the length of the room opposite the front door. Walking slowly toward the bar, John sensed the ambient noise drop and noticed that Murphy's watery eyes acknowledged his presence without the usual defiance. Murphy didn't speak but tilted his head sideways toward an office adjacent to the bar.

They stepped inside the small dingy office with a single cluttered desk and windowpanes gray from years of cigarette smoke and grime. A low-watt bulb extended from a cord in the ceiling. A spittoon half full of dark brown liquid, attracting flies, sat against one wall. As Murph stood by the desk without sitting down, John questioned, "What can I do for you, Murph?"

"Sheriff, you know goddamn full well that I ain't one to complain to no fuckin' lawman. Anyhow, when a man starts hurtin' my business, well, goddamn, it's time to do something! A man's gotta make a living, protect his business."

"Go on, Murph," said John, bemused.

"The point is, *Sheriff*, some dumb bastard done beat up my best girl *twice!*" snapped the portly barman.

"Which best girl?" asked a now deadly serious John Woodward.

"Naomi Hess, my best waitress," Murphy responded.

"Tell me about it, Murph," John requested, pulling a pad from his coat pocket.

"Well, let's see," Murph mused, looking down, "she got beat up bad one night last week—Tuesday night, I think. Anyhow, two nights ago, the same damn thing happened, only not as bad; but, shit, she done missed two days when I needed her fat ass in here. She's real good at gittin' the boys to buy more beer, and when she ain't here I lose money."

"Who did it?" asked John, eyes narrowed.

"Fuck, Sheriff! If I knew that, I wouldn't be a standin' here talkin' to you! I'd done handled it myself."

"What'd she tell you about it?" asked John, knowing Murphy's words were true.

"She don't say shit. That's what I don't understand," Murphy answered, then added quickly, "Or I do understand too."

"You don't understand; you do understand. Which is it?"

"Well, since she won't say who done it to her, I figure that bitch probably thinks she's in luv!" Murphy explained.

Typical whore mentality, John thought to himself. Then he ventured, "She told Doc Smith a Negro tried to rape her."

"Shit," Murph responded disdainfully.

"You don't think that's true?" asked John, incredulous himself.

"Hell no, it ain't the truth, Sheriff. Ain't no niggers come around here, 'cept that Jamie that passes all the time, but he don't count 'cause he's some fuckin nut, and she don't go where any niggers are at. So that's bullshit," opined the proprietor of the Knot Hole.

"Is she working now?" asked John.

"Yeah, and I told her to talk to you and tell you the goddamn truth!" answered Murphy.

"I never thought I'd see this day, Murph!" John said dryly.

"Me neither," responded Murphy, stepping toward the door, "I'm gonna send her in here."

John stood in the middle of the office as Naomi Hess strolled in. Not surprised by her abused appearance, John looked first at her neck, seeing barely visible marks as she assumed her bad girl knobs stance. Expecting defiance, he simply asked, "Who beat you up, Naomi?"

"Sheriff, I'm gonna tell ye that same thang I done told the boss man, it's none of your fuckin' business!" she answered, looking directly into his eyes.

"When somebody gets assaulted, it becomes my business, Naomi," John responded calmly.

"It ain't if I ain't pressin' no charges, and I ain't pressin' none!" she shot back.

Understanding her mentality as part hooker, part knobs girl, John knew it would be impossible to get information if he solely challenged her; yet if he showed what she perceived as weakness, it would likewise be fruitless. He critically needed to know who had assaulted her! Could it *possibly* be the killer? He had to elicit something from this belligerent mountain girl. He had to approach her in a balanced way. "Naomi," he began slowly in a monotone, "I know you don't want to rat on anybody. And I know that you can take care of yourself most of the time, but it's very possible that you're in danger."

"I'll be the judge of that, Sheriff," she answered, unflinching eyes still locked on his.

"Well, you can, Naomi, but let me give you something to help make that judgment. The killer who murdered three women left marks on their throats like those left on your neck."

"Thought the first one was rotted! How come you knowed about her?" challenged the belligerent Naomi her eyes narrowed, as the trace of a smile started to show at the corners of her thin lips. John realized that the murders had been tavern talk as well as parlor conversation.

"I misspoke, Naomi. Two of the women, the last two, had marks on their throats. You're right about the first girl; her body was decomposed," said John, realizing Naomi was a lively adversary, more of a challenge than he had imagined. He added, "But if she was killed like the second two, and right now I assume she was, she was choked too."

"Well, Sheriff, 'course I knowed who done this, but both times we was drunk and horsin' around, and I got my own licks in on him too. Wasn't nothin' but some tusslin'. You know what I'm talkin about, man-and-woman stuff," she explained to John's fascination.

At that moment the rotund form of Murph Murphy filled the door. Without looking at him, John maintained eye-to-eye contact with the young woman and said, "Naomi refuses to identify the man who beat her up so there's nothing I can do, Murph."

"What the fuck is wrong with you?" Murphy shouted at Naomi.

Ignoring her boss's question, Naomi turned toward John, answering, "'At's right, Sheriff. I ain't pressin' no goddamn charges. Now if the boss man don't want me a workin', I'll jes go home."

"Git the fuck outta here and go back to work!" yelled Murphy, jerking his head toward the barroom. Naomi, shooting a triumphant glance at John as she stepped by him, disappeared into the smoky room. "Well, ain't this a hell of a note! I call on the goddamn law like any honest citizen, and you don't do jack shit for me!" he said, turning his anger toward John.

"Let me explain, Murph. Even if I identify lover boy, she won't press charges. You know what that means. Got any suggestions?" asked John, still frustrated by the girl who just *might* possess critical information.

"No, I don't got suggestions; I got a question. Why the hell did I call you for?" asked a sneering Murphy.

"Listen to me, Murph," began Will, dropping his voice. "Do all you can to find out who beat her up. And if you do, I guarantee you I'll take him off the street without her complaint. I'll solve your problem and never involve you. Somebody *must* know who attacked her, maybe one of the other girls. Are you willing to help me help you?"

"Yeah, you got a deal, Sheriff," answered the unlikely cooperating citizen.

Chapter 26

On Thursday afternoon Susan Shipley called Colley Brothers Grocery to make a special order for a small gathering of women she would host in her suite. She requested the food from a person she assumed was writing down the involved order along with her instructions, but Eugene Johnson remembered each item and her requests without taking a note.

The next afternoon Johnson stood at the door to suite 212, where, holding the heavy bags, he knocked with the back of his hand, calling "Colley Brothers."

A pleasant Susan Shipley, opening the door, requested, "Please put them on that long table." Entering Eugene caught the refined smell of her subtle perfume and felt excited; yet, paradoxically, he was threatened too, and anger began to churn deeply inside as he left to gather the remainder of the order.

Blocks away, Doc Smith sat in the sheriff's office, sipping coffee with his friend. One part of Dr. Dietrich's report lingered in John's mind, which he read aloud to Press, "If you have conducted a significant number of interviews, you have probably interviewed the killer." They sat in silence for several minutes until John said, "If this recall does take me out of office, please make this point known to whoever becomes Sheriff."

"That's not gonna happen, John," Press answered, not confident that his words were true.

"I don't know, Press. I just don't know." John sighed in quiet resignation.

At three-thirty Natalie White walked down the second-floor corridor of Hotel Abingdon, looking for suite 212. For inexplicable reasons, she felt as if she were being watched. Seeing the gold numbers of the suite on the darkly stained door, she dismissed her intuition. As she knocked lightly, Natalie failed to see that the door was ajar at the end of the corridor under the "Exit" sign. The 212 suite door opened quickly as Susan stepped forward and embraced the younger woman. Soon they laughed, chatting easily, preparing for the reception.

On Friday Frederick Price failed to arrive at work. Because the Prices had no telephone, Will, unable to leave the office, asked Jean if she would drive out to check on Frederick, who was needed badly because the freight volume was heavy on Fridays.

"I'm Jean Deaton from the Express Office," she explained when the door opened, exposing a frail woman with gray hair. Her lined and weathered face suggested a woman who had lived a hard life, but her deep blue eyes were soft.

"Oh, you're from the Express Office where Freddy works. I see. You can come in if you want," offered Mrs. Price, opening the door.

Sitting on the edge of a worn fabric sofa, Jean explained to Mrs. Price that Frederick had not come to work. The older woman, clearly taken by Jean, exclaimed, "My, I didn't know women worked for the railroad." Jean smiled politely, nodding in the affirmative as Mrs. Price began an explanation. "Since Freddy divorced and moved back here, in with us temporary, he comes and goes as he pleases. He's a grown man. I don't ask him no questions anymore." Looking at Jean for a response, but getting none, she continued, "He didn't come home last night. That happens sometimes. He said one time that he sleeps in the Express Office when he don't come home. Freddy's a good boy, never been in no trouble 'cept when he was a youngster."

"Except when he was a youngster?" repeated Jean.

"Yes, you know, in Roanoke he got caught for peepin'," answered Mrs. Price in a matter-of-fact tone.

"Peeping?" asked Jean, not sure she had heard clearly.

"Yeah, you know, peepin'; peepin' in windows, like a Peepin' Tom. Well, he was peeping in windows. Then he started a silly prank, but you're not interested in all that," offered Mrs. Price.

"Yes, I am interested, Mrs. Price. I would love to hear about the silly prank," responded Jean.

"Well it wasn't much of nothin', just, for a prank, he sole stuff from clotheslines . . ."

"What kind of stuff?" interrupted Jean, her mind flashing back to the day that now seemed so long ago, the day when she and Georgia and Eliza laughed about the underwear stolen from Natalie White's clothesline. She could see Georgia's merry face and twinkling green eyes as Mrs. Price's voice yanked her back to the present.

"Well, actually it was undies. He was seventeen or eighteen, but that didn't keep his daddy from tannin' his hide! It taught him good—that and going to court," Mrs. Price reported, leaning back in her seat.

"He went to court?" questioned Jean softly.

"Yeah, they *convicted* him. Is that how you say it?" she asked, frowning slightly.

"He was convicted?" Jean pressed.

"Sure was. Poor thing. I felt sorry fer him, but I never told him that," she revealed.

"He was convicted of what, Mrs. Price?" asked Jean quietly again.

"Petty theft," said the older woman, clearly enjoying Jean's interest.

"What about the peeping? Was he charged with peeping?" Jean continued.

"That got dropped 'cause nobody could say it was Freddy," answered the older woman, her words quicker.

"Why?" Jean questioned, still confused.

"Cause Freddy was really kinda smart for a youngun," she responded proudly. "Well, what he done was, he wore this flower sack over his head, with little-bitty eye-holes cut out to see through. Nobody could say for sure it was him. Course, I knew cause later I found the mask, and he admitted it to his momma. He left home not long after that, and he's been gone ever since. That is, until he come home this time," explained Mrs. Price.

Jean's intuition told her to seek more information as she questioned, "Did he come here from Roanoke?"

"No, Richmond," responded his mother quickly.

"What did he do up there?" Jean questioned patiently.

"Well, mostly learned cookin', I guess. He works at Kit's on the weekends. He's a grand cook. Did you know that?" asked Mrs. Price, smiling broadly.

"Yes, I've heard that. Is he divorced?" asked Jean.

"Oh, yeah, Freddy is, but he don't have no younguns. Said he was gonna git him a good mountain girl this time. That city trash don't make good wives, you know," she answered.

"Who does he see?" Jean questioned.

"It's some girl who works in a tavern in town. I do know that," she answered, smiling again.

"Kit's Café?" Jean questioned.

"No, a tavern. Kit's is a fine café, ain't it?" asked Frederick's mother.

"Oh, yes. It sure is. Does his girlfriend work at the Knot Hole?" Jean responded.

"Yeah, that's it," exclaimed the woman, rocking back and forth, delighted in remembering the name. "I heard him a callin' up there, a asking fer some girl, but I can't remember her name," answered the woman.

"We tried to call out here, but we couldn't find a phone ring for you," Jean explained, confused.

"Used to be three shorts and a long, but they took the phone out. Freddy got mad a while back and hit the phone with his fist. Broke it up pretty bad. Anyhow, they done took the phone. Say we can git another one after Freddy pays for the one he busted up," explained Mrs. Price in tired resignation.

"I see," said Jean, smiling as if she understood. "Well, I should be getting back to the Express Office. I want to thank you for helping me. If Frederick comes home, please tell him we need him badly for the last train," Jean requested.

"I'll sure do that," Mrs. Price assured, standing and extending her hand.

"Thank you so much. I enjoyed talking with you, Mrs. Price," said Jean, shaking the older woman's hand.

"I enjoyed a talking to you too," responded Mrs. Price, standing on the weathered porch, watching with admiration as Jean climbed onto the carriage. Then smiling and nodding toward Mrs. Price, Jean charged the team forward toward the depot.

It was after four when Susan said good-bye to Natalie White, the last to leave. "I'll see you at dinner, Susan," said the girl as she stepped into the hallway.

As Natalie turned she thought she saw the door at the end of the hall close slightly. As she approached the landing, the unmistakable feeling of danger came upon her, the feeling she had the night she was chased, but she quickly skipped down steps until she reached the lobby. The young desk clerk watched her admiringly as she glided past in her feline way, wishing he could watch her cross the lobby again.

Susan, exhausted, lay on the large bed in her underclothes as the slowly turning oak blades of the ceiling fan sliced the heavy air. A soft, prickly electronic sound pulsated in concert with the circular motion, emitting its own sultry music in the fading summer light. Susan drifted away slowly as the street sounds below grew softer and softer until she thought she heard the sound of a door lock, a key turning slowly; yet she wasn't sure.

She heard it again, the cold, metallic sound of a lock clicking! Now she was awake! As her feet reached the warm floor, she thought, *Did the floor creak in the entry hall!*

Reaching quickly toward the lamp, she knocked it to the floor. Again she heard a sound, this time like a door closing, gently, covertly. Susan dashed to the wall, feeling frantically for the switch that illuminated the room, then raced to the lighted entry. There she saw the key lying on the entry hall stand and the deadbolt unlocked. Had she heard the door? she wondered. Had someone entered the suite? Had the falling lamp made the intruder leave?

Refusing to become a victim of her own fear, Susan dismissed those thoughts. After a tepid bath, she walked down to the lobby to await Arthur White.

Chapter 27

"A scoundrel and a villain goes around with crooked speech, winking the eyes, shuffling the feet, pointing the fingers, with perverted mind devising evil, continually sowing discord; on such a one calamity will descend suddenly; in a moment, damage beyond repair."

Proverbs 6: 12–15

E arlier in the afternoon before the reception started in suite 212 of Hotel Abingdon, Jean returned to the depot, where Will listened intently as she told about the strange meeting with Mrs. Price. Jean was surprised to see that he took notes from time to time, but he didn't interrupt until she finished. Leaning forward, his expression intense, Will asked, "Is that all? Are you sure there's nothing else?"

"That's all, everything she told me, every word," assured Jean confidently.

"If Price comes by, call me at John's office," he ordered, walking away before she could respond. Will wasn't sure what the information meant, if anything, but he wanted to relay it as quickly as possible to John Woodward. Like Jean, he sensed it could be important.

Ten minutes later Will arrived at John's office, where Thunder stood outside. He found John and Press in an intense discussion about John's encounter with Naomi Hess.

Jean's keen mind and attention to detail enabled Will to render a faithful version of the old woman's words. As Will spoke, he saw Press and John exchange surprised glances several times. When Will finished, John asked, "Is that everything, Will? Everything she told you?"

"That's it." confirmed Will.

"We need to find Price as soon as possible, but it looks like he may be out of pocket. He's not home, not at work, and not at the Knot Hole, at least not when I was there. While we're looking for him, I want another lead covered," John stated, gazing intently ahead. "This information about Richmond," John began, "there's a possibility Price was in the state prison there. That's probably where he learned to cook. Will, you have his background, his full name and his date of birth, right?" asked John.

"Right," Will responded.

"Send a telegraph with my name to the warden of the state prison. Ask if Price was in prison there, and get his criminal history if he has one," directed the sheriff.

"What else can I do, John?" asked Will.

"I realize you don't understand all that's going on here, Will," John began in a low voice, "but a lot of that information is significant, especially the part about the mask. The man who chased the White girl wore a mask. Stealing women's underwear is important too, but I don't have time to explain now." Looking from West to Doc Smith, John said, "Price *could be* the one who beat up the Hess girl."

"The Hess girl?" Will asked quickly, trying to follow the conversation.

John quickly explained about Naomi Hess, then continued, "Back to your question, Will. There is something more you can do. After you send the telegram, you can help my deputies and me look for Price. Do you have a weapon?"

"Yeah, I have a thirty-eight and a shotgun, but I prefer the shotgun," answered the station master. "I've been trained in Roanoke by the Northwest and Western Railroad Police. I keep the shotgun in my office because we have a lot of cash there. The shotgun is a twenty gauge and loaded with double ought-buck, each pellet the size of a thirty-eight round, and there's about eight or ten of them in each shell. I've had experience with the shotgun, and I know how to use it properly," Will explained to an interested coroner and an appreciative sheriff.

"Suit yourself, Will," said John, "I'll need to deputize you, and I'm telling you the same thing that I'll tell the deputies. We only want to *question* Frederick Price. Legally, there's nothing I could charge him with now. All I want now is to discuss the assault of Hess, but if he's on parole, he may be reluctant to talk about anything."

"John," Will offered, "you may be aware, Price is seeing Helen Hanson."

Eyes narrowed, John began, "I've heard about them before, but at the time, it had no significance. Now she's a logical lead to locate him." John didn't remind Press that the Dietrich paper said the killer might have a relationship with a woman. "Will," he began again, "you go send the telegraph. While you're doing that I'm going to pay a courtesy call on Mr. Murphy at the Knot Hole to see what he knows about Price and Naomi. Then we'll meet at my office, where I'll deputize you."

Approaching the Knot Hole, John leaned high across the English saddle to pat Thunder while talking to him, "Maybe we're getting close, old friend." He dismounted at the rail, where a dismal group of undernourished horses stood with sagging backs and sad, tired eyes. Flies hovered around their ears and peppered their quivering, runny nostrils. Thunder, standing untied with reins dangling toward the ground, jerked his head skyward several times, shrieking a high-pitched, elongated whine. "Okay! Okay! I'll be careful, old boy," John called, glancing back as he approached the door.

John Woodward walked into the Knot Hole, finding the noise elevated even for a Friday night, heightened by the cacophonous racket of an ancient mountain fiddler scratching out a Scottish Highland tune. Barmaids moved about the damp, smoky room, flirting and pushing groping hands away. Overhead two ceiling fans turned slowly, slicing through grayish yellow veils of Burley tobacco smoke and stale air smelling of sweaty denims and spilled beer

Scanning the vulgar crowd, John did not see Price as the noise subsided abruptly. He quickly checked the barmaids, standing in place with hateful scowls, but Naomi was notably absent. Slowly walking forward in his three-quarter–length coat, tie and western hat, John *looked* like a lawman moving toward the bar.

The room fell silent except for the mournful, off-key lament of the fiddler as the lawman approached Murph Murphy, who stared contemptuously through intense, pig-like eyes. Clearly drunk and obviously in a mean, defiant mood, Murphy would be unpredictable and dangerous, John knew.

"Murph," John said, nodding his head and smiling slightly.

"What's your problem, Sheriff?" growled the sweating Murphy, mild laughter rumbling from his personal theater of the absurd.

"Murph," John began in a low voice, "there isn't a problem . . ."

"The problem is that you come walkin' in here on the best goddamn night of the week, and you ain't never good for bizness, Sheriff," Murphy responded.

"Murph, step in your office, please. I have to talk to you, but I don't want to interrupt your business," John stated, hoping to salvage the moment, desperate to learn what Murphy knew about Frederick Price.

"I ain't going back in no fuckin' office!" snarled Murphy to the sounds of affirmation and laughter.

As each step of John's western boots was heard as he walked toward the bar, Murphy was unaware that in the eyes of John Woodward, he had just morphed from an annoying petty thug to a significant obstructionist involving the most important case of John's career, a case he viewed in terms of life and death. Every eye locked on John as he slowly lifted the hinged bar top and stepped behind the counter. Murphy tossed a heavy mug aside, yelling, "What the fuck do you think you're doing? Get the hell out from behind my bar!"

Murphy's eyes widened in the split second John lunged toward his dirty white shirt, his large hands thudding hard against Murphy's big chest, yanking so hard, that the back of the shirt split apart. Simultaneously John jerked the astonished, wild-eyed Murphy forward, causing him to stumble forward, vainly trying to keep his footing. With the grace of a Spanish matador, John stepped back, allowing the falling bull to pass and crash into a table of startled mountaineers. Rolling to his side with surprising athleticism, Murphy instinctively sheared the top off a beer bottle, creating a sharp weapon. The big man struggled to lift his heavy body as John's western boot struck hard, driving the heel into Murphy's broad upper chest, knocking him backwards. John's second kick removed the jagged bottle from Murphy's powerful fist, leaving him defeated, holding his swollen hand, blood spurting from a sizable cut.

"Get him up!" John shouted, causing several men to scramble to lift the heavy body of the Knot Hole proprietor. "Help him to the office," he ordered again. Three men, straining to keep Murphy on his feet, stumbled to the office. Once inside, Murphy collapsed in a seedy fabric chair, still holding his hand, which one of the men hastily wrapped in a dirty rag. Soon, the rag changed colors from gray to crimson as the men scurried from the office.

Still in the fight-or-flight stage, John kicked the door closed, ordering, "See Doc Smith about that hand. I'll pay for it."

"Fuck Smith, I see Webb," snorted the subdued bull.

"Okay, see Webb," responded the sheriff.

"I'm gonna have your goddamn job, Sheriff! I'll tell you something else: don't ever turn your back on me!" Murphy growled, wide eyes bulging.

"Murph, I'm going through this once. If you fail to cooperate, I'll lock you up right now, and then I'll close this public nuisance permanently."

"You'll never git it closed!" Murphy countered with a sneering smile, suggesting he knew something John didn't.

"Try me, Murph," John contended.

Holding his injured hand high in the blood-soaked rag, Murph asked begrudgingly, "What do you want to know?"

John realized Murphy remained a threat who would kill him if he could and claim self-defense before Judge Harris. Protecting his holstered weapon, John responded, "Why didn't you tell me that Frederick Price has been seeing Naomi?"

"Well, shit! I didn't even think about it. Look Sheriff, do you have any idea *how many* men that bitch sees? What's that got to do with anything?" Murphy demanded to know.

"I'm asking the questions," John responded. "What time did Price leave here last night?" asked John in pretext.

Murphy scowled, rolling his eyes upward. "Last night? I don't remember see'in that son-of-a-bitch in here last night. I don't think he was in here. No, hell no. He ain't been here in a week that I can remember."

"Are you positive?" John pressed.

"I know good and well it's been several days. I know that much," responded Murphy.

"Where's Naomi now?"

"That's a goddamn good question, Sheriff. Why don't you tell me where that bitch is? I ain't seen her in two days. I'd like to kick her fat ass myself," railed Murphy, with renewed ire.

"Listen to me closely, Murph," John began again. "If Price comes in tonight, call my office right away. If you don't, I'll lock you up. Do you understand?"

"Yeah, I understand," Murphy answered reluctantly.

As John walked toward the bar, the crowd moved inward to engulf him subtly, incrementally, with no one looking him in the eye. Each time he moved forward, a body with a face looking the other way stepped in front of him. John knew the coarse men were trapping him near the bar far from the front door. They were deadly serious, responding to Murphy's shame and humiliation. Like moving confidently by a mean, mongrel dog, John's instincts told him not to panic. If he drew his weapon before someone yanked out of his holster, deadly force would likely follow.

As the mob encircled him, few saw both of John's little fingers enter the corners of his mouth to stretch his lips apart and downward. His high-pitched, shrieking whistle penetrated ears as startled faces jerked toward him. Outside Thunder's head yanked upward, mane flying, in response to the familiar command, but as be trotted toward the door of the saloon, he stopped abruptly, intimidated and frightened. The whistle shot out the second time, to the dismay of mountain men looking at each other, smiling darkly, bemused by the antics of their trapped prey. Outside the Appaloosa jerked about, prancing frantically in place, whimpering and whining. He trotted toward the door again but bolted back wildly. Now Murphy's ugly volunteer army commenced again, facing John with mean, unflinching eyes. Stepping backward, John felt the edge of the bar as he whistled once more, loud and long, blending the two notes together up a high octave.

As John's fingers left his lips, the crash exploded at the opposite end of the barroom! Thunder, eyes wild and flashing, burst through the swinging doors, knocking over the nearest table. His shod hooves slipped several times on the hand-hewn floor as his spotted rump dropped downward, threatening to fall, but he managed to lunge forward awkwardly until he acquired solid footing again. Drunken patrons jumped blindly to the side as the room exploded into bedlam. Running forward in the open path, John grabbed the flying reins as Thunder, highly excited, spun about in a circle, kicking backwards and sideways. He leaped on the horse, drawing the reins in, afraid Thunder would fall on the slick floor. Still trembling, nostrils flared, the horse was momentarily under control. The wrecked saloon looked like a smoldering battlefield as dazed men stood like wounded soldiers, staring vaguely, trying to understand what had happened. All gazed at the Sheriff of Washington County, mounted surrealistically on the Appaloosa, as Thunder began a slow, hesitant walk. As the nervous horse approached the door, his tail rose, gracefully arched, like a Tennessee Walking Horse, and they were gone.

Chapter 28

As John allowed Thunder to break into a full run on the way back to the sheriff's office, Eugene Johnson crept up the back stairs of Hotel Abingdon. Slowly cracking the door at the second floor landing, he peeked into the dimly lit hallway. Reaching the door at suite 212, he paused, listened inside and heard nothing. Then he slowly turned the knob. Finding it unlocked, he slipped inside.

Press and Will were startled when John walked into the sheriff's office. "John, are you okay? You're pale as a ghost, like you're in shock," ventured Press, taking a step closer.

John removed his hat, yanked loose his tie, and tossed his coat on a chair. "Getting these clothes off will help, and you're not going to believe what happened. I may be in shock, literally, but I'll tell you about it later. Do we have anything yet?" asked John as he poured a glass of cold water with trembling hands.

Press began quickly, "The warden from the state pen called you back. Frederick Price was in prison for second-degree murder. Killed a man in a bar, claimed self-defense, and got ten years but never finished serving his term. As a trustee he escaped from the kitchen, where he was a cook! Eight years ago Price was the suspect in the murder of a prostitute in Roanoke. The victim was strangled and beaten."

"One victim?" asked John quickly.

"Only one," confirmed Press.

"Bite marks?" asked John, studying Press's face as if anticipating his answer.

"No bite marks," Press responded, "but, remember, the bites could become part of the MO of one whose violence escalates. Price was never charged in that case. He went to prison soon after that girl's death. If he were responsible for her death and hadn't gone to jail, there might have been more victims."

John looked steadily into Press's eyes. The communication did not have to be verbal. *This is it*, were the unspoken words.

"Gonna call the commonwealth's attorney?" asked Press.

"No, Price is an escapee. If we find him, we can lock him up. Where are the deputies?" asked John, turning to look at Will West.

"Out looking for Price," answered Will, speaking for the first time. "They said they would do nothing if they find him until they contact you."

"Do they know?" asked John

"Yeah, everything," answered the coroner.

"Okay, Press. If you will, stay here near the phone and coordinate for me. Will, I don't have to explain that Price has to be considered very dangerous."

"Right."

"Here's what I want you to do, Will," John said gravely. "If you spot Price, don't approach him. Come for me first, and I'll do it alone. I get paid to do this; you don't."

"I'm not worried about that, John," offered West.

"I know you're not, but that's how I want to handle it. Now, if you do spot him, you may have to stick with him for a while if you can. If that happens, you'll have to determine where he's going or where he stops, and remember Price doesn't know what we know. He has no reason to be running unless there's more we don't know now. Remember, take no action on your own."

"Got it, John," Will responded quickly, looking directly into the lawman's eyes.

At that moment Susan Shipley stood facing the front of Hotel Abingdon after saying good night to Mary and Arthur White. Walking down the hall, she glanced toward the stairway door at the end of the hall. It was closed. After she turned the key in the lock, the door opened. Stepping inside and locking the deadbolt, she had no way to know that the door was unlocked before she inserted the key.

John left the west end of town open for Will and himself without assigning sectors. There could be redundancy, repeating the same route, but one might spot Price in the location the other had covered only moments before. John decided to ride by and check Kit's Café first.

As John neared the café, Will approached the depot. Glancing toward the darkened Express Office, he saw that the Norfolk and Western freight wagon was gone. Checking the stalls, he discovered the team missing too.

When Shirley Shipley entered her suite, she felt the presence of another person; yet she was not gripped in fear because the feeling was passive, strangely benign. Turning to the light in the parlor, she saw nothing revealed but the ghosts of the afternoon party, silent echoes of the happy voices of women. Moving down the hall to the bathroom, she reached inside to feel for the wall switch. The sudden light made the large porcelain bathtub loom starkly white.

At the bedroom she reached out her hand to feel the warm switch plate, where she pushed the button in, lighting the room. It was hard for a woman to disregard her intuition and feelings. *Perhaps*, she thought, *it's this town.*

After undressing slowly in the hot room, Susan saw it for the first time on the night stand, sitting behind the base of the lamp. The small box, two inches square, was bound neatly in gold wrapping paper and tied with a green ribbon. Opening it tentatively she discovered a single piece of dark chocolate fudge, gooey in the hot temperature. It was a pleasant surprise to see such a lovely gesture in the hinterlands. Susan did not look on the bottom of the small box, did not read the stamp, "Colley Brothers," before she turned the light off and soon fell asleep. She would not sleep long.

During their patrol, Will and John visited Helen Hanson separately at Kit's Café. Busy with the demands of Friday night, she could speak but briefly to each of them. Helen told both she hadn't seen Frederick Price in several days. John mentioned nothing to her about the warrant, but he told Kit, who promised to call Press if Frederick came in. Saying he would explain later, Will cautioned Helen never again to be with Price alone.

Will passed the information about the missing Norfolk and Western team and wagon to John, Press, and the other deputies. There was no way to know if Price had the wagon, but it should be easy to spot. Will rode by the Price residence, seeing no wagon and no activity. John checked the Martha campus, finding it mostly dark, the students now girls of summer at their homes.

The full, translucent moon illuminated the night sky of August with silvery incandescence, leaving John thankful for the bright sky. Having searched before for fugitives at night, he viewed the beaming, pockmarked moon and its searing brightness as a blessing.

At a quarter to twelve as Will rode south on Depot Street past Kit's, toward the square, he could hear laughter spilling outside into the warm night. Pausing, he glanced down at the sawed-off 20-gauge shotgun hanging to the right of the saddle. Moments later he nudged the horse forward, moving in the direction of Hotel Abingdon, housing the darkened room of Susan Shipley. He had no way to know that his path was being paralleled at the moment half a block away.

Moments before, moving west on Main Street, John aimlessly turned Thunder left into an alley running south from Main, paralleling Depot Street. Now both men rode south, John toward the rear of the hotel, Will toward the front canopy.

At first John didn't see anything in the long, ink-dark shadow cast by the three-story hotel, but a primal alert stirred inside him. Stopping Thunder, he surveyed the blackness. When one of the horses flicked its head jingling the ornate Norfolk and Western harness, John pushed forward in the saddle, trying to see what was behind the veiled outline of the horse. *It's two horses,* he thought, possibly the Norfolk and Western team, but now there was no movement. Maximizing his night vision, John looked slightly away from the object he wanted to distinguish, suddenly perceiving the unmoving form of a man in the high wagon seat, a man sitting immobile, frozen, facing him. As if the awareness traversed both ways, the team jerked forward. Holding both reins in his left hand, Frederick Price sat high in the padded leather seat. John's heels dug backward as Thunder lunged forward toward the heavy wagon, closing on Price's left.

"Price! Wait!" yelled John. As the wagon stopped abruptly, Price rose with a quick, fluid movement, his arms extended forward with deadly grace, as both beefy hands clutched an enormous revolver. In a split second of infinity, a suspended, surreal moment of recognition and insight, John saw clearly the muzzle of the Colt .45 caliber revolver.

Instinctively, like darting aside to deflect a punch, John jerked away from the danger, yanking hard on the reins, wrenching Thunder's head and neck sideways. As the horse plunged into an unexpected stop, John slid across the slick English saddle into the flying mane. Falling sideways to his right, he frantically grabbed the animal's neck, struggling to hold on as a round erupted from the mammoth handgun, propelling the bullet through the midst of explosive gases at mock speed.

John felt the deadly impact as the massive projectile tore through bone and sinew just below Thunder's left eye. The horse's noble head exploded in the August night. Splintering bone fragments and flying chunks of torn, bloody flesh spewed onto his last rider as Thunder made his final descent to the ground. John's arms clung to the neck he had groomed so many times as his beloved horse hit the ground with a bloody, dead thud. With his body leading the fall, and no way to escape, John hit first by a heartbeat as the carcass of Thunder collapsed on top of him, pinning both of his legs. Trapped on his back, John could not see Frederick Price spring from the wagon, pumped and anxious to pull the trigger again; but sensing Price's approach, John clawed for his .38 revolver, finding the holster empty! In blind panic he frantically raked the ground, both arms flapping like a giant moth trapped in the rocky soil. Abruptly John felt a prevailing sense of calmness, waiting helplessly, resigned to die.

Price advanced cautiously, crab-like, his muscular arms extended forward, large hands cradling the deadly, smoking magnum. He instinctually turned his massive body sideways to minimize his target area moving toward Thunder's fallen form, now a shield for John Woodward. John could not see his adversary, but he felt the cold, deadly closeness. Instinctively, John extended both arms into the air, hands empty, fingers extended, as he lay pinned on his back. Struggling to raise his head, John looked into the eyes of Frederick Price, who appeared to be enjoying the moment as, smiling darkly, he raised the .45 toward John, who was still in the universal sign of surrender.

Will West held his long-barrel .38 revolver high in the air as his excited horse raced at full speed toward Price, who fell on one knee behind John. Price's powerful left hand clutched a patch of John's graying hair, jerking his head upward like a humiliated puppet. The big man pressed the smoking barrel of the .45 hard against John's temple.

"Drop your piece, West! Now!" Price yelled with the command presence of a field general. Will, like John, yanked hard on his horse's reins, bringing the animal to a faltering stop. "You heard me! Now!" screamed Price, rising slowly, with the weapon now aimed downward toward John's chest.

Will tossed his revolver to the ground in the moonlight and extended his arms upward as John had done moments before.

"Get off the horse!" Price demanded, walking forward, his weapon now aimed at Will's chest. "Slow, and hold the horse!" Price barked again, as Will complied, dismounting slowly. He stood holding the reins, the horse behind him, as Price advanced.

"Price! Freeze!" shouted the sheriff, bending upward from the waist, both arms extended, empty hands gripping an imaginary handgun. As Price whirled toward John, Will yanked his shotgun from its holster beside his saddle as his horse bolted sideways. Price spun back toward Will, his gun rising. In another suspended moment of infinity, Will could see Price's smiling face, as in slow motion clarity, he saw the fire flashing from the muzzle milliseconds before he heard the deafening, explosive report and felt shock waves as the projectile sped past his head into the August night.

Raising his sawed-off shotgun, Will *jerked* the trigger prematurely, causing the blast to hit the hard ground, but several pellets ricocheted into the groin and thick thighs of Frederick Price, who simply looked surprised, staying on his feet. A natural warrior, Price raised the .45 as Will aimed, looking steadily down the slick barrel at the single bead fading across the image of Price's calm face. Will *squeezed* the trigger this time, sending the spreading mass of .38-caliber projectiles to implode the face of Frederick Price into a bloody mass of splintered skull and mutilated flesh.

Silence engulfed the night after the competing reports of the hand gun and shotgun blasts. Will stood motionless, his gun emitting spindly, blue-gray threads of smoke from the short barrel. Momentarily confused and trying to ground himself in reality, Will could not wrench the details from a consciousness that chose not to remember the moments before.

The body of Frederick Price lay still, the upper portion a heap of obscene, bloody mutilation. Will's eyes fell not on the head wound that had torn the face and life from Price, but on his brown belt and his black boots. Unaccountably Will pictured the big man pulling the boots over his woolen socks the last time he dressed. He envisioned Frederick standing, cinching the brown belt around his considerable girth. *Had he last dressed early this morning or was it sometime later?* Finally, unable to divert himself any longer, Will looked down at the misshapen, fragmented skull of the former human being, the man he had just dispatched from life.

As the shotgun clanged to the ground, Will fell to his knees, then forward, as his open, ashen palms slapped the hard alley surface. Turgid warm liquid erupted, spewing from his mouth as he wretched violently, thrusting the contents of his raging, acidic stomach onto the ground beside the steamy, graying brains of Frederick Price.

Curious onlookers like upright, silent insects crept toward the bizarre scene cautiously, tentatively, as Will stood slowly, wiping his mouth with a red railroad bandana.
John! Will suddenly thought, running falteringly toward the downed Appaloosa. As Will drew near, John raised up as far as he could. Their eyes met, then John fell back, still pinned to the earth. Will knelt on one shaking knee, looking down into John's teary eyes. Neither man spoke for a few seconds, until Will, seeing John's bloody shirt, began, "John, are you . . . "
"No, no, I'm not hit. Are you all right?" asked the confused sheriff.
"I'm okay . . . . Later, I hope I'll be okay," Will uttered truthfully. "John, your legs . . ." he stammered, slowly becoming conscious of the reality before him.
"Can't feel anything," John answered, looking down toward his waist.
Will's cracking voice broke in unsure, gasping patterns, "Price was a madman. Tried to kill us both." Abruptly Will remembered the sheriff's desperate, high-risk effort to free him from the big man's control. "John, my God, if you hadn't called, yelled out . . . risked your life, we'd be dead!" stammered Will, his voice breaking into muffled sobs. John reached for Will's forearm, clinging to it tightly as his friend wept. That was how the deputy, the first person to approach the triad, found them.

Chapter 29

As always, the first curious onlookers had no idea what had happened as they gazed at the carnage, unable to understand the strange and deadly situation. None recognized the body of Frederick Price. All were confused by Will West's involvement because he wasn't a lawman. His shotgun, a harsh symbol of violence and death, lay in the alley near Price's body. How, they asked, did the Appaloosa get killed, and how in the name of God could the sheriff end up under his horse? Later, as the parts of the deadly puzzle were pieced together, men debated at length about the British riding saddle, posing the question: Had it caused John Woodward to lose control facing a deadly adversary or had it saved his life?

Press Smith plunged to his knees beside the trapped sheriff and Will West. The doctor quickly determined that both men were in shock, but he was unable to assess John's injuries because of the heavy horse carcass. Although John quietly explained that he felt no pain, the doctor worried about broken bones and circulation as he assured John he would soon be freed.

Frank Hutton, the chief deputy, knelt beside Doc Smith looking down at John, who uttered, "Frank, get something to cover Thunder. He was too proud; he wouldn't want to be seen like this." Then, his voice trailing off, John added, "And *I* don't want people to see him this way."

Moments later the deputy ran from the hotel with two sheets. Knowing his boss' concern, Hutton first covered Thunder, then draped the other sheet over the body of Frederick Price.

Waiting for John to be freed, Press wanted to remove Will from the scene. Turning to the closest bystander, a refined looking woman in a flowered dress, Press asked her to help Will into the hotel. Will and Susan Shipley exchanged nods without speaking as, holding his forearm and touching the small of his back, she assisted him toward the hotel.

Soon four men arrived with lumber and quickly leveraged Thunder's dead weight, freeing John Woodward. After sunrise, as the veterinarian removed the body of the horse, a deputy would discover John's .38-caliber Smith and Wesson six-shot revolver still warm from the heavy body.

When Helen Hanson tentatively ventured behind the hotel, she was unaware that her former lover lay in bloody desecration under the sheet. Motioned back by a deputy, Helen saw Will West as he walked slowly toward the hotel with the support of a woman in a flowered dress. Helen ran after them.

As two hospital workers lifted the stretcher into the emergency wagon, John instructed Frank Hutton to order a deputy to stay with Thunder's body. Later Thunder would be removed to John's small farm, where he would be buried with dignity. Like Frances Wertz months before, reluctant to release Georgia to the undertaker, John hated to think of another person, especially one with no concern or feeling, handling his Thunder, even for the last time, even in death, even though he was an animal.

John ordered Frank to call George Wertz to photograph the scene then and in the morning.

"Ain't gonna be no trial," mused the deputy.

"We don't know that, Frank," countered John sternly as Press waited patiently. John also instructed Frank to secure the Norfolk and Western wagon at the depot. "Look good in the wagon; make sure you don't miss any possible evidence," John called as the hospital rig pulled away.

"Okay, boss. Don't worry. Let Doc take care of you," called Hutton.

George Wertz began, once again, to photograph death rather than life. This morbid duty was his first assignment since losing Georgia. To steady his fragile emotions, he thought of his granddaughter, Christy, at the moment sleeping in Georgia's room. She reminded him not only of Georgia but also, inexplicably, of the mother he had left behind so many years before in the forests of Bavaria.

Finally, most tasks at the scene were completed with only two things left to do: remove the body of Thunder and secure the Norfolk and Western wagon. Frank directed another deputy to stay with Thunder until morning when arrangements could be made to haul him away.

"The rest of the night? Stay with the horse the rest of the night?" questioned the junior deputy.

"Yeah, boss's orders. You know how he loved that horse. We can't leave Thunder alone. It'd break the sheriff's heart if the horse lay out here all night by himself," explained Hutton.

Inside Hotel Abingdon Susan Shipley poured a cup of steaming black coffee for Will West as Helen Hanson sat quietly by his side. Earlier Will called his sleeping wife from the front desk as the two women remained at a respectable distance in the lobby. Mrs. West had not liked the idea of her husband's participation in the sheriff's secret group. He was, she pointed out, a railroad man, not a lawman. When he told her about the secret operation, she warned him that he owed it to her and their son not to get involved. Home this early morning would not be a refuge for Will West.

As Frank Hutton approached the wagon in the Norfolk and Western warehouse, he walked to the back and looked inside. It was parked directly under a light, allowing him to see a tarp stretched from one end of the wagon to the other covering freight items. The room was dark outside the bright circle of light above the wagon.

After climbing onto the front, Frank inched his way back on the wagon's frame, where he stopped and tossed the tarp to the side, revealing neatly stacked twenty-pound sacks of flour, so he jumped to the ground and headed for the office. Walking toward the door, Hutton suddenly thought of the sheriff. He could hear his boss's voice in the morning asking, "Was it all flour? Anything else?"

"Hell, better check it again," Frank muttered aloud, climbing back onto the wagon. Flipping the tarp back to the other side, he looked dumbfounded into the vacant, glazed eyes of Naomi Hess. Staring in disbelief, heart pumping wildly, Frank leaned forward and saw that part of her thin lip was bitten savagely at the side of her mouth, where dried blood had clotted. Her thick neck was discolored and bruised. The nude body of the stocky mountain girl lay prone, her feet resting against a feed sack. In shock Frank failed to see the purple bite marks on her thighs, but he spotted the brown wooden cigar box that lay lodged between Naomi's full, rounded hips and the flour sacks beside her. Hands trembling, he slowly lifted the small box from the wagon floor.

Inside he found a small bundle of cash wrapped by a rubber band. A leather change purse contained the identity of the owner, Helen Hanson. That made no sense to the bewildered and shaken deputy. He did not know the identity of the victim, but he did know Helen.

Later it would be determined that the money, almost forty dollars, represented Helen's life's savings. Humble mementos were also in the box.

Frank stared again in disbelief at the ghostly white body of Naomi Hess sprawled naked before him in the harsh overhead light. He could tell by her pale color and the blood that she had been dead for several hours. It did not occur to him that her soul had gone ahead of the soul of Frederick Price. Wherever her soul had gone, Price's would not travel with it.

* * * * *

Harold Kane quickly realized the possible connection between the dead man and the multiple murders, but when he went to bed early Sunday morning, he did not have Price's identity, and he didn't know about Naomi Hess. When those facts came to light the next day, he ran back to the office to prepare another special edition of *The Virginian*.

On Sunday morning Doc Smith examined the body of Frederick Price, but he did not conduct an autopsy, knowing well the cause of death. Press checked Price's pockets and found a Hotel Abingdon key. *Strange,* he thought as he raised the key toward his glasses to examine it more closely. On the wooden plate hanging to the key was a word MASTER. *My God!* Press thought, realizing it was a master key to all the rooms. John would later discover that Price had taken the key from Helen Hanson's room. Press and John would come to ponder how many women were vulnerable at the hotel.

Naomi Hess was buried in the steep, rugged knobs where she was born. Her difficult journey, like those of other victims, including Georgia Wertz Thompson, came to an abrupt, early end. The family displayed her body in the ramshackle frame house by the rushing mountain creek late Monday afternoon. From the time she was brought from the funeral home, the pathetic, ragtag family and countless friends wailed and cried, until late in the night. Regularly the men passed among themselves a green-tinted Mason jar with clear moonshine, courtesy of Naomi's former boss, Murph Murphy. The confrontation with John Woodward over Naomi and Frederick Price did not enter his mind as his life moved on without reflection and examination. Naomi's death to him and the others was, after all, simply another of life's passing events. Several times, nudging his fellow mourners, his pig eye winked as he proclaimed, "Thank God, buddy, for good shine!" The response was uniformly the same, "Yeah, thank ye a lot, Murph. That's for sure!"

Late that night, a fistfight broke out in the Hess yard between drunken knob men, and most stepped but a few feet from the front porch before urinating in the yard. All in all Naomi would have approved. It was a pretty good time of mourning.

In the white frame church on Tuesday afternoon, temperature soaring, the fiery preacher railed on against sin. Most of the men sat dazed, sick and hung over from the night before. Two went outside and threw up, neither bothering to move far enough away to prevent the congregation from hearing the retching just outside the open windows. Three women managed to faint, one in a trance-like swoon. "Amen" was offered by several men during the sermon. When Murph returned to his saloon late in the afternoon, patrons asked the same question several times. Always the dumb show played itself out in the same way. "What'd the preacher say about old Naomi, Murph?" bleary-eyed patrons asked.

"Said she was a good 'un and we're all goin' to hell, I guess," answered her former boss.

"Same old shit, huh, Murph?"

"Yeah, buddy, same old shit," Murph confirmed.

After unsuccessful efforts to acquire information from the sheriff, Harold Kane called on Mr. and Mrs. Price, perceiving that both grieved in a stoical way. It became apparent as Kane crafted pretext questions that no substantive information would be gathered. Like the sheriff before him, Kane concentrated on Mrs. Price. As he was leaving, she made a point important to her. "They's one thing men don't think about, Mr. Kane," she began. "You men don't ever remember, but you oughta. You have to remember my Freddy was a little boy one time. He was *my* little boy. That's all I can tell you."

Kane excused himself to begin the next issue of *The Virginian*, which carried a headline in bold letters: **MOTHER CALLS KILLER "MY LITTLE BOY."**

On Wednesday morning, the day after Naomi's funeral, the sheriff and the coroner met in the office of Herbert P. Mitchell, the commonwealth's attorney. At forty-five, Mitchell stood erect, lean, and suntanned from farm work performed when he wasn't lawyering for the commonwealth.

Press described his examination of the body of Naomi Hess but explained wearily that her family refused to allow an autopsy. He was reasonably confident she was murdered by the killer of the last two victims. Known as a sexually active woman, Naomi had engaged in intercourse shortly before she died. Press could not, however, tell if she were with the killer or another man. There was evidence of trauma to her vagina, and her thighs and lip had been bitten. He believed it was unlikely that she had had sex with Price. Because of the previous examinations, Press had checked her lower legs and found semen traces. The modus operandi was clearly the same.

Mitchell was concerned that the community would never reach closure without resolution beyond a reasonable doubt, as Harold Kane had written in his last special edition, speculating, "Was Frederick Price the Dark One or was he a copycat killer like some in London who killed after Jack the Ripper? Is the murderer lurking among the vulnerable citizens of our beloved community?"

The men agreed that if evidence of the other murders was in Frederick's home, it must be hidden, unknown to Mr. and Mrs. Price.

When John informed Mitchell of the master key from Hotel Abingdon, the prosecutor expressed thankfulness that Price had not victimized women in the hotel. He quickly drafted a search warrant for Frederick Price's room. John was the affiant, but because of his injuries, Doc said he should not to go to court. Mitchell would handle it himself, reading John's signed, sworn statement to the judge.

Unknown at the time, that offer turned out to be a blessing for John Woodward. Judge Harris was in a mean and foul mood. Angry, he demanded a complete briefing, far beyond the probable cause for the search warrant. Early on, showing considerable irritation, he asked, "What in the hell happened at the Knot Hole? I hear that place is a goddamn wreck!" Wondering why the judge would mention the Knot Hole in the context of a search warrant in a murder case, the commonwealth's attorney answered truthfully that he didn't know anything about it. After grilling Mitchell for fifteen relentless minutes, Judge Harris finally authorized the warrant, and a bewildered Herbert P. Mitchell walked briskly from the chambers with a copy of the warrant clutched tightly in his sweaty hand. It was drawn for execution the next day because of the funeral of Frederick Price that afternoon.

The next morning an apologetic John Woodward presented the search warrant to Mrs. Price as her husband lingered in the background without speaking. The warrant was narrowly drawn, including only Frederick's room, but John intended to look elsewhere if circumstances dictated. Mercifully Judge Harris did not go into a rage when reading the term "trophies," a word lifted from the Austrian doctor's paper. Trophies were among the items sought as evidence along with other "fruits and instrumentalities of the crimes." John sat with Doc Smith as the deputies searched, greatly frustrated because he could not move about freely without pain in his legs and back.

Doc came to assist the impaired sheriff and to help calm the Prices if they became emotional, but they accepted the warrant stoically. Under John's watchful eye the deputies searched the house and premises for several hours. First they searched Frederick's room for more than an hour, finding nothing. John knew that only the contents of Frederick's room would be admissible in court, but with Price dead, there would be no trial. They were searching for resolution. After Frederick's room the men moved quietly throughout the house, including the damp, cluttered cellar and the dusty, cobwebbed attic. Finally, at John's direction, a deputy inspected the crawl space separate from the basement, again finding nothing.

John, sensitive to the grief of the Prices, instructed the deputies to ensure they put everything back in place just as they found it. "These people have suffered enough without our causing them more pain," he said, in a tone of resignation. The deputies themselves, thinking of the murderous Frederick Price, found it difficult to feel sorry for his parents, but they hid that sentiment by blank faces, overt emotional detachment. They worried about the sheriff's physical condition and now his vast disappointment over the unproductive search.

*****

After the shootout, another story of Will West spread quickly. In this story he acted as a special deputy, under the color of the law. Herbert P. Mitchell allowed the release of general information about the shooting, revealing that Price was wanted as an escapee from prison. He and John agreed that if Price were not involved in the other murders, detailed publicity about his being a suspect could adversely affect any future prosecution of another defendant.

With that information fueled by street rumors, Will West became a reluctant hero. Regardless of his status as a deputized lawman in a situation demanding lethal force, actually self-defense, he wanted no public acknowledgment for killing another human being. The granting of hero status has nothing to do with someone wanting it, however, so Will was forced to endure his high community profile.

Meanwhile John pondered countless questions about Frederick Price. Had he lurked outside Jeanette Moore's cottage that stormy night? Was Naomi his first or his fourth murder victim? Neither Jamie nor Natalie could identify Price as the man who had chased her although his physique matched Jamie's general description. Could the *real* killer still be in their midst, laughing, amused at their ineptness, waiting to murder again? He was not the only person in town entertaining those haunting questions.

Like the incident with Grimes, John felt humiliation, this time as a law enforcement official who was rescued by the civilian railroad man. He thanked God that he and Will survived, not that Price died. As a matter of fact, John prayed for Price's soul, something he didn't understand but had acquired from the *Book of Common Prayer* years before. With a profound sense of humility, he uttered an awkward prayer for Frederick Price, the man one person still remembered as a little boy.

John's profession itself was dependent upon his solution of the multiple murders; yet technically, he could write off *only* the pathetic death of Naomi Hess. A month passed, but the public still demanded to know if the danger was over. Most believed Price was probably the Dark One, but "probably" fell short of resolution; thus, closure still eluded John and the community.

After the gunfight, John plunged deeply into abject grief over the loss of his beloved Thunder, which many found curious. After all, they noted, Thunder *was only an animal*. Joe Dunn, however, understood, quietly telling John that love crosses species, that love "between man and God's creatures" is another gift of life, one that can reach the same depth as love for fellow humans. John still fought the mist that fogged his eyes and the lump that choked his voice at unexpected moments when Thunder barged into his consciousness. At dusk several times he thought he caught glimpses of his horse prancing in the pasture, snorting and head bobbing. Finally, awash in loss, John remembered Joe's words and, knowing he had no choice, gave in to the grief as he would have over human loss.

Yet John recovered his focus quickly as his sole concern mounted to epic proportions; he *had* to solve the murders. After so much loss and so much pain, the solution, once seemingly in hand, now seemed ephemeral. Would it ever come? Would the years pass with no resolution? He had to do something, had to solve the case.

Sitting in his office on a sunny fall afternoon, John pondered the question once again, *But how? How, dear God, do I do it?* he asked, partly as a thought and partly as a prayer. The answer flooded into his mind, swiftly and clearly, racing into his consciousness: *Search again! Search again!*

Still unable to ride a horse, John traveled alone in his buckboard to the residence where Mrs. Price allowed him inside with the same quiet resignation she displayed before. They chatted quietly for a while, two people at opposite ends of the spectrum of understanding and grief. When she offered John iced tea, he accepted. She was stoically compliant as they talked about Frederick. With no forethought, as if another person were talking, John asked, "Did Freddie ever build things? Was he good with his hands?"

"Not anything that I can remember. But . . . no, wait a minute. I *do* remember he worked on his wardrobe when he first moved in with us," she recalled.

"His wardrobe?" John asked quickly.

"Yeah, he worked on it, but I didn't pay no attention particularly. I do remember that his daddy and me was at church when he done it," she recalled as if her vague thoughts were too remote to gather.

"When he did what? What did he do to the wardrobe?" John pressed.

"When he did whatever he did," she replied, sighing openly, honestly.

"You don't know what that was? You don't know what he did to the wardrobe?" John probed.

"No, only that he worked on it some way. He had tools and things. I think he had maybe some stain. I can't remember. Maybe he touched up the stain on the wood. I just can't remember now," Mrs. Price explained, finality in her tired voice.

"Mrs. Price, do you mind if I look at the wardrobe?" John probed.

"Well I guess it won't make no difference," she responded slowly.

John struggled to his feet, adjusted his crutches under sore armpits, and made his way to the filled wardrobe standing the way his deputies had left it. Conceding to himself that he could not examine the wardrobe on crutches and with a leg in a cast, he asked, "Do you have a phone?"

"Well, we got one, but it's broke," she explained.

"I can go next door and use the neighbor's phone."

"Yeah, they got a phone that works," she confirmed.

Reaching Press, John asked him to come as soon as possible and bring a claw hammer and small crowbar. Press said he would, without asking why.

Now John had a gut feeling informed by his years of experience. He was close to something.

Thirty minutes later John and Press entered the room alone. When John told Press about his conversation with Mrs. Price, the information didn't generate the same excitement with the doctor who asked, "You think that's got some significance, huh?"

John hobbled to the front of the large mahogany wardrobe and, turning to his friend, asked, "Press, please take everything out. Do you mind?"

"No, of course not," answered Press as he began removing the hanging clothes, which he neatly stacked on the bed. Soon the wardrobe stood empty as Press, on his knees, leaned forward, moving his head inside. Several moments of silence followed before the doctor spoke. "John, this floor is close, but it's not exactly the color of the rest of the wood."

"What do you mean?" John asked quickly.

"The wood stain is off slightly, I think," Press answered, his head still inside the large wardrobe.

"And look, Press! The floor seems higher than it should. Look how elevated it is from the floor of the house," said the sheriff, pointing a crutch inside the wardrobe.

"You're right," answered Press, still on his knees, reaching under the front panel of the wardrobe. "Let's see now . . . how hard is it gonna be to remove this molding?" he muttered while gently pulling on each end. To his astonishment the panel of molding slid forward. It was not nailed; it was held in place with wooden dowels on each end. Glancing quickly at his friend, Press jerked his head up. The panel was altered for easy removal! As Press slid the front molding back, John saw it first! The floor panel was not stained on the front side, the side hidden under the molding. The end of the floor panel stood out harshly as bare unstained wood, new wood, in contrast to the mahogany floor color. Press pulled on the floor which slid forward easily, smoothly.

John leaned forward on his crutches as Press removed the floor panel revealing a white pillowcase. Reaching inside the sub-floor compartment slowly, carefully, Press removed the pillowcase. Faint blue letters identified it as property of Hotel Abingdon. Press paused, looking up at John from his knees. Then he stood slowly, without speaking, extending the pillowcase toward John. "It's okay, Press. Go ahead, open it yourself," John said quietly.

After they examined the contents of the pillowcase, Press reset the false floor and the decorative molding. Then he carefully put everything back in the wardrobe. Although they had no warrant, John seized the pillow case and its contents. He did not bother to leave an inventory. Mrs. Price looked up without speaking, without comment, when John thanked her as he and Press quickly left her home. George Wertz would go back later to photograph the wardrobe's secret compartment.

Chapter 30

The commonwealth's attorney was satisfied after John presented the contents of Frederick's secret compartment, explaining each item. "That'll do it. We can close on that. Write off all four murders," directed Herbert P. Mitchell.

First John had displayed a solid-gold, heart-shaped locket, its fourteen-inch gold chain broken. The locket opened to reveal on one side the face of a handsome, unknown college boy with an abundance of dark hair. On the other side was a picture of Anna Marie Holmes. A date was inscribed on the back of the locket: *August 8, 1909.*

The connection with Jeanette Moore was as compelling. In a small brass frame, which was wrapped in a pair of black panties, John found a G. N. Wertz Studio portrait of Jeanette. Mitchell saw that George Wertz had managed to capture Jeanette's essence as he had in his pictures of the college girls.

The parents of Vivian Grant positively identified a small linen handkerchief that she had bought on a trip to Knoxville. It was, they said, in the pocket of the dress she wore the night Price wrenched her life away. Later when it was released to the family, Brett Grant, with the approval of his parents, burned the handkerchief. Her possession, simple and elegant, became defiled when the monster snatched it away from her along with her life.

A second pillowcase was found, one dyed black with holes cut for eyes, along with six pairs of women's panties and four bras.

John related that the cigar box found with Naomi Hess contained the life savings of Helen Hanson. She had maintained some relationship with Price, he advised, the exact nature of which was still unknown but probably intimate. Both John and the commonwealth's attorney agreed that Price had stolen the master key from Helen, who used it in her job as a charwoman. John pointed out that "like a true sociopath," Price had not only exploited her fragile emotions and her frail body but had also stolen her meager savings. Finally John presented a blue denim shirt taken from Price's wardrobe with all white buttons except one. The button he found at Holmes' grave was identical to the other stark white buttons. John acknowledged that it was a most common button; nevertheless, he pointed out, one of Price's buttons was missing, and the one found at the crime scene matched the others on the shirt.

After briefing the judge, with Herbert Mitchell's authorization, John briefed Howard Kane, as he had promised he would at the conclusion of the case. Kane wrote that the sheriff held many items of "feminine attire" in case any ladies wanted to see if they had been victimized by Price's fetish-driven thievery. None came forward as neither John nor Press noticed that one bra bore the label from a department store in Richmond.

The plan was Will's idea, but John liked it right away. Two days after Harold Kane's detailed stories were published about the solution of the case, Will paid a visit to Byron Byrd, part owner and manager of Hotel Abingdon, quietly noting that his visit was confidential. Will, who routinely referred passengers to the hotel, revealed the recovery of the master key, pointing out that the sheriff and the commonwealth's attorney had taken great pains to protect that information. Price, he noted, had acquired the master key through deceit, the same way he had stolen Helen Hanson's life savings. Helen, however, a young and innocent girl, simply made a mistake of the heart. She appeared, Will pointed out, to be a lonely girl who was an honest employee and a hard worker. Yes, Mr. Byrd agreed, he regretted having to let her go.

Will artfully related to his friend the proposal being offered. *If* Byron Byrd kept Helen on at the hotel, the information about the key would be held in the strictest possible confidence. Byrd gratefully agreed to restore Helen's job, along with a modest increase in pay, noting that he would be immensely appreciative if the sheriff and commonwealth's attorney would in fact keep secret the information about the master key.

Returning to the depot, Will considered telling Jean about getting Helen's job back, but he chose to keep the secret. Suddenly he was flooded with a sensory memory of Jeanette. For a passing moment, he could smell her perfume and hear her hearty laugh. She would be pleased about what they had done for Helen.

The same day Press assured the sheriff he would have severe life-long complications if he didn't show more respect for his broken leg and stiff back. Ordering John to stay off his leg at least one full week, Doc stated emphatically, "I want you off your feet. Do you understand that, John?"

"I do, Doc, I do," John answered quietly. Then he gave in, actually relieved at last. Finally it was over, and he wanted to go home.

The third day of his rest, late in the afternoon, John sat on his back porch looking toward the pasture where Thunder used to graze and frolic. Across his lap was a copy of *The Virginian*, which he read earlier with great interest, finding that Kane had written a complimentary article about him. Now that they could discuss the case, Kane had also interviewed a reluctant Will West and written of John's life-threatening risk as "bravery beyond the call of duty." He also described the sheriff as "a true law enforcement professional in the final analysis." The editorial stated that it was not only John's "admirable persistence, but also his intellect that solved the cases and allowed the community, at last, to

breathe a collective sigh of relief." Several town leaders stopped by to see Kane, compli-
menting his article and his proven ability to change his mind. "Hell, I was wrong, that's
all. Wasn't the first time and won't be the last," Kane stated dryly. And that was that, the
slate wiped clean, at least for the moment.

As John sat, his cast resting on a footstool, Joe Dunn walked onto the porch. John
respected the priest's intellect but also greatly appreciated his ironic sense of humor.
"How's the patient?" asked Joe, smiling broadly.

"I'm doing fine, thanks," answered John, looking up, pleased to see his friend of
many years.

"Well, that's strange. You don't look so good!" Joe responded. "Remember, I've
told you before, no good deed goes unpunished!" he said, laughing, the corners of his
eyes crinkling from the lingering smile. Sitting down, Joe extended his hand, saying,
"I brought you something."

John took the small object, wrapped only in tissue paper. It was a framed engraving in old English printing. The engraving had oil-painted animals in the borders, as
did the ornate porcelain frame.

John read silently:

**God who is infinite, unbounded Love,
will not allow the love which exists
between his creatures to perish.**

The mist and the lump came rushing back as John said softly, "Thanks Joe, thanks
a lot."

"You are more than welcome," the priest answered softly, relaxing in the padded
wicker chair.

A short while later as they sat sipping iced tea in the late-afternoon shade of the
porch, John broke the silence. "You know, Joe, I've been thinking about George and
Frances Wertz a lot this afternoon."

"You have? What about?" asked Joe, turning toward John.

"Well, you know we have our married daughter, an only child like Georgia was. I
can only imagine how Frances and George suffer, and when I think about them, I feel
guilty because I have such grief over Thunder, as much as I would for a person. That's
what made me think of them - not knowing how they can endure the loss of Georgia,"
John related, his voice trailing off almost to a whisper.

Joe Dunn didn't speak for a while, reflecting on John's words. After several moments
he began softly and slowly, as if telling a secret. "When my little white mutt Terrier died last
year at fourteen, I came to realize that grief is grief, John. Once one passes the superficial
thresholds and plunges into the well of his being that holds grief, when one goes deeply
enough into his soul, there is no choice but to grieve. So, regardless of the source of the
grief, if it comes from the depth of your soul, it's pure and, for a while, devastating. Grief

comes from love and loss. And again, love is love, whether for a person or an animal. Real love, healthy love, doesn't have to get complicated and analyzed in terms of the beloved. And loss doesn't remove love; it just takes away, often painfully, the object of the love. The essence, the spirit of the love, continues as long as memory remains. The blessing, and you know this well, is to have the love in the first place. That's a gift from God. And it's true in all our relationships, whether we speak of our love for other human beings or our love for God's other creatures."

"But what about Georgia?" John asked softly, glancing at Joe's profile in the afternoon shadows of the porch. "She loved Bentley Thompson, and she died for it. Love, it seems to me, caused her to die," offered John, his thoughts drifting to the face of Hannah Holmes.

"John, we've talked before about the inescapable ambiguity of life. Often our vision is clouded. First Corinthians says that sometimes 'we see through a glass darkly.' Often we just don't know the answers. Sometimes it is as if we drop a stone into a dark pond then we try to see our own reflection, but the rings travel out from the point of impact and the image of ourselves and others, indeed, like life itself, is murky and distorted at best. It is frequently that way in our perception of life. I'm not sure Georgia's love caused her to die. I see her love as causing her to create another human being although that was not her conscious intent at the moment Christy was conceived. A gift, John, given lovingly, freely, as Georgia gave her gift of love to Bentley, is not diminished because the receiver fails to value and cherish the gift. The gift is not negated because of betrayal, even deadly betrayal. It is not the giver of the gift who loses, but the beloved who, for whatever reason, rejects the gift. If some choose to distort and pervert love, the greatest gift of life, it does not diminish the goodness and the spirit of the giver. Think of the countless people who go about their lives quietly, day after day, month after month, year after year, loving deeply, loving with abandon. The acts of the men like Bentley Thompson and Frederick Price will not make the rest of us question love. Actually, through our losses, we hopefully resolve to love less selfishly, to love more purely, to give agape love all that we can."

The two sat silently, looking at the pasture as the falling ball of burnt, orange-red sun eased downward slowly, split in half by the distant Blue Ridge it slipped behind. Shards of light spiked through fall clouds majestically cast above, as below the end of day faded into a gauzy softness. The hue of the Blue Ridge was deep and magical for a moment before it surrendered to the night.

The End

LaVergne, TN USA
10 February 2011
215883LV00003B/130/P